CONGO SONG

CONGO SONG

by
STUART CLOETE

HOUGHTON MIFFLIN COMPANY · BOSTON
1943

CL

PRINTED IN THE U.S.A.

CONTENTS

CONGO SONG

Chapter 1

The COLLECTOR

^^^^^^^^^^^^^^^^^^^

THREE MEN SAT ON THE STOEP. THEY WERE DRINKING TEA. They were drinking it from white enamel, half-pint cups with dark blue handles. There was a can of condensed milk — Nestlé's — on the table and a bowl of sugar.

They were talking of women. That was because there were no women here. One did not count, as women, the native women going to the water, naked but for their little aprons before and behind, with red earthen pots on their heads. One did not, even if one used them upon occasion. Even the administrator, who had six bastards and enjoyed the droîts de seigneur over a district the size of France, had been known to complain that there were no women. He was away on leave at present.

Only Sebastian and Channel were talking. Bentinck, who was a hunter and kept the store — it was also an hotel — seldom spoke at all, and then never of women, which was the real reason the others came. They required a listener. To ask for a sympathetic listener was too much. A listener sufficed. Naturally they did not listen to each other. Each was polite in maintaining silence while the other spoke. This was a convention which had been arrived at without discussion or arrangement: something mutually accepted on a basis of trial and error. It was accepted as Marais' neatness of dress was accepted, or Olga's beauty, or the professor's absent-mindedness. It was comic, that he should be so absent-minded: like

the professors in the jokes. But his absent-mindedness was
accepted as the administrator's bastards were accepted, or the
fact that the beautiful black females that went to the river
were not women. In the Congo one accepted or one died.

It was established between them what women were. This
had been done a year ago, when Sebastian first came here from
nowhere: arriving on foot with his paints, some rolled canvas,
and stretchers. Channel had been here a long time, nearly
ten years, but in a day they had discovered their common
interest: the one as a painter, the other as a Frenchman, very
spirituel, a doctor, and an observer of natural phenomena,
particularly that which concerned what he called 'the relation
of the sexes.' In addition, he had other interests: his collection
of medical specimens; his passion for hypnosis; his love of bad
music.

On that first day, when this endless discussion had begun,
they had decided that it would be necessary to define women.
White, to start with. Only white women were relevant.
Young, naturally, but not too young and not over forty except
in special cases. Chic, of course. To sum up — women who
were desirable. That was the basis, but since then they had
gone a long way. The subject had been approached from all
angles and still nothing was solved except Sebastian's more
immediate problems. This had been done by obtaining two
Batanga girls to take care of him; but since they were outside
of the specification so academically arrived at, they rarely
entered into the discussion. It would have been dishonorable
to particularize in any way, and it was tacitly assumed that
certain conventions such as this must be observed, even upon
the equator. Basic natural functions and facts were acknowledged. After all, one could not deny them. It was also
acknowledged that the tropics, contrary to all popular fiction,
were not conducive to love-life. But these acknowledgements
were in parentheses, asides, because — and this also had been
insisted upon, not on the first day, but during the first week —

the conversation must remain objective and scientific. There might be an occasional necessity for referring to actual experience; this, however, must not consist of the glorifying of personal exploit, but only be used to enlighten or to give concrete examples which would illustrate an hypothesis or serve to develop one of those theories which had been put forth.

Channel poured himself another cup of tea. He had beautiful hands. With the long fingers of a surgeon he grasped the handle of the metal teapot.

'One day I will make some studies of your hands,' Sebastian said. He looked at his own hands as he rolled a cigarette; they were large, strong, rather dirty, with fingernails bitten to the quick. 'One day also I shall stop biting my nails.'

'They should have put alum on them when you were small.'

'Who should? The good Sisters? They were only interested in my soul. Leonardo made good studies of hands — and Rembrandt. Only a great artist can draw hands.'

'It is frustration that makes you bite them,' Channel said. 'In addition, it is a disgusting habit.'

'Frustration. I am a painter. Naturally I am frustrated. All artists are frustrated.'

'They are escapists. It is a mechanism of escape. To become a criminal is another escape.'

Bentinck got up and came back with a rifle. He set the sights at three hundred yards, leant it on the stoep rail and fired.

'Get it?' Channel asked. He had not turned round or moved when the shot was fired.

'Yes. A duiker. Convenient, isn't it?' It was a little idea of Bentinck's: that patch of bright green beans planted on a hillside three hundred yards away. The only crops he ever reaped were the buck that came to graze upon it. The land had been planted for that purpose. Without orders his boy had left the house, knife in hand.

'It is a terrible thing to kill,' Sebastian said.

'I do not kill for fun. I have to eat. I kill for food or for money to buy food.' You had to explain things to Sebastian as if he were a child.

'Whisky,' Channel said.

'And whisky. It will go up if there is war.'

'That is an interesting reflection,' Channel said. 'Whisky will go up because of war. Therefore, you will have to kill more animals to make more money in order to obtain the same quantity of alcohol.'

'Or I could give it up.' It amused Augustus Bentinck to be considered a heavy drinker. Sometimes a bottle lasted him two days.

'You could, but you won't.'

'No.'

'Rhino horns: an aphrodisiac for the Chinese,' Channel said. 'A remarkable survival of homeopathic medicine. The bigger the horn...' He did not finish his sentence.

'They still buy all they can get. But there are no rhino here; have to go to Kenya.'

'I too have killed,' Sebastian said. 'I have killed men... Guadalajara... It is better to kill such men than deer.'

'Deer, Sebastian, lose their horns. The duiker is an antelope. Cephalophinae.'

'In the old days they ran up to six feet,' Bentinck said. 'I have been told that. A horn as tall as a man.'

The boy came back carrying the duiker. 'It is a wifie, Baas,' he said, 'and it has horns.'

'A pity he cleaned it,' Channel said. 'I should have liked to see its ovaries. They may have been affected.'

He looked down at his hands. Sebastian was right. His hands were beautiful — worth drawing; but he saw them as instruments of God, in whom he did not believe: instruments that saved life, that alleviated pain. There was so much pain in the world. A doctor was a student of pain, of disease. He concentrated on his hands again. He drew a small file from his pocket and rubbed it over one of his nails, that of the second finger of his left hand. Hands. Sebastian's great spatulate fingers were also instruments, and Bentinck's. How expert they all were, each in his fashion! Masters of their trades isolated in this place, insulated illogically from the contemporary world, taken out of it like a phrase from a book — a bar of music from a song. He wished he could have examined that duiker. A female carrying the secondary sexual characteristics of the male was always interesting.

There would be war. Munich had made it certain. The only question was when or where it would break out. It would be amusing to observe its repercussions here. Would the relative values of aphrodisiacs — of rhinoceros horns — adjust themselves to the new price of whisky, for instance? Would the cost of one force up the price of the other? Everything was a matter of balance, of adjustment. Inevitably things adjusted themselves, but there was always an error in the time factor, a lag. He clapped a little wooden pill box over a fly on the table and slid it to the edge where he put on the lid. It looked like a new variety. It was time to go. He was tired of being here. And he wanted to examine the fly.

'Let us go, Sebastian,' he said.

Sebastian got up. 'In Spain,' he said, 'when I was with the International Brigade . . .'

'Yes,' Bentinck said, 'and if you want some meat, send down a boy. I only want the saddle. You could take it now if you weren't in such a damned hurry.' Hurry was something he did not understand. It never did any good.

'Not now,' Sebastian said. 'It would be warm.' The idea of riding with meat so recently alive repelled him.

As they got into the car, Sebastian was thinking of his women. Whenever he left them he thought about them. When he was with them they annoyed him. That was the worst of women, white or black. He had bought them the

kind of clothes they liked: silk taffetas, one each, of primrose-
yellow and cerise. They wore them gathered tightly over
their sharp, pear breasts. Their shoulders were bare. They
wore bustles on their croups and rustled as they walked.
They were young: virgins when he got them, buying them with
the proceeds of some paintings he had done for the Belgian
Government. Both the payment for the virgins and the pictures had been on the instalment system. But he had got the
girls when two-thirds of their price was paid. He had used
them as models to complete the pictures, and he had used the
final payment on the pictures to end the protracted transac-
tion between himself and their father. They were sisters and
much attached to each other. They were satisfactory, very
acquiescent, but they were not women. In fact, they only
accentuated the lack of women, and they were abominable
cooks. Still, he was always glad to get back to them. They
would betray him one day, of course — to that extent they
were women; but it went against the grain to make their
downward path too easy. In a way, his care of them was a
moral duty. He was their father. That was what they called
him when they wanted something. He had learnt a little of
their language and from him they had learnt to swear in three
tongues. Nevertheless, they were pleasing to look at: like that
deer Bentinck had shot. Their native names he had abandoned as being too barbaric. He had rechristened them Nina
and Maria, a compliment not only to the girls themselves,
but to those after whom they had been named. How happy
they would be if they knew what he had done! One day he
would write to them.

Channel pulled up the car to put more water into the
radiator. It was boiling with the climb. He kept a can in the
car.

Sebastian thought of the duiker. It would have been warm.
The women were warm. It was blood that made things warm;
blood was very spiritual. The spirit ran out of living things

with the blood. This no one could deny. He thought of his own thoughts. Of the beautiful concatenation that had led them from the warmth of the newly dead antelope to the warmth of his women: from thence to the profundity of blood. Only von Brandt, the Nazi, and he cared about blood. How he detested him with his heresy! Blood had nothing to do with politics. It was better to believe nothing than to have wrong beliefs. Blood was of God.

He looked down. It was almost a precipice. Below them was Bentinck's store and the big tree by which it had been built; and the village, and the banana plantations — brilliant green, the dead leaves orange. Bentinck's little land where he had shot the duiker was a spot in the distance, a pin-point in the endless forest. Gauguin had gone to the South Seas to paint. He, Sebastian, had come here. One day he would be heard of. 'That,' people would say — 'why, that is a Sebastian. That is a work of genius. How did you ever get it? Strange that he should have lived and died in the Congo. Tragic. Still in his prime.' There would be stories, scandals about him. People would come from America to see his grave, would risk sunstroke in order to stand hatless beside it: the solitary grave of the master. Tears came into his eyes. It was a beautiful and sacred thought.

He had great respect for Americans. It was much better to shoot a Fascist than a deer. A deer was one of God's creatures as were his Batanga girls. To him everything beautiful was of God. This was the beginning and the end of everything, of all belief. God was beauty. He had spent two hours once trying to convince Owen that his girls were of God. But missionaries were very orthodox. They were without souls. But it was easy to forgive Owen. It was natural that he should have some resentment against him for having taken the girls from the mission and hard for him to understand that a life of celibacy and chastity was unhealthy for such young and beautiful creatures. That deer was of God, and the bananas, the forest orchids, the spotted leopards. God was beauty, beauty was life. All living things were God. It was all so incredibly simple, if one had a soul. He thumped his chest. 'A heart,' he said. 'A soul.'

'Your heart is good,' Channel said. 'I tested it only a week ago.' He was turning a corner.

'Yes, my heart is good. It is big' — Sebastian extended his hands as if he were measuring a fish — 'big.'

'If it was dilated, I should have told you.'

'Big — and my soul . . .' Sebastian's head sank on his chest. No one understood him. Not even Channel.

As they turned another corner, he said: 'This is where I will be buried. The view is magnificent.' Cecil Rhodes . . . the Matopos . . . what are they compared to this? People will come here to the grave of Sebastian the painter.

'You are not likely to die,' Channel said, 'and do not always talk as we turn the corners.'

'You do not know. Only I know. I am an artist, sensitive to premonitions. Stop the car. I want to show you the exact place, then there will be no mistake: we will mark it. I . . .' Of course he talked at corners. Where else should one talk but when a new vista opened before one's eyes? Each turn giving a new impact to one sensitive enough to appreciate it.

Channel did not stop. He would never understand. You could not go beyond the material, the scientific with him. Sebastian suddenly felt very charitable towards Channel. Sad for him, for his lack of vision and understanding, but what could one expect from a surgeon, a man who spent his time peering into human entrails, who when he saw a duiker only wished to examine its ovaries? Ovaries were of God. They should not be tampered with. He had seen everything worth while in the world, all beauty, but he had never seen an ovary. To look at such things was an indecency, an obscenity.

'I have never seen an ovary,' he said.

'I'll show you some when we get in. I have some nice ones.'

That was like him. Everything bottled in alcohol, every-thing tabulated and named. A man without a soul, a man with a fly in his pocket. Flies should fly around. They were of God. They should not be put in little boxes. It hurt him to think of that fly's confinement. He wondered if it had enough air.

'I do not wish to see,' he said. 'I do not believe in them.'

The car was pulling up. He could see his girls: one in cerise and one in primrose taffeta. They were standing outside his house.

'In what, Sebastian?'

'In ovaries.' Now what had the girls been doing? He would never know. One could do much in a short time.

He stopped on his way to the girls and turned back.

'There is no reason why there should not be a little shrine.'

'A shrine?'

'Yes, it would keep the sun off their heads when they come to my grave. I should not like anything to happen to them.'

'To whom?'

'The Americans who visit it. And there could be a little shop beside it ... my sketches, native curios ... souvenirs of all kinds. In this way they would remember it. It makes an impression on people if they spend money.'

He turned towards the girls again. They had not moved. He would never know what they had been doing.... A tableau vivant representing what? What was the phrase he sought to explain them? And what did it matter? The impli-cation was clear in his mind ... things inexplicable ... in-scrutable.... There was a man in ancient Greece who having carved a statue embraced it and it came to life. Here was the opposite. The living statues whom he possessed but never reached ... of whom he knew nothing. Perhaps because there was nothing to know. They stood looking at him. Only his dog ran forward.

To none of his questions was there an answer. Ovaries. It
was extraordinary how people spoilt things for you. He hoped
his girls had not touched his paints. They were like children,
but beautiful. Deer ... Fascista ... the green of young
bananas ... With primrose a pale mauve would be better.
But they did not like mauve. Complementary colors ... How
the sun struck the satin of their brown shoulders ... dark
pools at their feet ... pools of shadow ... Shadow was wet
like black water ... A springing deer arrested by death ... a
hunter ... a hunter upon a hill ... Guadalajara ... Movement was life ... life was God ... Suddenly he was thirsty for
cold beer: for beauty.

Channel watched Sebastian going towards the women.
Then he went into his house. He was still thinking about the
duiker. He went through the sitting room into his office.
Nowhere in the world was there a finer private tropical collection than his. There were bottles and jars [of all sizes on
the shelves sealed with red wax. The room smelt of alcohol
and formalin. The result of ten years' work on the equator.
A Watusi hand, a Pigmy foetus ... There were tumors particular to this region ... organs, specimens of every kind.

This country was a doctor's paradise: sleeping sickness,
elephantiasis, abdominal growths, goitres, bladderstones,
scabies, worms of infinite variety; hernias, some of which hung
below the knees; head lice, crab lice, yaws, jigger sores that
eat whole feet away ... And there were some strange facets
to this practice of his. There was no cancer here and no
appendicitis. With gonorrhea almost universal, there was
no need to disinfect the eyes of newborn children. Try as he
would, he could find no explanation for this. This desire to
explain had obsessed him — as a young man. How many
years ago it was that he had begun to follow in the footsteps
of Mesmer. In his search for truth he had come very near to
it. Too near, perhaps.

He transferred the captured fly into a killing bottle and sat down at the table to write. 'July 12th. Went to the store with Sebastian. Discussed women. Bentinck shot duiker female with horns. N. B. try to obtain another for examination — query: physical damage to uterus affecting ovaries, possibility of old age. Change of sexual characteristics caused by age unlikely in wild animals; horns more pointed and less thick than in males. Should have examined teeth. Sebastian expressed desire to be buried mountain-side. Premonition of death perhaps due to seeing buck shot. It is interesting to note that in all our conversations Olga is never mentioned. Why? Possibly because thoughts of her are always present. No one ever speaks of Olga, except factually...'

He put down the pen. Olga was woman. So much so that she became representative, generic, symbolic, diffusing a sexual aura. A woman alone among men. He thought about the beauty of women. Men were infinitely variable in their taste. One man's woman was not another man's. What does he see in her?... How often did one ask that of oneself when one looked at the wives of one's friends! But the women who were considered really beautiful — actresses, film stars — were simply those who by their symmetry appealed to a great number of men instead of a single man. Olga was of that type.

Was it a proof of civilization or of decadence that for a woman to be a woman — that is, female — was no longer enough? The higher races no longer mated; no longer coupled in the spring and fall. They made love in their minds before they made it with their bodies.

He closed his diary. Sometimes he wondered why he kept it. Out of habit: he had always kept a diary. He wrote too much. His books — his notes. Was there any point in writing — in assuming that experience or knowledge could be communicated? They all wrote too much. Jean, Retief — himself. Lacking the variety of companionship offered by a normal life, they ran to their diaries, their journals. Introspection and speculation, if it did not come naturally to them, was forced upon them. The things they were unable to say they wrote.

Tonight he was dining with Olga and the professor. Retief would be there, naturally, but would there be anyone else? Probably not. They would play bridge. It was a pity she had not let him kill Congo. Before he went to bed, he was going to try another drug — Bentinck had got it for him. It was said to induce visions.

He went back through the sitting room and out onto the veranda. He had a desire to see pigeons flying, a flock of them twisting and turning in a cold, blue sky. Pigeons were so reasonable, something you could understand. You fed them bread crumbs. They billed and cooed on the streets, in the parks. They blew out their chests and bowed. Why should he think of pigeons now? Why did one think of anything? Tumblers... It was supposed to be a disease. They became dizzy and fell and then recovered. But why should the whole flock of pigeons become dizzy at once? Japanese waltzing mice going round and round. And dogs; gun dogs, pointers, setters... a form of catalepsy. Pekingese, English bulldogs, fancy goldfish... What queer tricks man had played on Nature and on himself! Here was a subject worthy of investigation. Not the phenomena, but the instinct of man to produce phenomena... Dwarfs artificially crippled; boys castrated to sing in cathedrals; eunuchs for harems... His mind went back to pigeons again circling in a cold, blue sky. The two were associated in his mind. The African sky was burnt out, incandescent. It did not cover you. It beat down upon you. It would destroy you if it could.

One got these fits of depression... these nostalgias. The past was past. It could not be brought back. He doubted if he would ever again see pigeons wheeling in a cold, blue sky. In this new Europe he would be an anachronism.

Bathe, dress, dinner, bridge. In the garden a boy was tying up a climbing rose.

When the car had gone, Bentinck poured out another cup of tea and lit his pipe. Funny the interest Channel took in things like that. A buck was a buck. If he knew as much as I do, he thought, he would not worry. But that was it. All scientists believed they would find the truth if they went on long enough. Yes, it was funny. Sebastian came nearer to the heart of things than Channel. So did Owen. Jan had the duiker hung by its hind legs to a tree and was skinning it. Its belly was a black void.

They would send down in the morning for the legs. He kept them in game. When he shot something, he ran a white flag up on the staff he had fastened to the top of the big marula. You could see it easily with glasses from the Station. Meat did not keep long, and it had to be fetched at once. If they had not been in such a hurry, they could have taken it with them.

He was looking forward to his supper. The saddle. He would make holes in it and fill them with twists of bacon and a little garlic. That was the way to cook a saddle. He would do it himself and not leave it to Jan. He wondered when they would come back. They came once a week, sometimes oftener: just to pass the time of day; to talk to me, he thought. But they did not talk to him, they talked to each other about women, and it passed the time. They did not know anything about women. They did not know anything about anything. He knew about women. He had loved one woman and married her. And she had died. That was how you learnt about women: from one woman; from loving her. It was nearly thirty years since Mary had died. She was buried in Kimberley.

Chapter 2

The HUNTER

wwwwwwwwwww

THE STORE HAD BEEN BUILT BY A BIG MARULA. THE TREE HAD
been there for hundreds of years. Beside it the store looked
very insecure. The tree was rooted fast in the deep red soil.
The store had been run up ... a frame building mounted on
hardwood blocks; sheeted in corrugated iron, it stood sun-
beaten, ant-rotted, hot as an oven in the blazing glare of the
African noonday. It cast no shadow. Only the great tree
cast a shadow, a black lake out of which the trunk rose, smooth
as an elephant's leg, climbing into the main fork, breaking
into lesser forks, into branches, into the twigs that carried its
bright green foliage mass.

The ground round the tree and the store was bare —
tramped hard. But the tramped ground stopped abruptly;
and where it stopped, the long harsh grass began; tamboukie
grass, turpentine grass: sour grass as tough as wire; and in the
grass stood trees: thorn trees, timber trees, Mopani scrub,
vaal bos, Podo, olive and camphor, Kameel doorn and
mimosa. Beyond the trees was the line of dark green that
marked the river bank. In one place the river itself shone; it
glittered, a sword part drawn from the scabbard of its course.

Silberman's store, they called the place. Silberman had
built it and had died here of fever many years ago: his, the
first of the eleven graves that stood in an irregular line behind
the building. They were not in alignment because those men
had been buried by their Kaffirs, who were unaware of the

importance of a straight line. Between the store and the graves was a cairn of bottles, dark green, brown, white; whisky bottles, gin bottles, beer bottles. The sun struck at them indiscriminately. They struck back shimmering and indestructible.

Sometimes Augustus Bentinck went out to look at the graves. His own would be the twelfth. Sometimes he forgot about them for weeks. He liked living here where the cards were stacked against him. All his life he had played against Africa, pitting his strength and his wits and his skill against the infinity of the wild. His life had been long, and this was his final triumph, that he should continue to live here, trading a little, sleeping and reading his remaining days away in peace where so many had died before he came.

He was dozing now, on a deck chair beneath the tree. His hat was pulled over his face; his belt was loosened — slacked like the girths of a horse. He was dozing while he waited for someone to come. A quarter of an hour ago he had seen a man running over the low hill that bounded the far side of the river. The man was a native. There was only one place to which a man could run. He was in that place, and while the man ran, he dozed. When the man came, he would know why he ran. Until he did, there was no reason to disturb himself.

The flies buzzed ceaselessly. They settled on the long dark hairs of Bentinck's forearms, but he never moved. They sat on his veldschoen and crawled up his bare ankles. They blackened the inside of an empty can that lay near him. The flies were an integral part of the bush where he lived; part of the grey-green sea of scrub and forest that ran from the blue escarpment of the mountains to the green velvet of the coastal swamps; to the mangrove thickets that mantled the sluggish estuaries of West Africa, fifteen hundred miles away.

The flies were a part of this life, as were the buck, and the lions that coughed in the night; as were the vultures circling

endlessly in the sky; as were the stones of the marula fruits
that littered the ground beneath the tree. For hundreds, for
thousands of years these things had gone on: the lions roam-
ing, the buck grazing in the dawn, the vultures circling, and
the ripe fruits falling from the trees, each in their season.

Three go-away birds rose out of a bush with fluttering
wings. *Go Away! Go Away!* they cried.

Bentinck sat up. The wait was over. The man had come.

He stood beneath the tree in front of him: a Masai.

'I see you, chief,' he said.

'I see you, warrior,' Bentinck answered.

They watched each other, staring into each other's eyes.
The sweat ran down between the warrior's breasts. He
raised his hand to wipe it away, pushing it down in a little
stream with the bottom of his hand; it ran over the heaving
muscles of his belly. He was naked: his nakedness was apparent when he moved. Over one shoulder he wore a blanket
of tanned hide. His hair, dressed with fat and red ochre, was
drawn up in the shape of a Roman helmet; a pigtail bound
with thread hung down his back. He was a Moran, a warrior.
In his hand he held a spear, eight foot long, all steel but for a
little central shaft of brown wood. He also held a shield. It
was made of buffalo skin painted with designs of red, white,
and blue. Above him the vultures circled. Behind him the
store burnt in the sun. A draggled cockerel stood near, its
beak open, its wings held away from its sides. The go-away
birds were gone. They had given their warning.

To the Masai time was nothing. He was unconscious of it.
To Bentinck time was meaningless. He knew of time, but he
had given it up. This was a moment of meeting between two
men. It had purpose. It had design. The Masai knew why
he had come. Bentinck knew whence he had come. A man
did not run sixty miles through the little paths of Africa for
nothing.

Meanwhile, they measured each other, missing nothing.

The Masai's flanks still heaved. His sweat still ran. His nostrils quivered as he drew the hot air into his lungs. Changing his spear to his left hand, he raised his right and placed it, palm to palm, against Bentinck's.

Bentinck said, 'Whence come you, warrior?' He knew whence he came and the Moran knew that he knew. It was a politeness: a convention.

'I come, chief, from Seluca on the banks of the M'Loco.'

'You come from the place of reeds on the banks of the M'Loco River,' Bentinck repeated. 'That is far.'

'It is far, lord.'

'A young man does not travel so far and so fast; so swiftly, to such a great distance from the maidens of his race, for nothing. The warrior did not come for nothing.'

'He did not come for nothing, chief.'

'Then go.' Bentinck pointed to the store. 'My servant will give you food and water. Rest, warrior. Compose yourself. When the sun is there' — he raised his hand and pointed to the top of the bush on which the go-away birds had perched — 'we will speak together.'

'I go, chief.' The Moran turned towards the store.

A fine people, the Masai: a beautiful people. Perhaps the most beautiful in all the world, Bentinck thought, as he watched him go. Cattle-raisers; blood-drinkers; milk-drinkers. The blood they took hot from the veins of their beasts, drinking it and plugging the wound with a thorn. This man was a member of a tribe which, isolated from the rest of the nation, lived on the plains watered by the M'Loco. The messenger had probably run without halting, but would have been too proud to ask for rest or food.

Bentinck pulled the hat down over his eyes. The flies returned to his bare ankles and the long dark hairs of his forearms.

The sun moved westward. The shadow of the tree lengthened towards the east. Slowly, like a living thing, it extended itself from the trunk. It grew longer and longer. It grew grotesquely long as it crept over the hard, bare ground. Because the ground was red, the shadow was purple. Bentinck was no longer in the shade, but he still slept.

The Moran was back; he stood, spear in hand, on one leg waiting. His eyes were fixed upon Bentinck. Nothing moved: nothing but the flies — they were tireless; and the vultures. Then Bentinck woke. His eyes met the staring eyes of the Masai.

Bentinck said, 'You are rested?'

'I am rested, O chief.'

They were silent again. Bentinck wondered what the Masai was thinking. He might be thinking of how best to state his message. He might be going over in his mind the speech he had memorized: the Masai were lovers of beautiful words, and of maidens, and of war. His lips moved as if he said phrases over to himself. Or he might be thinking of a love speech that he would make when he got home.

Bentinck gave him time. He was lost in his own past. He thought of the old days when he had hunted with Freddy Selous . . . of the ivory they had sold . . . of the great herds of elephants they had seen. He thought of the later days when he had become a hunter of medicine for the Kaffirs. That had been after Mary's death.

Hippo fat was a favorite love potion: the maid or man smeared with it became irresistible. This was well known. Elephants he had poached for the small tubes inside their livers. Even if an elephant had light tusks — and the day of big tusks was over — it had liver tubes. Sections of these also sold well as love potions. He thought of crocodiles whose brain mixed with snuff was a swift and certain poison; and the fat of a crocodile which was a safeguard against poison — not merely its own, but all poison; and the little stones, some- times as many as a hundred, that were found within its belly which insured long life. Crocodiles' eyes were also good medicine and so was the heart. The eyelids of the buffalo dried and powdered would make a man face any ordeal with the appearance of innocence, and a little in a woman's food would make her weep with desire for the giver. Tigers' whiskers were another poison. Python fat was in demand as a cure for earache, as was the fat of the blue monkey. Hyenas were always wanted. A strip of hyena's skin was a good thing to burn by anyone planning evil; while the burning of an eyelash of this animal by a young man would make the girl he loved sleep and awake wanting to kiss him. This was how he had got his native name, by hunting strong medicine for Kaffirs. Some he sold to buy powder and shot. Some he gave to his friends among them and as rewards for service. Yes, he thought, I sell poison, but only to my friends for use upon their enemies. Not that he believed in these poisons — he had taken some himself to try them — but they killed people. It was all a matter of faith. He had no faith in his poisons, therefore they were harmless to him. But he had a name among the witch doctors as a purveyor. It interested him because the natives had real poisons, vegetable ones which they seldom used. These must appear too unsophisticated to them: too simple. A witch doctor had to consider his technique, his prestige. He was an artist, a craftsman. But on the whole they were nice people, men of great principle and integrity. His poisons he kept at the back of the store, behind the shelf of jew's-harps, wrapped in newspaper parcels. No one would steal them: they were too mixed up. He used the *Times* for wrapping. It did not tear easily. He got the *Times* about two months late: not the weekly *Times*, but the regular daily paper. He read one copy a day.

His past was spread out before him as his recollections unrolled: the ribbon of his life that was watered with the blood of accidents, that was ragged with adventures, stained with the offal of his thousand killings. He wondered how much he

had killed ... how many elephants, lions, hippos, buck ...
how many? How many miles had he travelled hunting,
transport riding, prospecting, trading? How many men had
he known, and how few were left alive? In all those years
how little things had changed! There was not so much game,
but that was less due to man than to the rinderpest of '96.
Everything had died then — game, cattle, everything. The
lions had taken to eating garbage, and many of them had
died too. It was all long ago, very long ago.

He looked at the young Masai again. 'Speak,' he said, 'I
will hear you.' It was never any good trying to hurry a
native.

'There is news from Balan; it came by runner,' the Masai
said.

'And what is the news from Balan?'

'A man has come. A man in a motor car.'

'Aah,' Bentinck said. 'A man.' He paused. Was this man
the one he wanted? For a year now he had been waiting for
someone. But after all, if it was, what had he to tell him?
Just straws in the wind; just the faintest spoor on the rocky
ground. If this man was the right kind of man ... if he could
convince him ... if ...

'What manner of man is this?' he asked.

'A very tall man. White, an Englishman.'

'And where is he?'

'He is two days away and his motor car is sick. Its leg is
broken.'

'But he comes this way?'

'Lord, what other way is there for him to go? Come he
must, unless he turns back running upon his own spoor that is
yet warm.'

'That is true. Give greetings to the Elders,' Bentinck said.

'I will give greetings.' The Masai raised his spear. 'I go.'

'Go sweetly.' Bentinck filled his pipe and settled back in
his chair.

Two days, he thought. That was one day by car, fifty miles over those roads was not bad going. He would be here tomorrow. The Masai were very reliable. He had had a lot of information from them, one way and another.

It would be interesting to meet a stranger. It was a long time since he had seen a new face. Well, whoever it was, he was coming on a good day. There was going to be a party for the doctor tomorrow night. Jan brought tea out to him. He poured himself a cup, scraped the flies off the condensed milk can with his finger, and poured some into the cup. He stirred it till it melted, put in two spoonfuls of sugar, and stirred the cup again. The idea of the party amused him. They were always having parties at the Botanical Station. They would all get drunk except Olga. He might even get a little drunk himself. She would watch them contemptuously and go out to play with that damn gorilla of hers. Von Brandt would lay down the law — he always did — and talk about German West when it was German West. Channel would become sentimental about Paris. He thought of Retief watching Olga, of Sebastian roaring about beauty and art, of the professor pottering around, and Owen as miserable as hell. Those parties were no place for a missionary, but Owen always came. Partly out of loneliness and partly to save them, if he could. Poor Owen, the talk always got round to women, a difficult subject for a minister.

He drank his tea and poured out another cup. If I was younger, he thought, I'd be after Olga myself. As it was, the race was between Retief and von Brandt. They were like dogs snuffling after her, following her.

'Jan!' he shouted.

'Baas...'

'Jan, tomorrow a Baas comes this way. He will stay with me. See that the place is clean.'

'The place is clean, Baas.'

'I mean cleaner. It must be washed. The floor... clean, I say.'

'With water, Baas? I must wash the floor with water?'

'Ja, Jan, with water.'

He thought about his visitor again. Frazer must have sent him. Things were moving at last. He felt very cheerful. It was not that he had been bored — not exactly. But you got tired of just sitting on your stern waiting for things to happen. What a lot of company he was having! Yesterday Channel and Sebastian. Today the Masai and the boy who had come to fetch the buck. Tomorrow a stranger. It was hard to get real privacy.

He had told Frazer he was too old for the job when he had sent him here. But his argument had been no good. 'It's because of that I want you to do it. You know the country and the natives. You know German. No one will think anything of it if you take over the store. It's the kind of thing a man like you would do.'

And it was. But it was funny in a way, too. After a lifetime of hunting animals to hunt the biggest game of all ... to end your life hunting men, and to find it dull. He knew what people thought of him. *Old Bentinck, old rough-neck, old-timer ... that's what men come to when they live like that away from other men. He drinks, of course; they all do.* It made him laugh. He never drank till sundown.

What people thought! How little one really knew of anyone! And what could they know of his past since he never spoke of it? It was a good thing he was working with Frazer. With anyone else there would have been endless questions, demands of proof, and then the whole thing pigeonholed and forgotten. Frazer let him alone. 'If there's a blood spoor, I'll find it,' he had said. But he was tired of spooring. It was time they closed in a little — gave 'em a run for their money.

It was long since he had been home: twenty years. And he hadn't been well treated in the last war. None of the hunters and scouts had been. What hundreds of lives they could have

saved if their advice had been followed! But that was not the
point. If the Government needed him, he would do what
they asked. 'No one is going to suspect you,' Frazer had said.
But he had sent in no reports for a long time. He had always
been the same, wanting to make sure before he fired. Nothing
hit or miss about old Bentinck... old Augustus, to whom a
Boer was impatient. Magtig, how angry he had made some
of them in his time! But patience paid. He thought of his
notes. Olga had them. That was certainly the last place anyone would look for them: the last place and the most dangerous. Olga was a good friend of his.

He went into the house to eat. Tonight was the last night
before the coming of the stranger. He felt his coming would
end a phase. Something would end and something else begin.
The hunt was up. The hundred strings he had thrown out,
the snares he had laid, must be drawn tight. When he had
made up his mind about the man who was on his way, he
would see Entobo. He was a first-class witch doctor and
universally respected. It made him smile sometimes to hear
people talk about witch doctors. Behind all that mumbo-
jumbo there was knowledge. 'And what do you think about
it all, Bentinck?' they asked.

'What do I think, young man? I think that I would not
like to be cursed by one. I think that when a lion-man comes
and asks me for an ox, I would be a fool not to give him
one.' The last time this had happened had been at Heath's
Hotel in Jo'burg. There had been another old hunter there.
They had smiled at each other. Aloysius Horn it had been.
He wondered what had happened to the old skelm.

Jan came to take away the saddle of buck. He had had it
cold tonight. When the boy left, he turned the lamp higher
and began to read. The book was 'Bleak House.' He was
reading it for the eighth time. He read a chapter and then
put the book face down on the table, pushed up his glasses,

and stared out of the window. He was listening to the drums:
the Congo drums. News was being passed through Africa:
news of the stranger, perhaps. He lifted the bottle to the light:
there was another drink left, a nightcap.

Chapter 3

The AMERICAN

 ◆◆◆◆◆◆◆◆◆◆◆◆◆◆◆◆◆

HENRY WILSON DROVE SLOWLY. HE HAD TO. THE ROAD WAS bad. He was in a bad temper, due to the road, to his recent breakdown, and to his own idiocy which had got him into this. Why in God's name had he come out here into the bush like this? If he had wanted a motor trip, there were plenty he could have taken on decent roads. And why had he agreed to Frazer's proposition? He had not even the excuse of drunkenness.

Every event had a visible source . . . granted it only became visible afterward when it was too late: granted also, that preceding the visible cause there must be a number of invisible, unappreciated psychological reasons which drove you to that beginning which was the visible source — to the place where you could say categorically, 'It all began there . . . when I did that.'

But even this philosophic conclusion was no particular comfort. To know you were a damn fool was not much good. A hornbill flew across the road in front of him with a clattering cry. Some vultures, clustered round a dead cow twenty yards away, stopped scuffling over the entrails they had drawn out of it, flapped their wings, and as he passed them settled down to their feast again. This was the real Africa which so few tourists ever saw . . . silent except for the cry of an occasional bird, empty save for a dead beast here and there. Its bare ugliness punctuated by beauties that took your breath away.

Of course the divorce was the real beginning. Or Anne was. Or the Warrens where he had met Anne. Or his mother, perhaps. The Warrens had been friends of hers. His mother certainly, because if he had not had a mother he would never have been born. And if she had not known the Warrens, he would never have dined there. If he had not dined there, he would not have met Anne. How lovely she had looked in that white lace dress! Not regular lace — but a queer material, all tiny stars like snowflakes fastened together in a web of white. And if he had not met Anne, he could not have married her, and there would have been no divorce. No divorce, no Africa. Anyway, it was silly to think you get away from things by travelling. . . . And no Africa, no Nairobi . . . no Frazer . . . and no damn-fool business like this.

But it had really begun, or this part of it had, when he had bought the car. He went back over the last few days in his mind.

'Yes, I'll take it.' He had looked at the car. There was something funny about buying a dark red Ford V8 in Nairobi. He couldn't figure out why it was funny, but it was. It wasn't what he had expected. On the other hand, he wasn't quite sure what he had expected. Nothing had turned out the way he had thought it would.

He had wanted to get off by himself. He had been afraid to for the last six months, but now the sooner it began, the better. The night before, Frazer had asked him what he was going to do. He had had no plans. But Frazer's question had crystallized something that must have been in the back of his mind for a long time.

'Buy a car and drift around. See the country a bit.'

'If you're going to buy a car, get a Ford. You can always sell it again.'

Buy it. Use it. Sell it. Change. That was what he wanted,

wasn't it? It was, and it wasn't. He wanted something real, secure: something that would last. But things didn't last. It was no use expecting them to. Perhaps one should be able to live for the moment, forget the past and not worry about the future. He wondered why he had never seen it that way before. Even your friends changed. He thought of the people he had known seven years ago . . . fourteen years ago. Wasn't a man supposed to change completely every seven years? You changed. They changed. The friends you kept were the ones who changed with you: who went your way . . .

'You'd better have two spares,' the man had said. 'In this country . . .'

'Yes, two spares.' Well, two spares hadn't been enough.

He was an immaculate young man with an Oxford accent, like all motor salesmen. They were a special variety of young man. Wilson wondered what went on in his mind . . . in any of their minds. They spent hours leaning, beautifully dressed, against the fenders of the cars they were selling: just waiting for someone to come in. They spoke in a special way. Nice car . . . new features . . . trade-in . . . just try it and you'll see what I mean . . . no comparison. Then he had said just what Frazer had said the night before: 'If you come back this way, we'll buy it back . . . cheaper really this way.'

Cheaper than what? Hiring, he meant, presumably.

'Tomorrow morning do?'

'Yes.'

'At the Salisbury. Nice hotel, isn't it? We'll see to the insurance and everything. You've got your license, haven't you?'

He had looked forward to getting the car. As soon as he had it, he would go. He was tired of Nairobi. He had seen everything: the herds of game; the Macmillan Memorial Library; the Museum, another memorial; the four golf clubs, the country club, the polo club, the Aero Club. He was tired of Delamere Street and Harding Street. He must get on.

What a lot he had seen already, one way and another: the
big hole at Kimberley, the Game Reserve, the Falls, Zimbabwe. He had had letters. He had been passed from one
man to another. He had been entertained till he was sick of
entertainment. 'Beautiful, charming, wonderful . . . No, I've
never seen anything like it before.' He had used up his ad-
jectives, used up his politeness, his critical faculty. He had
met some nice people: so many nice people that they had
blurred into each other. They were now one composite nice
person. And he was going to get out of it. Into the blue, he
had thought. Funny how you used expressions like that to
yourself. But it was right in Africa.

He slowed down. The distances were blue. The hills and
plains, the mountains were all blue. When you got there,
they were brown — khaki-colored. This was where khaki
had been invented . . . the Boer War. But there were always
more blue distances beyond, more mountains and plains.
You saw a range and crossed it, but there was always another
range in front of you. That was like life, always something
beyond. And it was always disappointing.

Anne would have liked this trip. But it was no good thinking of Anne. That was over. He must get it into his head.
That was why he had come out here. It is over, he thought.
He had run far enough. He could not run away from himself
forever. The time had come to think, to remember and clear
away the débris of his life. Tidy it up, the loose ends, the
little incidents. It was a pity people took sides in a divorce.
It was such a personal matter. Something no one could
understand. So many hopes, so many illusions. He was glad
he had not taken a boy with him. Kampala, Rutshuru,
Stanleyville . . . How Anne would have liked Kilimanjaro . . .
There had been a cocktail party at Lady Soames' that evening,
and then that final dinner with Frazer which had torn it.
He went over the party in his mind. I wonder when I'll go to
another one, he thought.

'How nice of you to come, Mr. Wilson,' Lady Soames had spoken past him. Someone had followed him in.

'My dear Francis, how delightful!'

There had been a lot of people there already. Many of them he had met before. You always met the same people or some of the same people. Even the people you had not met looked just like the people you had met, spoke as they did and of the same things — polo, horse-breeding, shooting... 'You know that new coffee shamba Hastings bought...' 'But I got him next shot...' 'Then H. E. said...' He had seen Colonel Renton. He had a crippled arm. It had been mauled by a lion three years before. Gentleman farmers, sportsmen, almost all of them had been soldiers; some civil servants, officials. More fragments of conversation came back to him... 'Of course he denied it, but everyone knows ...' 'But, my dear!' 'No, darling, it's been going on for years.' A boy in white with a scarlet tarbush and sash carrying round a tray. A Martini. The choice was Martini or sherry. Lady Soames moving through her guests. She was a remarkable woman with a figure like a young girl's and a pigskin face — like a saddle. She had this place where she bred a few horses, about twenty miles out; and a big farm up-country. She had a manager there. She had had a lot of managers in the last ten years. They never lasted long and were all young men. Sir Alfred had died soon after they came out... so sad.

Wilson had found himself talking to a young girl in blue. 'She's my aunt, you know.' She nodded at Lady Soames. He had not known.

'And how do you like it out here?' he had asked.

'I love it. I simply love it. I don't ever want to go back.'

'I don't think you'll have to.' She had been very pretty.

'I hope not. Anyway, I've got three months more.'

A young man brought her a drink. 'This is Reggie French. You know Reggie, don't you, Mr. Wilson.'

'I think we've met.'

'Yes, we met last week at dinner ... the Johnstones'. Staying long? If you are, I've got some ponies ...'

'He's got some lovely ponies,' the girl said. She had looked from Wilson to Reggie. 'I ride them, don't I, Reggie?'

'Exercise,' Reggie said. 'Can't ride 'em all myself. Niggers got no hands. Ruin 'em. Come out and see them sometime.'

'I'd be delighted to, but I am leaving soon.' There had been no need to tell him he was leaving tomorrow.

'Shooting?' Reggie asked.

Another man joined them, and a girl in pink. The man was a little drunk. Then he had seen Frazer and excused himself.

'Thought I'd find you here,' Frazer said. 'I hear you've got your car. I think you were right to get a Ford. Always sell it again.'

More people had come. The room was full of people and smoke. There was a lot of noise. Nairobi. It might have been London, or Paris, or New York. The women were well-groomed. They were groomed like horses, and the men all had that horsey look. They were sunburnt and trim in white. Hard as nails. It was funny the way you could spot horsey men. He had never liked horses. But they seemed to do something to the men who associated with them.

'See you later,' Frazer had said. 'I'll take you home. You haven't forgotten you're dining with me, have you?'

He remembered wondering why he had come. The same people, the same talk, the same offers ... Ponies to sell ... nice farm, plenty of grazing and good water ... someone else with a rifle they wanted to get rid of. Women looking for a new man ... any new man. All very well-bred, but ... The stories you heard about the place were true: too much money; too little to do; the climate. Not that there was anything wrong with it except the altitude, five thousand feet, and on the equator. Of course, there were some real farmers and planters, but they stayed clear of all this sort of thing. This kind of life was very hard to understand. But why should it be? He had seen enough of the same sort of thing elsewhere. That was it — elsewhere. Everything was exaggerated here. Everyone knew everything about everyone else.

He had had another Martini. Frazer had signalled to him and he had made his way across the room. Lady Soames had been talking to Colonel Bellairs as he left. They were all colonels.

'Got to go? I'm so sorry. Hoped you'd stay on. There's some food, you know...'

'I wish I could stay. It has been so delightful.' He had said something like that. The evening had seemed very quiet when they got outside.

After dinner they had sat in the big room that Frazer called his library. There was a fire burning in an open fire-place. That always struck him as extraordinary — the way it got cold at night here. He had watched the flames.

'Expect you're glad to be going,' Frazer said.

'In some ways.'

'Any plans?'

'No real plans yet. Congo, I think.' He had been certain of only one thing: that he wanted to get away.

Frazer had lit a cigar. 'You're half American, aren't you?'

'Yes, but I've spent most of my time in Europe: England and France.' America was a long way off tonight. Anne was in America. He had wondered what she was doing. What time was it in New York now?

This was a very nice room... books, lots of them; some heads, some nice hunting prints. How had Frazer known he was half American? He was proud of it, but somehow re-sented the fact that he had been discussed. A hunting picture seemed to be no good unless someone in pink was falling off

a horse . . . grey horses, bay horses, chestnuts, but always a
man in pink going over its head.

'Do you mind my asking you something personal?' Frazer
asked. 'Why are you out here? You're not the ordinary
tourist. You're not shooting.'

'I was divorced six months ago,' he had said. It had been
hard to say.

'I see.' Frazer had got up. 'I'm sorry,' he said. He had
stood with his back to the fire. He could see him now. It was
a very English pose. They stood like that even if there was no
fire. He did it himself — due to his English father, no doubt.
It was funny that he had never thought of this before.

'The reason I asked you is because I want you to do something. I want you to go to Mokala and find an excuse for
staying there a bit. Something is up and I want to know
about it.'

'Why do you?' he had asked. Frazer had never struck him
as a curious man. But how had he known about the Ford so
quickly or that he was half American?

'Because I want to know about everything. You see, I'm
in the Intelligence. A lot of Germans came back after the
war. Have to keep an eye on them.' He had seemed embarrassed about it.

A more unlikely man it was hard to think of.

Frazer had smiled. 'Surprised, aren't you? I'm dull. Bit
of a bore with my stuff about rubber and sisal and coffee and
cotton.' They had talked of rubber at dinner.

'I should hardly say that.' He had hoped it sounded con-
vincing.

'No, you wouldn't say it, but you think it. Now listen to
me. There's going to be war. It's not my place to talk about
Munich or Chamberlain. As a matter of fact, I blame
Baldwin for most of it, but that's between ourselves. I have
no opinions. I'm supposed to be a statistician . . . I send nice
little reports to the Colonial Office about the native produc-

tion of cotton and coffee and things. I go out a lot as I did today. I bore people to death with my figures while I listen. Of course, no one reads my reports: not those reports. But it gives me an excuse to go about.

'You speak like an American,' he went on then. He leant back in his chair and drew on his cigar.

'I've lived there as a child,' Wilson said. 'My mother was American, you know. And my wife.' He had not thought it worth while to add that he had been to an American university.

Frazer said nothing. He seemed to be thinking. Wilson concentrated on the prints again. He did not want to think of Anne or his mother. He did not want to think of America.

'I think it would be better if you were an American,' Frazer said. 'Let people think it at Mokala, I mean. You wouldn't mind, would you?'

'No, but I don't see why?'

'If there's anything going on, they would not suspect an American. Neutral, see? No European commitments.'

'All right.' It was true it would be easy enough. And if it would make Frazer happy ...

He asked Frazer about Mokala. Frazer ... Good Lord!

'I've got a man there,' Frazer had gone on. 'An old hunter. Drunken old devil running the store. You might look him up. And there's a Botanical Station on the mountain. Interesting people, I hear.'

'You think I could help?'

'I don't know, but it might keep you from brooding,' Frazer had said. And that had been that. Another highball, and when he said good night Frazer had wished him luck. That had been all.

Mokala began, and began rather badly about two miles east of the store. There seemed to be no particular reason why it should begin here, or why it shouldn't.

The bush road opened out before this point into savannah country. It was like all African roads, engineered by men who avoided obstacles instead of overcoming them. It wound about, and then there was the notice — a white board with black, roughly printed lettering ... MOKALA. Wilson slowed up to read it. Frazer had told him that it was a big district — part low-country, part swamp and rolling bush dotted with fever trees, and part mountain and forest. A land of gorillas, okapi, elephants, and lions; Pigmies and giants. He had reached his destination.

And where do I go from here? he wondered. He meant to stay for a while. He had promised Frazer he would. But after? There was always an after. One got so tired of things. He would have to think up something to do here. He had taken anthropology at Columbia and here was a chance of making use of it. Who were the Watusi? Was there any relation between the Congo Pigmies and the South African Bushmen? And had the rock paintings in Spain anything to do with those he had seen all over the Union and Rhodesia? These questions interested him vaguely. He did not hope to solve them. His was not the true scientific approach. He was a dilettante, an experimenter; a passer of the time. That was what money had done for him. It made him ashamed in a way. When you could do anything, you did nothing.

Though he was in no hurry, being held up yesterday had upset him. He was in a queer state of mind.

Well, here he was. Now for Mr. Bentinck, Augustus Bentinck. Anyway, as Frazer said, it would give him something to do.

A blind turn, because the trees were thicker, and there was the store standing near a big tree. A man lay asleep sprawled in a deck chair beneath it.

As the car slowed down, the man pushed back his hat from his eyes, and sat up. Then he rose. He was a big, loosely built man with an untrimmed grey beard.

Wilson got out and went towards him. 'Mr. Bentinck?'
he said. Doctor Livingstone, I presume, he thought. Or was
it the other way about? Who had found who? A white man
meeting another white man in darkest Africa. The human
mind was a funny thing. Come to that, the human being was
funny altogether.

Wilson looked at the tree. It must be a landmark. There
was a flagstaff lashed to its upper branches; a thin wire rope
ran through a block and was fastened to two big nails driven
into the trunk.

The man put out his hand. 'Augustus Bentinck,' he said.
'I'm Wilson.'

They shook hands.

'I've got your room ready,' Bentinck said. He waved his
hand at the store. 'Hotel,' he said. 'Bentinck's Hotel. Silberman's Post, it was. But he's dead. Then van Rensburg's,
then Frenchman's ... everyone called him that. Then some
others. All dead.' He stared past Wilson. 'Had it specially
cleaned out for you. Jan!' he shouted. 'Jan, tea ...'

'My room?' Wilson said. 'You expected me.'

'Been expecting you for a year.'

The man was mad. A year ago he had been in New York.
Happily married ... a year ago ... He did not want to think
of a year ago. Fishing with Anne in Florida.

'I don't see ...' he said.

'No,' Bentinck said. 'Have some tea.' He led the way to
the store. A colored boy was putting a brown enamel teapot
on the table. He brought two white enamel cups with blue
handles, a can of milk, a bowl of sugar, and two spoons.

'Milk and sugar?' Bentinck asked. The boy stood at the
door watching them.

'Yes,' Wilson said, 'cream and sugar.' The tea was nearly
black.

Bentinck turned to the boy. 'Get the Baas' things out of
the car and put them in his room.' The boy went out.

Bentinck lit his pipe. He concentrated on it. Then he looked up. Wilson could feel himself being examined. The dark eyes went over him a point at a time.

'Taking you to a party tonight,' he said.

'A party? What sort of party?'

'Cocktail party.' Bentinck drank his tea, sinking his face into the cup and then wiping his moustache and beard with his hand. A cocktail party here! That was just what he thought he had got away from.

'Yes,' Bentinck went on. 'It's the fourteenth of July.'

What had that to do with it? Then he remembered.

'It's a French holiday,' he said. But what application had it here?

'It's Channel's party. He's French.' Bentinck went on smoking. He seemed to think everything was satisfactorily explained.

Wilson looked round the room. Except for a rack of rifles and two shelves of books, it was empty. There was the table at which they sat, four chairs, and a bench, but nothing except the books and guns that gave any clue to the kind of man Bentinck was. Through the door he could see the store.

'Books,' he said, and got up to look at them.

Bentinck turned his head to watch him.

There was a complete set of Dickens; some Thackeray, Thoreau's 'Walden,' Whitman's 'Poems,' a Bible, Wells' 'Outline of History,' and two books by Selous.

'You can tell something about a man by his books, can't you?' Bentinck said.

So he had guessed what he was after. 'Sometimes you can,' he said.

'More tea?' Bentinck filled both cups. The boy came through the room with two gasoline cans of hot water.

'Your bath,' Bentinck said. 'Expect they'll send for us, or we might drive up in your car.'

He was evidently talking about the party.

'Where is it?' Wilson asked.

'Settlement. Up the mountain. Botanical Station, they call it. Nice place,' Bentinck said. 'Healthy. Not like this.'

'How long have you been here?' Wilson asked. He seemed to expect this question. He was evidently proud of living here.

'Three years. Longer than any of the others except old Silberman. Show you his grave. Can't kill old Bentinck. That's what they always said about me, and, by God, they're right.' He took the pipe out of his mouth and polished the bowl against his nose. He looked at it with pleasure.

'Better have your bath now,' he said, 'and shout if you want anything.' He waved towards the door.

Wilson went in. A tin bath was in the middle of the floor. There was a bed with a mosquito net over it, a box that served as a washing stand, and some nails were driven into the walls for clothes. His suitcases stood near the bed.

On the wall opposite the door there was a big hairy spider. It was as big as a saucer, its body the size of a silver dollar. When he went towards it, it raised two front legs like a boxer. Knotting a towel, he smashed it.

'What's that?' Bentinck shouted from the next room.

'Spider,' Wilson said. He was learning to talk as did his host. It pleased him.

'Lots of 'em,' Bentinck said. 'Poisonous.'

Cheerful place. He poured the water out of the petrol tins into the bath. Spiders ... cocktail parties ... Bastille Day ... Doctor Livingstone, I presume ...

He wondered what he would wear. The white flannel suit with a black pin stripe would be best, he thought. And what they called correspondent shoes in London — black calf and white suede.

So this was Mokala. He had done what Frazer had asked him. He was here: very much so. Bentinck seemed almost as unlikely an agent as Frazer himself. Funny people, the English. He began to be sorry for his mother. Perhaps

Englishmen should never marry. His father and mother.
Himself and Anne. Living the way he had, he had never
really thought of himself as anything.

He sponged the dust off himself. He wondered what he
had thought secret agents looked like. He had never met any
before, but he had had his ideas about them: slick ... Phillips
Oppenheim ... Sax Rohmer ... Bull-Dog Drummond. That
was it — international, sophisticated. More like me, he
thought. That was really it. When he read things like Somer-
set Maugham's Ashenden series, he had always seen himself
in the hero's rôle. Well, now he was in it. He watched the
red mud run into his navel with satisfaction. African dust
plus African water made mud, just like Texas dust and Texas
water ... He mustn't think about Texas. That was where he
and Anne had gone for their honeymoon, to the Andrews'
ranch. Texas dust ... Anne in Levi's, and a belt studded
with big turquoises set in silver ... But mashing that spider
was a good omen. He would be a successful American.

Chapter 4

The WOMAN

~~~~~~~~~~~~~~~~~~~~

OLGA WAS AWARE OF HER POSITION: THAT OF WOMAN. NOT OF
a woman, but woman. Willingly or unwillingly, the lives of
all the men here were affected by her: some closely, some less
closely. They hummed like tops, circling towards her, away,
and towards again; like flies towards the honey pot. The
natural selection, of taste, in ordinary society did not function in Mokala. The law of sexual gravity, which oriented
men and women towards each other into pairs, was inopera-
tive here. Only desire remained. But desire, distorted,
alternately weakened by fever and stimulated by circumstance, was inconstant, inconsistent, flaming up and dying
down, burning first bright and then dimly. Reason, as it was
understood elsewhere, was without application. Reason
there was, but it was endemic reason, specialized, of a kind
which only appeared reasonable because of this particular
situation. Here the white man was the exotic. Everything
was in reverse. It was the negative of life, where black appeared as white. Factor piled onto factor, event onto event,
influence onto influence, and the dark stream of each individual life flowed without guidance, without the influence
of public opinion, without news of the outer world. There
was the radio, but its news appeared irrelevant. The voices
that came over the air, though clearly audible, were so distant. There were papers like Bentinck's *Times*, Channel's
Petit Parisien, and Owen's *Saturday Evening Post*, but they did

no more than arouse dormant nostalgias. The past for all of
them was a book they opened only with regret.

There were few speculations about the future, since it was
inevitably based upon the past, and the past they had known
was dead. Even trips home could no longer be looked forward to. They lived in the blazing twilight of today, in the
pursuits of today, in scientific research, in art, in business.
Their only anchor was their work. That was the men.

On Olga's part, she was woman. To be woman was her
interest, a part she played to perfection and with charm.
Also she played it without difficulty. 'I did not choose,' she
thought sometimes. 'I am as I am. I am what I am.' To
be herself, to be that, was what obsessed her. Only to her
mirror did she not lie, and this was reciprocal.

She had long conversations with her mirror. It was an
Empire mirror, circular, gilt-framed, surmounted by an imperial eagle that held two chains in its beak. They ran to the
left and to the right, giving the illusion that the eagle supported the glass. It hung low over her dressing table and reflected the tortoise-shell and silver-backed brushes, the comb
and toilet articles that lay scattered upon it — the spilt
powder, the little enamel snuffbox in which she kept her
mascara, the long case that held her hairpins, the silver tray
that stood in the middle of the table for oddments, and Olga
herself, sitting beneath the perched eagle of Napoleonic
France. She talked to Congo too. These were her confidants:
her mirror and her gorilla. To the others she spoke at great
length, but without frankness. The others were men.

Her husband she scarcely counted as masculine. She had
little reason to. Nearly thirty years older than herself, she
treated him as a child. She was grateful to him. He had never
objected to her keeping Congo. The exact position of Congo
she had never analyzed. He was not a pet. He was not a
child. He stood somewhere intermediately between the two.

He had a bedroom of his own with barred windows. He

wore clothes — sailor suits, as a rule — that were laundered
with the rest of the household washing. He ate at the table
when they were alone. There was no question about his
having a mind. He had mental processes like everyone else.
Of course he could not talk, but on the other hand he could
express himself. She did not like to think of how he had come
into her life and she could not think of life without him.

She was brushing her hair. It was very long, reaching below the stool at which she sat. She had to hold it out to brush
it. It was like the tail of a golden horse with something of
that living texture, a pliant, perfumed crispness. As she
brushed, it crackled. Putting down the brush, she shook her
head, switching her hair out into a shining fan. Then she
began to brush again with her left hand. She wished someone
could watch her. A man. A woman looked her best as she
brushed her hair. There were reasons why this should be so.
The play of light on the hair itself, an hypnosis caused by the
synchronized movement of the white arms, the face reflected
in the mirror . . . that was the face he knew, but changed by
the transposition of the features: perhaps even the emanations
of the hair itself. As you raised your arms, the breasts were
drawn up, taut, sharp, provocative. Then there was the implication of hairdressing, of the toilette, of the putting-on or
the taking-off of clothes: the implication of past or coming
nudity.

Meanwhile she brushed. There was no man. But there
had been men . . . there would be more. She smiled into the
glass; it was a smile of recollection: not of the past as a whole,
but of incidents within that past, pearls withdrawn from the
drab context of those years. When she was dressed, she must
continue the decorations for Channel's party.

She got up and stretched. She opened her green silk
dressing gown. It was green piqué, apple green. She ran
her hands over her thighs. Satin soft, the feel of herself delighted her. Ivory, gold, and green. The Empire mirror was

still her friend. The time came to all women when their
mirrors were enemies, but it had not come to her yet. Today
nothing was more charming to her than her mirror. She
could have stared into it for hours, delighted at the mirror, at
herself, at the subtlety of the relationship between them: between a woman and her reflection.

She had designed her room as a setting for her beauty —
as something utterly different from what one would expect
in Central Africa. The great Spanish bed, the polar bearskins
on the floor, the curtains of green brocade, the pink shaded
lights were not mere accessories. They were a part of herself:
an expression, luxuriously couched, of her contempt for
Africa: the challenge of a woman to a continent.

Next door the gorilla was hammering on the wall with his
fists. He wanted to be let out. She looked back at the mirror.
The mirror was a vertical pool reflecting beauty: her beauty.
Since the Empire it had reflected many scenes. She wondered
if it had ever hung opposite a bed. If walls had ears, then
perhaps mirrors had eyes that finally were dulled by the
repetitions of human life — the repetitions of despair, of orgy,
of hope they witnessed: even of beauty. She thought of old
mirrors, blotched, tired old mirrors that had seen too much.

Olga looked round the sitting room with some satisfaction.
She had finished it this morning and had only come in to see
that nothing had been moved. She liked to decorate: to arrange.

Of them all Sebastian was the only one who had no flag,
no birthday. He had no papers except one which stated that
he was not a Hungarian subject, and a citation for valor with
the International Brigade. These appeared to suffice him.
He knew nothing of his birth. 'Since I am here, I was born,
madame,' he said. 'That is incontrovertible. But when or
of whom I have no knowledge. I belong to a great family:
the greatest: the family of artists.' Of them all he enjoyed

the fêtes the most, for he was without regrets. His birthdays'
since he did not know it, did not make him sad. Without date,
his life was much simplified. He lived unpunctuated: a
human manuscript, comma-less, without breaks, dashes,
marks of interrogation or exclamation. He lived. He painted.
He spoke French with a Spanish accent, Spanish with a
German accent, German with an Italian accent, English with
a French accent. But he spoke them all to perfection. Words
poured out of him in all tongues, a profusion of artistic
criticism, of panegyrics, of curses. He was a wonderful curser.
His ambition was to paint her nude. He spoke of it continually. 'If I could paint you like that, I would be done with
you, madame.' That was why she would never let him do it.
When first he came, she had slept with him.

The long table against the wall would hold the sandwiches,
cold meats, fruit salad and drinks at the far end. Behind it,
hung on the wall, were the flags. The French Tricolor was
in the centre, since the party was for Channel. On one side
of it was the Belgian red, yellow, and black for Retief, on the
other the Union Jack for Bentinck. They were flanked by
the Swiss white cross on its red ground for her husband, and
the Polish flag for herself. Then at the ends came the flag of
Holland for Marais, and the German flag for von Brandt.
On the other wall, again above a table, but a smaller one, was
the American flag. That was for Richard Owen, the missionary. Later she would go and gather roses to put in the
vase beneath the Stars and Stripes. Just now she wanted to
enjoy looking at her work.

It was all very cosmopolitan. That made her laugh.
What a life... what a place! What a collection of people!
And these parties! But it was amusing. With men of so many
races there were so many national fêtes. The Fourth of July
for Owen — that was only just over; and now this one, the
Fourteenth, for Channel. Empire day for Bentinck. Her
fête... her husband's... Retief's... Marais'... fête after

fête. Then there were the birthdays. It was odd that Channel should have been born on July the fourteenth. Yet, why odd? One had to be born sometime. Then there was Easter and Christmas and New Year.

And always here: always in their house because it was the biggest, because she was the only woman . . . *and because I like it*. The noise, the smoke of the cigarettes and the black cigars: the subtle breath of alcohol fumes evaporating, the movement, the smell of eau de Cologne, brilliantine, and masculine perspiration: the tremendous tension of races at odds, but bound socially by proximity and economics: a league of nations. *Oh, la la*. And Armistice Day, they had that too. That was difficult, when they drank to their dead, when they glared at each other. Marais who was Dutch, her husband who was Swiss, and Retief who had been too young, had not fought. But even those who had not were soldiers. They had made their service.

She liked soldiers. She liked their backs. The back of a man who had been drilled was different. It was something that remained with him always, even if he got fat.

She wondered about this new man. He had arrived today and was going to stay with Bentinck at the store. What was he like?

And how would he get on with Owen? As Americans they would have something in common. It was lucky that there was a flag for him. It would make him feel at home. She admired the American flag. It was very artistic with all those stars in a corner. That it was there would make her seem a better hostess. It was one of those fortunate social accidents like having the right photograph out when someone called. She wondered how old he was . . . was he tall or short? Was he dark or fair? And what was he doing here?

She must see that Congo did not get out. He would soon wreck her arrangements. He had done it once, three years

ago. She tried to remember whose fête it had been. Mon
Dieu, a gorilla loose in a room that was arranged for a party!

The roses. She got a pair of scissors out of a drawer and
went out. How astonishingly beautiful it was: still beautiful
after all these years. And certainly if you had to live in
Equatorial Africa no place could equal this. She wondered
if she had hung the English flag the right way up. If she had,
it would be for the first time. The Union Jack was confusing.
But the English were a confusing people. Right or wrong,
she would know this evening when Bentinck came. That
would be the first thing he would notice.

She went down the garden steps. The roses were on the
third terrace. What a time she had had making this garden
on the mountainside! Olga's hanging garden, Channel
called it. 'A little Babylon mignonne.' There were always
implications in Channel's speeches. But he charmed her.
What a man he must have been when he was younger! You
forgot his small size when you were with him. A dagger was,
after all, as much a weapon as a sword. Everything about
him was sharp. His moustache was waxed into points. He
never had a hair out of place. His eyes went through you,
they saw you naked. Not merely physically — all men's eyes
did that — but mentally. He read your thoughts. Disil-
lusioned, bitter, a cynic. But what was that but the idealist?
No one who was not an idealist could ever be a cynic; it was
a defense: the scabbard that protected the harmless blade
of a warm heart. There were the things that he had done.
He thought no one knew of them. But she knew. They
were not in keeping with his protestations.

She cut the roses with long stems low down on the bushes.
General Jacques Minot . . . there was nothing else on this
terrace. Dark red, almost black, velvety with an intoxicating
perfume. How it would fill the room! Should she wear the
red dress to greet them? This was almost the most delightful
moment of a party . . . the indecision of what to wear . . . the

oscillations of the mind hesitating between one perfect con-
fection and another equally perfect: the adjustment of mood
to color and texture; and all of it but the overture to the
triumphant effect of the finale, the greeting — when the body,
bathed and perfumed, gowned and shod, stood separated
from the mind by the very brilliance of its finish; when the
face, under its studied maquillage, was a mask, but of such
subtlety no one even guessed that it was not your own ... The
lip rouge, the eyebrow pencil, the eye shadow were as much a
part of the costume as the dress itself, as carefully considered
as the fall of the dress, the rustle of the silk, or the final adjustment of a jewel.

She paused among the roses to consider the party. It
would smell like this, of the roses she was gathering. She
heard the whispered, 'Ah, Olga ...' as Fritz bent over her
hand. She felt Retief's eyes on them.

Could you love two men at once? Why not? Why could
you not love two opposite qualities: gentleness and savagery,
tenderness and brutality, even if that brutality had never
been exposed? You could feel it. It excited you. That was it:
the one calmed, the other excited. The one was a torrent,
the other a placid lake. Too much of the one would bore you;
too much of the other would destroy. The only practical way
was to take something from each, balancing the one against
the other and attaining, if not satisfaction, then a mean ...
an average that justified by its fulfilment. When one was
married to a professor, one became very scientific. Jean said
everything was a matter of mathematics; that everything
could be demonstrated by a graph, explained by an equation.
This was her sexual equation. Certain aspects of mathematics
could be interesting.

And I do not really know what love is, she thought. This
amused her. If anyone should know, I should. I have had
enough, in quantity ... in quality ... in variety; and I started
young, hardly sixteen. She put that thought away from her.

The roses were lying on the grass that separated the beds. She stared at the mountains. Over there was the great African Rift. The mountains lay in ranges, one behind the other. The nearest were a brilliant green. The broken silhouettes of the more distant were blue: pale blue, dark blue, lilac, purple, their peaks indistinct with mist. When the mists cleared, the snowcaps glistened white. Those were lakes there, mountain lakes, hyacinth blue. Divided by green volcanic cones, they were set like jewels between forests and thickets of bamboo. This was the rocky backbone of a continent: high mountains, deep secret valleys, lowlands, forest plains cut with sluggish rivers, broken by morass and swamp — tortured mountains intersected by lakes, forest-clothed, snowcapped: terrifying. The forest... this was the land of the forest and other things.

They would have strawberries too. She had had them picked. How well they did here! Strawberries on the equator — a big bowl of them with maraschino — the Chinese bowl Fritz had brought her from Zanzibar.

Yes, she would wear the red — the decision had come suddenly — the dark wine-red that almost matched the roses.

She thought of Owen. He got an extra party at Thanksgiving because she was so sorry for him. He had so little pleasure living by himself in that miserable little mission. Of course, he had his birthday too. They all had that. She had a list of them in a drawer, and of their national holidays. Poor Mr. Owen. Life was not easy for him. Had he ever had a woman? She was sure he had not. That he had not made him extraordinary: something of a phenomenon. What things must go on in his mind! When you did not know, you wondered. She wondered at his wonderings, at his imaginings. How he must confuse the issues, thinking the act itself complex when that was the ultimate simplicity! That which preceded it, the passages of words and of increasing contacts, were the real complexity. The prologue to love was infinitely

variable, its achievement an anesthesia, its epilogue a tragedy.
And Owen knew nothing of this — nothing. He would never
know.

She thought of Warsaw. How good the chocolates were
there! She thought of a French make. She could not remember the name, but the trademark was a black poodle
jumping through a hoop. André had bought her a big box
once. Why should she think of chocolates? Because of the
party? There should be bonbons in little silver dishes, at a
party ... marrons glacés, chocolates, sugar almonds of pink
and white ... caviar, vodka, sweet champagne, Rhine wines
... a roast boar's head, its tusks shining on each side of its
snout, a bouquet between its jaws ... and a Tzigane band.
It was years since she had thought of these things — of
servants who were not black, of the three-horse sleighs, the
furs, the wraps, the carriage rugs ... the sound of a wolf
howling in the distance. *I was a child then.* You never forgot
what you had seen and heard and smelt as a child. You were
always seeking the safety you had known in childhood. Then
there was always someone who could help you — a mother,
a father, a nurse, a servant, a stable boy who admired you, a
lover when you were no longer quite a child. Nothing was
irrevocable then, though most things seemed so. She sat
down on a seat. She had had it put here for this purpose, so
that you could sit here amid the perfume of the roses and look
out over the world.

The process of her mind intrigued her. First, clothes.
That was easy. It was the first connotation of a party: the
dress one would wear. Then men ... love ... the love of
men. Then the decision of the dark red dress, probably influenced by the roses she had been picking. Owen had followed, because he was a man who had not loved ... Warsaw,
where she had first been loved, was mixed up with the roses
of the convent garden. But the chocolates? That, too, was
Warsaw ... and then from one kind of chocolates to another

kind ... from one kind of man to another kind. She wondered
about the American again.

It would be amusing if she was taking all this trouble for
nothing: if he was ordinary. She was always careful of her
appearance, but what had been in her mind was more than
carefulness, more than merely being well turned out ...
soignée ... And as to tracing the concatenation of her
thoughts. She had wanted to stop thinking of Channel and
Congo. The mind was like a dog: it must pursue something.
So she had started the hare of Owen's celibacy ... of the loss
of her own virginity. How academic that sounded! A boy
rolled with a girl in a hayloft for a moment and this terrible,
irrevocable thing occurred.

She picked up the roses and turned back from the view; she
was tired of it. She looked at the house. It was the biggest
of the five that comprised the Station Botanique. Channel's
house was about a hundred yards away, standing on a little
plateau with his hospital behind it; Sebastian's was between
them. Then there was the guest house. It had fallen into
disrepair. But the group was attractive — whitewashed,
thatched, surrounded by trees, flowering shrubs and creepers.
Each set in its own lawn, they clung to the hillside. The
actual experimental station was below her. On terraces arranged at intervals her husband tested all kinds of plants ...
coffee, tea, gums, timber trees; and down in the valley was
the rubber. There were other experimental patches of rubber
in the true forest. What cruelties had been perpetrated for
rubber! — all in the name of progress. What horrors! But
the administration of a colony was hard for a woman to understand. Things were better now, but the stories remained. A
folklore of lashings, of murder, of extortion and atrocity.
There was still exploitation. The big companies like Huileries
du Congo Belge were only interested in results.

It was a fantastic country: a fantastic position in which to
find yourself. At first she had felt this constantly, but now

only upon occasion. And this was one of them. It was almost
certain that there would be war in Europe, and what then?
What of Africa? What of the men who were here, each held
by a European allegiance? The news got worse each day.
Hitler ... Only a few months ago his troops had gone into
Austria. Then Czechoslovakia. Now Poland, her father's
country, was threatened. And when the trouble started,
where would it end? War in Europe would mean war here.
She had seen war ... Her life had been destroyed by it, her
home burnt, her parents killed — slaughtered like pigs:
Marie, her sister, raped. She saw herself running — running
in the snow, a little wild animal. She had joined other wild
children, living as they could; stealing, even killing. What
could a man alone do if he was set upon by a pack of children
of all ages? A hundred children could overwhelm him, pull
him down like a deer.

She remembered very little of it all. Only incidents that
were without continuity ... blood running on the tramped
snow ... meat cooked in a cellar. A bigger girl had taken
care of her. If she hadn't, I should have died, she thought.
And the girl's name — what was her name? Anna. That was
it ... Anna. She had been about fourteen. She had had a
lover, a thick-set boy with red hair. And then the Nuns.
They had found her. It was odd that both she and Sebastian
had been brought up by the Church. That was after Anna
had abandoned her to go off with the red-haired boy. The
Sisters had educated her, and then she had run away from
them: with a man, naturally. Sixteen, I was then, or about
sixteen. A baby ... It had been born in Paris, and he had
left her. One had to live as one could. In brief, one had to
live. The baby had died. Then she had been lucky — a rich
man ... André Dulac, an industrialist from Lille. Clothes,
an apartment in the Avenue Victor Hugo ... Le Touquet ...
Cannes ... It was André who had caused her to become an
agent for the British. He had been interested in the rearma-

ment of Germany — had assisted in financing the young ora-
tor, Adolf Hitler. She had obtained documents from him and
sold them — out of patriotism — out of pique — he had said
he would divorce his wife ——

It had been in Cannes that she had met her husband, the
professor. He had been there on business: something to do
with cantharides, or was it cochineal insects? It appeared
that they lived on cactus ... There had been a scheme of some
kind ... she could not remember it. Jean had married her.
He had said, 'I will say you were my secretary; that will explain things.' She had never seen how it would explain anything, or to whom. It had always seemed to her that her
appearance was self-explanatory. He had told her he was
going to the Congo; would she go to the Congo with him?

The Congo, Burma, China, Iceland, Zanzibar, Malacca ...
it had been all one to her. She was a married woman: something inconceivable. Within the circle of that little band of
gold was safety. It was a pity she was not different. It was a
pity she betrayed him so much and so often. But he made it
so easy for her that it had seemed a waste not to. She had
been insulted by his trust. Women ... what did he know of
them? What did anyone know, even women of themselves?

Then the other baby ... and Congo. That surely was the
strangest trick that could be played upon a woman. Channel
had wanted to bottle Congo: to preserve him in alcohol.
Channel, the surgeon whose curiosity had undone her.

Why was she thinking like this ... Why in the name of
God? What had come over her? The party? It was Channel's
birthday. It was the fourteenth of July.

She must prepare Congo's food — plantains, tomatoes,
ears of corn, ground nuts. If he was good, she would give him
a cup of coffee. He loved coffee with a lot of milk and sugar.
And of course he would have to stay shut up in his room.

She wondered how she would do her hair. In two long
plaits wound round her head ... or curled like shells over her

ears ... or down? Once she had worn it down at a party ...
a sensation. 'It is like corn,' Fritz had said: Fritz von Brandt.
'Like golden German corn, sun-ripe, sun-bleached.' Perhaps
she would wear it down again.

But what was the party to her? What were these people
to her? Men wanting her because she was a woman: because
she was beautiful. She could have been much less beautiful
to be desired here. She was young, she was white, she was
healthy. There were few healthy women here, even among
the blacks. It was the German noncommissioned officers in
the last war who had brought venereal disease with them.
Or so it was said. But she thought it must have come before.
The French and Belgians had brought it earlier. The Germans had merely spread it. It was a very civilized disease.
It came everywhere with progress, with the Bible of the missionary, and the police of the administration, with the traders.
It came, and no one seemed to mind.

A flight of wild duck cut through the air. They were so
near that the whistle of their wings made her turn. They
flew in a wedge, in an arrow point; they flew, and then they
were gone.

She was glad the decorations were done. She was tired. She
felt very alone. No matter how many people were near you,
no matter how many grasped at you, touched you, you remained alone. Your personality was inviolate, untouchable,
stone hard, however much you wished things otherwise. She
would feed Congo and then rest. She would feel better after
a bath ... cleaner.

The bathroom was very modern. The professor was well
off, and at her request it had been modelled on the best
American pattern: needle sprays, plate glass, chromium plate,
and tiles of apple green — her color. The bath itself was
enormous, partially sunk. She had a passion for bathing.
She wondered how much the desire for baths was prompted
by cleanliness and how much from the desire to be released

from the hampering grasp of clothes. Though she wore few clothes, sometimes only a small girdle to support her stockings under her dress, she wore them well cut and close. She liked to feel the embrace of her clothes, to feel she filled them. To have clothes well cut and tight, and then to take them off, were two sides of a single pattern — restraint balanced by abandon.

The sitting room had looked nice. It was best to do everything very early here or late. She had only left the roses till evening. During the day one rested. One read novels, one played the piano, one sang a little, one did one's nails. One paid those attentions to oneself that were required.

She turned off the water. She tested it with a bare toe. Long-legged as a deer, she stood balanced. Withdrawing her foot, she slipped on her mules and went back to the bedroom. From a hook behind the door she took an electric prodder and opened the door of Congo's room. He was safe. Yes, he loved her. But he was strong. That was the real danger, that he loved her so. Perhaps it was always dangerous to be loved too much.

The gorilla was sitting in a chair waiting for her. He had been hammering on the door again, but he had heard her coming. He did not wish her to know of his impatience. He was dressed in a white sailor suit with a blue striped collar. On his head he wore a blue cap with a red pompon: the cap of the French sailors.

'Come, Congo,' she said, 'you shall have a treat. You can watch me bathe.'

He came towards her, semi-erect, balanced on his knuckles. He was happy.

The bathroom smelt of steam, of geranium, of woman... Bouquet de femme, Channel had called it. And now of gorilla. Congo seated himself on a white enamel stool.

Chapter 5

The GORILLA

~~~~~~~~~~~~~~~~~~

THE MIND OF A GORILLA IS THE MIND OF A GORILLA. BUT THE mind of a gorilla that has drunk woman's milk is the mind of a gorilla that has drunk woman's milk. It is conditioned. Not only by the heredity of the forest, but by circumstances that are human.

Also, Congo was male. Not yet fully, but approaching maleness, aware of an unease that caused him to flex himself, to extend his arms, to test his strength by lifting objects, by breaking them. He was unaware that he belonged to Olga. In his opinion Olga belonged to him. She was an extension of himself, of that personality which existed within him. When he was with her, he was happy. He felt completed, though restless. Alone he was unhappy.

His eyes were on the prodder that leant beside the bath. To him the prodder was GOD. It was power. The prodder and the snake were the only things he feared.

If it had not been for the prodder, he would have lifted Olga out of the bath. He did not like her to be in it. It might hurt her. He did not know why, but there was a memory of water. Water was dangerous. This extension of himself should not be immersed in it. There were many memories in his mind, half-formed pictures of hanging lianas ... of branches, of great leaves dripping with moisture, of fruits, of nuts, of fat white grubs. Sometimes he had a pain in his chest. It seemed as if it would burst. Then his eyes were suffused

with blood and he beat upon it with his fists. That was at
first.

Later he had come to enjoy the sound he made as he ham-
mered at it. One day he knew what he would do. One day
he would tear down those posts that closed in his windows.
One day he would catch someone passing by the arm. One
day . . . His strength was mounting; he was gorilla, almost a
man. How nearly he had missed being man, no one would
ever know: some accident some million or so years ago: a
sport, or the lack of it. But he came near. No one knew how
near. No one knew anything of him: of his emotions, his
pains, or of his desires.

He loved Olga, an extension of himself. His mother.

He liked the smell of geranium.

His belly was full and his heart, and he was strong, happy
in his fullness and his strength.

Soon she would dry herself. He did not like that either.
She might get hurt.

He did not like the prodder or the snake. Sometimes she
frightened him with the snake. There were memories of
snakes in his heart.

He took off his cap and twisted it in his hands. Olga said,
'No, Congo.' He put it back on his head.

Later he would show her something that he had taught
himself. He would take a book and sit down with it, turning
the leaves. Meanwhile, he sat there on his stool watching;
smelling the odor of geranium bath salts, of hot water which
smelt different from cold, of woman, of Olga. These smells
disturbed him. They were not the right smells for a gorilla.
His nostrils, unknowing, longed for the scent of moist undergrowth, of rotting vegetation, of the steaming forest, of fruits
ripening and sun-warmed, and above all for the odor of
female gorillas and young ones, and the smell of the old male,
the head of the family, whom one day he would kill. The
dark forest should have been his, with its giant trees, its thick

bush tunnelled by the paths of his kind, the forest where he
was king, where all but the driver ants gave him place,
where neither the leopards nor the lions would face him.
That was his home ... not a room barred with logs, nor a
boudoir, nor a bathroom delicately perfumed. It could be accepted that he knew nothing of all this; but it could only be
accepted because it was more pleasant that way.

His eyes never left the woman in the bath — a woman in a
pale green bath that had come from the United States. Under
his silvering fur his blood coursed. His lips moved. He
raised his black hand to touch his big canines. These were
his weapons — his teeth and his hands, and the latent energy
concealed within that thick-set body. He loved, he hated; he
was, within himself, moved; motivated as much by his immense hereditary past as this unnatural present: as much by
memories of forest scents as by this perfume of woman and
geranium.

Chapter 6

The PARTY

'YES, MR. WILSON . . . NO, MR. WILSON . . .'

It was a good party. Olga was amused by the American. He was rather like a Saint Bernard: very large, strong-looking, with fine wide shoulders. She was amused at his suit and his shoes. Of course it would never have occurred to Bentinck to tell him about dressing. She was amused at his embarrassment. What a soldier he would have made! It was not that she cared for soldiers, but drill certainly improved their appearance. There was something about him. She wondered what it was. She stared at him and said, 'Yes, Mr. Wilson,' again.

He was telling her about America. Of course what he was telling her was unbelievable, incredible: but nevertheless interesting. She liked his voice, and he had charm. She hoped he would stay for a while. There seemed no reason why he shouldn't. So far they had had very little conversation. He had told her a great deal and she felt that he considered her attractive and intelligent. Her turn to talk would come later. Most women made the mistake of talking too much and too soon. Men had to do the talking. It gave them a sense of superiority to do so — and of security. They were like children, comforted by the sound of their own voices. She wondered what he would say when he saw Congo.

'I do hope you will stay, Mr. Wilson,' she said. 'You will find so much to interest you here. And it is so beautiful. Is

it not beautiful?' She pointed out of the window at the rolling
forest, black now — and white, checkered in the moonlight;
and to the mountains beyond the forest, their dark mass white-
tipped with snow. 'Beautiful,' she repeated.

'Yes, Mrs. Le Blanc, it is beautiful.' It amused her to be
called Mrs. Le Blanc instead of madame. Le Blanc, she
thought; I am not Le Blanc. I am Olga Severenisky. That
also amused her. And the others, sometimes it was madame,
and sometimes it was Olga. It depended on who it was, on
who was there, on how much they had been drinking: depended, in fact, upon circumstance, upon the place and the
hour ... *enfin* ... it depended. Everything depended.

Wilson had been in love. She was sure of this: less from
what he said than from what he did not say. But they would
speak of love later. She determined suddenly that he must
stay.

'Channel,' she said. He was standing near her.

'Madame?'

'I am so glad you have decided to ask Mr. Wilson to stay
with you. Later on he can have the guest house. It will do
it good to be used. I will arrange it tomorrow. It will only
take a few days to put it in order.' Nothing had been said to
Channel about it, but he could be counted on.

'I don't want to be any trouble,' Wilson said. 'I was going
to stay at the hotel.'

'Trouble, Mr. Wilson? It will be no trouble. It will be a
pleasure. And it's unhealthy down there unless you are
salted to fever like our friend' — she nodded at Bentinck.
'He will not even use our doctor's serum.'

'Madame is fond of pleasure,' Channel said. 'She has a
capacity for it.'

Olga smiled at him. 'You say such charming things,
Doctor.' The man was a serpent. He knew too much about
women. But Wilson would not understand. For the moment
all that was necessary was that he should remain. She put her

hand on his knee, just for an instant, letting it pause there: a white, red-tipped butterfly of a hand, hesitant in its flight from her lap and back again.

'You will stay, won't you, Mr. Wilson? The doctor is right, it will give us pleasure. Mr. Bentinck will not mind. I will arrange it with him.'

Retief was watching her with sheep's eyes from across the room. No, not sheep's eyes; with spaniel eyes. It was curious the way she called men by their surnames even in her mind. It was his eyes ... they were so pathetic ... which had made her ... but now they only irritated her. They were so sad. She thought of von Brandt's eyes, brilliant, shining. Eyes of china blue: the eyes of a Prussian.

'I will be delighted, Mrs. Le Blanc, if you are sure it will be no trouble.'

Wilson was surprised to hear his own words. He had meant to stay with Bentinck. He hoped this change would not offend him. But the Station was intoxicating. It was not just the cocktails and the Pernod that had followed them. It was the place itself. The atmosphere ... the grandeur of the scenery; the altitude; the paradox of snow on the equator; of roses and strawberries; and above all, of the strange people who were gathered here. What a charming woman Mrs. Le Blanc was! So understanding and sympathetic. And he had promised Frazer ... There was a lot he wanted to see here, he discovered. To see was a way of forgetting. For the last two hours he had almost forgotten that he had to forget. For two hours he had been free of his past: free even of the future. He had lived for the moment alone. He had come a long way in more ways than one since yesterday. And there was something in what Mrs. Le Blanc had said about its being more healthy. It would be stupid to get a go of fever when there was no necessity for it.

The professor came up to him. He was in a very good mood, a delightful man.

'Yes, Mr. Wilson,' he said, 'they laugh at us because we
are working on rubber. They say rubber is finished. That
may be so for the planter, but we work for the Government.'

'Quite so. Of course, if you work for the Government it's
different. Still they told me at the coast that it cost about two
shillings a pound to produce f.o.b. and that the top price has
been about eightpence. Wasn't there even a rubber restric-
tion scheme a few years ago to try to hold it at eightpence?'
He remembered how bored he had been when Frazer had
told him all this. What a dinner it had been! It had only
been at the end of it that he had spoken of Mokala.

'You are very well informed,' the professor said. 'But there
are matters that go beyond commerce.'

'Not for the planter.'

'Yes, in the end even for him. There is Geography. What
are the sources of rubber? They are Malaya' — the professor
ticked Malaya off on his finger — 'South America, and
Africa.' He held up three fingers.

'That's right.'

'But suppose Malaya, Ceylon, and the East Indies were cut
off by war — what then?'

'I still don't see it. It doesn't pay, and you can't afford to
subsidize to that extent.' He was not going to be led into a
discussion about the possibility of war. Either it would come
or it would not come. And, anyway, he must remember to
act neutral — as an American. It was curious that having to
play this part was making him feel so English. He wished he
had put on a dinner jacket instead of the pin stripe. Bentinck
should have told him that they dressed.

'Not subsidize: experiment. I will tell you something of
what we are doing.' He was very excited. 'Let us take a
Ceara, for example — a Manihot Glasiovi of three years of
age. It should yield some hundred and eighty grams of wet
rubber. You agree with my figures?' he asked.

Wilson nodded. He was not in a position to argue.

'Do not imagine,' the professor went on, 'that I hold any brief for Ceara; it is nothing like as good as the Hevea Braziliensis — Para; but it produces a little quicker, and I have just taken it as an example. If you like I will give you Hevea figures too. But to take this Ceara tree again — three years old and giving one hundred and eighty grams of wet rubber. That is nothing, eh ... nothing. But suppose we could make it produce two kilograms. That would change things, would it not? That would make the Congo important, would it not?' He was chuckling. 'And do not say that it is impossible because we are coming near to it, and it is cheap — you would be astonished at how cheap it is. I tell you this, my friend, that in science nothing is impossible, and that within a year or two we may have fourteen-year-old trees giving three kilograms of dry rubber.'

The butler brought him another drink. The servants were in white, with red sashes across their bodies. Le Blanc lifted his glass.

'Good luck, Mr. Wilson, and may your stay with us be pleasant and long.'

Wilson raised his glass. 'Thank you, Professor. It is very good of you to ask me to stay with you.'

'It is nothing. A stranger does us good. We get tired of each other, don't we, Captain von Brandt?'

Von Brandt clicked his heels and bowed. 'Tired, Herr Professor? Never.' He too raised his glass. ' ... Prosit.' He drained it at one gulp. He stood very straight as he drank, his heels still close together and his elbow very high. His bent arm was parallel to the ground.

Channel was watching the grouping and regrouping of his guests: the ebb and flow of human protozoa. They joined, they parted; they came together, divided; they ebbed, they flowed. They moved according to their instincts: drawn to the table by a desire for alcohol, forced towards Olga by their lusts, driven to the sandwiches by hunger, or out into the moonlight by the pressure of their bladders.

Nothing could have been more human. A cavalcade. A charade, a comedy with that element of latent tragedy which gave it point. There could be no tragedy without humor — no comedy without sadness. The play changed from one to the other according to the relative values of the ingredients in counterpoint to each other. The world was a stage. Life a performance played for his particular benefit. That was the way he liked to think of it. In the life of an animal there was no tragedy except perhaps among dogs. But they had for so long been associated with man that they could scarcely, in psychological terms, be considered as animals. On the contrary, men could more easily be conceived as various species of dog. The professor with his carefully tended beard was a poodle, very intelligent, capable of learning anything. Sometimes he hated him. If it had not been for him, he would not be here.

Retief, a hunting dog of some kind. A retriever with a good mouth that could be trusted to carry an egg without cracking it. Von Brandt, a German boarhound, courageous but stupid. Marais, the young American, and Bentinck were harder to place. And himself. I wonder what kind of dog I am, he thought. He gave up his train of thought. Dogs. Yes, dogs. And Olga the female dog. Perpetually in season, coloring everything with the miasma of her perfume. The sexual impertinence of women still astonished him. What ends they reached and through what ignoble means! The yellow Pernod clouded as he added water slowly, dripping it through the lump of sugar he held upon a pierced spoon. What a lot we owe to Pernod Fils! he thought. We, the men who are without women or past them. He wondered if there was any explanation for the difference in the effect of Pernod and other drinks. For only with absinthe did you get that detachment of mind, and release, usually associated with the completion of the sexual act: that disembodiment and mental clarity which could only be achieved when the dissociation of the mind and the body was complete. He drank.

It was coming, that clarity ... Down there was the forest — he looked out of the window; down there was the dark, silent, sylvan world. He thought of the great mahogany trees that rose tremendously girthed, towering columns, their stark trunks bare of branches; of how abruptly and in unison they spread their canopies, layer upon layer, each with its own life; each independent of the others; each separate, but all closing out the sky from the ground below them; each closing out the sunlight; each closing out the life that lived there. You saw nothing of the birds that flew, that mated and nested and fed there; nothing of the monkeys that swung screaming from branch to branch. How dark it was under the trees, solemn as a cathedral! There were only the tree-trunks, still grey in the dusk of midday; and the creepers strung like rigging from the trees: endless lianas, orchids, ferns, and the tree-trunks buttressed into the black humus of the soil. There was also a silence made greater by the cry of an unseen bird; by the hum of an insect.

Down there the forest, and up here in this room the forest too. The dark forest of Freudian obsession, of repression, of fear and hate and love and lust, of hunger and pain, of quick-snatched joys and long regrets. Up here too was life canopied and secret where each was alone. All you knew of anyone was the little rustlings you heard ... the whisper, the soft laughter, the closing of a door.

He was drunk, of course, but it gave him pleasure. He rode his drunkenness like a horse. His body he had arranged — disposing it comfortably in a chair — while he rode the Pegasus of his mind, galloping it through the space-time of his memories, leaping metaphysical obstacles, wrenching at the branches of half-seen knowledge as he thundered through the forest of his imaginings ... thundered on towards the oblivion of sleep where each night each man died in his bed alone. Yes, died. And was alone were he bedded with ten women. Man was always alone.

The party was in full swing. The moment had come — the precise moment. He was drunk enough and not too drunk. His mind was in full alcoholic flower; later it would blur. The perfume would be lost.

'Messieurs, Mesdames ... Damen und Herren ...' he was standing, a small, sharp man. Trimmed — neat as a yacht in his dinner clothes — a composite mess kit, half civil and half military, that he had designed. He could see himself in the mirror. 'A toast,' he said. 'I ask you to drink to France. It is the Fourteenth of July. To France,' he said. His glass was held high. He was flexed on his toes.

'To France.' The glasses were raised and emptied.

'Another,' Olga said. 'Another to our doctor. It's his birthday too.'

Channel smiled at her and sat down. This comedy had been repeated so often, for so many years. Each played his part — the cues were known. It was routine.

'Channel ... the doctor ...'

He stood up and bowed. He was very moved. One was always moved by alcohol. The inhibitions which restrained tears were removed. The nerve centers, lacking control, permitted the glands to function in an uncoordinated fashion, independently of each other. He liked to consider his own actions. A reflex. It is my birthday, he thought; sixty-five years ago today he had been born in Paris. What hopes they had had of him! How far he had gone! How deep had he sunk! His eyes flamed; still moist with tears, they burnt. He could feel the hatred in them. These people. These irrelevancies. And now they expected a speech. He would flay them with the scalpel of his tongue, laying bare their sadisms, their fornications, their masturbations, their gluttonies. He would show them up for what they were, strip them naked down to the blue-white sinews that joined their absurd frames, articulating them like dolls. Was he not a surgeon — once the greatest in Paris — in all Europe? Did they know themselves for the animals that they were . . . dolls animated, driven by atavistic desires, rationalized into what they thought was order? Flesh like all other flesh, like that of a cow or a bull. Like that of a dog, a bitch, a tiger cat. Meat. Carrion to rot if he could not save it with his medicaments, his serums, or his shining case of knives. He began.

'The Fourteenth of July.' He laughed. 'I will tell you about another such party. It was at Lourenço Marques. The new French consul had put a notice in the papers that he would give a dinner for all the French in that city. All Frenchmen were invited. The dinner was prepared. And figure to yourselves who came. No one but prostitutes. The street women, the cocottes. The only French in Lourenço Marques. Then afterward, three days later, he called on them all in his carriage, with flowers — a bouquet for each tied with a tricolor ribbon of silk. That is the France to whom we drink . . . a France that honors her harlots. *Vive la France!*' he raised his voice. '*Vive les femmes de France . . . les prostitues . . . les grues des Boulevards . . . vive les poules de Paris . . .*'

He emptied his glass and sat down. France that honored her whores and destroyed her doctors . . . Paris . . .

Paris . . . How near Paris came today. Paris in May with the chestnuts in flower. White phallic candelabra. The Champs Élysées . . . the Avenue des Acacias . . . the lakes . . . Armenanville. Paris in the autumn. The fallen leaves in the Bois: himself, a child kicking his way through them. A herd of goats following a piper. Winter — the chestnut vendors in fur caps bent over their charcoal stoves. The chestnuts hot, in newspaper twists, one in each trouser pocket warming your legs. The riders in the Bois. Women, men, officers of Chasseurs in sky-blue with scarlet breeches. Sarah Bernhardt driving in a victoria with a uniformed coachman behind two bay mules. The children playing, the Nou-Nous in bright clothes with streamers from their caps... the peasant wet-nurses, each wearing the costume of her district. The heaps of sand in which the children played. The top whips, with lashes made of fish skin and the spinning tops. The little girls with short dresses that showed their frilled drawers as they ran. Paris. The Paris of his childhood, of his youth. The Lycée... the university... the faculty... hospital... honors... the little red ribbon that they had taken away from him...

Le Quatorze Juillet... the day of the Bastille — my birthday. He thought of the birth of a child.

At a birth there were flowers and gifts, the medicine man, the acolytes and wise crones. The same odd panoply, that varied so little in principle, accompanied all birth and death. For the woman it was the end of her pregnancy, the logical end of a biological act. For her it was an end of one thing and the beginning of something else. There was before the event and after it. There was the intolerable, forgotten pain of parturition. There was the easing of her distension, the relief of being free of a burden. The seed swollen within her was burst forth... was extant. For her there was a certain sense of pride and accomplishment... by it she was inscrutably fulfilled: one of her ends accomplished. There was little memory in her: none of conception. The whole past was concentrated into her instant milk, into the pain of her breasts and the sucking lips of her child. The unseen blood cord was broken. Physically loosened from her, the child was now psychically bound. It was a child, no longer a foetus. It was a male child, and, therefore, doubly a child... a sower of seed. In the dark recesses of her mind a ravisher, a conqueror. He was very small: very weak. But in her mind he was not small and weak. She saw him as he would be... potent: the flower of the rooted female tree.

And the child? What of him? Nothing of him. He was

nothing but a complex organism. Mindless, but subtle with
potentiality. A hero lauded ... an assassin to be duly hanged.
That was the child. Sixty-five years ago today he had been
born ... in Paris.

To Owen the party was intolerable: a debauch. He wondered why he had come. He always wondered why he came.
Yet these parties had a fascination for him. He tried to understand them: to relate them to his knowledge of God; to his
religion; to his own life, that he led at the mission twenty
miles away. It was a long ride on his bicycle. He thought of
it, propped up against the wall outside. By now the boys
would have stolen his repair outfit and spanners. He should
have put them in his pocket, but he always forgot.

He tried to form a pattern, a conception of life into which
his life and this life fitted. He was a man of God and these
were Godless: unbelieving or worse, worshipping their own
false gods. The professor believed in the god of science ...
of latex ... the god of the trees ... a Druid in the employ of
the Belgian Government. Channel, also a man of science, had
gone farther: he was cynical even of science and dabbled in
the occult. Sebastian was plainly mad, painting abomina-
tions with an inspired brush. Marais believed in money. He
was frank about it. Von Brandt in force. He was equally
frank. Bentinck was an old man and perhaps the only good
one, but even he never came to the mission. Retief was in love
with the professor's wife: a fornicator in mind if not in fact.
To lust after a woman was to commit adultery with her. And
Wilson. If only he had been quicker, he might have got him
to come to stay at the mission instead of remaining here.
Madame Le Blanc, Olga ... the whore of Babylon, with her
ape and her big black snake. He thought of the first time he
had seen her playing with it. It had been curled round her
arm and neck. Its head had turned this way and that. It had
seemed to kiss her with its forked, darting tongue. She kept it

to intimidate Congo. But she liked it. And why did she keep Congo?

He was ashamed of his thoughts, of his lack of charity. Who was he to condemn? Perhaps he could help her. Perhaps... What chance had she had? Married as a child. And who knew what had gone before that... what horrors? The revolution... war... she had never confided in him fully. His own life had been so sheltered, so safe. Even temptation had passed him by. No woman had ever looked at him softly.

The room was hazy with smoke. Everyone was shouting. His ears throbbed. If I took less quinine, he thought. But he could not take less quinine.

He thought of the temptation of women. It was strange that Christ had never been tempted that way. The temptation of the soft flesh — the yielding. Of wet lips... of breasts upright, firm with desire...

These things had passed him by, but he knew of them. He had seen the results and tried to rationalize the cause. Woman ... women... the curse of Adam. The horror of it! He saw in his mind that terrible lascivious intimacy, that drawing together of bodies ultimately entwined. He looked at Olga in her red dress: the scarlet woman. If only I could help her... He was trembling.

Sebastian, completely at ease in his blue painter's blouse, white canvas trousers and sandals, was enchanted. He said so, he kept saying so to everyone: 'I am enchanted.' It was so much better than drinking alone. There were people here: his friends to whom he could talk of beauty. They could not get away from him. He had just driven Marais into a corner. He was trying to explain color to him. No one understood color. 'Color vibrates like music,' he said. 'It strikes blows upon the soul. Then there is the juxtaposition of pure color ... the arrangement... the symphony. It is not an accident that bulls are sent mad by red.' He thought of the bull-fights he had seen ... of Spain ... of Guadalajara. 'Mother of God, Spain,' he said. Tears came into his eyes.

Olga in red. He wanted to dress her in more red ... in brighter red ... to lay her on a red couch in a red room garnished with gold-framed mirrors and to strip the red from her so that she lay white and tawny, a pearl in a scarlet shell. He pointed to the window.

'And green, meneer. Do you know how many greens there are down there? How many gradations?'

'It is dark,' Marais said.

'Of course it is dark. But what has that to do with it? The greens are there, meneer. Livid arsenic greens, purple-greens that are nearly black, grey-greens, blue-greens, yellow-greens ... green ... green ... green!' He was shouting.

'I do not understand modern art,' Marais said. 'Rubens ... Van Dyck ... They were great painters. They —'

'They ... they! Mother of God, they ... with their sepias, their men in cloaks, their fat women!'

'I like fat women,' Marais said. 'They are comfortable. They are good-tempered. They are good cooks. They keep a house shining. A house should shine.'

'A house,' Sebastian said. 'A house is pedestrian, it is bourgeois, it is unnecessary. What, after all, is a house? It is a box. It is without beauty. Only a cathedral is good because it is built by the spirit. Take Rouen, take Cologne, take Notre Dame, take Canterbury — even Saint Paul's.'

'A place of worship should be simple and without ornament,' Marais said. 'That is how I see it. I belong to the Dutch Reformed Church. With us ...'

'Who spoke of worship? I spoke of beauty. Sometimes I seem to be the only man who understands beauty: alone in my knowledge and appreciation.' He struck his chest. 'It hurts me here.' Marais annoyed him. He was so neat, so precise, so meticulous, so ... so ... so infinitely boring ... so clean. He said it. 'You are too clean, meneer. You shine like a tin pot.'

Sebastian drew himself up to his immense height. He towered
over them all. He was great even if he was alone in his knowledge of his greatness. 'You are a trader, meneer,' he said: 'a
trafficker. You produce nothing. To me you are of less importance than a worm. A worm weaves a silken cocoon from
its bowels . . . it becomes a butterfly. You will never be a butterfly. You are a shining pot.'

He turned on his heel, hesitated a moment, and drove towards Olga: a red flame hovering near Channel and the
American. Art might mean something to the American.
They were a great people, those Americans. He had known
them in Paris. American artists. He had known them in the
International Brigade. And they bought pictures. Someone
had to buy pictures. It became brilliantly clear to him why
people had to buy pictures. They had to buy them so that
artists could sell them. One had to live. To live one had to
have money — even in Mokala. He would approach this
American. He would show him his work. He would paint
him a picture — a new one specially for him . . . a black nude.
He saw her in his mind: tremendous, Nubian, voluptuous,
with hanging pear-shaped, green-shadowed breasts . . . heroic.
He named the picture in his mind. SHEBA, that's what I'll call
her. His fingers moved through space. He pressed on space
with his great spatulate thumbs, pressing the black woman
out of the smoke haze in front of him — modelling her. In
this instant he had given birth to a woman. He was a mother.
This impressed him enormously. I will tell the American, he
thought. His coming had been like an answer to his prayer.
One minute he had been thinking of the Americans who
would visit his tomb. The next, an American was dropped
like a ripe plum at his feet.

'Mister Wilson,' he said. He bowed.

'You know Sebastian, don't you?' Olga said.

'Mr. Wilson,' Sebastian said, 'I beg to inform you that I
have become a mother. She is black — shining, immense.
I will sell her. Two hundred francs.'

Fritz von Brandt was enjoying himself. It was amusing to be in a group like this where the hostess, unknown to anyone, was your mistress. When he caught Olga's eye, he smiled at her. His woman. The professor's wife, but his woman. Among them all he was the only man: the only one who understood the new world that was being formed ... a world of order, of discipline, of blood and iron, of sacrifice. Because of this, he was the only one who dared to be proudly male, a pure Aryan type, a begetter of men. He stood with his shoulders back, his belly drawn in. His only regret — that he was not able to wear his uniform. Uniform had been forbidden. But the day would come. Then all would be changed by one stroke of the Leader's pen. By one order the legions would march and those in secret authority like himself would strike, gun and whip in hand. The masters! As he now tamed wild beasts would he then, when the time came, train men, break them, and bring them fawning to his feet.

Bentinck was drinking brandy. He did not like it, but it made a change. He was content to sit and observe. Drinking was much the same all over the world. A Kaffir beer drink. A cocktail party. Did the truth really come out as the drink went in? And what was the truth? Did the truth not vary; depend upon mood and place? Was not today's lie tomorrow's truth?

He had been talking to Wilson about hunting. Wilson had said he was tired of it. That was the attitude of the amateur; of the sportsman. He had tried to explain the professional hunter to him, the man who lived in the wilds and by the wilds, one to whom the veld was home; to whom the beasts that peopled it were more real than men and women. A hunter loved the beast he killed. He arrested it suddenly, cutting the thread of its life with the knife of his bullet. It was a sacrament.

He thought of the beasts he had killed, of the ivory and skins he had sold. This was a train of thought that was continually returning to his mind, one that fascinated him with its mystery, though at the time — when he had been hunting — it had not seemed mysterious. The relationship of the hunter to the hunted was not ordinary — the chase itself symbolic of something that went beyond the chase. The savage cry of triumph at the kill. The mort sounded with such panoply at a French hunt: the blooding of English children, the rites of the mask and brush, the pride in the trophy. These had no simple explanation.

There had been a certain dignity in his life: a reality. He saw the camps he had made — thousands of camps in his life. He thought of the treks. But his eyes never left von Brandt. His head did not move. He sat still and he watched. At how many water-holes and pans and fountains had he watched like this! How many spoors had he followed! He had learnt patience from the Boers and finally had excelled them. Old Jannie Beyers in Angola had taught him patience. 'A hunter,' Jannie had said, 'is like a hound. When he has the spoor, he stays there, neither hurrying nor checking. He follows and finally he kills.'

Von Brandt had drifted across the room. He was with Marais now. They were very friendly. They were talking in German. He saw Olga turn her head and raise her hands to her head. She leant towards the mirror to tidy her hair. That brought her nearer to von Brandt, her elbow touched his shoulder.

Bentinck lowered his eyes to his glass; the bubbles clung to the edge — little balls of gas. He touched the scar on his cheek: Heidelberg. But scars on a professional hunter were easily accounted for. The tie between the Nazi and the Dutchman was business. Marais thought of nothing else.

They were talking of wild animals. Marais sometimes got hold of one. Apart from being a German, Bentinck detested von Brandt on professional grounds. To capture animals alive was brutal. It meant running them down or trapping them. It meant killing a female to obtain the young that ran at her side; and once captured, so many died. The idea of it disgusted him.

He raised his glass and drank. He would give Wilson a few more days before he said anything. But he liked the look of him. That was the important thing. He could detect his quality. The American had quality... blood, you'd call it, in a horse. The only question was, had he staying power? The bubbles in his brandy-and-soda had formed a crescent. Some had combined with others, forming bigger bubbles. More were rising from the bottom. Within the glass an orderly process was taking place. There was no chaos: not anywhere. The idea of chaos was due to a misconception of time. Vastly delayed... infinitely slow according to human concepts, the spinning wheel of each apparently irrelevant event fell finally into its appointed place.

He thought of justice. There was none. There was only the law of orderly accident. Those bubbles, for instance, that clung to the edge of his glass — molecules of alcohol, gas, and water. Why should they be chosen for this fate and the others — those in the centre — be chosen for another? It was accident that brought the buck near to the waiting lion ... accident that had brought Wilson here today. He had just told Olga that Frazer had sent him.

The professor was asking Olga to sing. 'Sing to us,' he said.

'Oh, no, Jean. No one wants to hear me. They are tired of my singing.' She always said this, but she would sing. She always sang.

'Mr. Wilson has never heard you,' the professor said. 'My wife has a beautiful voice.'

'Please sing, Mrs. Le Blanc.'

Do not worry, my friend, Channel thought. She will sing.

Her husband was right. She had a beautiful voice: a husky contralto, very supple, very moving. He pulled himself together. He was tired of this nonsense.

'Sing, Olga,' he said. 'After all, it is my party. It is the Fourteenth of July, and my birthday.' It was a hundred and fifty years since the Bastille had fallen. He felt very patriotic.

She was turning to him. He could see the white blur of her face above the red of her dress. Between the face and the dress was a hectare of white breast. It made him smile to think of those here who had seen the rest of her in one way or another. All of them had except Bentinck, Owen, Marais, and Wilson: I as her doctor ... the others in other ways for other reasons; and Wilson, he thought, soon would, from the way things were going.

'What shall I sing, Doctor,' she was saying. 'Since it is for you, I will sing in French.'

Sometimes she sang in German, sometimes in Polish or Russian. Above her breast came the slender column of her neck, then her head. She carried it thrown back, and on her head the rolled glory of her honey-colored hair. When it was down, she could sit on it. It covered her like a cloak.

'Sing *Mon Ami Pierrot*,' he said.

She went to the piano and sat down, her fingers ran along the keys. She began ... *Au clair de la lune* ... *Mon ami Pierrot*. He could see into her mouth as she turned it toward him: dark, sharp with white teeth, bounded with wet scarlet. But how beautifully she sang. Freely as a bird, as clearly. She must have been well taught, he thought. Well taught in many things, in a hard school, perhaps; but that no one would ever know. 'I am Olga Severenisky,' she said of herself. 'I was secretary to the professor. Yes, I am Polish, and of good family.' That always seemed to amuse her. 'My mother was French.' *Ma chandelle est morte.* How many candles were dead! The words went on repeating themselves in his mind. *Ma chandelle est morte ... je n'ai plus de feu ...*

Ouvre moi ta porte ... pour l'amour de Dieu ... Open your door
for me ... I have no more light ... for the love of God. A
folk-song, a cradle-song, the first song that a child learnt to
sing, but like so many of its kind one whose psychological
values were scarcely veiled by its simplicity. A mother sang
it to her child ... But a girl might sing it equally to her lover,
or a lover to his mistress.

The song always made him think of his mother. He remembered running to get her music for her. It was kept under
the music stool. He saw the stool of dark wood with a pink
plush top. The top was hinged. You lifted it and there was
the music ... in loose sheets and in books. There had been
two candles on the piano. Sometimes she had let him light
them. They had been on brass swivelled brackets.

Olga closed her mouth. Her chin dropped a little. She
was breathing faster, but the air was still filled with music ...
with memories of music. People ... Olga ... People ... the
more I see, he thought ... He wished he had a dog. But dogs
were no good here, the leopards got them. Only one — Sebastian's yellow cur — had survived.

Owen came to say good night.

'You mustn't mind Sebastian, Mr. Owen. He is like a
child.'

'You should not have him here, Mrs. Le Blanc. He is a bad
influence. He has no morals. He ...'

'He amuses my husband,' Olga said. 'And he's a good boy
except for those girls. It's a pity, I know,' she said, 'but it's
life.' She shrugged her shoulders. He was staring down between her breasts. He blushed when her eyes met his. He
took her hand.

'Thank you so much,' he said. 'It makes a nice change to
come here.'

Change. Yes, it must be a change from the mission. Poor
Owen, he did not know what he came for. How upset he
would be if she told him he came to see her breasts!

The party was over. It had gone well. Olga watched her
husband undress. She wondered how many more fêtes there
would be like this. Where would they all be this time next
year?

Leaving the bedroom, she went to the wired-off cage on the
veranda where she kept her snake. It was cool and smooth
in her hands — it curled over her bare arms and round her
neck. The snake which terrified Congo had a calming effect
on her. In the moonlight it shone like silver as it coiled and
uncoiled — a cold, living ribbon, something alive, but without emotion. By now Jean should be in bed. She put down
the snake.

She wondered about Wilson's wife. Before he left he told
her he had been married. American women were so differently brought up: raised, as they said, in a spirit of rivalry, of
competition. And they married men their own age so often.
Young women were older than young men, and the superiority they gained in youth over their husbands they held in
age. A girl brought up in a convent respected men, since she
knew nothing of them. She was submissive, humble. As a
rule she married a man much older than herself who taught
her to love. Then she took a young lover who, when he was
older, would teach some young girl. It was a cycle ... a system centuries old and not without a certain civilized charm.

Wilson, it was obvious, knew nothing about love. How
could he? Love had to be learnt. Everything had to be learnt.
She thought about the ménage à trois ... about Retief. It
upset Retief to be her lover, but he was an exception. Most
men liked such a situation. Pleasure without responsibility ...
the excitement ... the uncertainty. She thought about con-
vents again. It was amusing to think that there could be no
better preparation for men than a life of religious instruction
and utter insulation from them till the moment of full ripeness
occurred. The romantic notion of the bud was absurd. The
budding woman was merely a bud. A woman must first

flower fully ... must desire. A full ripe bloom to be savored, not a bud to be worn in the buttonhole.

The American was going to be amusing. She was glad he was going to stay. She wondered if she would tell him that they were collaborators.

Chapter 7

The MORNING AFTER

~~~~~~~~~~~~~~~~~~

WILSON SLEPT WELL: HEAVILY: THE SLEEP OF THE DRUNKEN. He came out of his sleep slowly. He fought his way out of it and into a headache that threatened to split his skull, and from the headache into a resolution of future temperance. It was not that he did not enjoy drinking. He did. But it was not worth while. If only one could remember that.

Where was he? He was staying with Channel: Bentinck had seemed pleased with the arrangement. He wondered how Bentinck had got back, and then remembered that Retief, the professor's assistant, had driven him home. He had hardly spoken to Retief last night. He wondered if he had been rude. It was certainly good of the doctor to put him up for a few days while Mrs. Le Blanc fixed up the guest house for him. That was nice of her. A charming woman: a very beautiful one to find here. But was she really beautiful? Her grey eyes were so widely spaced, her hair so pale in color, her cheekbones so high, her mouth so wide. Her lips looked as if they had been put on from the outside. She was so alive. She moved so well. And her voice was lovely.

Last night continued to take shape in his mind. By an effort he superimposed it onto his headache. He had never seen anything like it before. There had been talk of a gorilla; that she had one, a pet, somewhere. Who had told him that? Sebastian. Who was Sebastian? Sebastian who? Sebastian what? He said he lived with two colored women. He said he had bought them guaranteed virgins. He had said, 'Is it not interesting that only in the darkest Africa is a virgin guaranteed?' Yes, the night was coming back. Crazy, inconceivable. An 'Alice Through the Looking Glass' party.

The light poured in through the windows. He looked round the room. It was very bare. The walls were whitewashed. The only furniture was the bed on which he lay, a washstand with an enamel jug and basin, and a chest of drawers. There was a lioness skin on the floor. The doctor went in for nothing superfluous in his guest room. But at least there was no spider.

What he wanted was coffee: strong coffee, and a lot of it. As he was thinking of it, the door opened and a boy came in with a tray. Channel, in a blue dressing gown embroidered with white dragons, followed him. He had a glass in his hand.

'You slept well, I hope,' he said.

'I slept wonderfully.'

'Now here is your medicine,' Channel said. 'Fernet Branca . . . nothing like it after . . .'

'That's what I feel like . . . after . . .'

'And coffee. Then we will have breakfast on the terrace. That is something magnificent: unique. You will see. And do not dress. What a night! What a party! Certainly I feel sixty-five today. Yesterday I was sixty-four. Now I am sixty-five. Time passes, my young friend. One grows old. One looks back and not forward. Memories . . .' he said. He kissed his hand and flicked it in the air.

This was a strange place.

Channel pointed to the skin on the floor. 'I shot her last year,' he said. 'I like the skin of a lioness the best. You do not fall over the mane . . . Till breakfast.' He went out.

'And what do you think of zis, Mr. Wilson?' Tink, Mistair Vilson, was the way he said it. 'Behold the world below you. Behold us eating here on a terrace in the centre of this spinning

globe. On the equator at an altitude of two thousand metres
eating cereal, strawberries and cream, paw-paw, cold venison,
eggs, bacon, bread and butter with marmalade, while we
listen to the voice of Josephine Baker. That is sophistication.
Ça a du chic mon ami . . . ces quelque chose . . . but yes, it is something. Down there gorillas, leopards, okapi . . . up here,
Josephine. Did you ever see her?' He gave Wilson no time
to answer. 'What legs!' he said. 'What a voice!'

He hummed the song she was singing. '*J'ai deux amours . . .
mon pays et Paris.* Paris,' he said. 'Paris in May.' His hand was
trembling as he raised his coffee-cup.

The servant who stood near the victrola wound it with a
pink palmed hand.

The tune began again. 'The Folies Bergère,' Channel said.
'What a spectacle . . . what production! What nudity! — for
the foreigners, the tourists naturally, but still nudity, and of
great interest. Many of the girls catch terrible colds in the
winter: on their chests.' He tapped his chest. 'I have at-
tended some of them. They had beautiful chests. Kept by
rich men, they could afford the best attention, naturally, since
the men paid. But personally I always preferred the Concert
Mayole. It is more intimate.' He drank coffee. He peeled a
nectarine, cutting the skin in a single long snake with a silver-
bladed knife. Wilson said nothing. There was nothing to say.
He looked down at the immensity of the Congo. Channel
went on.

'I like to play such records as I have my petit déjeûner.
Maurice Chevalier . . . Josephine Baker . . . it is amusing. It
makes a paradox, for you must remember that it is not a
dream. The girls are there each night at the Folies Bergère;
the actresses and the little whores in the vestibule. We are in
Africa, but they are there in the streets, on the boulevards,
in their little apartments. We have the advantage of them,
for we know of them and they know nothing of us.' He shook
an aspirin out of a bottle. 'Have one?' he said. 'Aspirin, the
antidote to civilization.'

'Africa for them is Algeria and Morocco,' he went on. 'They think in terms of Spahis and Chasseurs d'Afrique. The Legion even is nothing to them, for the Legion has no money. They like money, those little chickens. They will permit anything for money. "You want that, monsieur," ' he imitated a woman's voice, ' "then it will be so much more." More, always more. I have made a study of prostitution,' he said. 'Eighty per cent are servants before they begin. Afterward they become charwomen or flower-sellers or Madames if they have saved enough. Some marry. Name of God, it is better perhaps to marry one who has been a harlot than one who has not. At least she has finished with it.'

'Isn't that the store?' Wilson asked. It seemed to him that he could see the road. A red pencil line drawn across the green mass below them, and the big marula. Channel followed his finger.

'That is the store. A brave fellow, Auguste Bentinck. A hunter of great renown and a man of education. We have a bet between us. I said when he came that he would not live five years down there. He has been there three. It surprises me. I tell him he does it to annoy me.'

He was silent. Then he said: 'I think you will like it here, Mr. Wilson. You will like it because you will know that you can leave at any time. For us who can't, it is something else. Frankly and between ourselves, we hate it. Down there,' he pointed, 'you die of fever. Up here you go crazy because of the altitude. You lose your balance, your poise, your sense of perspective. Ha!' he shouted. 'Ha, Sebastian! Here comes the painter. He breakfasts with me, but is always late.'

'Hola, Laertes! Bring more things. Prepare for Monsieur Sebastian. My boys are named from Shakespeare, Mr. Wilson,' he said. 'Laertes, Hamlet, Polonius, Othello, Capulet, Mercutio... And your women, Sebastian? They are well?' He did not wait for an answer.

'I will tell you something of man's illusion of fair women,

Mr. Wilson.' The doctor held up his hand. 'No, do not stop
me, it is a pleasure to have a stranger here who has not heard
it all before. Much of it is fear ... the torment of unease.
The tension between the desire to get it over and the fear of
not being able to. There you have it, fear; not of the act,
but of the force that activates the act ... fear of the knowledge
that you rut like a stag, and that for a time at least you are
in no way master of your environment or your acts. Out of
this springs the desire for orgy. That is very old,' he said.
'How old, no man knows. Then, when mankind was young,
it was the desire for the unlimited female. Today we are
civilized.' He laughed. 'Today it is in the imagination an
orgy with only beautiful women. The "harem bath" by
Ingre,' he said. 'And do not pretend you have never had it.
It is common to all men ... this desire for mass beauty, for
total extinction within that mass. It is the nightmare born
of the dream of endless voluptuousness and unimaginable, ex-
haustless potency. Then, on the other side, more reasonable
but born of the first, is the search for the perfect woman ...
the one who combines in a single and more manageable body
the qualities of all women ... the woman who is the Golden
Fleece. This is the rationalization of the orgy, for what is
she, this perfect woman, but the microcosm of the first illusion.
You can laugh, my friend, but it is so. Sexual extinction is
one of man's desires.

'It is even possible that men hate women. Hate them for
having brought them forth, as they hate the Jews who are
responsible for the laws of Moses which set the yoke of morality
upon their shoulders. The act of love itself is an attempt by
man to return whence he came ... to seek in woman the
oblivion from which woman flung him. This among higher
men only. The low and the savage bear their fate patiently
with the beasts, acting according to the urgency of their desire
and contented by their consummations. But for the civilized
man, that is another thing. His spirit is shackled by his body,

his body by his spirit. For him, with his understanding, there is no middle course ... no happiness, nor even much content. He is the burnt offering to the future' when these forces will be more fully understood. He is the last phallic sacrifice standing midway between the fertility cults of the past and powers that the distant future will make clear. Sensuality and libertinage are the products of reflection, of leisure, of riches, of civilization. They are meaningless and irrelevant to the laborer. He works too hard to be clear about his desires. It is too hard for him to live at all. It is only when the mechanics of actual living are economically solved that psychic factors begin to govern the circumstance of life.'

He lit a cigarette. 'Once,' he said, 'I was paid for lecturing.'

He turned to Sebastian. 'I suppose it is your women who make you late every day. They delay you. Each morning you leave home like a business man embraced by your brides.'

'It is not the women today. It is that last night I drank a little.' Sebastian spoke seriously. 'It was a mistake. My hand shakes. I cannot hold a brush.'

'Coffee and Fernet Branca,' Channel said, 'and an aspirin, perhaps. You remember Mr. Wilson?'

'Certainly I remember. I sold him a picture last night. A nude. Immense black with ...'

'With pendulous green-shadowed breasts,' Channel said.

'Yes, but how did you know?'

'You only paint one picture. It is your obsession, this woman, but you will never find her.'

'Two hundred francs was the price. It will make him the envy of New York. You live in New York?' he asked Wilson.

'I am afraid I live in Philadelphia.' This was not absolutely true, but he had lived there as a child. He regretted he was such a bad liar. He was going to have to lie a lot before he was through.

'That is most interesting. So there are two towns. I always understood there was only New York.'

Laertes came with fresh coffee.

'I must leave you,' Channel said. 'I have several operations. One is a beautiful ulcer. An interesting case. Sebastian will entertain you.' He bowed. Wilson watched the embroidered dragons till they disappeared.

Sebastian ate with concentration and in silence. He reached for food with big hands. He poured out cup after cup of coffee: three big cups, and gulped them. Then he pushed his plate and cup away and began to draw on the white cloth with his thumbnail. Because it was so bitten, it looked as if he drew with his knuckle. He seemed satisfied with his work: completely absorbed.

'There,' he said. 'There it is done, a masterpiece...a woman. On a tablecloth. What could be more ephemeral? That goes for all the works of man. In a minute a black will take it. He will see nothing. Tomorrow it will be washed. Tomorrow...next week. It will be washed sometime, but today it exists.'

He had been talking to himself apparently, for now he turned to Wilson. 'I am ready to talk,' he said. 'Ask me anything. After all, you are an American, my patron. I am a great admirer of your President Wilson.'

'Roosevelt,' Wilson said. 'A lot of people don't like him. He's ruining the country, they say.'

'A man of great vulgarity,' Sebastian said. 'A rough-rider. A man who came out here to hunt. They still speak of him. A stout, vulgar little man. I saw him as a child in Paris.'

Evidently politics were something Sebastian did not follow.

'Things have changed since Wilson,' Wilson said.

'Wilson.' Sebastian was suddenly excited. 'A relation. Perhaps you are related to the President. In that case I could come back with you. We could have an exhibition. We could...Dali,' he said, 'Salvador Dali...There are greater painters than Dali.' He began to draw on the cloth again, pushing things still farther from him.

'I must shave,' Wilson said.

'Shave? Why must you shave? There is no necessity. The blacks like a bearded man. It is a sign of virility. My beard fascinates them.' He touched his red beard lovingly. 'Also it is something they cannot do. The psychology of the black is like all other psychology. I who speak know these things. I know them here.' He struck his chest a great blow. 'These scientists . . . The professor, Retief, Channel — what do they know? Little things they have learnt in books . . . fumblers. Only the artist knows. Now I also must leave you. Here we all work. I go to my studio' — he waved his hand towards his house. 'I leave you. Au revoir. Auf Wiedersehen. Reverdici. Till I see you. Vaya con Dios.' He held out his great hand. 'I speak in many tongues,' he said. 'I have many gifts. They were given to me by God.'

Wilson was alone with the view: alone with Africa. The table had been miraculously cleared. The victrola was gone. He lit a cigarette. It was a pleasure to be able to do something so ordinary. Channel's words came back to him. The altitude. Perhaps that was it. Or because they were right on the equator, or . . . Was it birds of a feather? Was lunacy infectious? And he was committed to stay at least some weeks. The guest house was being repaired for him. Bentinck seemed sane enough, and the professor. The German, von Brandt, was like all other Germans of his type. Channel was a cultured man, but warped. There remained only Sebastian, who unquestionably was mad. A genius, perhaps. That remained to be seen. And Mrs. Le Blanc. A beautiful woman, a superb hostess. And then there was Marais the Dutchman. He was so correct, so ordinary, so impeccable that here in these surroundings he was easily forgotten. Instead of standing out by his difference from the others, he faded from your consciousness. Your mind simply refused to accept him. What was it, then? What the hell? You couldn't put your finger on it. Then there was a gorilla. He hadn't seen it yet, but no doubt he would. A pet gorilla was conspicuous. And why was this extraordinary? This was gorilla country. Still he had a feeling that it was not an ordinary pet.

It's just the set-up, he thought. He looked down into the valley, at the red pencil of the road, at the big marula. I'll get the car and go and see Bentinck, he thought. Considering the amount he had drunk, he felt very well. His hang-over had gone. A shave and a bath. In a day or two he'd get the hang of things. He looked toward the professor's house. There was Mrs. Le Blanc. A string of natives, in single file, were moving past her. Each had a great bundle of grass on his head. She is having the guest house rethatched for me, he thought. This was hospitality indeed. He must try to get something out of Bentinck. He might mention Frazer. But somehow he felt he had better leave things to Bentinck. He did not seem to be the kind of man who liked to be hurried. What had he meant when he said he had been expecting him for a year?

If he was going to stay, and he knew he was now, he would have to find something to do. That idea about anthropology was a good one. And then maybe he would write a book. It was funny. Ten years ago, he thought, I would have given anything to be here. These people were experts, scientists, observers, hunters. He would get help from them. No doubt the idea of a book would amuse them. Let it . . . anyway, he would be running true to form. People always wrote books when they had been a few weeks in a country. Impressions they called them . . . He got out his car.

There were three men on the stoep of the store. It was a crazy world. The men were Channel and Sebastian; they were sitting with Bentinck. They were drinking tea.

'Have some tea,' Bentinck said. 'I thought you might turn up.'

Channel said, 'The woman died.'

Sebastian said, 'I lost it, monsieur. I lost my inspiration.

In consequence behold me here. We were discussing pleasure. Proceed, Doctor.' He turned to Wilson. 'I do not agree with the doctor, but I like to listen to him.'

'All pleasure,' Channel said, 'comes under three heads. Either separately or in combinations.'

'What are they?' Wilson asked. This was an extraordinary place.

'Yes, three,' Channel repeated, staring past him. 'The sensual, the aesthetic' — he ticked them off on his beautiful surgeon's fingers — 'and the dangerous. Everything that gives pleasure to the senses is the sensual . . . sensuous: the warmth of the sun, the touch of soft material, the feel of a young rabbit in the hand, the softness of a woman; good food, wine, perfume. The aesthetic is everything beautiful. It is a conditioned cerebral pleasure and is of infinite variety. It is philosophy and art. It is religion.'

'And danger?' Sebastian asked. 'I do not like danger. It makes me afraid. Cows are bad,' he said simply.

'Danger,' Channel said, 'is the most difficult to analyze. It comprises all sports, pastimes, games . . . hunting and war . . . gambling in which men risk their fortunes or their lives . . . love affairs in which they risk their reputations. It has elements of masochism; of prayer to the god of luck; of dedication.' He smiled. 'When you understand all this, you begin to understand pleasure, and the days of your pleasure are done. For if to understand everything is to forgive everything, to understand is also to betray the hidden motive which was the cause. The time comes,' he said, 'in a man's life when he has done everything. When he has sampled all things and knows that there is nothing in the future that will be better than what he has had in the past. When the most he can hope for is that things will be as good as he has known them, and when he realizes that even this is improbable. That is the parting of the ways. Some men never reach it. Most do not. Most die as senile adolescents, having lived their lives in terms of repetitions which they have not comprehended. The body can only repeat, and with the years the repetition becomes weaker and weaker: discovery belongs to the mind. Only in the mind, if it is well trained, is there no repetition. As our bodies disintegrate and if we are wise, we cultivate our minds, abandoning the fertile earth of our youth for the aesthetic acidity of the soul. The strong body and strong mind are rarely found together, since they are in opposition and mutually destructive. When the nut-milk is gone, we polish and carve the husk into little ornaments. In youth the bedroom,' he said. 'In age the study.' He laughed softly.

'It seems inevitable that we should talk of women,' he said to Wilson. 'If you were an Englishman, you would say it was because we are foreigners,' he said. 'But you are an American and therefore more open-minded. You are the only Europeans. Europeans in Europe are French, German, English, Spanish. In America these strains are blended. America is the proof of Europe, of a world civilization and culture.' He raised his hands and examined his fingers. He held his hands palm side up, then he turned them over. The cuffs of his white shirt were frayed. He looked at them with annoyance: first one and then the other. He wiped his forehead with a red silk handkerchief, and said, 'It is hard to live without a woman and remain neat.'

'I have two women, and I am never neat.' Sebastian spoke seriously. 'No woman could keep me neat. They have tried. Clean, yes, I like to be clean, but not neat. Neatness is bourgeois. It is without profundity. I spit upon it. All the same, it would be better if there was no woman here.'

'There are no women here, Sebastian. And if you mean Olga,' Channel said, 'I like to watch her. She is very graceful.'

'She disturbs me. A woman has no place in Equatorial Africa.'

'And have we?' Channel asked. He answered himself.

'Yes, we have. As much here as elsewhere. We are misfits, my friend. Masters of our professions, we have sunk to these depths because of our superior specific gravity. There is no place in the world for the master.'

Sebastian appeared to agree with him. Bentinck as usual was silent.

Wilson looked at the bananas growing near the store: at their great green flags, at the finger of ripening fruit — they pointed upward, at the ribbed, corrugated stem that ended in a purple flower. It had a bloom on it like a grape. One petal was turned up. It was crimson scarlet.

The silence seemed to embarrass none of them. Sebastian sat with his big head held in his hands. Channel was mani-curing himself. Bentinck smoked a foul, strong tobacco. He held his pipe far back in his mouth, gripping the stem with his molars.

'I am going to study,' Wilson said. 'If I'm going to stay here, I must do something. I want to take up anthropology again where I left off. I took it at Columbia.'

'Columbia,' Sebastian said. 'What is that?'

'A university,' Wilson said.

'In America?' Sebastian asked.

'In New York City.'

'Are they interested in the fine arts at the university? Per-haps we could ... I have great gifts. I have given many lec-tures...' So he, too, was a lecturer. Wilson imagined intro-ducing Sebastian to Doctor Nicholas Murray Butler.

'Anthropology,' Channel said. 'An interesting subject. The science of man.'

'I have no confidence in man,' Sebastian said. 'Only in artists, and they are sterile. Look at me. Not a child at thirty-seven years of age.'

'I thought you did not know when you were born, Sebas-tian,' Bentinck said.

'I do not know, but I have my ideas. It is my idea that I am thirty-seven years of age.'

'Medically speaking,' Channel said, 'he is right . . . granting an error either way. He has lost only two teeth. He has no hair growing out of his ears or nostrils. His beard is still low on his face and has not crept up onto his cheekbones. Under forty, I should say.'

'That is not the point, Doctor. The point is that the artist, the flower of humanity, is sterile, speaking in the widest terms. Talent can be passed on: genius never. And I am childless.' Tears came into his eyes.

'More tea?' Bentinck said.

Sebastian held out his cup.

'Among the Watusi,' Channel said, 'a man two metres in height is average. They are Hamites, said to be the descendants of the men who swept over Uganda three hundred years ago. It is even possible that they are related to the Masai and Banyankoli. You will have plenty to occupy you, Mr. Wilson, and please remember that I am at your service.'

'If you write a book, it will require illustrations,' Sebastian said. 'A camera tells nothing. A photograph is dead. Only a drawing lives. The camera and cinema have destroyed us!' he shouted. 'Take the first giraffe I saw. Was I surprised? I was not surprised, I had seen them on the films. Nothing surprises me any more.'

'Did you ever see a white giraffe?' Bentinck asked.

'No,' Sebastian said. 'They look better spotted.'

'I have seen a white one and several black.'

'Albinoism and melanism,' Channel said. He got up. 'It is time we went home. Come, Sebastian.' They both bowed. 'We will see you later. We will have more discussions.'

They went to their car. It was a Model T Ford with a box body. Very practical, Channel called it. They seemed to have no reason for their coming, or their going.

Bentinck said nothing for a while. He took some loose tobacco out of his pocket and loaded his pipe again, ramming it home with his thumb. He fitted a little perforated metal cap over the bowl and lit it. It was fastened to the pipe by a chain and a ring that ran over the stem. He smoked without speaking. Then he took his pipe out of his mouth.

'This is a queer place, Wilson. God-damn queer. If I was you I think I should get out. There's nothing to hold you here.'

'I don't think I'll go.'

'No, I don't suppose you will. I didn't think you would when I said it.' He put his pipe back into his mouth and went on smoking.

'Well, if you're going to stay, I'd better tell you a few things. I must say you've done very well. It's all been most realistic. And your being an American is good. American passport and everything, I suppose.'

'Of course I have a passport.' He had done that very neatly.

'Frazer tell you anything?'

'Not much. Only to come and see you.'

'Clever man, Frazer. Everyone thinks he's a fool. Most fools go about trying to make people think they're clever. So he left it up to me, which is all right, but I must say you've been a hell of a long time coming.'

What was the old man talking about?

'You see, I'm getting old,' Bentinck said. 'And things are coming to a head. Come inside.'

They went through the store into his bedroom. It was furnished with a camp bed, covered with a silver jackal karos; two wicker armchairs; and a rack of guns against the wall. A signed photograph of Frederik Courtenay Selous stood on a brown chest of drawers. It was very faded. The rest of the room was piled with junk. Cases of stores, some tusks, assegais and fish spears, a great pile of newspapers, the accumulation of years it looked like; more packing cases, a barrel of gunpowder piled with geological specimens which showed traces of minerals and a prospector's hammer.

'Use it as a storeroom,' Bentinck said. 'Convenient. Sit down.' He sat down himself. 'Going to be war, Wilson. We all know it, but we pretend not to know it.' He paused, and then said, 'What do you think von Brandt is doing here... collecting animals?'

Wilson had not thought of von Brandt. He had only met him last night for the first time.

'That's his story,' Bentinck went on, 'and I must say he knows his job. He has sent home a couple of okapi, some leopards, and a lot of common stuff. But there's a tie-up with the Belgians. He has authority; no one interferes with him.'

Wilson wondered where all this was leading. It was evident that Frazer must have promised to send Bentinck someone a long time ago, and that he was annoyed at the delay.

'Know anything about niggers?' he asked suddenly.

'Nothing,' Wilson said.

'All the better. But remember this. Treat the Masai well: as gentlemen. If you don't, they will kill you. Come back in a day or two and I'll have things fixed up. And don't make a mistake with von Brandt if you see him. He's one of the best men they have.'

When Wilson left, Bentinck thought him over. The American was all right. He would do. Frazer had made a good choice. He was bored and angry with life. Something had happened to him. For a job like this, that was a good thing, and he looked tough. At present he had no plan in his head. He only had the outline of one. They might go on a little trip. What could be more natural than a rich American taking an old hunter and going into the bush to have a look around. To shoot a bit, take some photographs. He had the feeling that in a few days something would happen. He believed in his hunches. Nothing must ever be hurried, a new pattern formed as a crystal did ... slowly but unmistakably. He was satisfied that already something had begun. A little waiting and

watching, and then he would be able to make a plan. Till
then he could rest in peace. There were so many things he
wanted to think about. How was it, for instance, that the
ivory on the West Coast was hard and that on the East Coast
soft? The elephants were the same. Was it due to what they
ate or the climate? And how was it a waterbuck was safe from
crocodiles? It was all very well to say that they had the habit
when chased by Cape hunting dogs of standing at bay in the
water and that the crocodiles waited to catch the dogs as they
came after them. He knew that. Everyone knew that. But
how had it begun? That was what always interested him: how
things began. Everything began somewhere, even a political
situation.

That was what he was doing here now, seeing that nothing
began in this particular neck of the woods. Well, he would do
it. Me and the American, he thought. He put the political
situation out of his head and thought of some of the things he
had seen... a springbuck trek, locust clouds that blackened
the sky, Masai lion hunts, a family of gorillas in a forest clearing. He thought of the Germans. He knew them well. A
slave people who by overcompensation thought themselves a
master race. Slave and master was the only relationship they
understood. He thought of them as colonials, of what they had
done to the Hereros. All these things he saw as part of a single
pattern, the result of urges, of pressures. Animals... men...
This was his conception of life. He saw it all as one thing, animal life merging into human, and merging back again. There
might be no hard-and-fast line anywhere, no actual right or
wrong, but there was a better and a worse. The German idea
was worse. They were destroyers. They were the modern
Zulus. Hitler and T'Chaka had a lot in common as the world
would see one day. He loaded his pipe slowly, polished it
against his nose and lit it. Some more machinery had gone up
to Marais yesterday.

He went into the store. He looked at the canned food, the

bolts of striped calico, the three-legged iron Kaffir cooking
pots, the cups and plates, the bushknives, the ammunition, the
rolls of brass and copper wire, the jew's-harps and mouth-
organs . . . Everything seemed to be in order. If anything had
been moved, he would have noticed it. When he had first
come here, he had thought he would get no trade, but he had
been wrong. He got plenty. More than he wanted sometimes, but, then again, having the store made the coming and
going of his informants inconspicuous. Most of the trade was
barter — the exchange of beads, of cooking pots for chickens,
goats, mealies, monkey-nuts, Kaffir corn, ivory, or gum. Then
the stuff he got had to be traded again to be turned into actual
money. Marais took a lot of it. Some operations were even
more complex. He would sell some material for mealies.
Then he would buy with the mealies earthenware pots the
women made, the standard price being as much grain as
would fill it, and sell the pot for something else. He looked at
the bags of salt. Salt was in great demand. The natives
scooped it up in their hands and ate it like sweets. Scented
soap was another good line. The pigmies loved to eat it and
the other natives bought soap from him to trade with them for
skins and ivory which they sold back to him. Jan was asleep
in a corner on some bags of mealie meal. Everything was in
order. He was proud of his store . . . and he was pleased about
the American. Frazer might be slow, but when he sent a man,
he sent a good one.

Chapter 8

The MEETING

THE LAST THING WILSON WANTED TO DO WAS TO FALL IN LOVE
with Olga. It was not just that she was married. It was not
that he did not want to have anything to do with women. He
had had several affairs since leaving Anne. Not that there was
any chance of falling in love with her. But the very fact that
he put it this way to himself showed that it was possible. He
recognized the possibility. He often found himself thinking
about her. He was still staying with Channel and getting used
to him. But he had seen a lot of Olga — Mrs. Le Blanc, he
corrected himself — lately. Inevitably, since she was fixing
the guest house for him, he was being consulted all the time,
sometimes unnecessarily it seemed to him. 'How do you like
this, Mr. Wilson? Do you think that will be all right? Of
course, if I had had more time...'

Her voice had a curious effect on him. He found himself
longing to hear it when he was away from her. She had a way
of smiling when she spoke.

They were together now. She was in a white linen dress.
Her hair was knotted behind her head. She had a maroon silk
scarf round her neck and high-heeled white buckskin slippers
on her feet. In her hand she carried a white felt double terai.
She was showing him the house. It was almost done.

'You'll be able to move in tomorrow,' she said; 'and meals
...' she paused — 'you will take with us, of course. Except
breakfast. Channel wants you to have breakfast with him.
He gets tired of Sebastian undiluted.'

'That will be very nice, Mrs. Le Blanc. Very nice indeed.
Are you sure I shall not be . . .'

'A nuisance? No, Mr. Wilson. You will not be a nuisance.
You are a new type to me.'

'You think men can be divided into types?' he asked. She
had a funny way of speaking.

'Both men and women, Mr. Wilson.' She changed the subject. 'And you are sure you like the curtains?' They were a
rose-patterned cretonne and looked very fresh and pretty
against the whitewashed wall. The room was charming: a
little effeminate, but charming. It was hard to believe that
it was not a Long Island cottage; that it was not in England or
in France. It was anything but African. The furniture even
was imported. She must have moved a lot of things from her
own house. In addition to the bedroom there was a bathroom, a sitting room, and a stoep. From the windows you
looked down into the valley and over the vast expanse of
forest. It was a wonderful view, but a frightening one. It was
so big.

Olga stood beside him as he looked out.

'You feel it, too: the immensity.' She stood so close that he
could feel her body against his thigh. The faint smell of geranium that he had come to associate with her was in his nostrils. It disturbed him. He had wanted to get away from
women: to forget about them. Or, if not exactly that, he did
not want to be seriously involved. It had not been hard when
he had been travelling. The fact that there had been so many
women had made it easy. They had neutralized each other.

'To understand it you should go down into it, Mr. Wilson.
Yes,' she said, 'you should go into the forest.' She pointed.
Her hand was beautifully kept, the nails lacquered dark red
to match her scarf.

'That,' she went on, 'is where Congo came from. I will
show him to you in a day or two.'

'I'd like to see him,' Wilson said.

'You will see him. But I had to wait till he got used to you. He seems to know your smell now. Of course, he has watched you as you move about. He is probably watching us now.'

So that was it. He had often felt he was being watched. He felt it at the back of his neck and along his spine. If I was a dog, he thought, I should be bristling. What he did feel was a vestigial remnant of the power which raised the hairs of animals in fear. He looked at his hostess: she was smiling. Did she ever do anything else? Her face was always expressionless or smiling. You could read nothing in her face. He was astonished that at first, on meeting her, he had questioned her beauty.

'Then you are satisfied?' she asked. They had been staring into each other's eyes. Satisfied . . . it was ambiguous. 'With your new home,' she continued, as if she had read his mind, 'and I hope monsieur will stay a long time.' She swept him a curtsy. 'My husband will be so pleased, and now I must go. You will let me know if there is anything more I can do?'

He was relieved to be alone. But he was not alone. She had left a fragrance behind her: a faint scent of geranium. He had always been susceptible to scent. Anne used Chanel 5. Where was she now? Palm Beach was the last he had heard, indirectly, of course, but that had been some time ago.

It was hard to escape one's memories. The sooner he started work, the better. 'Congo Basin,' or something like that, he would call it. How did you write a book? Make notes and then coordinate them, he supposed.

No word from Bentinck yet. He did not want to go and see him again too soon. Nor had he seen the other people he had met at the party: von Brandt, Marais, or the missionary. Sebastian he saw continually and his girls. They smiled shyly at him when he passed them. Channel he liked. He liked his reminiscences, his lectures, his long thoughtful silences. Von Brandt was never mentioned. One of the best men they have got, Bentinck said. Retief he liked, too; and the professor,

utterly absorbed in his researches, was a man of great culture
and charm, but a queer husband for Olga. His mind was back
on Olga again. And he did not like the idea of Congo watching him. There was something frightening about anthropoid
apes — manlike! so nearly men. Odd that the sex of a gorilla
should be so hard to detect till it was nearly adult, and then it
was mainly by the secondary, rather than the primary, sexual
characteristics. That was something he had learnt at college.

How had Olga got her gorilla? He came from down there,
she had said when they were looking at the steaming forest.
But the 'there' had been vague; it had embraced the whole
horizon. Anyway, he would see him soon. And tomorrow he
would move in here. He wondered what it would be like taking meals with the Le Blancs. He had dined there several
times, but when you took all meals with a family your status
changed. He wondered how he would fit into their scheme.

Closing the door of the guest house he went back to his room
at Channel's. He had read a little. There was a book he had
seen. It was published by the Carnegie Institute at Washington: 'Gorillas in a Native Habitat.' If he was going to
write, he would have to do some reading first.

Wilson never knew how the conversation with Channel
began. He only knew when it had ended. For an hour he had
been talking about himself, about Anne, about their life together and its dissolution. Had Channel guided the talk in
this direction? How was it you could talk to a stranger so
easily, say things that you wouldn't dream of mentioning to
your best friend? There had been a curious comfort in it: a
release; that of confession. He now saw his own mistakes as
much as hers. He had been almost objective. It astonished
him. There was a quality about Channel's interested silence
that had drawn him on. His approach to these things was that
of a man approaching a problem. He seemed to blame nobody. He offered no advice.

When it was over, he said:

'My friend, you are suffering because of the time into which you were born. A hundred years ago this would not have happened. A hundred years hence I do not think it will happen. This period in which we live, you as a young man, I as an old one, is a period of flux, an interval in the development of the human being in which the established ways no longer function and the new ways are as yet unformulated.' He lit a cigarette. 'You must not blame yourself, or your wife. This is an unhappy time, a time of many means and without ends.

'To start with,' he went on, 'why this assumption of happiness? Happiness is not compatible with self-consciousness and the human race ... a great part of it is becoming increasingly self-conscious, individualized by circumstance rather than by desire; driven by literacy into introspection, more and more men are thinking and finding themselves unable to reconcile the life they live with the knowledge they have acquired. You have talked for a long time. You have told me much of yourself, but you have told me nothing new.'

Channel began to walk up and down the room. Wilson got himself a brandy-and-soda. He was beginning to get used to brandy ... fine à l'eau. But he still kept wishing it was whisky. He thought of Bentinck. He was the only other whisky-drinker among them. He wondered if he could buy some from him. Channel went on.

'A woman,' he said, 'becomes bored with her husband. This boredom is new, the result in part of those mechanical devices and luxuries, what I called the means just now, on the one hand, which have taken her home interests and work away from her, and of contraceptives on the other, which, releasing her from the burden of continued maternity, have thrust her back to sex, the source of maternity. Women are not bad when they seek lovers. They are only simple, acting according to the simplest of all natural laws. Physical release is their psychic object. "Boredom. Oh, I am so bored!" is the rationalization that has thrust them back into sexual circulation. Back to nature, where nature plays for the accident, for failure, for divorce, by which the cycle will be broken and a fresh start can be made. Forget just once, be carried away just once, be careless just once too often, and then...' He shrugged his shoulders. 'There is wilful forgetting, my friend: nine hundred and ninety-nine times precautions and the thousandth none. Surely the habit would be inculcated? Therefore, the accident is often no accident, though the woman herself may believe it to be one. Many women deceive their husbands.' A smile flitted over his face; he was walking towards Wilson as he spoke. 'But they do not deny their husbands. They give their husbands their rights. They find them distasteful but bearable, and to recompense themselves for their distaste, they spoil the delight of their husbands; till finally, by the subtle intonations of such intimacies, they neutralize them; castrate their husbands; by psychologically rendering them all but impotent so that then they have the excuse to turn upon them. To their lovers they give delight. But even here they temper the joyous wind, since there is no loyalty in this relationship. It is ephemeral, its purpose pleasure, an end which is ignoble. It can perhaps be said that the upper classes are being sent slowly mad by contraception. It is at least an interesting hypothesis ... that of mankind fettered by its new freedom as surely as it was fettered by its previous lack of freedom. Once women died because they bore too many children, now they become hysterical because they have none. No ends and far too many means,' he said again. 'But one day the balance will be struck.'

He stopped walking up and down. 'That is poor comfort, is it not?'

'It doesn't help me much,' Wilson said.

'No, it does not help you. All I hoped to do was to try to show you a small section of the design of life today: to present it in its right perspective ... to show you that you are not only the child of your time, but also its victim. Before you can think of yourself, you must think of others: of the whole world. Generalize first and then particularize. You are not the only unhappy man. Your unhappiness is part of an immense phase of unhappiness due to the dislocation of human relationships that will in time, and by the process of trial and error, rectify itself. We might even call this period the period of error. It would be a good name.' He sat down. They smoked in silence. Then Channel said suddenly, 'Olga asked me to bring you over. She wants you to see Congo.'

'She said in a day or two.'

'Then she has changed her mind. Perhaps Congo is in a good mood.'

Wilson hoped he was. He did not want to meet a gorilla much, anyway, but if he had to, then it would be best if it was, as Channel said, in a good mood. Evidently it must have bad ones or there would have been no point in his remark. First a lecture on modern woman and then an introduction to a gorilla. Channel took it all as a matter of course.

'How does Sebastian get on with it?' he asked. He said it for something to say; he did not really care.

'Sebastian and Congo? They get on very well. They have much in common. They are both very simple in their outlook. I get on with him, too. It is a matter of extremes. But he does not like von Brandt.'

Channel gave him his helmet. Not to use a helmet or double terai was dangerous even if the day was cloudy or there was a mist. Before ten in the morning or after four in the afternoon were the only times one could take a chance, for then the sun's rays struck only glancing blows. To go out beneath a vertical sun uncovered was to court madness, even death. It curdles the brain, Channel had told him; melts it into idiocy.

They went out together. Wilson was strangely excited. Because he was going to see the gorilla? Because he was going to see Olga again? Because he felt that by seeing them together he would learn something of her, come nearer to her? Before he could decide, they were there.

Olga met them as they opened the screen door of her stoep. She had on a cream dress of heavy Chinese silk with a wide, bright crimson sash. It had a square peasant yoke, but was cut low. It had short sleeves. Wilson was interested in women's clothes and the effects achieved by them. This outrageous simplicity, for instance, was an example ... An example of what? Of a woman who wished to show by concealment. Of a woman who ... He wondered how many times a day she changed.

'I'm glad you could come,' she said, as if he might have been lunching at the club or have gone to the races. She took both his hands in hers; they were soft and cool. Then she kissed Channel.

'Papa Channel,' she said: 'doctor, counsellor, and friend.'

'You insult me, Olga.'

'I insult you?'

'A man should be either much less than that to a young woman, or much more.'

She laughed. How pretty her laughter was! A girl's laughter. Wilson wanted to take her in his arms ... to touch, to hold, feel ... He was astonished at the range of feelings her laughter had aroused. But they had come to see her gorilla; to see Congo.

'He's in a good mood this afternoon,' Olga said, 'so I thought it would be a good chance. Don't be afraid of him, Mr. Wilson.'

'Never be afraid of any animal,' Channel said. 'Animals can smell fear. It is even possible that people can smell fear or love in others, though they do not know it.'

Olga was leading them through the house. 'He has his own room,' she said, 'and a toilet.' She paused and said, 'He uses it too. He is very clean.' Picking up the prodder, she opened the door.

Wilson never knew what he had expected to see. But whatever he had expected, it was not this. To start with, he had no idea that a young gorilla was so big. Congo was immense. His arms were thicker than a man's thighs. He was grotesquely manlike as he came forward, holding onto a long table that was bolted to the floor. Dressed in a white sailor suit with a sailor cap on his head, he was terrifying. His small sharp eyes peered out from under the ridge of his brows. He was making soft little noises through black pursed lips. For all his tremendous bulk, he moved with absolute quiet. But he moved: he was coming nearer. Olga interposed herself between them. How fragile she looked beside this animal! Beauty and the beast. That's what she wanted me to think, he thought. Congo put a tremendous arm round her waist and lifted his face towards hers. She bent to kiss him. Congo seemed delighted. He stroked her hair with a black hand. He touched her lips, forcing them open gently to see her teeth. All the time he muttered to himself.

'Come nearer, Mr. Wilson,' Olga said. 'This is Mr. Wilson, Congo. You understand. He's staying here and you are not to hurt him. He is a friend. A friend,' she repeated.

The gorilla looked from her to him. He took off his cap and scratched his head. His eyes remained fixed on him.

'Kiss your hand to him, Congo.'

The gorilla put his hand to his mouth and blew him a kiss.

'Once he's done that, he's safe,' Olga said, 'unless he gets angry. Blow the doctor a kiss too.'

Congo blew Channel a kiss.

'He knows Channel very well,' Olga said. 'Doesn't he, Doctor?'

'He ought to. After all, I delivered him. Sometimes I wonder if he is grateful.'

Delivered him. What did he mean? And why did they call him 'him' all the time. Not 'it.' Him: a person.

Channel went up to it. The gorilla letting go of Olga put

his arms round his neck and rested his head on his chest while
the doctor patted his shoulder. Channel said something in a
low voice. The gorilla muttered an answer.

'They talk to each other,' Olga said. 'Except for me, Channel is the only one who understands him. Sebastian does too,
a little, but in a different way.'

'I've brought you something, Congo,' she said.

He looked at her.

'Have you been a good boy?'

The gorilla nodded his head.

She gave him a magazine: a *Saturday Evening Post*, one of
those he had seen in the sitting room. He wondered where
they came from. Owen, no doubt. But it was extraordinary
to think of. Here was a gorilla in Equatorial Africa turning
the pages of a Curtis publication. He seemed to be able to
read it, too. Of course, he couldn't, but he seemed to be able
to. He had run to a corner with the magazine, but now he
brought it back to show Olga a picture that he liked.

'If you meet him outside, you need not be nervous,' Olga
said.

'No,' Wilson said. But he was not entirely satisfied with this
introduction. It seemed inadequate.

'Are you sure?' he asked. 'I mean he's really all right?'

'As long as you don't annoy him,' Olga said.

Annoy him. He wasn't the kind of man who would annoy
gorillas.

They left Olga with her pet. When they got back, Channel
began to laugh. 'It is not everyone who has met a gorilla
socially,' he said. 'And one day you will be glad of it. It is an
experience.

'When a man dies,' he went on, 'he thinks of all the things
he has not done. The bad man wishes he had been good. Not
because he suddenly sees that virtue is preferable to vice, but
because he has never tried it and now will never be able to.
The courageous man thinks had he been less courageous he

might have lived longer. The miser wishes there was time to
spend his money. He has never tasted the joy of spending.
The virgin wishes she could be raped just once. The prostitute
dreams of her virgin girlhood. The spinster wishes she was a
mother. The anarchist thinks of an ordered world, the conservative wonders if perhaps he would not have been happier
as a communist, and the man who has not met a gorilla wishes
that he had. That is life, my friend, and death. Only the very
old and experienced can accept death for what it is ... a
change, the final, the last sensation — the only new thing left
to them. The young fear it because they have not done everything they wished to do: because they have neither loved
enough nor suffered enough, because for them there is still so
much untasted. Living by creeds, by slogans, most men miss
life. Living by dogma and principle, they have failed to see
pattern. It is a strange thing that many men are happiest
when they do wrong. Only by it are they uplifted into a
sphere of consciousness and reality. The burglar while he
burgles is more alive than the banker while he banks; the
adulterer more alive than the husband; the child stealing an
apple more alive than the child given an apple for dessert.
The fruit of the Tree of Knowledge is always stolen fruit, bitter fruit; a fruit, double-edged like a sword, bringing success
and destruction in a single blow. Women can partake of it
more easily than men, having except in certain instances
neither morals nor the faculty of true memory.' He paused.

'You will wonder what I mean,' he said. 'I wonder myself
sometimes. But I think I mean that life should be lived fully,
and that perhaps there is only one great sin — brutality, cruelty, call it what you will: the sin of causing pain and suffering
to others without suffering pain yourself.' He sat down. 'That
is the worst of living like this, Mr. Wilson. One gets ideas.'

'I like to hear you talk,' Wilson said. 'It does me good. I
have never really tried to figure things out for myself. I lived
as everyone else I knew lived.' That was exactly what he had

done. And it had led him to do as the others did . . . to reach
the same ends by the same road. All roads seemed to lead to
Reno. It was a depressing thought. It was no good just letting things slide and hoping for the best. And that was what
he had come here for: to try to think things out; to be by himself; to try to understand. What a muddle he had made of his
life! This spy business he had engaged upon seemed ridiculous, unimportant. They were like a lot of little boys playing
Indians and cowboys.

'Take Olga,' Channel said. 'She takes that baby gorilla
instead of letting me preserve him. Her breasts hurt her. The
baby seizes them. She was woman. The two came together —
her pointed nipples and the gorilla's mouth. The gorilla
sucks. She gives milk, and a link is forged in a chain whose
end no one can foresee. No man would have done that. A
man would have reflected.'

A man would not have had breasts full of milk, Wilson
thought. Then he saw the significance of Channel's words.
So this was the story of Congo; suggested in phrase. She had
raised him at the breast. He was revolted. He was strangely
excited by his imaginings. Suddenly he wanted to see Olga's
breasts. Channel could talk about logic and sense, but a man
was no more sensible than a woman. The turn the conversation had taken had made him very aware that it was a long
time since he had held a woman in his arms. He was ashamed
of his thoughts. After all, she was his hostess: one could not
go about thinking things like that about one's hostess. One
couldn't, but one did. That she had suckled a gorilla made
her hateful and at the same time more desirable.

It was the place. It was the conversation of these men about
essentials. Women, birth, death . . . At home one never talked
about essentials, one never even thought about them. Sex was
old Bill getting into bed with that blonde. Hoping he
wouldn't get into trouble over it if he was a friend, hoping he
would be caught if you disliked him. That was about the long

and the short of it. But these people got down to things. They
lived nearer to actuality, nearer to the earth, nearer to death,
nearer to God, nearer to other strange factors that were the
opposite from God. He found he could not say the Devil or
Satan. He was amused at the way he avoided it. Forces of
evil... primeval... witch doctors... leopard men were all
jumbled in his mind into something undefinable and amor-
phous... something bad which was against man and which
would destroy him if it could. It was always there... in London, Paris, New York... but here it was palpable. This was
its raw, natural actuality — without frills.

Channel was calling him.

'Come here, Mr. Wilson. I want to show you something.'
Channel was in the adjoining room, the one he called his museum. It was also his workroom and laboratory, from the look
of it. There were two microscopes on one table and a typewriter on another. There were rows of jars and bottles neatly
labelled, filled with gruesome-looking medical specimens
bleached white by the alcohol in which they were preserved.
It was the first time he had been into the room.

'Look at these.' Channel pointed to a row of skulls on a
shelf. He took one down and put it into his hand. 'Gorilla
skulls. One of the finest collections in the world. Look at the
development of the canines. There are differences as you may
notice between them and us, but there are great resemblances.
It does one good to think about the apes. How nearly are they
men. How nearly are we apes.'

He pointed to another row of skulls. 'Chimpanzees. And
here are two Pigmies: the hardest of all to obtain. No one
knows their burial customs. No one ever finds one dead.
These two, a male and female, were brought to me wounded
and died in hospital. It is not so long since du Chaillu shot
the first gorilla... he was an American too.' He held a gorilla skull in his hands again. 'This is Congo's father, we shot
him later; and this one' — he took out another — 'is his

mother. His father was one of the biggest ever recorded. Three hundred kilograms and a height of two metres: a splendid creature; one capable of taking a rifle barrel in his hands and bending it like a piece of wire.'

Wilson was not sure that he liked all this talk about gorillas. From now on he might meet it anywhere, Olga said. He would ask Channel.

'Does she really let it run about?'

'Who? Congo?'

'Yes.'

'Not all the time, but often. He will not bother you, he is very shy. Unless he falls in love with you. That is a little embarrassing. He is generally in love with someone. Sometimes it is me; sometimes Sebastian; sometimes one of the boys. But it does not last; only his love for Olga lasts.' He put his specimens back on the shelf. Evidently he wanted to be left alone with his skulls and bottles.

That night Wilson undressed slowly. He had forgotten that gorillas were so human; that they fell in love; that they menstruated like women and had the same gestation period; that they lived approximately as long as a man, fifty or sixty years; that they made houses, nests at least, in which to sleep. Channel had talked of nothing else at dinner. And what was the full story of Congo and Olga? The subject he had studied at college bore very little relation to the actuality of experience. He had wanted to ask. All that he knew so far was that she had brought him up, as a mother brings up a child. But how? Why? How had the circumstance arisen? How had she come upon a newly born gorilla? How was it she had had milk. That meant a baby. She must have had a baby ... the professor's ...

There was a lot in what Channel had said about women. If he had thought more, things might have gone better with Anne. He missed her still. He wanted her.

He thought of Frazer again, of Bentinck, of what Frazer wanted him to do. What had it to do with him, anyway? If there was war, and it certainly looked like it, it would be their own fault. They had sabotaged the League between them. They — after all, who were they? The politicians. But it was people like himself who were responsible for the government. He thought of Sebastian's idea that he might be a relation of President Wilson's. His assumption that he was still President was funny. The Batanga girls. Congo. Olga. He wanted Anne; he thought of Olga. He wanted Olga. Of Olga and Congo, beauty and the beast. She meant me to think that, he thought. Then he slept and dreamed of Anne ... who turned suddenly into Congo as he held her to him. Olga, in white, was laughing at him.

Chapter 9

The MOTHER

〰〰〰〰〰〰〰〰〰

OLGA HAD SHUT CONGO UP FOR THE NIGHT. THE PROFESSOR was sitting in his favorite chair reading a detective story. She sat looking at him with her legs crossed and her arms folded round one raised knee. She was filled with a tenderness for her husband. It was a mood. She knew it would pass, but they came every now and then. At these times she saw him for what he was — a very distinguished man, an authority, a man of good heart and poor physique who had been very kind to her. In her heart she was more of a mother to this old man than a wife. She was a mother to Congo, too. This was the strange trinity of her motherhood: mother of a dead child, an adolescent male gorilla, and an aging savant. Her eyes went from one object to another in the room: from the lion, okapi, and bongo skins on the floor to the spears and shields; to the Pigmy bows and arrows on the walls; to the leopard skins thrown over the backs of the chairs; to the pictures — a Matisse, two Renoirs, and a questionable Corot: she stared at the Chinese porcelain vases on the mantelpiece, at the bookshelves lined with her own yellow-backed paper novels, her husband's detective stories, and thick scientific treatises. The furniture was all beautiful, imported, or made of heavy native woods polished till it shone like glass. You hardly missed the things that she had put into the guest house.

In a corner there was a carved West African god. It was, if you thought of it objectively, an amazing room, she decided. It represented the Far East — the Orient and the West in its pictures and books. And Africa, the Centre, in the skins on the floor and the hanging weapons. This was the womb of the world ... her dark, moist womb. This was a breeding place, a spawning place, lush, dark, hot, fetid: a place where tremendous mushrooms grew in a night; where flights of locusts blackened the sky; where the forest rose in towering primeval majesty out of the black earth; where the rivers ran darkly, slowly between walls of solid jungle; where everything was strangled by its own fecundity. Lianas choking the trees with thick brown arms, garroting them; where orchids in scentless, decadent surrealism clung to dying trees; where ferns grew like green fur on the pungent skin of the secret earth. The settlement was above all this, but it was round you. You felt it. You could not avoid thinking of it. To come here or to go from here you had to pass through it. And they lived at the Station, taking it all as a matter of course.

Retief, who was writing at a small desk in the corner opposite the carved god, she had scarcely looked at. She knew him so well: he was a country she had explored. It was the American she was thinking of. Yes, I like him, she thought. And he likes me. The word 'like' amused her. She was thinking in English. That also amused her, to think in different languages: in Polish, in French, in German, in Russian, in English. 'Je l'aime,' she thought, switching to French. I love him. 'Il m'aime.' He loves me. She conjugated the verb in her mind: I have loved ... I will love.

The professor looked up. 'At the end of August, Pierre and I are going into the forest again,' he said.

Retief turned towards them. His face was lit from the side by the lamp on the desk. He looked like a grey-haired Christ: so good, so long-suffering. It was astonishing how grey he had become in the last few years. She thought of Fritz von Brandt ... of the American. If Jean was going into the forest ...

'You will be away long, Jean?'

'A month . . . It all depends on how things go.'

'Of course,' she said. A month . . . and Wilson would be having meals here: all meals except breakfast. He was starting tomorrow. It was a boring life. Dull. Mon Dieu, how dull it was! She took her petitpoint from the brocade bag that hung from the back of her chair. The design on its wooden hoop was half-done. And when it was done, there would be another and then another. But it kept her hands occupied. Would Wilson stay as long as that?

Her husband said: 'I am not going to read any more today. I wish to think it out. I am convinced that I know who committed the crime.'

'Who do you think did it?' Retief asked. He shared the professor's interest in detective fiction.

'Why, the butler, of course.'

'That's what I thought too.'

'You mean he didn't do it?'

'I did not say he did not. At one point I certainly thought it was the butler.'

How impractical men were . . . with what little understanding did they move through life! And both these men were famous in their way: famous, but children. It had been amusing to watch that Wilson with Congo. But Channel was wonderful with him. Of course, he had known him since the beginning, but there was more in it than that. He seemed to be able to hypnotize him: even in his bad periods. They came with the new moon and he could still handle him — still dominate him. He could dominate me, too, if he wished to, she thought.

And now she had made a mistake: she began to unpick the stitches. Her husband was sitting staring into the fire, thinking no doubt about the butler in his book. Retief had turned back to his writing. She could hear his pen moving on the paper. She put her work back into the brocade bag. She found herself staring into the fire too. She was thinking. She was dreaming. What was it to a woman? What did a woman get out of it? What were her sensations when she was made love to? — when she made love herself?

A woman was less analytical than a man: more ready to accept the conditions that she had planned for. About this there was no question: about the planning. It was amusing that men always thought that it was they who planned. But you got a certain sense of peace out of love: first excitement and then peace. You also got pleasure out of your personal beauty and the fact that it was being used. Beauty should not be wasted. Nor should youth. She felt Wilson was thinking of her; of me and Congo. She would make him think of her. Now alone in his room he must think of her. She would have many opportunities, many excuses, to see him in his house.

Her husband was getting up. He was preparing to go to bed. He was saying good night to Retief. In a minute Retief would come over and say good night to her. Jean would put his detective story back in the bookshelf, first looking at the page and memorizing the number. He never used a bookmark. It irritated her that he should do this. She turned down the pages. 'Coming?' he would say. 'It's getting late.' Then they would undress. They would have baths. They would go to bed. The light would be turned out. Another day would be over. Another night begun.

'Good night, Olga.' Retief was bending over her hand. He looked at her with his brown spaniel eyes. The American had nice eyes: grey. Jean was memorizing his page.

Retief had left them. She heard his door close. 'Coming, Olga? It's getting late.'

Yes, she knew every gesture, every intonation of all these men: she could foretell each thing before it happened.

She got up to follow Jean. He must think of me. He must. Channel had talked to her a lot about telepathy, about suggestion, hypnotism, extra-sensory perception. Did he think he had to tell a woman of such things? His theory was that a woman was, by her nature, a mother: very near to the earth. The mother of men, of gorillas. The wife, the mistress, but always the mother. Even little girls playing with their dolls were mothers. Mother coming out of mother, all beads on an endless umbilical cord that stretched back without a single break in the sequence to the infinite prehuman past. The woman of today — she herself, he had said — was irrevocably joined to mothers who must have looked like Congo, to others that were less human, to ones that were not human at all, to the first protoplasm that had increased by subdivision, to the mosses and lichens, to life itself. What was the male but an incomplete female? What was he but a wanton fertilizer of the female soil? Channel was a fool.

It had taken her only a minute to undress. Her husband had not even looked at her. She wondered sometimes if he ever saw her. She was running the bath. She would bathe, come out of the bathroom, and get into bed. Then he would bathe. Sometimes he told her to leave the water in for him. Sometimes, but only sometimes.

She lay soaking in the warm water. She raised her foot to look at the enamel on her toes. They were as carefully done as her hands. Some men had a foot fetish.

Her husband was calling her. 'What is it, Jean?'

'Leave in the water.'

So she was to leave the water in. How simple he was! How patterned his life!

Chapter 10

The GUEST HOUSE

THE DAY BEGAN FOR WILSON WITH BREAKFAST. IT WAS A MEAL
that he enjoyed. But breakfast today began with Sebastian,
who met him as he came out onto the terrace. Sebastian in
the full glory of his rage, of his furious energy, of his artistic
depression: a man woman-mad: frustrated, thwarted by his
inability to portray the visions that he saw.

'Jesus,' he began when he was ten yards away, 'I have
known some beautiful women. How beautiful! How beautiful! It brings tears to my eyes to think of them ... fair
women with hair like ripening corn ... ash blondes ... dark
women with sherry-colored eyes. Whatever they do, those
beautiful ones, they are beautiful. That is because they are
perfectly made ... graceful as deer even when they scratch
themselves.'

'Beautiful women are fools,' Channel said from the table.
He put down his cup. He had not waited for them. 'They
cannot help it. They are never contradicted. Men look into
their eyes and agree with them. It is a provision of nature
that they have no brains,' he went on, 'which, in part at least,
saves man. If they had brains as well as bodies ...' He
shrugged his shoulders. 'They are dumb in the American
sense' — he looked at Wilson — 'even if they are not silent.'

'So is a flower dumb,' Sebastian said. 'Would you have a
lily speak? Do you consider that necessary?' He examined
the dirt in his bitten nails. 'A beautiful woman should be

accepted. She is of God. A rare accident sent by God to please men by her presence. It is the men who are fools to expect a lovely woman to be different from any other in bed. They are not for that. They are there to be looked at.' He sniffed the air like a dog. 'To be enjoyed as flowers are enjoyed. Their utility is that they are without utility, though that, no doubt, is beyond your understanding. Only artists have understanding: all other men are mad. I say,' he shouted, 'that the worst artists, men like Landseer and de Lazlo, had more sense than all the bank presidents in the world rolled into one. Common sense. Common is right... that is the mot juste ... the vulgar sense which brings material profit to the vulgar, to those who believe in things ... in objects. And what are things?' He was still shouting. 'What is this common sense? Where is the inspiration ... where is the inner light to be found in a banker?' He ran his hands through his hair, leaving it on end — agitated, a poked fire. 'I will leave you to vomit,' he said.

Wilson never knew if he really vomited or if he meant that they in their materialism had made him vomit spiritually.

'What about his breakfast?' he asked Channel.

'He will come back for it later. Then he will complain that it is cold ... that it is badly served ... that to live here is worse than being in a concentration camp. But he will eat everything.'

Channel removed the black seeds from the paw-paw he had just cut in half. 'He is a child,' he said.

'Yes, like a child,' Wilson echoed. He was watching Channel's hands as he lit a cigarette. His hands were beautiful. He looked at them holding the match box; at the fall of his wrist. An artist's hands. They were adjusted to greatest precision of touch, sensitive as antennae. They were much more artistic, whatever that meant, than Sebastian's with their bitten nails and the muscular strength of his fingers. But that was where his strength came from, Sebastian said.

From his thumbs. Wilson thought of him drawing on the tablecloth with his thumb. It was only lately that he had understood what his mother meant when she had talked of men's hands: saying, he has beautiful hands — he has ugly hands. It had always embarrassed him as a boy without his knowing why. Perhaps you had to be over thirty and your mother to be dead before you could understand. His mother had been a beautiful woman. Women were caressed by the hands of men. They were the penultimate instruments of love. His mother must have been caressed by hands. Not just his father's, perhaps. He was himself the outcome of a caress of hands. It was inconceivable that love could be made without them. He tried to think of the love of a hand-less man. Yes, women looked at men's hands. And when they looked, they thought . . . even your mother. All mothers. All women. It was queer that your mother had to be dead before you knew she was a woman. When she was alive, she was your mother. Only when she was dead did you under-stand her, and that was the measure of your regret. If I had known she was a woman, how I could have pleased her! he thought. How happy I could have made her!

He wondered what Olga thought of hands. He had dreamed of her. He thought of his mother again. It was a funny thought to have here on this terrace in Central Africa. He wondered if his mother had ever thought of him being here. He knew she had not. She had thought of him as being a member of Parliament, as being a judge, an admiral. She had thought of him getting married. She had lived to see him married. But Africa had certainly never entered her white waved head. And these people. What would mother have thought of them? Of Sebastian and the doctor, of Olga, of Bentinck? Mother would have been charmed with them all, but I should never have thought so while she was alive because I considered her only as a mother and not as a woman.

The white-gloved hand of Othello removed his plate of

bacon and eggs. The other boy changed a record on the
victrola. Still Josephine Baker, but this time *La Canne de
Sucre. En voulez vous de la canne* . . . she sang. *La canne de mon
pays* . . .

Sebastian was returning with great strides.

'You see what I told you,' Channel said: he pointed with
his cigarette. 'Our painter returns. He is a simple man. He
is hungry, so he returns to his food.'

Sebastian sat down, filled his mouth with buttered toast,
took a gulp of coffee, swallowed it, and said, 'I have made
them beautiful things . . .' He refilled his coffee-cup. 'Too
beautiful: they did not understand them . . . Lark's song . . .
swan's song . . . my God, what beauty I have made for women!
Yes, they inspired it. Women do inspire men. They clear
the minds of dross. A woman when you have had her leaves
you alone with God. Then you are frightened. I have seen
God many times,' he went on. 'The earth trembles beneath
you . . . you feel yourself falling. What inspires you . . . their
softness like satin, their curves, the light on their skins? Some
are no good. Beautiful they may be, but they absorb light.
They do not refract it. A naked woman should be pink and
green . . . apple-green. No, not what you think, but of a
subtlety . . . a cool, white greenness and a warm pinkness . . .
not Renoir,' he shouted, banging on the table, 'not hot-bath-
lobster-salmon-pink. After all, a woman is a human being;
she is not a boiled shrimp. Pink and green must be suggested,
like garlic in a salad. And I spit on those who are afraid of
their breath. There are men who are afraid of garlic. Americans, English . . . I have met them. They say I stink. I do
not care if I stink if I can paint; besides, it is good for the
intestines, it kills worms in the bowels, and I like it.' He
drank again. 'But those women of mine. When I go home I
find Maria has scratched Nina. I go to my box that I keep
locked to find a present for Maria to make her quiet. I give
her a goblet . . . Venetian fifteenth century . . . a thing of great

beauty. No, I do not know where I got it. I stole it, perhaps, or a woman gave it me. Rich women give you things sometimes for sleeping with them. Sometimes it is worth it. One must eat to paint: one must sleep to eat. But what did she do, that Maria? I will tell you. She threw the goblet at Nina. It cut her face, and both of them so God-damn foolish they do not know what it is that they quarrel about. It is very hard for a man of genius to find a woman... very hard.'

Wilson thought he was going to cry, but he went on eating.

'Savages,' he said. 'Naked savages, but beautiful naked... And the others, the civilized, they are only beautiful half-naked. Then they are like the advertisements for corsets... those that you see when you have not had a woman for a long time. Once I was a month... thirty-one days... that gives you a pain in the belly. But I do not like them,' he said. 'I do not like them at all. Now I am going home.' He pushed his plate away. He had cleared the table, there was nothing left to eat on it.

'Home,' Channel said, 'to the women.'

'Yes,' he said. 'I must beat them. Then they will become amorous and I am no longer in my first youth. I would prefer to give them presents if they would leave me to work. It is hard to know what to do with them,' he said. He was standing up, staring down into the valley. His yellow dog that he called Bernadotte was standing behind him; its tail was wagging slowly.

Channel looked at the dog with distaste. 'Even the leopards will have nothing to do with that dog,' he said.

Sebastian left them.

They talked of dogs. The servants went on playing the victrola. The doctor smoked; Wilson smoked. From Sebastian's house came screams, shouts, and laughter.

'You see,' Channel said. 'They mock him, those little brown girls.' He was tired of talking of dogs. After all there was not much point in it, Wilson thought, in a place where you could not have one.

'Behold Leonardo tormented by black nymphs,' Channel said. He had turned his head to listen to Sebastian's roaring and the girls' laughter. 'A great man and a great fool,' he said. 'Poor man, he can speak of nothing but women and love.'

'There is too much talk of love,' he went on, 'and too little thought. Open a book, turn on the radio, what do you see and hear? Love ... love ... romance ... boy meets girl ... boy is parted from girl ... boy deserts girl ... boy is jilted by girl. Endlessly you hear it. Endlessly you read it. But have you noticed the curiously defective thinking behind this theme? Romance stops at a given but unspecified point. I have often wondered at which point? The first kiss? I think not, for kisses are included. The second ... the hundredth ... the intimacies which follow the kisses, perhaps, but which ones? When a man touches a woman's breasts, as inevitably must happen, or when he touches her legs? Man is very tactual. His love process follows a pattern, but at some point all talk about it stops. This idyll whose initial episodes are so charming and romantic then becomes a wickedness that the sacrament of marriage merely palliates. When a woman says, "So you wish to marry my daughter ... you love her," she knows very well in her heart that she says, "So you wish to sleep with my daughter and to possess her." I find it very interesting this amputation by taboo of a process in mid-career. It is admirable to mix the flour and water and yeast and shortening to make bread, but it must not be put into the oven. Yes, it is interesting,' he said again, 'but I can find no explanation of it.' He lit another cigarette. His plate was filled with stubs.

Wilson had no answer for him. He wanted to talk about women less than ever. It made him think of Olga. Yet the talk turned to women continually. Perhaps these men, so different from each other, turned without knowing it to their one common denominator. Sebastian speaking flamboyantly

of beauty that he professed to worship, but which he only used
for inspiration. Channel cynically, his mind as precise as his
fingers, speaking of the pleasure to be obtained from sensual
gratification which according to him could be savored as
wine. Owen, the man of God, speaking fearfully of something
he did not understand. How upset Owen had been with
Channel when he had said at the party, 'But what can you
do, since they carry it about with them ... since when a man
and woman meet they have on their persons the requisites
for pleasure?' Of course, Channel had been drunk, but what
about me? he thought. Me and Olga. His dreams of her.
He had been making love to her almost, but each time had
waked terrified, as Congo had dragged him away from her.

There was silence at Sebastian's house. The sun was growing warmer. The mist below them was dissipating. Had his
mother-in-law really thought, when he had said he wanted
to marry Anne, that he wanted to sleep with her? Channel
had flattered Mrs. Delaynay: to imagine she ever thought
anything was to flatter her.

This place was a microcosm of the greater world. It was
the small town infinitely keyed up, thrown out of perspective
by the circumstance of geographic location, by the intellectual qualities of the protagonists, and then projected
against the screen of his mind which was itself abnormal owing
to his emotional state.

He realized he was seeing educated men acting in a manner
which was almost entirely uninhibited. Even if they clothed
their acts in the vestments of a formal attire, it only exaggerated the processes of their minds. They dressed for dinner.
Their servants were clad in immaculate white. They played
music, symphonies and Josephine Baker; but where they
dressed their bodies, they undressed their minds. There was
little pretense ... little endeavor to impress. In such a restricted society it was impossible for anyone to pretend to be
other than what he was for long. The idea of it all, of what he

was seeing, shocked him. It was so logical. Each of them was the direct result of his past, his environment and heredity. Congo the gorilla no less, and no more, than Channel the doctor, Sebastian the painter, Bentinck the hunter, or Olga the wife. And he found himself in the middle of this mael-strom trying to steer his way between the Scylla of his mem-ories and the Charybdis of actual involvement. But he was being dragged into it. He could feel the pull.

First, Frazer. It was he who had given him the initial push. Now Olga was dragging at him with soft, white, red-tipped hands. The climate, the scenery, the conditions of life were weakening him. Sounds, perfumes, all had their particular impact on his personality. The wild, occasional shouts of Congo. The doctor's lectures. Sebastian's women. Sebastian himself with his outbursts. The professor's botanic objectivity. Bentinck's hunter's patience. The scent of geranium that came from Olga. The soft touch of her hand upon his bare arms. The look in her eyes. The line of her neck when she turned. The perfume of the roses that came in at his window. The choking cough of a leopard. The rustle of great leaves in the evening breeze . . . And the feeling that war was coming in Europe. That which he had at first thought of as a joke, as playing Red Indians, was going to be the real thing: a matter of life or death. The feeling that before it was done, one, perhaps more than one, of these people among whom he lived would die. There was no getting away from it. He was in-volved, whether he liked it or not. From an interested ob-server, from an umpire in the game, he had by slow degrees, over the few days he had been here, become an actual partici-pant. He no longer regretted it.

Channel had finished eating and was staring into space. Conversation scarcely existed here. There were lectures, arguments, monologues, exclamations, but no one talked. They said at great length what was in their minds. Then, when they had said it, they shut up and ate or smoked or did nothing.

Throwing his cigarette away, Channel said: 'Well, you're leaving me today. I am sorry. It has been pleasant having you as my guest.'

'I'll still be having breakfast with you.'

'Breakfast, yes.'

'We will not forget you, comrade.' Sebastian had come back. 'We are not the kind of men who forget their bene-factors, and besides you are only going a hundred yards away. What is a hundred yards?' he asked. 'Now I must go back to work. I have settled the girls. The attack!' he shouted. 'Work should be attacked with energy, with fire.' He strode off. His dog ate a piece of bread that had fallen on the grass, and followed slowly.

'Moving will be no trouble,' Channel said. 'My boys will do it, and you will be more comfortable over there.' He nodded at the guest house. 'Olga is a wonderful hostess.'

'I'm sure she is.'

'I've told the boys,' Channel said. 'In fact they seem to have begun.' Wilson turned. Channel was right. There they were. Othello and the other black Shakespeare characters were proceeding in single file, each carrying something: a coat on a hanger, a pair of shoes, a rifle. A picannin followed the bigger boys staggering under a suitcase that he held on his head.

'Do not forget to come in whenever you feel like it,' Channel said, 'and take any books you want. The professor has some books that you might like: ethnology interests him too. And detective fiction for relaxation.' Channel went slowly towards the hospital.

Wilson got up. Another phase was over. He was going to be installed, as they called it, in the guest house. He had better go and find Olga. He had given up calling her Mrs. Le Blanc.

He found her in the garden. Congo was with her, following her with bent legs, his knuckles touching the ground as he walked. For a moment Wilson almost turned back. The gorilla scared him.

'Come and look at the roses, Wilson.' She had seen him.

It was absurd. Everything was. It did not make sense to be here on the roof of the world looking at dark red roses with this girl, with a half-grown gorilla chaperoning them. And what a chaperon! 'If I touched her he'd tear me to pieces.'

They walked down the grass path.

'General Jacques Minot,' Olga said. 'The sweetest-smelling rose in all the world.'

They were the roses she had used at the party on the first night: they were the ones she always had in her house. Every time he had dined there, she had had them on the table. He knew that he would never forget their scent; that it would be forever associated with this woman.

She picked a bud for his buttonhole. As she put it in, her geranium smell, now blended with that of the roses, came to him.

'I love perfumes. Nothing can remind you like a perfume. Roses remind me of my first love affair, with my cousin. It was in Poland. Beautiful Poland. Later he was killed, but when I walk in this garden he is with me. He walks on the grass beside me holding my hand.' She did not tell Wilson that she had been five years old at the time.

'I am sorry,' Wilson said.

'Sorry? Why? It was beautiful. Sorry that he died? Do not be sorry. He died young, in war, before he had known disillusion. And you?' she asked. 'You have loved, have you not? I can see it in your face.' She was standing beside him. His hand went to her waist.

'No. Not now. Not with Congo. He will not let anyone touch me. Not even my husband.'

What did she mean ... 'Not now'? That meant later. A

reference to her husband. Her question about his having loved ... He found himself answering her.

'Yes, Olga, I have loved. It did not go well. My marriage went wrong.'

'Does it ever go right? And why should it? Why not be satisfied with beauty while it lasts? I have loved many men. I have never been sorry.'

There she was again. The suggestion. The half-promise. He did not know what to say. He wanted to make love to her and he wanted not to. If once he began ... and besides with that damn gorilla beside them. He looked away.

She came closer to him. 'I could love you, Mr. Wilson,' she said. Her breath was on his cheek. 'Yes, I could love you. Do you think you would like it?' she laughed. 'I could send you mad for me.'

Didn't she know she had done it already? He said nothing. He did nothing. Congo was close to them, sitting behind them plucking a rose to pieces petal by petal.

'You see,' Olga said, pointing to him. 'She loves me, she loves me not.' She laid a hand on his arm. 'Do not be afraid. It will not hurt you to be mad for a little while. It will be something to look back on later ... something to look forward to now.' Another experience, like meeting a gorilla socially. Channel's talk of memory, of young men and old, of regrets at the things that had not been done came back to him. Her eyes were on his. Her lips were parted. She wetted them with the tip of her tongue. He noticed the contrast in color — the pink tongue, the bright scarlet lips. He could read nothing in her eyes except a faint amusement, a faint ironic promise. She was a woman offering a small boy a rather dangerous treat. The blood was hammering in his ears.

'Come,' she said, 'let us take the roses to your house. What is a house without flowers? I hope you will be happy there.' She looked back over her shoulder.

'I'm sure I will,' he said. What were they saying to each

other by implication? What did the future hold? When would it happen? He was certain that it would happen; that she would arrange it; that he was already caught in the swirl of the vortex. He watched her walking in front of him. The swing of her hips, the swaying of her dress. They went into the guest house.

'You wait,' she said to Congo.

Wilson closed the door. As he closed it, she was in his arms. He had never known anyone could kiss like that. She trembled as he held her, but not with nervousness. She trembled like a flame in a draught, burning up and then down. She slipped away from him. Her hand went up to her hair. To tidy it.

She pulled out a rose to shorten its stem.

To look at her, nothing might have happened. Her hands arranging the flowers were steady.

'You see I was right, Mr. Wilson,' she said.

'Yes, you were right, Olga.'

She put the vase in the window and turned quickly.

'Let me know if there is anything you want, won't you?' she asked.

He was alone once more. The morning he spent arranging the few things he had in his new home. His eyes kept going to the vase of roses. He kept smelling them. That was clever of her.

His lunch came over from the main house on a tray. With it was a note: *I am sending your lunch over, as I am indisposed and the professor is out.* No more than that. No signature. Her writing was firm, dark, and up and down. He smelt the paper when the boy had gone. It smelt of her.

In the afternoon he went for a walk, climbing the mountain behind the house. It was hot, too hot really for doing this, but he felt impelled to go; to get something out of his system by violent exercise. He forced his way through the thorn scrub, clung to lianas, scrambled over rocky outcrops and

followed little paths that went like tunnels through the bush.
When he had gone far enough, he sat and smoked. Olga had
upset him. She had made thought impossible. Another cigarette and he returned, taking an easier path that led directly
down to the settlement. One of Sebastian's girls passed him,
the younger, that he called Maria. She was walking fast:
he wondered where she was going, and then forgot about her.

Dinner at the Le Blancs was uneventful. Olga was the
charming hostess, nothing more. Cocktails were served as
soon as he arrived. The professor's welcome was warm;
Retief's friendly. There was no one else there: just the four of
them.

'We have stopped treating you as a guest, you see,' Olga
said.

'That is nice of you. It's always awkward being a guest
when you can't return hospitality.'

Not that this conversation made any sense. He was more
a guest than ever; his obligation increasing with each meal.

'The return of hospitality, Mr. Wilson,' the professor said,
'is to have you here with us. I sometimes think it's hard
on Olga to see the same faces all the time ... to have to
listen to conversation of men who are completely absorbed in
their work. You can tell her of the world. Talk to her of
London, of Paris, of America.'

Wilson took a second Martini, so did Retief. Olga did not
drink. Dinner was announced. He sat on Olga's right. The
professor was opposite to her and Retief opposite him.

Hors d'oeuvres, petite marmite, grilled trout, guinea fowl
Marengo, and a compote of fruit. The wines were a Sauterne
and a Pomard. The meal was relatively silent. Being foreigners they enjoyed their food. What conversation there was
was desultory. Olga did not speak at all, but sat with her eyes
downcast and a faint smile on her lips. 'Enigmatic,' Wilson
called it to himself, 'like a Sphinx.' Then he was angry that

he could not think of anything more original. Once her foot
touched his under the table. It could easily have been an
accident.

Retief, after dinner, as they had coffee and brandy, told
him about the possibilities of the country: about its immense,
potential riches. He was enthusiastic. 'There is everything
here,' he said — 'gold, tin, silver, copper, valuable timber,
rubber. The ancients knew this country well. They knew all
Africa. Did you know, Mr. Wilson, that with the exception of
the Rand every mine in Africa has been found by developing
the ancient workings?'

Wilson had not known it. With one part of his mind he
listened to Retief's talk, thought of this ancient land, of Sofala,
of the traders of the Arabian, Indian, and Chinese ships that
had touched on the East Coast for centuries, of the old trade
routes of the interior. Ancient, mysterious, bad — there had
been so much wickedness here, so much cruelty. The slave
trade was supposed, since its inception, to have taken thirty
million lives on the West Coast. There were no particulars of
the East Coast, where the Arabs had dealt in men for a thousand years and more. Who had built Zimbabwe? Had those
dead miners been Phoenicians ... Jews? Who were the
Bantus? The Hamites? Gold, ivory, slaves, ostrich plumes,
gums ... men and women shackled, marching, driven by
whips through the endless paths of Africa.

He answered Retief. He asked questions. But in another
part of his mind he was occupied with Olga. She had on a
white and red-striped taffeta evening dress. He had never seen
her look more beautiful. An amethyst cross suspended on
a fine gold chain rose and fell as she breathed. Her hair was
coiled like a golden snake about her head. She had silver
slippers on her feet. She sat with her legs crossed, her head
resting on her hand, her elbow on the arm of the chair. He
wondered what she was thinking: if she was listening to what
they said. She had hardly spoken to him all the evening ex-

cept when he had first come in. Her foot had touched his once at dinner — he kept remembering this — and as they had sat down in the sitting room she said, 'Don't stay too long tonight. The professor is tired.'

What had she meant by that?

If she didn't want him to stay, he wouldn't. But he did not want to go. He could have sat here watching her forever. She was beautiful in repose. It was impossible to associate this calm, cold woman sitting quietly in her drawing room with the woman he had held in his arms this morning. What was she thinking? What did she ever think of? Why did one torment oneself about what went on in the minds of others? He got up to say good night.

'You will be seeing so much of me now,' he said, 'I don't want to outstay my welcome.'

'You are very welcome, Mr. Wilson,' Olga said. 'Isn't he, Jean?'

'Certainly he is,' the professor said.

In his own house after dinner he put Olga out of his head and went back to what he had been thinking earlier: of the bonds that tied these men. Channel and Sebastian were tied by their interest in women. Channel and Marais, though he had hardly seen them speak, had a precision of mind that was shown by the neatness of their clothes. Von Brandt was a soldier, and therefore allied in a curious way with the others who had also been soldiers. The professor and Retief and Channel were all scientists. Bentinck was a hunter with a vast knowledge of the wild. He was practical; they were theoretical. Also he got them their meat. Sebastian being an artist was, as Channel said, in a sense a child, and as such had an appeal. This was apart from his work, which was worthy of respect even if he as a man was not. Then all of them were tied by economics. They made their livings here and could not afford to quarrel. Channel doctored them. Bentinck shot for them. Owen ministered to their souls, or wanted to. The professor, because he had started the Station, was responsible for their being here. Olga represented woman to them all. Inevitably she affected them, whether they wanted it or not. He saw something here that he had never seen before. The interrelations of social intercourse, of expedience, taste, and economics. No one of the group could be affected without its in some way affecting the others. It was funny to be thirty-three ... to have lived all over the world, to have been to a university, and then to have come here by accident and really begin his education among a lot of men who were, if they were nothing worse, at least eccentric.

But what did surprise him was the fact that for the first time he was beginning to understand people, the functioning of their minds, their hopes and desires — the way they tried to achieve their ends. All his life he had lived among too many people and had been unable to see individuals because of the crowd. He had known other artists. Sebastian was only those men extended, psychically prolonged, drawn out to the limit. Channel was other doctors also extended, or it might be reduced, dissolved in the acid of his experience till only the hard core of his personality remained. And Olga was all women. In all women, even in Anne, he now could see as he looked back, there was some Olga.

In placing them, however, he had not yet succeeded in placing himself. He did not know what he wanted, or even what he hoped to get from life. He had never had to fight for anything: never been exposed to real danger or hardship. In terms of experience he was virgin, adolescent. Hunger, cold, fear, anger, love, hate, in their real sense, he had not known. He had reflected the emotions and ideas of the people with whom he had mixed. He had no ideas, no reasons. He was Episcopalian because his mother was; Conservative because his father was, but he had never bothered to vote. He had never considered religion or politics. He had accepted them. He had never thought about love. He had been in love with Anne in a way. But it had been too easy. He had never analyzed what he felt, never tried to see whence it sprang, or where it would lead. Marriage for him had been a mixture of going to parties and to bed with a woman. When you, or she, got tired of going to parties and bed together, you got divorced. Anne had got tired of it first. But he wondered now if it was not because she was tired of their life being so purposeless. So little was actually achieved by people changing their bed and party partners. The more it changed ... Either life must have purpose or it was infinitely boring. That was what Channel had meant when he spoke of women: when he had said, 'I am so bored ...' Boredom was due to the idea of futility which revolted the unconscious urge for creation. But it was damned silly to have had to come here to find these things out: paradoxical that to get any understanding of civilization, a man must leave it. What he felt for Olga was not love. It was lust, and yet it was more than lust. She had a representative quality. He felt somehow that he could learn from her. Or was this just a rationalization of his desire? That was where thought got you. You fooled yourself. If it came to that, he had been fooling himself all his life. But it was a beginning of something, he did not yet know what it was, when you knew you were fooling yourself. He had advanced one stage along the road to maturity.

He went out into the garden. The African moon was shining. It was very big, much bigger than even a Southern moon. It was in keeping with the land on which it shone. The leaves of the elephant ears were painted white by it, the moonflowers were mystically illumined. The night air was cool, fragrant, and from somewhere came the throb of a native drum. It was not talking. By now he had come to learn when a drum was sending messages. This man was just tapping his drum: getting some obscure satisfaction from it; from the noise ... from the feel of the taut hide beneath his hand.

Had the call of the moon brought him to tap in the silent night? Why was Congo uneasy when it was new? Why were there so many old stories and legends of men becoming moonstruck? How did the moon affect the tides? What was the relation between the waters of the sea and the blood that ran in the bodies of men and beasts? What made dogs and wolves bay the moon? Why were there so many superstitions about the weather and the moon, about the sowing and reaping of crops according to its phases? Why did the Hottentots and Bushmen dance at its fullness? What was a harvest moon? Why should witches be associated with the moon? What was meant by moonlight being romantic? Did its light excite desire? Moonstruck, moon-mad, moony, mooning, honeymoon ... So many words, phrases, legends, superstitions could not be without foundation.

And why had he never thought of these things before? Why did he suddenly wish he knew more? That he had read the *Golden Bough* more carefully. That he had really studied Freud, Jung, Adler, Gerald Heard, and the others? Anne had wanted to. She had tried to, and he had laughed at her. He saw now that she had been trying to understand something; that she had been trying to find a reason for her own existence. A woman had rhythm. Her life, punctuated by her menstrual periods, was broken up into twenty-eight-day moon-months, divided into compartments by her conceptions, pregnancies, and parturitions. A man's life and his thoughts bore no relation to a woman's. He had thought he understood Anne, but it had taken tonight and the African moon to show him that he had not understood her ... that man would never understand woman. Man and woman met on the approximation of their homosexuality. Sexually they met as animals: but mentally, in the negation of their sexual attributes, in the measure of the resemblance and the totality of their differentiation. No woman was entirely woman. No man entirely man. Together, added up in an hormonic sum, the couple totalled a complete man and woman. But where physically the woman in woman called to the man in man, mentally the woman in woman called to the woman in man, and the man in man to the man in woman.

He listened. The drum had stopped.

Someone was coming towards him. It was Olga in a green dressing gown. Her hair was down. It hung like a cloak over her shoulders. It reached her waist.

'You were expecting me?' she asked.

'Perhaps,' he said. 'I was uneasy.'

He hadn't known that he had been expecting her, but her coming had not surprised him. In his heart perhaps he had been expecting her, been hoping she would come. She had drawn him into the black shadow of a palm.

'To say good night,' she whispered. 'To kiss you good night, mon amour.'

She was warm, supple in his arms, fluid against him. His hands were on her breasts, his lips on hers. Her mouth clung to his.

She broke from him, laughing softly. 'Tomorrow is also a day, Mr. Wilson. Till tomorrow. Bonne nuit, and sleep well.'

She was gone. If only one thing was certain, it was that he would sleep badly.

Chapter 11

The PROFESSOR

〰〰〰〰〰〰〰〰〰

PROFESSOR LE BLANC ENJOYED HAVING WILSON AT THE
Experimental Station. Olga seemed much happier with him
here. In addition, he was a quiet young man, retiring and
studious: altogether a charming guest.

It was his presence which made his proposed short trip
possible. The main trip which he took every three months
that he had spoken of to Olga remained unchanged. This
was a short trip. The idea of it had come to him suddenly.
There were some trees that he had not seen for two years.
They did not fit into his regular safaris. They were out of
the direct line he took and too far away to see without making
an actual expedition which would last at least a week. Yes,
it was a great relief having that Wilson here.

He began to think about the trees. They were a variety
of Burma teak that he was trying out under natural forest
conditions. Perhaps he should have gone to see them before.
But if he had, he would have interfered with them. If they
had shown signs of being swamped, he would have tried to
help them. He could never be really objective about his
trees. They were like children to him. Retief was just as bad.
Still now, after two years, they would either be all right or
they would be dead.

He was very excited. They would go tomorrow. And
Retief had been right, it was not the butler. Naturally,
Retief having read the book knew it was the young man, but

it was nice of him not to have told him who it was. It would have spoilt his pleasure.

Certainly he was lucky to have such an assistant, and to have that Wilson here. The trees should have done well. He was sure they should. If they left tomorrow, they would know in a couple of days. No, not tomorrow, next week. It would be rude to go at once, before Wilson had really settled down. Yes, he was lucky. Lucky to have such a beautiful wife, such a nice home, such a pleasant job, to have money of his own so that he could concentrate on his work; lucky in the honors he had received, in the way his works were considered textbooks in several countries — notably Switzerland, Belgium, France, England, and the United States of America.

He sighed with satisfaction. His scheme for the internationalization of botanical knowledge; for the exchange of information; of seeds, plants, runners, rhizomes, tubers, cuttings, and suckers between botanical gardens, research stations, and Departments of Agriculture throughout the world was actually on the point of operating. Even before his idea a lot had been done. Salt bush had come to Africa from Australia, following the blue gum and the wattle. Rhodes grass had gone from the Union of South Africa to the United States. The spineless cactus, perfected by Luther Burbank, had come from America to Africa. Kikuyu, umfufu, and elephant grass had gone from this region to many tropical and subtropical countries.

But this was only the beginning. Useful plants, beautiful trees and shrubs were the common property of the world. They should be allowed to grow wherever they could be of use. The limit being, not the political situation, the national ownership, but the geographic and climatic conditions of the areas involved.

His work was mainly connected with rubber. But all plants and trees were his interest. All grasses from the finest to the giant bamboos that clothed these mountaintops and those of

Asia. All trees, from the slender aspen to the great baobabs;
all flowers, cacti, succulents, mosses, lichens. He could sit
like this and dream for hours, watching his beautiful wife and
thinking about the miracle of growth, of the fantastic marches
and migrations of men which could sometimes only be traced
by the trees and plants they had left behind them. A race
might die out, but some of its agriculture was likely to remain. He thought of seeds carried, carefully hoarded, by
pioneers as they trekked; of weed seeds brought in the forage
of invading armies. Khaki bush from the Americas and
blackjack from Australia had come to this continent in the
South African War. The casuarinas — Australian pines,
as some called them — had spread to the East Coast of
Africa, Australia, Polynesia, from the Indies; sorghums,
millets, Indian corn, Kaffir beans had spread everywhere:
potatoes from America: cinchona trees, breadfruit, paw-paws,
bananas. The list was endless. Wistaria from China. Rhododendrons from the Himalayas. Big blue poppies, Arctic
poppies, bougainvillea, hibiscus — fruits of all kinds, flowers
of all kinds. These were the great sources of nourishment for
the body and the soul.

He had better tell Olga.

'Next week Retief and I will take a trip, Olga,' he said.

'Next week, Jean?' She looked up from her petit point.
'I thought you were going next month.'

'We are, but this is just a short trip. We shall be away less
than a week. It seems a good time, with Wilson here to keep
you company. You like him, don't you?'

She was sewing again. He liked to watch her hands as she
sewed.

'Yes, I like him, Jean. He is a very interesting man.'

That he was interesting had never occurred to the professor.
He did not interest him. He was remarkably ignorant. But
he was good-natured, and a godsend at this particular moment.

'He is willing to learn, Olga,' he said.

'Yes, Jean. It seems to me that he is the kind of man who learns fast.'

'Then you do not mind?'

She looked at him out of clear, wide-spaced grey eyes.

'Mind? I always mind when you go. Life is not the same without you, but I know if you say you must you must. Voilà tout. . . . What is it this time?'

'The Burma teaks. I have not seen them for two years. It is terrible to think of those little things in competition with the jungle, fighting for their lives in these exotic surroundings. Of course they have their heredity.'

'They will be all right,' Retief said. 'You will see, Professor.'

'You think so?' He was perturbed at this endless struggle for existence. Plant fighting plant in its efforts to reach the sunlight, in its search for nourishment from the soil. Despite what he had said to Wilson about rubber, he was still not satisfied with his work — it was not enough. He was also working on a formula for synthetic rubber. It was expensive to make now, but later it might not be.

The idea that anything was synthetic amused him. It was the same or nearly the same product arrived at by different means. Coal and oil were a basis for rubber. But what were coal and oil but the product of an ancient vegetation — of cellulose? Coal to his mind was scarcely a mineral. They had come near, today, to alchemists' dreams of changing matter, of transmuting it. It had been proved that matter could be changed, that the elements themselves were subject to change, if their atomic structure could be rearranged. But it was the grasses that really interested him: grasses for feeding the cattle that made meat, grasses and canes that could be compressed into timber for building. The grasses that would one day be processed for human consumption. The grasses from which he was certain that rubber could be made.

Olga looked up from her work. Jean was dreaming again.
Her husband was an idealist: a man who thought in vast
generalities. That was his path to happiness. He pursued
his happiness through knowledge. So did Channel. Owen
sought his in religion. Fritz also sought his through religion.
His fanatical National Socialism could only be considered as
religion. Sebastian stood halfway between the scientific and
the religious principles. Bentinck was a natural and practical
philosopher. The American as yet was nothing. But he
would be. She would make him into something. That
rarity — a human being, perhaps. She would teach him
what he had not been able to learn from his wife: something
that no man could learn from a wife ... the universality of
woman ... next week when her husband had gone. She had
made a beginning already. She thought about Channel again.
Science, yes, but he went beyond it, into the mystic, into the
esoteric. He was trying to control the forces of life and death.
They were all, when it came to that, trying for something
beyond man — even Fritz with his talk of a superman, of a
Herrenvolk. And in all this she, the woman, was the stabiliz-
ing factor. Channel said that world regeneration when it
came — if it came — must come through woman, as life
came through her. She was the source. She made men in
her body. She trained them. The child was the father of the
man. It never forgot what it had learnt at its mother's knee.
Men changed again later according to the women with whom
they associated. Women put a spell upon men. They made
them or broke them. In the end it was always the woman as
it was in the beginning. Even in detective fiction ... Cher-
chez la femme ... It had not been the butler in her husband's
book. It had been the young man, and behind him the
woman. Behind every figure, small, in private life, or great,
in public, there was a woman. Or there was no woman. No
woman was the same as a woman. The man who avoided
women was so susceptible to their influence that he feared

them. Therefore, with him, too, it was woman. How right Channel was — and how wrong! His logical arguments seemed so good — till you thought them over. Then, if you were a woman, you still thought them good, but knew that he had missed the salient point.

She held up a green thread to match it against her design. Jean talked of competition among plants. The same was true among men: each sought the sunlight of his happiness. Each sought: few found. Even Congo sought. Gripped by the periodic unhappiness of his frustration, he became unmanageable. Generally he gave warning; tried to get her away as his play got rougher. It was as if he knew that later he might hurt her; as if he knew that he had no self-control.

Outwardly life was the same as it had been for some time, but the coming of Wilson had precipitated the solution of their lives, had clarified the liquid of their association. Wilson — and the approach of war. Sometimes it made her laugh. She knew so much. It was she who had told Frazer to get a man like Bentinck. She had woven many complex patterns, been part of so many things, making of her life a tapestry that resembled the pattern she held upon her knee. She was a woman. A brain and a body. A subtle brain and a beautiful body. She liked to employ them both. In this occupation there was little conflict. The one was complementary to the other. The beautiful spy had gone out, they had told her in London. She had been there with the professor before they sailed for the Congo. A young man in a black coat, striped trousers, and beautiful wavy blond hair had told her so.

'On the contrary, monsieur, because of fiction it has come in again,' she had said. 'It is so obvious that no one would dream of using it except in the simplest manner with little prostitutes or sailors' trulls.'

He had laughed. 'Perhaps you are right, madame. A beautiful woman is not like a battleship, she can never become obsolete.' This had been after her previous record had been examined.

They had understood each other. It was often much easier to do business with a homosexual. One did not have to go to bed with them. She had left with a letter of introduction to Mr. Frazer at Nairobi.

She moved her chair to get a better light. The light was no better in the new position, but she had moved. When the professor and Retief were away, she would continue the education of Mr. Wilson.

She would also send Fritz a message. She wondered if she had been kind enough to Retief lately. The expression of his eyes had changed. They had lost something of what she had called 'their sick spaniel look.' Had she gone too far with him?

Chapter 12

The PEACH

'ANIMALS AND PEOPLE HAVE THE SAME FACES,' SEBASTIAN SAID
suddenly. He had brought a bottle of wine over to Wilson at
the guest house. 'They all have masks.' He pulled an envelope and a stub of pencil from his pocket. He had to draw
to show what he meant. He drew a face. 'Look,' he said,
'take a line from the corner of each eye to the point of the
nose ... a triangle. Take another from the outside of the eyes
to the chin. That is the mask, the frame; everything falls just
inside or just outside it. Forehead, cheeks, chin ... bone
structure ... a series of planes, curves, bulges, recessions: they
all fit round it. When you say a man looks like a bloodhound,
a fox, a rabbit, you mean just what you say. You mean that
his mask reminds you of those animals.

'It's the mask that gives expression. People and animals ...'
he continued. 'Where does the one begin and the other end?
Men meaner than dogs. Dogs nobler than men ... all eating,
drinking, breeding, moving — all enclosed within the same
space — all interrelated by their enmities and friendships, by
wildness and domesticity — all living side by side, preying
on each other, supporting each other.

'My God,' he exclaimed, 'when I watch those women of
mine, I wonder if they are really human or if I am ... we
can't both be. No, we can't both be. They have no souls.'
He drank again. 'And what is a soul? I have an immense
soul.' He stretched out his hands. 'I have tried to explain it

to the doctor. It envelops the world, but I have no faith. Those girls have immense faith and no soul. They are animals that believe in God. I am a man who believes in animals. They learnt about God from Owen. What a way to learn about God! They think that God can only live in a house with a corrugated-iron roof.

'Fantastic, that's what it is. So fantastic that it's incredible. I can't explain anything. I can't even begin to understand. So I paint. So I put things down. It's a great relief. That's because I do not believe, but they — those girls — don't have to put things down: they eat and fornicate and pray. Sometimes I try to think of what's going on in their heads. Something must be going on. They have heads, haven't they? There must be something in them. If they were killed, and their brains spread out, they'd look like my brains or a calf's brains: look so like that it would take a doctor to tell them apart. And what goes on in a calf's brain?'

He was silent. In a minute he would start again. A man possessed by devils, by fantasies. Words, thoughts, ideas poured out of him. He jumped from subject to subject. He hunted thoughts through the convolutions of his tortured brain as a dog hunts rabbits in a hedgerow. I am Sebastian the painter. I am the painter Sebastian... I am Sebastian. Had he another name? He was dragging his bitten fingernails through his beard.

'Do you know anything about those shrunken heads they get on the Orinoco?' he asked. He did not wait for an answer. 'I had a beauty once: that of a white man. I gave it to a woman. Lovely as an angel, she was. A red blonde, like one of those orange cats — like a cat: beautiful, cruel, lascivious. But they're all males. You never see a marmalade cat that is a female, or a tortoise-shell that is a male. What do you make of that?' he asked. 'I always look at them to see.'

Wilson could imagine Sebastian investigating the sex of every alley cat. He had something of the cat in him: a tom cat.

'It was all stamped out,' he said, 'and then a demand sprang up again. The tourists began to buy them. Supply and demand. Like toothpaste, or ospreys, or white slaves. If there is a demand, there will be a supply. But they are artists, those Indians. They do not kill at once, they want to study the features. They use a poisoned arrow or a spear that paralyzes the body, but not the face. Then they sit around and watch for days, before they kill. They want to reproduce expression. The mask again. And no one knows exactly how they do it ... take out the bone, they say, and then shrink the skull with hot stones put in from the bottom, through the neck or the roof of the mouth. No one knew who that white one I had was, but it was a funny thing to have, and I was offered a lot for it, and then like a fool I gave it to that woman, but she never saw the point. All she knew was that it was valuable.

'But it is a fine country — wide rivers you cannot see across, peccaries that will tree and kill a jaguar, rubber trees, jungles, orchids, anacondas, alligators, hummingbirds like little jewels, so small you could wear them in a ring, and blue butterflies as big as birds, that fly high up in the trees. Did you know some butterflies will come to carrion? A bit of rotting liver is the best way to attract them. When I was a boy, I used to catch them that way... purple emperors in the forest.

'And farther off, towards the Andes, there are cannibals that eat men raw. It cannot be good. Long pig I can understand, cooked slowly with herbs and yams, flavored with coconut. But of course the Polynesians were cultured people till we civilized them with syphilis... a great moral force is syphilis. You have to be moral if you don't want to catch something.

'I did a picture of the Garden of Eden once — Gabriel with a flaming spirochete in his hand... an allegory. I was drunk when I did it, but it was a fine picture. If I had it here, I would show it to you. You would like it.'

Where had he not been, this ridiculous painter? The South Seas. South America. Spain. France...

'Did I ever tell you how they fought over a blue blanket?' Now he was talking about his girls again. 'Not because it was blue, you understand. That would have been a reason. It was a wonderful blue ... cobalt with a touch of indigo; but because it was a blanket. Just savages,' he said. 'Pretty as pigeons, but savages. But I can paint them and I sleep with them. I cannot get on without a woman. It helps me in my work, and I would sooner have them wild like that. Once you get used to it, they are the best, and cheaper, too, not always wanting things and whining and being important. You do not get too fond of them and can get new ones when you move. It's a hell of a business being a man — a hell of a business. So much trouble getting rid of it. But if it was not there, there would be no men, so you are back where you started. And it is the fornicators that make the babies. Yes, that's the way new souls are made, by a man and a woman behind a bush. Only I cannot make a baby. Is that not an extraordinary thing? That I, Sebastian, have never had a woman who was not barren.

'Real drawing comes from the hands,' he went on. 'You learn technique ... of course you learn it. You teach your hands, drive them till they're like dogs that obey you and you need not think any more about them. Then you leave them to do it and work with your eyes and your heart. You work from your brain to your thumb directly, often hardly looking at your work. Your hands do it. I can draw with both hands. And I knew a girl in Geneva that painted with her toes. She had no arms ... she had been born that way, and was a great disappointment to her parents. They were good people and wanted her to be a side-show in a circus, but she would not. She was a painter. Van Gogh, Cézanne, Gauguin. Looks easy, does it not? That's why every man with a small talent thinks he can do it. They could draw, those

men, but then they went for something else. Their distortion
is meant, it is gift of God. They worked with their hands,
with their thumbs like me. And Picasso. There's a man who
is always doing something new, always searching. There was
a little bull-fight he did . . . just a little picture that I saw in
London. The bull with three heads, the matador with arms
all over the picture. But that's the way you see it. The human eye does not take in motion. It's too slow. It takes a lot
of separate pictures. Whoever saw a horse-race? No one
knows what a horse-race is really like. You see a head or two,
some shining shoes, a flash of color; you hear the sound of the
hoofs on the turf, the cheering, and then it's over. How can
you draw that? You can't. It is a feeling, an emotion, a
sound, but it has no form . . . it is without plasticity. It's
maddening!' he shouted. 'I tell you, maddening! It is like
trying to paint love. No one can paint love.' He looked at
Wilson.

'Some men when they reach a certain age have to get
women from other men. A girl is no use to a man of this type.
He needs a grown woman. He will take more chances, too,
because he has achieved success. He knows it to be failure
under another name. He is bored, frustrated, life is passing
him by. The days, that before stretched out before him, are
shortening.

'But it is all a mistake. Those men who feel like this should
do like me. Should buy a couple of virgins from a mission
and . . .'

'You didn't buy them from the mission?'

'Of course not. But I saw them there. Owen would not
part with them, so I went to their father. He wanted money.
It shocked me that he would take money for his daughters.
But I am not to be defeated. Not Sebastian!' he roared.
'So I went to the Government. They gave me money.'

'For the girls?'

'No, for pictures. Then with the money for the pictures I

went to their father and he went to Owen. He charged me
more because, he said, they could read. It was no use my
saying I did not want them to read. And they cannot read,
but he would refund nothing.'

He was silent, concentrated, drawing on the table with his
thumbs. He was drawing two pictures, one with each hand.

Sebastian started some queer thoughts in one's head. This
morning Channel had said:

'There can be no real love-making until the confidence
of mutual obscenity is established, until the man realizes
that his sensuality is counterbalanced by the woman's las-
civiousness, until he understands that his ideas and desires
are hers, that she is suffering from the same inhibitions. Shy-
ness, chastity, modesty, or good manners are all equally out
of place in bed. The act is atavistic and must be atavistically
performed without reservation, reserve, or afterthought of
embarrassment. There were few men and women,' he had
said, 'who did not, upon occasion, do things when they were
alone which they would refuse to acknowledge. But here was
an act that was shared, where two people knew not only what
they had done themselves, but what the other had done.
And what could be more ridiculous than conventional love-
making which consisted in getting the sexual act over and done
with as soon as possible? Thus the peak of life, all life — the
act whereby life was reproduced — was attained rapidly,
shamefacedly, and without pleasure in the darkness of the
night; often brutally, because of the resentment of shame, and
a pretense was kept up that what had happened had never
happened, or that it was something connected with functions
of the toilet. In this way do we render unto God those
things that are God's, and to Caesar those that are Caesar's
with this anticlimax — that all creation is shameful.'

Sebastian was right when he said you never knew when you
were happy. Not till afterward, when you were unhappy
again. It was like being well. You were never conscious of

being well, only of being ill. So that what we assumed was
positive was really negative, and what we took to be the
sculpture of life was only the matrix. But it took a lunatic like
Sebastian to put it across, and then it only made sense while
he was talking.

He had just pushed the table away, almost upsetting it,
and was weaving his way back to his women. To satisfy himself he must satisfy them. The empty bottle lay on its side on
the stoep.

Wilson watched a big hawk moth hovering, its long tongue
curved into the white trumpet of a flower. Tomorrow the
petals would begin to fall. Tomorrow the seed would begin
to swell.˙

And Sebastian did this to paint. He destroyed his body,
producing more bodies, to free his soul. Only he did not
produce more bodies. The hawk moth was more successful
than the artist.

Besides, a man did not want two women. He wanted one
woman. He wanted comfort and safety. He wanted to be
cosy with a plant in the window and a baby carriage in the
hallway, and then, when he had it, he didn't want it any
more. Then he wanted to live dangerously, to have other
women, exotic women, women of another race that talked
with an accent. There was something exciting about foreign
women. Wilson had never forgotten Poinder. He had met
him in London. Poinder had been a planter in Java and had
all sorts of mistresses — Japanese, Chinese, Celonese, Java-
nese. He had talked about them like the horses he had had,
or the dogs. It was strange, this desire to live exotically with
women . . . with all women. More women, to stifle the
memories of other women, as if you could create memories
to lacquer over the ever-living past. What was the difference between children and adults? Children came together
tenderly, diffidently, half-scared at what they felt and wanted.
But a man and a woman were not like that. They knew and

manoeuvred for position. An affair was like an exhibition
bout, where each played for a hold that would put the other
in his power: where each knew every move and had a counter
for it. You knew what her looks meant, her actions, her
devices, and she knew the same about you. Both carried
subtlety beyond subtlety till it became honesty, and honesty
beyond honesty till the truth was a lie. That was what
frightened him about Olga. She was so good at it. The difference between an affair and being in love was that if you
fell in love you deliberately left yourself open to pain.

It was a queer way to spend the morning — talking, drinking, and then thinking about what had been said. It was
very civilized in a decadent way. But it got you down. These
people had too many ideas: theories, hypotheses; and what
did they do with them? Nothing. The ideas, as far as they
were concerned, seemed to be ends in themselves.

Wilson went over to the house for lunch.

Olga, very fresh in a pale green linen dress, got up to meet
him, uncurling herself from a big chair as he came in.

'And how is our visitor today?' she asked. 'I meant to
come over, but I saw you had Sebastian there. I thought it
would be a pity to interrupt.'

She led the way into the dining room. 'Tête-à-tête again,'
she said. 'How my men desert me! It makes a scandal. It
must be dull for you to talk to a woman all the time.'

The lunch was chicken curry, rice cooked with saffron,
chupaties, mango chutney, and hock to drink. The boy
passed him shredded coconut and onions cut up very fine.
Another boy brought Bombay duck.

'Rotten fish,' Olga said; 'dried on a line like washing, but
it's good, isn't it?'

'Yes, it's good,' Wilson said, 'when you get used to it. I
used to go to the Waldorf in London for curries. They had
them every Friday. And there was a place in the Tottenham
Court Road . . .'

'The Delhi,' Olga said.

'Yes. How funny your knowing it.'

'Yes, isn't it? Quite a coincidence.'

He thought she was being sarcastic, but all the same it made a kind of bond between them. People were associated by mutual experience even if that experience was only eating in a certain restaurant.

'How do you like my husband?' Olga asked.

The curry was hot. Wilson's head was pricking.

'I like him,' he said. What an extraordinary thing to ask!

Olga laughed. 'Oh,' she said, 'how funny you are! You should have said "I hate him." It is normal to hate husbands ... At least, it is polite to pretend you do. Yes, you like him,' she went on, 'and so do I. He has certain admirable characteristics. He is very patient, very unobservant, he ...' Then she changed the subject. 'And Retief,' she asked. 'You like him too?'

'Yes,' Wilson said.

'And the doctor and Sebastian. Oh, yes, I know, you like them all. Like ... like. It is very ordinary to like. You should love, hate, admire, despise ... And me? Do you like me?'

If she wanted the truth, she should have it. 'No,' he said.

'A la bonneheure, that's better. You might fall in love with me. You do not want to, and you have.'

'I haven't,' Wilson said. He was furious with her. She was making him behave like a small boy. He lit a cigarette.

Olga clapped her hands. The butler came in to take the plates away. The second boy brought clean plates and finger bowls. The butler came back with a dish of fruit. Coffee came. Olga was peeling a peach reflectively. Wilson didn't want any fruit. He wanted to get out of here. To get out and see something normal: to smell gasoline in the streets: to see a policeman again: any kind of policeman as long as he was white; a London bobby, a New York cop, a sergent de ville

in Paris complete with pistol and sword. Policemen made
sense. And he had always hated policemen. Now I want one,
he thought. I want to find one and say, 'Officer, this woman
is going to seduce me, please stop it.' He had drunk too much
hock. But she was right, he loved her . . . he wanted her.
Only not this way: not as a game.

How pretty she looked with her eyes downcast, her lashes
over her cheeks, her slim fingers on the peach turning it in
her hand! When she had done, she put it down on the plate
and sucked her fingers one after the other while she looked
at him as innocently as a child, as if butter wouldn't melt in
her mouth. And how had she succeeded in making him look
wrong . . . in making him feel he'd done something, been
awkward . . . done something!

'I shouldn't tease you, should I?' she said. 'It is not kind.
And love . . . why should I say love. What, after all, is a kiss?'

What, after all, was a kiss? But there were kisses and kisses.
She kissed with her whole body. And besides, it was lunch
time. He decided he hated foreigners. Americans and English were the only civilized people: the only respectable
people.

She was laughing now. Before he could say anything, she
had jumped up, had passed behind his chair, and stooping
quickly had kissed his neck.

He heard the door of her room close. When next he saw
her, he would be embarrassed. He would not know what to
say and she would look at him in that amused way that annoyed him so much. He was in love with her. And he had
been right in his idea that it would hit him hard.

Chapter 13

The VISITOR

~~~~~~~~~~~~~~

WHEN YOU TOOK MEALS WITH PEOPLE REGULARLY, YOU BECAME one of the family. Wilson was getting used to it, but Olga seemed to be avoiding him; though when they were all together, she reversed the process. Then she took a great interest in him. Kept asking him about his book, his health, what he proposed to do next.

He was reading all he could about the natives of Central Africa. His mind was filled with names, with customs, with the various contradictory theories about their origin. He was also reading all he could about anthropoid apes. The professor bewildered him with his erudition. Channel thrust more and more books at him. Sebastian continued to talk about women and art.

The Le Blancs lived formally. They dressed for dinner, but, as Olga said, 'with our tongues in our cheeks.' It was done as a gesture of defiance. It was as much such a gesture as the refusal to dress in a civilized country. Out here you could only go two ways — the super-formal or to pieces after the fashion of Sebastian. To shave every day, to change your clothes, to dress well, was an answer to those strange tropic gods who responded only to boldness. There was a technique of life here as elsewhere, and over the years this little society had evolved this system by tedious trial and error.

But it produced odd stresses and strains. It changed the ratios from hour to hour and required an adaptability that Wilson was not sure he could achieve.

He thought about dinner parties. They were like a ballet.
They consisted of various movements; the bigger the party
the more complex the ballet; but there was always the
formula. There was the first movement — the arrival of the
guests in pairs, the removal of the wraps, the hand-shaking
and chorus of introduction. The second movement was the
cocktail movement. Then the tempo increased. The religious
formality of the first movement was replaced by a staccato
fluttering. The third movement was the parade, the coupling
of pairs about to eat. Then the ritual of eating.

So it went on, a ceremony utterly divorced from the necessity of consuming food. He thought of the gestures. The
women's hands synchronized, as they pulled down their
girdles, the men their vests. He had never thought of this
before, but now, looking back, he saw how every social function was stylized, subject to its own particular dogma. The
laws of correct dress, of correct conversation . . . of correctness.
Here in Mokala it was more obvious. That was what had
made him think of it, perhaps, getting up when Olga came in,
waiting for her to sit down or to lead the way into the dining
room. The changes of dress, the exchange of compliments, of
chatter; of questions about health, activities. Life at Mokala
was passed through a filter which, while it did not eliminate
the inessentials, showed them up. And all of them were
aware of it. It was in this that they differed most from the
people at home. They knew they were acting in a play. And
they acted as if they enjoyed it.

He kept wishing Olga would come over to his house again.
He was tired of reading anthropology. He was looking forward to the professor's going tomorrow. Then they would
be alone: he did not count Channel or Sebastian. The old
man seemed very excited about going: like a child going to a
party. They were taking the five-ton truck and a couple of
boys. For the last few days he had watched the preparations
being made. Cases of food, rifles, cameras, tools, instruments,

medicines, blankets, mosquito nets, camp beds, were being got ready. The professor was already wearing his bush dress, khaki shorts that showed his white bony knees and a shirt like a Boy Scout's. Wilson put away his book and decided to go for a walk. The hill behind the house intrigued him. It was a hill set like a boil upon the mountain.

He always took the same path, walked and climbed till he got up a good sweat, and then came back and had a shower.

Quite near the house he came on something strange. He had not noticed it before. A few yards from the path, the bushes and trees were dragged down, smashed and piled into a kind of semi-arboreal cup. Something heavy had lain in it. Either Congo or one of Congo's relatives had rested here. There were defecations on the ground and a scent that was unmistakable. He had smelt it in the house when he was introduced to Congo, only then it had been mixed with Olga's geranium perfume.

He looked at some of the broken branches. They were as thick as his arm and had been snapped like twigs. What was it he had read? The gorilla sat down and dragged the branches towards him, putting them under him until he had enough to make himself comfortable. Was it Congo or were there other gorillas? He hoped there were others, because the chances were they would run away if they were not interfered with. He wanted to go back, and then, refusing to be frightened, he went on till he came to the place where he usually sat to smoke a cigarette. There were his stubs on the ground. They gave him a sense of security. He smoked two cigarettes and then turned towards the house again. Halfway back he met Maria. He smiled at her, but she did not seem pleased to see him. She was going the other way.

'To my father's house,' she said. 'I go to make a visit: he is sick.' He had met her several times on this path.

She brushed past him. When he looked back, she had disappeared. If it was safe for her, it was safe for him. He

put his hands in his pockets and began to whistle. He felt
much better. The exercise had done him good. When he got
back, he would go and see what Sebastian was doing.

'Did you know there was a Saint of my name?' Sebastian
asked, when Wilson came in. 'He was a martyr. They shot
him full of arrows and then they beat him to death with rods.
Yes,' he said, 'they shot him and they scourged him. Sebastian is an unlucky name. I have never understood why
the good Sisters gave it to me . . . This other Sebastian en-
couraged those who were being put to death for being Christians. He was a Roman captain. After they had shot him, a
woman nursed him. Her name was Irene.

'I knew a woman called Irene once. She was dark with
eyes the color of sherry — Amantillado. When he recovered
he went and faced the Emperor — Diocletian, I think it was
— and upbraided him. It was after that they beat him to
death. So Irene had wasted her time.

'But she was lovely . . . straight as an arrow. She moved
like a deer in a wood. Daintily but strongly. That was in
Paris.' He was talking about his own Irene now. 'She worked
for Worth. That is, she did before I met her. It went on for
a year. It began in summer when the trees were in leaf. The
trees were as solid as dough . . . like green dough. Chestnuts,'
he said. 'On every little branch there is a mark like a horse-
shoe . . . and the nuts in their prickly cases, lying in their
white beds of kid . . . chestnuts like horses, shining; and some
of them brown and white — piebalds. But they change as
you watch them like the hoofs of a newborn calf . . . and they
are so beautiful to touch.

'Irene and I used to pick the fallen leaves from the planes
and sycamores, green and yellow and red and brown . . . Men
sweep them up into heaps with brooms made of birch twigs.
How they smell when they are wet! . . . It is rich, that smell
of rotting leaves.

'I like you, Mr. Wilson. I can talk to you now that I know you. At first I was tongue-tied.

'The artist is unequipped to meet strangers without warning. By the nature of his work he is forced to walk abroad unarmed, keyed up to receive the impressions of the outer world, ready to feel the flight of the birds, to know the impress of their wings upon the rushing wind; ready to see the play of light and shadow on the street, the color of a woman's dress reflected in her eyes. Only unarmored can he receive these things and know them. But to meet men and speak with them, he must have time. He must change the clothes of his mind, for they are his armor. He must school his eyes and close the secret parts of his brain. He must make ready for some hours to sacrifice all that he holds dear . . . make ready to step from his world of color, of sound, and fantasy into that other world of ordinary life which is to him but a spectacle.

'More alone than other men — separated from them by his visions — the artist has only the compensation of his dreams. By them he lives. In them he lives . . . untouchable, isolated equally by the suspicion of others and his suspicion of himself. He knows only his failure, the vast chasm that exists between his conceptions and his achievements. His contacts are without certainty, for any day he may go drifting off on the wind of his necessity. One day when the sun rises, he is gone from his place. He has seen visions . . . he has followed a star. Possessions become meaningless when set against the purple of the horizon . . . the silver ripple of the singing stream . . . the wind that turns the leaves upward before rain . . . of such things as these is the mind of the artist made. He lives alone with beauty. But alone. And he dies alone, conscious that if he has failed, he has succeeded, too, for he has made some beauty. That men who never knew him have known his work . . . that from it other work will arise; that his work will sire other work as his own was sired. Art is derivative . . . it will continue to be derivative. Art, like other things, is in-

finite, without beginning or end. That the artist has had
women, has been drunken, will be forgotten, and rightly,
since such things are utterly irrelevant to his work — since
he himself was irrelevant to it, an instrument only on which
the chords of his art were played . . . the symphonies of color
. . . of words . . . of stone.

'That is how an artist lives and dies,' Sebastian said.
'Much loved . . . little respected . . . poor always, but rich
beyond compare. I tell you this because I feel that you should
know it. You are an American, a relative of the President.
Tell them over there that these were the words of poor
Sebastian. Tell them that a man may reason with his head,
but that he lives by his stomach and his heart. It is his belly
that turns over when he sees a certain woman . . . it is his
belly that contracts with rage at the sight of a certain man;
and both are without reason, both inexplicable. It is a man's
belly that turns to water with fear . . . that rises into his
throat with hope. It's a wise man who listens to the dictates
of his belly. All that matters most in a man is bound by his
belt. And there is more in the writhing convolutions of his
bowels than in those of his brains. For even if a man could
live by reason, he could not increase by it.'

He was silent, and then went on.

'The artist is an intellectual masochist, one who seeks out
the pain of beauty . . . searches for it, so that it may hurt him.
He lives by pain rather than by pleasure . . . lives by emotional impact upon a personality which is kept raw by impact
. . . a flagellant continually drunken with the ecstasy of
beauty . . . by the quality of God that is held within it.'

Sebastian began to cry; tears trickled between his hands
onto the empty bottle at his feet. He wept like a child, sobbing and choking. Nina came out of the house and stood
watching him. The yellow dog sat on its haunches, pointed
its nose to the sky and howled. Wilson went back to his house.
The visit had not been a success.

Channel had just given Olga her injection. She had one every month and attributed her excellent health to them, though, as he had told her, they were not essential at this altitude. He wished the professor had gone on with them, too, but he was an obstinate man. Still, it was something that Olga continued, though one case, even over a period of ten years, was not an absolute proof of the qualities of his serums, he was of the opinion that the results were comparable to the Voronoff glandular grafts, which might be why his friend Jean had stopped them, in which case the conversation he had planned with Olga was perhaps a little out of place, since it was possible that he was himself responsible for both the way she had kept her looks and her moral vacillations.

Lighting a cigarette, Channel continued his discussion of adultery. 'A woman can never keep a lover secret,' he said. 'She is a marvel at intrigue at the beginning, then she must show him as if he were a fish she had landed. Women are always being spiritually photographed holding the latest fish they have caught. After all, if they didn't, how would anyone know? There are their enemies, the other women who say they are passées. That will show them, the woman says. If I had gone off, I could not have got him, could I?'

Olga looked at her watch.

'This has been charming, Channel,' she said. 'Your solicitude ... your worldly wisdom. But I am afraid I must leave you. I have an appointment.'

'With Wilson?'

'With Wilson.'

Channel patted her knee. 'Ma chère, I give up. You are adorable.'

'So I have been told, Doctor.' She laughed and waved her hand. She waited till he had gone and went over to the guest house.

She stood in the doorway, looking at Wilson.

'I was hoping you would come,' he said.

'I hoped you would hope. That was why I did not come before.' She sat down. 'You need more roses. I'll get you some tomorrow.'

Tomorrow the professor would be gone.

'Give me a cigarette,' she said.

He gave her one and lit it.

'I have been talking to Channel about love...'

Wilson wondered if any of them ever spoke of anything else.

'What did he say?'

She jumped up. 'Perhaps I'll tell you tomorrow, when I bring the roses.' By now Maria should have reached Fritz with her message.

Soon after Olga left, Channel came in.

'You have had a visitor,' he said. 'A very charming one. I was talking to her before she came over.'

'So she said.'

'Ah. She told you?'

'She said you had been talking about love.'

'In a way. I was trying to make her leave you alone.'

Channel was treating him like a fool. He felt like a guinea pig in a hospital. They were all trying experiments on him.

'I like you,' Channel said. So did Sebastian when he lectured him about art. So did Olga. Sometimes he wished they liked him less. 'Yes,' Channel went on, 'love is both interesting and beautiful to watch — as is any natural process. But has it occurred to you that a male animal is not interested in the appearance of a female? He is interested in the fact of her femaleness. What, then, is it that makes man so susceptible to female beauty? He can do no more with a beautiful woman than a plain one.   He can make love equally to both. The limit of the love he can make is the limit of his own power. Quantitatively there is no difference. Both beautiful and ugly are female to his male. Yet he selects passionately. He discards the one and seeks the other. He seeks not quantity, not women; but quality, the woman. This selectivity is part of his humanity, part of the superiority that raises man above the beasts, differentiating him; it is therefore of the spirit and not of the body. The beautiful body is the symbol his soul seeks of that infinite beauty which is its final concept. Not sensuality, but spirituality. His sensuality is a means, not an end . . . a grasping for beauty . . . a groping of the hands in the dark on a woman's body for her soul . . . for the flight of a bird . . . for the perfume of the flower.

'This, then, is the end of his dream . . . the final disillusion that continues through life . . . the grasping for eternal beauty which ends in bed with a woman. Beyond the portal of her thighs he cannot go. Her thighs are of brass. To go there is the little death. Beyond it, at the end of life, is the greater, where everything will be clear . . . or nothing. Beyond woman there is death. In life there is only woman, the source of life, while suspended overhead, by the ever-weakening thread of years, is the bitter sword of impotence. So is a man's life balanced precariously, on the point of his biological necessity. His physical ends defeating his spiritual purposes. His means inadequate to his causes. His pain insatiable in the great waters of his desire. Endlessly wishing exploit, achievement. And without the means of exploit . . . of achievement. Capable only of gratification . . . of palliative. Grasping always at the substance, but wishing always for the shadow. Eating the bread, but unable to become drunken on the wine. That is the song of his life: the sum of it: its glory . . . its shame: its beginning, its end. Were it more than this, he would be a god. Were it less, a beast. Seeking all beauty, he fornicates, saying this will be no fornication. This is all beauty that will end all desire. This will be no fumbling thing. This will be the emptied cup. Finality. This will be death: the final exploit where all beauty meets all desire in one splendid leap to end them both. The wave broken on the shattered cliff.'

He spoke as if he were quoting. Wilson wondered if it was something he had written.

'Think it over, Mr. Wilson, before it is too late. Olga can hurt you.' He put his hand on Wilson's shoulder. 'Do not think I am jealous. I have never slept with Olga. Unfortunately, I am too old.'

When Channel left, Wilson was in no mood to work.

At dinner Olga said: 'I saw Bentinck's flag this afternoon. Mr. Wilson, perhaps you would not mind taking your car down and bringing up the meat tomorrow?'

'I shall be delighted.'

'Man does not live by bread alone,' Retief said.

'Nor by meat,' Olga said.

My God, one could not even eat in peace now. What was it she had said? Tomorrow they would talk about love. And Channel ... plain women ... pretty women ... male animals ... men ... Had he been a fool to stay? He had known that he would fall in love with Olga. When he had said to himself, 'I must not fall in love with her, it was too late. He had been in love with her then, but he could still have gone. Now he could not. And besides, there was his promise to Frazer — and the fact that Bentinck seemed to need him. Another rationalization. He knew he was lying to himself.

Chapter 14

The FLAG

THE PROFESSOR'S START WAS SPECTACULAR. THE BIG TRUCK was now fully loaded. The two boys he was taking were perched on top of the gear. Retief was standing by the radiator. He had just looked to see if it had been filled. He stood with the cap in his hand.

Sebastian was there with Channel. They were detached from the scene, observers of it, critical, interested, but in no sense a part of it as were the two boys or Retief.

Wilson stood a little way from them.

'He will come in a minute,' Sebastian said. 'I like to see him start on a journey. Just now he is saying good-bye to his wife. How many have said good-bye to their wives and never returned!'

How often have I done it? His eyes were fastened on a packing case branded 'Johnny Walker.' He knew there was no whisky in it. He did not like whisky. But it made him sad to look at it empty — empty of whisky, at least. Everything empty depressed him — empty bottles, empty birds' nests, empty houses, empty eggshells, the empty wombs of his women, an empty canvas. His ideal world was one of cornucopias, overflowing with milk and honey, with wine, with oil, with fat, with fruit, with spermatozoa — a world in ferment, seething, writhing, heaving, voluptuous with color.

'Yes, Channel,' he said, 'there is a tragedy in parting. I know it well.'

Channel ignored him. 'You have got the quinine and morphia, Retief?' he asked; 'and the permanganate?'

Retief said, 'Yes.'

Sebastian went up to the back wheel nearest him and kicked it with his sandalled foot. Then he bent down to examine his toe.

'They are too hard,' he said. 'You'll get a blowout. I had a blowout once in the Alps. I was on my way to Rome. I spit on Rome,' he said. 'I had a commission to paint a countess there. A beautiful woman with red hair. A Venetian who had been sold to the count by her mother. An evil woman.

'And the count was an evil man. He never paid me for the portrait. I should have known the blowout was a bad omen and turned back. Rome,' he said. 'That is where my father abandoned my sainted mother whom he had neglected to marry. It is where my sainted mother at a later date abandoned me to go with a singer — an Italian tenor. It is where I was rescued by the good Sisters of the Bleeding Heart whom I abandoned on attaining puberty — all life is a pattern of abandonment, of desertion. Oh, Italia, sad and beautiful country of olives and ruins and wine and tenors who seduce small boys' sainted mothers from them! Italy: the beautiful Italy of my childhood, with the trains running late, with people singing and making love, with beggars and malaria and wild cattle on the Campagna. How I loved it then — before the Fascisti! What would Garibaldi in his red shirt have thought of them? I have always wanted to paint a dark man in a red shirt. But it was sad saying good-bye to that countess. How she greatly cried! Litres of hot salt tears over my chest, into my mouth. I cried. Our tears mingled. It is beautiful to mingle your tears with those of a red-haired woman. Then her husband came in: the evil man! a Fascista without understanding. I left at speed. But they are not honest, those men. They are without decency, without integrity.'

'He could not have been annoyed at your embracing his wife?' Channel said.

'Why should he have been? We had always embraced, even at the first sitting. It was just unfortunate that he came in. He did not appreciate her. He treated her as a possession, as a bought woman: she told me so as she lay crying in my lap at the termination of the second sitting. So, you see, I know what is going on in the heart of the professor. I am a man of great understanding, of great sentiment. A man,' he said. 'A woman. A parting. It makes a tragedy.'

The tragedy was apparently over, for the professor came out of the house. Wilson could see Olga through the screening on the veranda. She had on her green dressing gown and was waving to him.

'Come back soon, chéri,' she cried.

'Soon, chérie. As soon as I have seen my little trees.'

He trotted towards the truck. He was in his bush shirt and shorts as he had been for two days, but he was strung with things. Field glasses hung over his shoulder by a strap. He had a map case, a water bottle, a compass in a leather case on his belt. A haversack. A specimen box of white metal. There were other larger ones in the car. In his hand he had a big green butterfly net with a bamboo handle.

'You are ready, Retief? We can go?'

'I am ready.'

The professor took Wilson's hand. 'I owe this to you. If it had not been for you, I could not have gone. Good-bye, and take care of Olga.'

'I'll do my best.' As he spoke, he wondered how much he would have to do to take care of her.

The professor shook hands with Channel. 'Get me some flies if you can,' Channel said. 'Anything new you see.'

Sebastian took the professor's hand. 'Good luck,' he said. 'Here, take these.' He thrust two rosaries into his hand. 'They can do no harm.'

The professor climbed onto the seat beside Retief. The engine turned over. Retief let in the clutch. Everyone was silent watching the truck as it turned the first hairpin bend.

Channel said, 'Where did you get the rosaries, Sebastian?'

'From the girls. Everyone must make some sacrifices at a time like this. We alone here without the good professor. Olga heartbroken, an orphan widow. The Station' — he waved his hand — 'masterless. And he, the good professor, risking life in the name of science.'

'I did not know that Mr. Owen was a Catholic,' Wilson said.

'Oh, he is not. The rosaries they stole from the Catholic Mission near the lake before Owen converted them from Catholicism. They think they bring luck. But they are good girls. Channel examined them before I bought them.'

The scene was over now.

Channel and Sebastian left together.

Wilson went towards his car. If he was going to get the meat, he might as well leave at once. He wondered what Bentinck would have to say when he saw him. Nothing, probably.

Bentinck interested him. He was obviously educated, well read. But he spoke very abruptly. as a rule, in a way that completely disguised any pretensions he might have had. His name, too, struck a chord of memory. It belonged to a great English family. The Portlands, he thought. The Duke of Portland must be a relation of some kind. He had been at Rugby. After he had left Germany — and he had warned him never to mention that he had been there — he had knocked about the world — China, the East Indies, Australia, for a year or two, and then had come to Africa where he had remained, hunting, trading, and transport riding. But mainly hunting. His knowledge of animals and their ways was amazing. It was just practice, he said. If you lived through a great number of accidents and incidents, you began to understand.

'There are rules that must not be broken, there are others that can be broken upon occasion . . .'

He had learnt all this by degrees — by a word dropped here and a hint there: from listening to Channel and the others as they spoke. But evidently none of them knew that he spoke German.

Bentinck's store was a clearing house for information. He collected and synthesized the news he gathered. Much of it was nonsense, lies told for the sake of telling lies, for reasons of drama. The natives were great actors. But in the chaff of their wildest stories there was often a grain of truthful corn. These grains he noted. In the three years he had been here, they had formed a core which made sense, though sometimes he wondered if he was all wrong. Perhaps there could be smoke without fire. He had sent Frazer a few hints, but no detail. He wanted to be certain of his facts. And the moment had come to verify them. Wilson's arrival had been opportune, but he knew that even if Wilson had not come, he would have acted alone.

Still, it was a good thing he had come. It would make things easier. Bentinck polished his pipe. He was very attached to his pipe. Then he took a letter from his pocket and read it again. It was an authorization to take Mr. Wilson out on safari to shoot one male gorilla. He wondered how Wilson would like the idea. Anyway, if he did not want to shoot it, he would do it for him. In the old days, before there had been any of these new restrictions, he had shot a lot of gorillas. The natives had asked him to, partly because they damaged their gardens, and partly because they liked to eat them. Plenty of them had been cannibals then. Cannibals had always been very unfairly treated, it seemed to him. He had never had any trouble with them, and, reduced to its ultimate simplicity, the principle of man-eating was, from their point of view, perfectly sound. You eat a brave warrior and you be-

come brave. His courage went into you with his meat. You
eat a gorilla and you become strong. It was, after all, the
basis of homeopathic medicine, of gastric inoculation. And
if you believed in it, it was strangely successful. If you believed yourself to be brave, you were brave. They believed,
and it worked for them. Incidentally, gorilla flesh was good:
more palatable than that of many buck, and, as they said, it
made a change. Still, Wilson might not like the idea...

He filled his pipe slowly from a lion-skin pouch.

Few people understood Kaffirs. It was hard to gain their
trust. But he had come here with a good reputation for fair
dealing, and he was even remembered by some of the old
men that he had known in the early days. That was where
he had the pull over von Brandt. It was a pity times had
changed so much. Once, he would simply have got some of
his men together, hunters and warriors, and cleaned the
place up, no questions asked; but now everything had to be
legal. You had to have licenses to shoot everything.

He regretted the old days. He was too old for these oblique
diplomatic approaches. There had been a time when a man
had been either a friend or an enemy. Now... Well, now
things were different. You had to meet men like von Brandt
socially. He thought of Channel's party: of von Brandt talking
about animals and telling Marais that there was some more
machinery for him on the way up. That old dredge of his
seemed to require a lot of spare parts. It was a mistake to
despise women as those Nazis did. Was there a tie-up somewhere between Marais and the German?

And that fool von Brandt thought because he slept with
Olga she liked him. A baboon might as well think that a
leopard liked him. The leopard liked meat. Olga liked men.
It was as simple as that. Most things were very simple...
nothing like as complex as people liked to imagine. Wilson
was unhappy because his wife had left him, so he ran away
from everything that reminded him of her. What was com-

plicated about that? Then, because a young man could not do without women, he was running after Olga. That was still simpler. Magtig, he thought, old Piet Uys was right when he said men were as simple as animals. But things were moving. In the last month he had had a number of reports. There was a lot more coming and going than was usual. 'When the buck move, a lion is stirring.' That was another piece of Piet's wisdom. And the man who was hunting the lion watched the buck. By the way they turned into the wind, by their restlessness, the twitching of their ears, he could guess the position of the lion. Von Brandt was combining business with pleasure.

But why did he go and meet that girl of Sebastian's so often? It was dangerous to double-cross a woman like Olga. What were those messengers doing that went so often between him and Marais? What had his two trips over to the lake meant? The porters had gone under their full loads of sixty pounds and had come back with next to nothing. And why this sudden hospitality among the coffee planters over the mountain? Party after party. Were they parties? There had been little singing or drinking.

The boy who had brought him the news had looked in at some of them through the window. 'They stood like this, Bwana,' he said. He had stood very straight with his heels together and had raised his right hand. 'They said, "Aalitler ... Aalitler." Then they went their ways.' There was no beer, no women, no dancing. 'I think it is a new god they worship, Bwana. And they have arms. They open boxes of small guns.'

Small guns. Those would be Mauser pistols, Lügers' Tommy guns. Unquestionably Mr. Wilson must go and shoot a gorilla. They would pick up some Pigmy hunters and he would take a few young Masai.

The white flag was on the staff. The dead buck hung in

the branches of a tree. Bentinck looked up at the Station.
Someone would soon come down to fetch it.

His plans were laid. He had just come back from three
days in the bush. He had been seeing his friends the Pigmies.
He had shot a buffalo for them. He had also seen another
friend: the witch doctor, Entobo. He had arranged to see
him again before they left. The threads of his inquiries begun
three years ago were coming together. He had told Wilson
it was von Brandt, but there must be someone behind him.
Von Brandt was a front. Was it Marais? Olga suspected him.
She hated him because he took no interest in her. Had she
stumbled on the truth by accident?

At Channel's party he had noticed a curious thing. Marais
had upset a salt cellar. He had picked a pinch and thrown
it over his left shoulder. It was a funny thing for Marais to
have done. If anyone else had done it, it would not have been
funny. He would, for instance, have done the same himself.
But it did not fit in with Marais' character.

Von Brandt was one of their best men — one of their best
second-raters. Still there was a long way to go yet. This trip
with Wilson — not that Wilson knew he was taking it yet —
was just to check the lay of the land. He wondered if Wilson
knew how dangerous all this was. He had an idea he didn't.
He would explain the whole business to him as far as it went,
when they were out in the bush. The permit to kill a gorilla
had been necessary to make the trip seem valid.

He was not surprised to see Wilson's car. He had thought
he might come when he ran up the flag.

'Glad you came,' he said. He shouted for Jan to bring tea.
They sat on the stoep.

'You've got some meat?' Wilson asked.

'Yes, a bush buck. Got him yesterday.' Bentinck was
polishing his pipe. 'How are things going up there? Professor get off all right?'

'Yes,' Wilson said. So he had known the professor was
going.

'Next week we're going off ourselves. I've got a permit for you to shoot a gorilla. Adult male.'

'Me ... a gorilla?'

'Give us a good excuse to poke about. Easy to shoot. They charge, but stop before they get up to you. Only dangerous if you wound 'em.'

'But I don't really like hunting ... I'm tired of it.'

'This isn't hunting. It's part of your book, isn't it? Can't write a book about the Congo without gorillas in it. And it's practical. Throw 'em off the scent. Damn them!' He filled his pipe slowly. 'They're up to something big. Listen, Wilson' — he leant forward — 'I've lived with savages, as they call 'em, all my life. Nearly all my life,' he corrected himself, 'but I've never met anything as bad as the Germans. That's why I'm in this business. Partly for money, but most because I don't like 'em. They killed a friend of mine — King of Duala. They hanged him and burnt a lot of his men alive in trenches. Soaked 'em in gasoline and burnt 'em. That was a German major — Dominik was his name. They don't change, those people. Never have changed. Same for thousands of years. Tacitus wrote about them.' He went on smoking.

'You know in the war we did some propaganda in Central Africa. I had to put it across. They said tell 'em that the Germans have raped all the women in Belgium. Can you imagine that?' he asked.

'True, wasn't it?'

'Yes, it was true, but what propaganda! I changed it round. I said we had raped everybody. They thought a lot of us after that. You have to be victorious to rape. If I had said the Germans were doing it, they would have assumed we could not stop them and were losing. Nobody likes to be on the losing side. Enthusiastic they were after that. More tea?' He filled both cups.

This would be a good time to talk about the whisky.

'What about letting me have a couple of bottles of whisky?'
Wilson said. 'Buy 'em, of course.' It was amusing that he
was really learning to talk as Bentinck did when he was with
him. He wondered if he would learn to talk as Sebastian
talked, or give lectures as Channel did. Get into the dog-
house if I do, he thought.

'Sell you a case,' Bentinck said. 'Put it in the car with the
meat ... Anything else you'd like?'

'Just whisky.' It would be nice to have a real drink again.

'Then we'll start next week. Take Jan and some Masai ...
few Pigmies. No good using the car. Travel light. Let you
know when everything's ready.'

He was silent again.

'Got a movie camera, I suppose?' he said.

'Yes. But how did you know?'

'Because all Americans have them. Like to take pictures.
Documentary evidence to show their friends back home.
Anyway, bring it.

'And don't forget, it's your idea. American. Hunter.
Hire me. Fiver a day and found. Run of my teeth ... Show
you everything,' he said, 'Watusi, Pigmies, gorillas, whole
bloody lot for a fiver a day and found. Means whisky, too,'
he said.

When Wilson got back to his house, he found it filled with
roses. Olga had said she would bring them today, but why
had she chosen the time he was away? And why so many
roses?

Chapter 15

The WOMAN WAITS

~~~~~~~~~~~~~~~~~

CONGO WAS SHUT UP IN HIS ROOM. THE PROFESSOR WAS IN THE forest. Olga always thought of him as the professor. She lifted her nightdress and looked at her toes. All nightdresses should be long and sheer, she thought.

Over it she wore a new dressing gown of green satin edged with white maribou. She was smoking. There was only a table light on in the bedroom. It had a pink silk shade. She had made up. Her hair was neither up nor down. It was twisted in a yellow knot low on her neck. Parted virginally in the middle, it was drawn back, but not too tightly, from her forehead. She slipped her feet into green mules that matched the dressing gown. They were also edged with maribou.

How many women knew that this white fluff they wore so seductively came from a great carrion-eating stork? She loved the paradoxes of life. When Fritz came through the window, he would bow and click his heels. They would have some champagne. There was a tray with sandwiches ready. They would speak very socially, almost formally: she appreciating the joke: he embarrassed by it. Where did the social end and the biological begin?

Though she was waiting, she was not impatient. Also there was a masculine side to her character which made her enjoy the masochism of provisional uncertainty. Besides, she was always curious, always trying to pin down the moment of change, when social intercourse turned into sexual: always amused at the way men were troubled at this time.

Of course, when it happened like this, the woman had the advantage. She was undressed and ready. People were funny about sex. Funny was the correct word. They all pretended that there was no such thing.

Meanwhile, she waited. She concentrated on nothing, but let her mind drift on the tide of her latent desire. Fritz was attractive to her. His German mind was incredibly easy to read. It was, as it were, only academically complicated. It was the mind of a superbly educated child, one that had immense factual knowledge, but no wisdom.

Of course, her upbringing and experience made von Brandt clear to her. Germans had a fear complex which drove them into brutal, tribal collaboration. More, the Germans had always been like that, brutal, sentimental, incapable of a middle course. Fritz believed that by his Heiling, his heel-clicking, his whips, he actually made something, when he was really only thrusting himself back into that ancient Germanic forest womb which had never brought anything forth but horror. Their artists — musicians, poets, painters — were sports, un-Teutonic, many of them Jews.

He would come soon. She put out her cigarette and lit another. As a man, he suited what was woman in her. For that time, when she was woman, his assumption of mastery pleased her. What he did not see was that he was only a master because he was a slave.

But this would be without application for the next few hours. She was ready to sink her intelligence into the void of sensation. She was sorry for Fritz. Men got so little pleasure and they were driven so hard to obtain it. Women had always known this, though in the last century it had been denied by most. Desire interested her objectively even when she was not personally desirous. That is, desire interested her both objectively and subjectively.

She was pleasantly philosophical. Four years ago, when he had first come, Fritz had interested himself in them because he had been told by his Government to find out certain things. And he might have found some of them from the professor if she had not deflected his attention. He had been warned about women, too, apparently. That was why he had been sent out of Germany. She had got it out of him later. He was a good Party Member, a man of great personal courage, but not reliable where a pretty face was concerned. She must tell him if he had anything more to do with those Batangas of Sebastian's, she was through with him. It was odd that in a way it was all her own fault. It was she who had brought Maria into direct contact with him by using her as a messenger. She had thought when Sebastian brought them back what a convenience it would be, since their father's village was not far from von Brandt's place.

She heard the window move. He was coming. Congo, she knew, would be listening at the door of his room. It amused her to know he listened. The window opened.

'I have kept you waiting!' he said. He bent over her hand and clicked the heels of his white tennis shoes together. He was happier in boots... happier still if he wore them with spurs. Like all Germans, the noise of metal gave him confidence. Spurs, sabres, lance points in the sun, the gleam of cannon... they needed that.

'Yes, you have kept me waiting,' she said. 'I do not like to wait.' In her mind she laughed. As if I cared... I knew you would come, and I had plenty to think about — men and women, your foolishness and the pleasure you give me and the way I despise you... a stallion, a bull...

'I may sit down?' he said.

She waved to a chair.

'I have had a hard day, Olga,' he said. 'Only with you can I get happiness. Ja, you are my happiness — you, with your hair like rich German corn... your breasts of cream...'

She held up her hand. He was capable of enumerating the

things he liked about her person. If he had not liked them, he would not have been here, and she was bored with the German corn simile. He was like a little boy coming to his mother for sweets. She knew where he had been — organizing the coffee planters. They should never have been allowed to come back after the war.

'Yes, you have a hard life, Fritz.'

He was eyeing the bottle in its bucket of ice.

'Open it,' she said. She took the napkin off the sandwiches. 'And you must be hungry.'

They were like animals, these Nazis. They thought with their blood. Hitler had said that.

The cork popped gently. He picked it off the floor and touched her ankle. She liked the feel of his hand on her. They drank.

He was sweating, red in the face and uncomfortable. It had gone on long enough.

'Perhaps you would like a bath, Fritz, after your walk.' He always left his car in the bush and climbed the last part of the mountain. There was a little path. To suggest a bath was a way of saving his face. Olga always prided herself on her kindness of heart.

He got up. When he came back, the light would be out, but before he left the room there was something to say.

'Listen, Fritz.'

He stopped.

'You had better leave them alone,' she said.

'Leave who . . .?'

'Sebastian's girls. No. It is not that I am jealous. It might even be that I am thinking of you as much as of myself.'

'I . . .' he began to protest.

'The bath is ready, Fritz.' She had turned it on long ago so that it should be ready. It would be lukewarm, just the right temperature.

Baths and light effects — or lack of them — were a device

which saved the embarrassment of that moment she had thought of before he came, where the social merged so atavistically into the biological: the moment where strangers met in bed for pleasure. Only lovers in mind and body could meet openly — completely. The rest, all this that was coming, was a mockery, a black mass, spiritually insignificant. She knew there must be something else. Something better. But that was for others, not for her.

Poor Fritz. She could hear him splashing. Congo was snuffling at the door, shaking it gently. Fritz was the happiest man in Mokala because he thought he had found certainty, security. His faith, his life, was pinned to a single man.

It was amazing how anyone could think any man perfect. It was still more amazing that women did. Hitler's asceticism drew them to him. His personal life, on the one hand, and the license that he gave them, on the other. There was something disgusting about women, especially about Nazi women who were so ready, not merely to betray their own sex, but the world itself, in this new hysteria that had come upon them. They called him 'der schöne Adolf.' They saw themselves as the 'Brides of Christ' — these women of the Anti-Christ.

Standing drawn up to her full height, she took off her dressing gown slowly. She stretched, and then, sitting on the bed, kicked off her mules. Her husband was in the jungle. Channel was either drugged or working; nothing would disturb him. Certainly nothing like this, even had he known of it. Sebastian was occupied fully, she imagined, with his Batangas. The American was no doubt sleeping the sleep of the just, the innocent and the well-dined. She had seen to that. To the servants she never gave a thought. Nothing could be kept secret from them, anyway, but they never talked. The idiosyncrasies of the white man . . . or woman, being to them something at once peculiar and profoundly uninteresting.

He would come out in a minute.

Tomorrow everything would be forgotten. Tomorrow, to-

night would not have been. There was no past, or future;
there was scarcely a present. There was only the anticipation
of immediate pleasure, of contrived anesthesia.

Olga smoothed the silk of her nightdress. She was interested in her own breathing. It came faster. Her heart beat
harder. She lay back in bed, lost in a geo-sexual dream. This
was the centre of Africa: its tropical, equatorial heart.

It was a country of contrasts, of mountains, forests, and
swamps: at once the centre and the end of Africa: a primeval
place: a hopeless place dark with age. Coming from the
north, men had reached here and, exhausted, went no farther.
Coming from the south, they attained the Congo Basin, and,
abandoning hope, remained. Here the twentieth century
merged into a fantastic geologic past where each new flotsam
of race superimposed itself on older flotsams. Nothing was
washed away; all remained to rot in the torrid heat, to putrefy.
Here were the remnants of all past African races. Here were
the results of their crossings — Somali, Arabs, Masai, and
Kikuyu bastards, and Negroid Arabs, Nubians, escaped Abyssinian slaves. Here, too, were the lost men, the scourings of
Europe, lying still in the dead centre of the African vortex:
lying idle, waiting for nothing: living until they died.

Only the Pigmies and gorillas belonged here. The others
were irrelevant to the Congo.

And I lie here in bed, she thought. It seemed right to her
that she should be here: at the centre, where the dark pulse of
life beat out a rhythm of its own. A woman waiting. A centre, pulsating, coreless. The earth rich, waiting for the rain.
The field, waiting for the random sower. What had the field
to do with the ploughman, the sower, or the reaper? The field
went on forever. A hundred sowed, a hundred ploughed.
They came and went. What was man to woman but this?
His penetration of her secrets but the planting of a seed. Her
desire for him but the call of the earth to the plough.

The splashing had stopped.

Chapter 16

The DINNER PARTY

OLGA LOOKED AT HER GUESTS. THIS DINNER HAD BEEN A GOOD
idea. Channel, Sebastian, Wilson — he had brought Bentinck
up in his car — and Fritz — Captain von Brandt as she called
him in public. Bentinck was spending the night with Channel. Wilson could take him back in the morning.

'You will enjoy the forest, Mr. Wilson,' von Brandt said.
Bentinck had spoken of the trip they were taking.

'Yes, it will be an experience.' Wilson did not feel enthusiastic.

'It is a good thing you are going with a professional hunter,
though, because it can be dangerous.'

'I wish you could have come with us, too, Captain von
Brandt,' Wilson said. That was clever of him, Olga thought.

'I wish I could, but I have my work.'

'Perhaps we shall be able to see your place on the way, Captain von Brandt.'

'Or on the way back,' Bentinck said. 'You would like to see
his animals. He has a way with animals.'

'I like to master them. It is simple, really: a matter of technique and courage.'

'Everything is a matter of technique,' Sebastian said. 'I
always say that.'

'I have often thought of fear and courage.' Channel lit a
cigar and sipped his coffee. 'Courage is often only a matter of
youth, possibly of glands. And it might be better if there were
less courage in the world.'

'The Germans are a very courageous people. It comes natural to them. In addition, it is inculcated now. Hard,' von Brandt said, 'like steel.'

Channel looked at Olga. 'So much is a question of time ... of age,' he said. 'We pass through phases. As you get older, time passes faster. It would seem as if we get practice in passing time. Practice in facing it. Practice in disappointment. Time only passes slowly if you want something very badly and are waiting for it. Perhaps as you get older you get to know that few things are worth waiting for; that what you get will not make the difference you think it will. People do not change in essentials. The child is the man. His character is the character he will always have. It will be modified ... changed, but it is still fundamentally the same. Mean or generous, he remains mean or generous. Clever or foolish, affectionate, selfish, passionate, or cold, he will not change. The man is the child, with the experience of his years added to his character. By the time a child is five or six, it is formed: before that, it can be moulded, but only then within the limits of its inherited field.'

'That is what we are doing,' von Brandt said: 'moulding our children. They are like steel, forged pitiless. In the Fatherland . . .'

'What sort of a child do you think I was, mon cher?' Olga asked.

'A charming child,' Channel said. 'Beautiful, intelligent, a lover of warmth, of color, of fine textures.'

'Are you suggesting that I was sensuous?'

'Yes, madame.'

'And you say that people do not change?'

'No, madame. They develop, they progress along certain psychological routes towards an end that is already predetermined.'

'And what is the logical development of the sensuous, Doctor?' Olga was examining her nails.

'That madame should know for herself. Rest assured, my dear Olga, that whatever it is, it is logical. Everything is logical. Do you remember how long it used to be between birthdays and Christmas?' Channel laughed. 'I remember when I was waiting for a pony. And I was right. The pony meant a great deal to me. Nothing could mean so much now. Nothing means very much now; so time, having lost its urgency and importance, has lost its psychological weight. Time is now without significance. There are no surprises. Things follow a pattern. Things fall into their place. Nothing is ever exactly duplicated, but everything has been thought of. Everything is an approximation of what has happened before . . . women, scenery, wild beasts, fires, floods, storms, birth and death, hunger, cold, love, hate. We remember our personal pattern and conform to it. We develop a formula for living. Each man will open the breech of a rifle, handle the reins as he mounts a horse, or make love to a woman according to methods that he has perfected in the past. He will light a cigarette or smell a rose, pat a dog, milk a cow, or deliver a baby, by the particular method that suits his individual temperament.'

'That's what I say,' Sebastian said. 'Technique. I work with the thumbs. I feel with them. I press with them. I mould, I create . . .'

'Take Sebastian,' Channel went on. 'Do you think anyone could have stopped him from being an artist? No doubt everybody did try to stop him, but they did not manage it. Only death,' he continued, 'have we no technique for. Because it is always new. It is only encountered once. But at last we get tired of playing hide and seek with death. When we are young, we fear him. We are hot then: hot with the will to live, the will to breed. But when those fires die, when we stop thinking in terms of achievement, then we get ready to meet death. It will be a change. It will break the monotony of life. It will be the only thing we have not met before. No, not death, but pain is the enemy. Especially mental pain. But you can bear all pain when you learn the trick of it. That's a technique, too: a game of mind over matter, with a spice of masochism and irony thrown in. A man can even profit by pain, if he is a great man. He can refuse to let it conquer him. He can laugh at it. He can deride it. He can despise his body and rise above it by his intellect. Look at them, not just the Eastern Fakirs, but the others: Milton, blind ... Stevenson ... D. H. Lawrence ... Keats ... Elizabeth Browning ... Byron ... Proust. Sick men and women, all of them. But greater than sickness, greater than death, surmounting it. They will always be remembered. They will never die.'

'And me, take me,' Sebastian said. He had been waiting for a pause. He banged on the table. 'And I, too, am immortal. But none of you understand the truth. You talk, you talk and talk. You speak of youth, but the artist is youth itself. Each love-affair is his first. That is the artist. He is without cynicism, perpetually hopeful. Adolescent. He is always in pain, always on the verge of self-destruction. I have had a hard life.' He gulped his brandy.

Channel said: 'Sebastian is right. The artist is always young. The portrait of the artist is always the "Portrait of the Artist as a Young Man" ... a man running. When you are young, the mind serves the body, driving it on. When you are older, the body carries the mind. But the artist is at once very old and very young. With him neither his mind nor his body is master: both are the servants of his art.'

'The true artist,' von Brandt said, 'is Aryan. Our Führer is a great artist.'

'The artist is international,' Sebastian shouted.

'Only the Jew is international.' These people infuriated von Brandt. If it had not been for Olga — and for his instructions to watch the professor — he would never come near them. 'Jews, Bolsheviks, and financiers ...' he began again.

Channel interrupted him. 'So few people understand change ... the building-up and the breaking-down. Suppose

you consider life as a slow-motion picture and then imagine it
accelerated . . . A baby growing, its first teeth coming in, falling out, its body fining down, fattening, thinning again, hair
growing on its body, hair coming out of its head; imagine it
swelling, pregnant, giving birth, suckling, getting fat, losing
its teeth, shrivelling and dying . . . Imagine that run off
quickly — seventy years shown in an hour like those nature
films that show fern fronds uncurling. Then you will see what
I mean. We do no more than a butterfly . . . it takes longer,
that is all. The relation to time and development are different,
so the difference is only one of degree.'

'Yes,' Wilson said. They were all mad. Only Olga remained calm, and Bentinck.

'And it's not only that,' Channel went on. 'Take courage,
we were speaking of it. What is courage?'

'Courage is fear,' Sebastian said. He ran his hand through
his hair.

'Courage, like love, is a secretion,' Channel said. 'When
you're scared, you release adrenalin into the blood stream:
that is what makes you angry, and when you're angry, you're
brave. That is why young men are braver than old. They
secrete faster and better.'

'Bigger and better glands,' Wilson said.

'Yes,' von Brandt said. 'That's how animals know when
you're frightened of them. They can smell it. To train animals you must be fearless. The Germans are the best trainers.'

Wilson thought of the latest body odor advertisements.
Funny ideas one got in one's head. But they were just ideas.
They weren't things one said out loud. He wondered if everyone had them. That idea of change that Channel had been
talking about was true. But what were those changes? Why
did a boy's voice break about fourteen? Why did girls suddenly become women? Why did a woman of thirty show
signs of a double chin or a man of forty begin to grow hairs out
of his ears and nose? It was what Channel said . . . all change,

but so slow, so slow that you hardly noticed it in yourself or your friends.

'Did you know that plants like some men?' Sebastian asked. 'Some men have green fingers. Plants like them. They can make things grow because they love them.'

Olga was smiling.

'With some men a flower will turn towards them, with others they turn away. It must be some kind of radiation, some emanation ... waves of some kind,' Sebastian went on. 'But I have it. I have green fingers.' He looked at his hands. 'Wherever I go, the flowers turn to me. "There comes our friend Sebastian," they say, and at night sometimes I go into the maize fields and the maize talks to me. It talks ... it whispers things, but I never can quite hear what it says. The tassels are like women's hair, soft and silky, but when you run your hand up it, it's cool and moist, not hot and scurfy. I'll paint them like that one day ... A whole field' — he spread out his arms — 'of tall, slim women in the moonlight with long, cool, green hair. I'll paint their whisperings, the rustling of their long green clothes. That's what I want. I want to paint sound. It can be done. Vibrations. Vibrations of color hitting the ear drum through the eyes.' He looked up savagely. 'And I'm not mad,' he said.

'Who said you were mad, Sebastian?' Channel asked.

'I don't know,' he said. 'But don't say it. Let nobody say it. Genius is of God.' He stared round the table.

It was amusing to watch them, Olga thought. Von Brandt stiff as a poker — her lover last night again. Sebastian, her lover when first he had come. Wilson, her lover to be. Bentinck and Channel, the audience of the emotional and political symphony she played. What an immoral lot we are! she thought. What an immoral lot every lot was! Suppose in a big restaurant you could read people's minds. How shocking ... how amusing it would be!

'Don't make any mistake, my friend,' Channel was saying

to von Brandt. 'A man's sexual impulse is irregular.' How had they got onto that? She turned to listen. 'The result of a metabolistic glandular irritation, whereas a woman is continually sexual. She is sex, and on rare occasions she is beautiful. That is by the law of accident, which some call the law of average. But sometimes she must by this law be so put together that the coordinated result of her various limbs and features are pleasing to the eye. Apart from that, and inclusive of it, woman is female, as female as a queen ant, built for and concerned only with the carrying and rearing of her young.'

Sebastian nodded his head in agreement.

Channel warmed his brandy, cupping his hands round the glass. It would have been inconceivable that he should hold his glass any other way. His head was bent over the rim as he sniffed the bouquet. He looked up.

'A woman's sexual life,' he said, 'is a slow, continuous rhythm from puberty to menopause. A man's,' he went on, 'is an occasional explosion. He may be motivated by sex, but he dissociates himself from it. That's the big difference. It annoys him. The fundamental tragedy is that humanity, if it succeeds in raising itself above humanity, ceases to exist. So equalizing the upward drive is the downward pull. However much man may strive heavenward, he is ultimately of the earth . . . earth-born, earth-bound, and earth-condemned.'

Channel twisted the points of his moustache — a nineteenth century gesture that seemed to fit him. He had no beard, but Olga always thought of him as wearing an imperial, neat and crisp, like a little goat's beard. And he did wear one spiritually, even if his chin were bare, just as his feet, spiritually, inside the neat black Wellingtons, were cleft. He had a capacity for incredible neatness under all conditions, which made him seem like an ancient toy, recently revarnished. Olga wondered what gave her this impression. She had always had it. Perhaps it was a worldliness that went beyond

mere tolerance, a sophistication that went beyond sophistication, an atheism that had completed the circle and become
religion. He had seen so much, done so much; was as brilliant
in the concepts of his mind as he was perfect in the minute
details of his person. Or was it just this place? Would she
have thought all this if they had been in Warsaw or London
or Paris or Brussels? He was a period piece ... Empire ... Napoleon the Third ... Winterhalter. How gracefully he would
have made love to the Winterhalter ladies! He was the kind
of man who could take flowers to a woman and present them
without awkwardness. It would never occur to him to have
them delivered. But it was really only Anglo-Saxons who sent
flowers. The others brought them.

'What we need,' Channel said suddenly, 'is a new religion,
a new God ... or the old one revived. Not Owen's religion,
which is afraid of life, but a religion which is life itself — perhaps even the religion of Jesus Christ. "Suffer the little children to come unto me," he said. Take that broadly, and who
is not a child? Let men once see that they are all equally condemned to live and let them make something of it. But first
you must teach them to think, not along accepted lines but
freely; not in terms of academic knowledge, not only in terms
of fact, not rationally, mathematically, but mystically. It is
not humanity that is wrong, but the leaders of humanity, for
the best men and women have no desire to administrate. They
want only to live, and then, before they know what has happened, they find they cannot live — that they have been ad-
ministered into war, into disaster.'

'War is not disaster,' von Brandt said. 'By war men grow.'

'Once I thought,' Channel went on, 'that the women would
do something with their vote. I should have known better.
I should have known that women are less civilized than men:
interested only in the immediate, in the conservative, in the
reproductive. That they deny this so passionately is the proof
of its truth. Women are interested in babies, not in ideas.' He
turned the glass slowly in his hand.

'As far as one can see,' he continued, 'there is only one pattern in life, only one purpose, and that is increase, apparently useless increase; from the simplest moss, fern, or protoplasm to the most complex living animal: the ultimate end an apparently purposeless duplication.'

Von Brandt nodded in agreement. The idea of increase appealed to him. Increase, then battle and the survival of the fittest.

Channel went on. 'This is all we can see. How it began or where it will lead remains unexplained, and, as far as we are concerned, unimportant. Eliminating the certainty of an after life which governed the behavior of older generations, we are left with only the present . . . with a heaven or a hell to be created here on earth, while we live, among other men, with the idea of a common humanity, a common life, and a common end — the pursuit of happiness, which means happiness for all, the pursuit of virtue and beauty, and finally, of justice, for in justice alone does man excel. This is all we can see, but there is something beyond this. With Sebastian's permission I borrow his words — Man is of God.'

Olga thought Channel's approach was a little academic, compared to von Brandt's, who was nothing if not direct. He had his hand on her thigh under the tablecloth. She touched Wilson's ankle with her foot. She saw his finger tighten on the cigarette he held. She liked his hands. He kept them well, but not too well. Fritz manicured himself continually, his nails had a brilliant polish. Also he slept in a hairnet at home, she had found out. So many Germans did. The difference between a German lover and a German husband was probably that the husband slept in a hairnet.

She got up. 'Don't you think we should be more comfortable in the other room?' The men all rose. They followed her.

She wondered what was going on in Fritz's head . . . in Wilson's. Fritz was even more arrogant than usual. It was not simply because of what had happened last night. That had often happened before. But he had a new confidence. His eyes were very bright, full of that blue Prussian fire. They were like bright blue stones: utterly expressionless. Why were Germans' eyes so different from anyone else's. She sat down and arranged her dress. It was a black silk moiré that swathed her to her hips and then flared out. She had a red hibiscus flower in her hair.

Olga was enjoying herself. The butler served more brandy and soda water. She held a gold kid pocketbook in her hand. Inside it was the little packet Bentinck had slipped into her hand when he came in. And why was Fritz carrying a pistol in his hip pocket? What was the world coming to when a man felt better because he was armed? He was behaving like a boy who has been given one of those soldier outfits that are sold on pieces of cardboard at Christmas.

Bentinck, who was near her, said, 'I think it's getting warmer, don't you?'

'Yes,' Olga said. 'I didn't know you were feeling the heat, too.'

'I didn't notice it,' Wilson said.

'Notice what?' von Brandt asked.

'The heat,' Olga said.

'You are feeling tired, madame?' The others had drifted over to Channel.

'Ja, Fritzie,' she said, 'a little.' She closed her eyes and looked up at him from under lowered lids. He thought he had done it and it made him proud. Like a cock on a dunghill. She put her hand out to him as he stood beside her. Yes, it was a pistol. She had wanted to make certain. How dared he wear a pistol in her house? How dared he sleep with Maria when she sent her over with a message?

Brandy always did that to Channel. What a low opinion he had of women! How he must have loved them to hate them so! It was always the same. Sex, philosophy, religion of a queer socialist kind, and then back again to women. Sebas-

tian was at least more consistent. How quick Bentinck was to
understand what she meant! It was certainly hotter. Like
that game you played when you were little: with your eyes
blindfolded. Warm ... warmer. Fritz must be afraid of something. Or less afraid. He was the kind of man who would
always go armed openly if he dared; he loved weapons: a pistol in his belt, a rhino sjambok in his hand, a kiboko. She
wished he would not try to touch her.

'Don't, Fritz. I want to think ... and I'm tired.'

'Tonight,' he said, 'later, when ...'

'No, not again.'

'But ...'

She did not let him go on. She called Channel. 'I want
you to give me something to make me sleep. I am very nervous tonight.'

'I'll get you something.'

Of course, she was not going to take it. But his coming
back with the medicine would break up the party. She had
enjoyed it, but Fritz was getting on her nerves. You could
have enough of anything, certainly of a Nazi. For an instant she thought of changing her mind. Then she decided
against it. Later. Let him wait. She would get nothing out
of him in this mood. She was glad she had not asked Owen
to come over: not at the same time as Sebastian again if she
could help it. He had no tact. He would keep talking about
the Batanga girls ... of how their education was progressing.
Their education in what?

Channel was at her side with a glass. 'Drink this,' he said.

'Later. Give it me. I'll take it in bed.'

They were going. Sebastian had followed Channel. They
would talk and drink till dawn at his house.

Fritz bowed over her hand. This time his heels did click.
She almost laughed as she thought of his tennis shoes. Wilson
was standing opposite her.

'Good night, Olga,' he said. He had given up that absurd Mrs. Le Blanc of his.

'Good night, Mr. Wilson. I wonder how I shall sleep. Parties always excite me.'

'I have not been sleeping well lately myself,' he said.

'Do you expect me to be sorry?' She was smiling at him.

He said good night again. She released her hand from his. The dinner party was over.

She heard von Brandt's car start. Then a door opened. Bentinck came out of the bathroom. She got up to meet him.

'The hunter returns,' she said.

'Poor old Bentinck,' he said. 'Simple old chap.' He sat down. 'You are a very clever woman, Olga. Warm, warmer ... It's getting very hot, my dear.'

Olga lit a cigarette. 'Danzig, the Polish Corridor. Yes, it's coming,' she said. 'Anything new?'

'Straws in the wind. But we'll know soon. That's what the trip with Wilson is for. You know he's in it, too, don't you?'

'Yes,' Olga said. She had guessed it. What a good idea the dinner party had been! Business and pleasure. And it would cover up her tracks. Give people something to talk about. Give her something to say to Jean and Retief when they came back. If the conversation got dangerous, she could always switch it. She was a little ashamed of her affair with von Brandt. Not of the affair, but that it should be with him.

'Have you put it away yet?' Bentinck asked.

'Not yet.' He was talking about the packet he had given her. She would put it in the wall safe in Congo's room before she went to bed. There could be no better place.

'I'll be going now,' Bentinck said. 'Sit outside and smoke a bit and then go over to Channel's. They'll still be talking.'

Olga sat on in the drawing room. Perhaps she had better let Fritz convert her. She had been toying with the idea a long time. She could lead up to it by saying she hated the Jews. Anyone who did that was well on the way to National Socialism. It would be enough to set him off.

Chapter 17

The PAINTER

〜〜〜〜〜〜〜〜〜〜

SEBASTIAN WAS SATISFIED WITH LIFE. IT WAS ONE OF THOSE
days when things looked as if they would go right. True, it
had only just begun, but it had begun well. And what hope
was there for a day that began badly? He had enjoyed his
breakfast even more than usual. The girls were not quarrelling; the sun was hot, but not too hot. The party last night
had exhilarated him, and the talk with Channel and Wilson
— Bentinck had joined them later. Drink, talk, women...
and work. The others were only a means to an end. Work
was the end. Yes, he was happy today: strangely so. And
pleased and astonished that he had no headache.

His masterpiece — the Nubian woman that he was painting
for the American — was going well. He was not even sure
that it was not finished. Most painters spoilt pictures by never
knowing when to stop. A picture was of God. Suppose one
went on adding things to a baby: putting on extra fingers,
extra hands, legs... adding to it, subtracting from it. When a
baby was done, it came out. It was ready: finished to the last
little fingernail. It could not be improved upon.

Anyway, he would do no more today. He would rest. He
would sleep. He would think, contemplate the tremendous
panorama of human nature, of history, of the animal and vegetable worlds. He would ponder on phenomena, he would
drink cold beer. He would even, so good was his mood, give

the girls some beer. He went into the studio — it had been planned as a garage — and looked at the Nubian standing on her easel. He bit his fingernails with pleasure. Of course, it would not last. At the moment he was pleased with her. To-morrow he would begin to see defects. The day after he would hate her. But now — he had made her and she was good. Enormous, black, voluptuous.

Unlocking the storeroom he got beer, six bottles. He called to Nina to bring the footbath and fill it with cold water. He put the beer bottles in the water. They tinkled pleasantly, half-floating. He dragged the bath to the edge of his bed. It was native-made of mahogany, latticed with rawhide strips. He felt in his pocket for the opener. He took it out and put it on the table beside the bed. Then he lay down. The bed creaked as it took his weight. The girls peeped in through the door at him. They think I am wonderful, he thought. They think how lucky they are to belong to such a man as I. They ponder on my generosity, my virility, my genius. He was very pleased with his girls. He forgave them everything. After all, they could know no better. In the corner of the room was his treasure chest. It had come after him by rail, by camion and by porter. In it was what was left of the beautiful things he had collected by theft, by being given them as gifts, and a few by purchase. Curious objects of art — Venetian beads, painted snuffboxes, red Bohemian goblets, a Dresden figure, little ivory gods, a bronze Venus. There was also an unreliable pistol of Belgian make, and a Moorish dagger. They were under some Chinese embroidered silks and a piece of blue brocade. There was nothing else in the room but a mahogany bench and a sacred picture he had painted — a cross-eyed Virgin and child. He had used Nina for a model. The astigmatism he had added because of some inner conviction at the time he was painting.

Stretching out his hand, he picked up the opener. He felt for the neck of a bottle. He drank and thought of his work.

When I paint, he thought, I do not depict. I do not photograph.

'I paint!' he shouted to the girls.

Yes, when he painted a horse, he painted all horses. He expressed all horses. The horse he drew might not be like the horse he was drawing. How could it be, since that particular horse was not all horses? A tree was all trees. It was the power of growth, the sap coursing through the trunk with terrible urgency, the bursting of the buds into flowers, into leaves — the fruiting, the seeding. A tree or a horse, as he painted them, embodied all that there was in the world of trees and horses. A woman was the same. When he painted a woman, it was all women. The virgin, the mother, the harlot. It was the complementary characteristics, the opposites, that he went for: the lascivious maternity of the spawning organism hidden behind the carefully made-up face, the schooled eyes and firm lips. This, or the reverse, the austerity of the loving mother: the prudishness of the prostitute. Always the opposites in combination, always paradox, always light against dark, dark against light, both technically and spiritually. In an old woman's face the child looked out, peeping from behind her wrinkled eyelids. In the face of a girl, you saw the woman ... the shadow of her unknown experience, the latent woman. In the seed he saw the tree. In the tree he saw the seed. He never saw himself at all. He was an instrument. He was, except for his work, without reality or significance. His anger at the Fascists, his participation in the Spanish War, had been due to his fury at those who prevented creation, who refused to let the world go forward, who interrupted its progress and with it his own.

But he was astonishingly happy here. The men he associated with were all creators. They all did something. Von Brandt even did something, though his profession of collecting wild animals alive was contrary to the will of God. Wild animals were of God. In addition, he was a Nazi. He said so

openly. Marais was a business man and as such uninteresting.
Wilson came under a different category. He was American
and therefore a patron. Patrons were of God.

He drank beer and thought of women — of Olga and his
two girls, of all the women he had ever known. They were
objects to be painted — models — and also, since by them a
man was rendered spiritual, emptied of desire and purified,
they were of God. Creating men out of their bodies, purifying
men by their bodies, women were admirably designed for their
specific purposes, which were both mysterious and inscrutable.
That they were actually human he doubted. He neither
understood them nor wished to. He liked them, he made love
to them. They liked him and allowed him to make love to
them. And what more could he ask? He felt himself modest
in his demands.

It was evening when he woke up. He must see someone.
He had a desire to explain himself: to develop the ideas that
had come to him in sleep, and out of the beer. Where was his
patron, the American? He would find him. They would discuss art. He might even show him the Nubian. He smoothed
his hair and went out. The girls were peeping at him from
behind the wall. He saw them: he waved his hand at them.
They flushed like birds in front of a dog and ran off fluttering
their skirts and screaming with laughter. They would sit at
the back of the house on the little mud stoep they had made
and begin to cook his supper. They were good little girls. But
it was a pity Maria had to go and see her father so much. She
said he was ill, and went nearly every day.

Wilson, in the guest house, was reading a book on gorillas.
He put it down when Sebastian came in: he was glad to stop.

'Why do you read about gorillas?' Sebastian asked. 'You
have one here, study it. Work from nature. Get close to it.
Embrace it. In an hour with Congo you can learn more about
gorillas than that man' — he pointed to the book — 'ever

knew. Even I can tell you more about gorillas than he can.
Congo is my friend.'

'Tell me about him, Sebastian.'

Sebastian sat down. 'To start with, he is a man. Yes, the
gorilla is not merely man-like, he is a man. He has a soul.
The hunter who slays a gorilla commits murder in the first
degree. The gorilla has affections, likes, dislikes. He has temperament. He learns to like alcohol and tobacco. This proves
that he has a soul.'

Wilson did not look convinced. His mind was set in its
ways. He was academic, contemptible. It was no use pursuing the subject. He would change and speak about himself.
That could not fail to interest him.

'I am before my time,' he said.

'Quite,' Wilson said. 'Sure.'

'A genius is always before his time. That's what makes him
a genius, one who, having ripped the entrails out of the past,
leaps forward into the future.' Sebastian jumped up. 'What a
picture! Can't you see it? — a male figure leaping, its arms
full of entrails. Salvador Dali, but beyond him. Don't you
see, if I could sell pictures, if people liked them, they would
be no good? I should just be a contemporary painter. Me
contemporary . . . me' — he tore at his beard — 'the crowd!
Me in the crowd . . . the Left Bank, Bloomsbury . . . Chelsea!
That lot, Mother of God . . . me a contemporary! I am
ahead,' he shouted — 'ahead of them all.' He pointed to a
half-naked child of four. It belonged to one of Channel's boys.
'My work is for him and his children . . . for the syphilitic
future. Today I am alone. No one resembles me, so how
could they understand? I am new . . . unintelligible . . . but in
a hundred years I shall be the master. In a hundred years I
shall be Sebastian.' He sat down again.

'People only like the accustomed, that to which they are
used, the conventional, the piddling, the mother's apronstring.
Only that which is known is accepted as reality. Look,' he

said. 'I draw a breast so.' He made a sweep with his broken thumbnail driving it into the wood of the table . . . 'And they say that is not a breast. But I say what do they know of breasts? Do they really look at them . . . have they touched them, examined them, looked at them from above, below, in sunlight, moonlight? No, they have not. They would be ashamed; they are afraid of the nude, afraid of it warm and soft . . . afraid of it even in watercolor.'

He was silent. He rolled a cigarette. 'You know,' he said, 'my secret is that I'm invisible. Because I am unseen, I can see what goes on undisturbed. It's my secret,' he repeated. 'I have never known that I existed . . . not even in the Spanish War. Yes, I was wounded twice, but none of it was real. I was there, but I was not there. Sebastian was not there. He was just watching another man called Sebastian who was there . . . laughing at him . . . mocking him. I love what I see and feel with my mind. The paint sings songs to me. You can't understand that, can you? How color can sing, and form can sing? — so that they hurt you and your thumb itches. But I am never anywhere . . . never at rest . . . always seeking, always invisible. My God! my God! I am never there. Not even with women. I can't lose myself in them . . . or find myself in them. I can't get rest from them or peace. I only get exhaustion. I get tired standing and watching myself. An animal can run away. A man can't. An animal has a choice. It can run or fight. A man has none. He has to stand still while he burns himself up.

'Come,' he said, 'let us go to my house. I have some Pernod there.'

Wilson followed him. They went to a table he had made under a tree to the right of his house. He disappeared for a moment and came back with a bottle, some glasses, water and sugar. He poured out the drinks.

From behind the house came the chatter of the girls: their laughter. There was a man's voice. Evidently they had a visitor.

Sebastian had made himself an extraordinary garden. Olga's terraces were lovely, were well kept . . . ordered. But this was a riot of color, of trees, climbers and shrubs planted at hazard, growing untrimmed, apparently untended. It was difficult to believe that he had done it in a year. Bougainvillea, honeysuckle, golden shower, coral vines, potato creeper, and Cape jasmine covered the house. Young bananas grew among the hibiscus, poinsettia, and transplanted palms. He had a patch of pineapples and a small land where his girls cultivated maracas, cow peas, sweet millets, and casava. Young paw-paws grew among the maize plants; pumpkin vines, hairy-leaved and yellow, trumpet-flowered, crawled over the ground. Green peppers, okra, sweet potatoes, and tomatoes grew in voluptuous profusion. The garden expressed its owner. Its piled masses of vegetation, its flowers and fruits, its vast disorder, achieved a magnificence of design. It was as if, casting his seeds, letting them fall where they would, Sebastian sowing blindly, inevitably made beauty. It was very still; the flowers hung motionless on the shrubs. The sky was cloudless.

'It is beautiful, is it not?'

'Yes,' Wilson said. He raised his glass. Sebastian drank with him. How pleasant it was to sit here with his patron! He would not show him the picture yet. He would save it up. Besides, the light was not as good as it had been. And this was an opportunity for further talk. The American was partaking of his hospitality. He could not get away. He was pinned down by his bourgeois good manners.

Now me, Sebastian thought. I would not be pinned down like that by a drink. If I did not want to stay, I would throw it in the face of my host. I would get up and leave. I would drink it quickly and then leave. I would . . . but then I am not bourgeois. I have never been called that. All other things, yes, but never that. He thought of nature, again of the beauties of nature, of animals. It was wonderful how Pernod cleared your mind.

'I am Sebastian,' he said. He pushed the glass away from him. It left a long smear on the dirty table: a smear of cleanness.

All right, he was Sebastian. But so what? Sebastian who? Wilson watched a fly settle on the edge of the smear. Did flies get drunk?

He watched Sebastian's hands playing with the glass. The bitten nails were dirty as usual. The sunlight coming through the leaves speckled them. It was very hot; it was very silent; only the flies buzzed, and somewhere someone was picking at a stringed instrument: not playing, just picking at it as if he hated it, as if he was picking the scab off a sore.

Sebastian spoke again. 'My wife once said, "Why do you drink so much, Sebastian?" and I said, "Because I like it. That's why I drink, because I like it." Soon after that I left her. But they're all the same.'

He leant forward. 'I have discovered something about time. You can drink it away. That's how you can fool it, and by working, and by women. I drink to get my dreams, women to crystallize them, and work destroys them. Your work is never the dream you had, it's a parody of it, an abortion, a miscarriage. You never get the child you begot. Only conception is glorious: the conception of anything; for then time stands still. In conception the sun and the moon and the stars hang static in a firmament of steel.

'I am going in now,' he said. He got hold of the table with both hands and got up slowly. He looked even taller than usual. His dog got up and stood staring at him. It was like him in a way, big, rough-haired, dissipated-looking, with yellow eyes. The dog stood staring. Sebastian stood swaying behind the table with his bitten fingertips upon it.

'I'll see you again later,' he said. 'I've got an idea. I only get ideas when I'm drunk and when I'm drunk I can't paint, but that's nothing. I'm teaching myself. I can teach myself anything. I'll see you again. I'll see you ... I'll see you.' He half-closed his eyes to stare at Wilson. Then he went out into the full light of the setting sun, was caught up in it, as if it were a hand. The dog followed him.

Wilson sat on. He forgot Sebastian. He thought of Olga — of her directness of approach.

That was what was the matter with most things. They were too wrapped up — everything in packets, packages. Everything had to be undone. Everything; not only cigarettes, but emotions, too, and you couldn't live that way. You couldn't wrap sex up in cellophane, put a ribbon round it, and merchandise it in the hot spots. What was the point of it? of European society, of the Social Register...? It all began and ended in bed. It was the same with a truck-driver, or a girl in the Ten-Cent Store; but rich people put frills on it. They punched a sort of social time clock — marriage, babies, divorce, remarriage. They fooled around with flowers, preachers, layettes, and cocktail sets, but what did it all amount to in the end?

There were more flies along the edge of the stain now, but it was dry. And there were the marks of Sebastian's sandals in the dust, and the marks of his dog's feet. The musician had stopped picking, Wilson saw him asleep at the side of the house, his instrument by his side on the earth floor; his mouth was half open.

Wilson's mind ran on; part of him said, 'You'd better get out of this place before something happens.' The other part said, 'What the hell? This is what you came for, isn't it?' That was the worst of it; whatever you did, you wanted to do the other thing almost as much.

A man's life was his own. He could use it or he could save it up. But what would he save it up for?

He thought of Olga's legs and hips. When you came down to it, all men thought of women like that, but they would not acknowledge it, not even to themselves. At least all men had some favorite bit... some men only looked at breasts and not

at legs at all; others only looked at faces. Women talking about
other women always talked about their faces. But perhaps
they only said that. Women were as interested in sex as men,
perhaps more so; but you couldn't tell them so. You weren't
supposed to know it, and you didn't know it till you had had a
lot to do with women, and you weren't supposed to have a lot
to do with women. You were supposed to have one woman,
some children, and live in a little house somewhere and commute. You were supposed to sleep with her once a week, at
night, on Saturdays, or on New Year's Day, or Washington's
Birthday, or Empire Day, and then lie in, to get over your
debauch, and maybe take her flowers next day to show her
you were sorry. And none of it was considered quite nice. It
was not to be talked about, it was not even to be inferred, and
yet everyone you saw in the streetcars, on the subway, in the
streets, had had these experiences. They all — every adult,
that is — lived with some other adult of the opposite sex. That
was a nice way of putting it. But in a lifetime a man was
likely to spend twenty years married; thirty was more like it,
but to be on the safe side call it twenty. Half that time was
spent with a woman alone, under intimate conditions, another euphemism . . . dressing, undressing, in bed with her.
That is, ten years of actual time.

There was something fantastic about this, not about it, but
that it should be ignored, glossed over as something else, considered obscene; if this was so, then conception was obscene,
then one's own parents were obscene, then motherhood, which
was so sacred in its accomplishment, was obscene in its begin-
nings, and the act of conception only mysteriously purified by
the nine months of pregnancy. If you slept with a woman at
eleven o'clock in the morning, it was a fornication; if you were
married at midday and slept with her an hour later, it was a
sacrament; but it was doubtful if the people themselves felt
very different . . . and things were changing. Fifty years ago it
would have been unthinkable to sit down to a meal without

saying grace...'For what we are about to receive make us truly thankful.' That was an idea, too... But there was certainly something funny about the whole of this man and woman business... Some fear of the atavistic, that was probably it.

That might be what Sebastian meant when he said, 'Animals are only frightened sometimes.' People were frightened all the time. They were driven by fear of death, of penury, by fear of love, by fear of not having love. There must be a pattern, form; perhaps he'd find it here. He had never lived without interruptions before. He wondered if he was drunk. If he was, it was in a funny way because his mind was very lucid... or seemed to be. In a way it was like being on board ship — the amount you drank; the slight effect it had; the restricted society. The Station was a ship set in a sea of bush.

The delightful sequence of his thoughts was destroyed by Sebastian. He was running out of the house, shouting,

'Maria! Maria! Where is that girl?' He came back to the table. 'Have you seen her?' he asked. 'The little one?'

'No,' Wilson said: 'has she gone?'

'Yes, she's gone. Again. And I gave her beer. Nearly a bottle of it. And then she slipped away.'

'She may have gone home,' Wilson suggested.

'That's what her sister says, but I have no confidence in her father. If he's sick, why does she go alone? Why don't they both go? And why did I not think of that before?' He bent over the table. 'There is another man,' he said. 'I knew today was too good to last. This morning I was too happy. Tonight I am betrayed, disgraced, discredited, abandoned... the garland is plucked from my breast... my garland, my little Maria.'

The other girl, Nina, came out of the house and said something.

'I must go,' Sebastian said. 'My dinner is ready.'

Everyone, Wilson thought, had his problems. If Sebastian's dinner was ready, it was time for him to dress.

He wondered what Olga would wear. She had a lot of clothes.

When Wilson got over to the big house, he found he was early. His watch must have been wrong. He sat down and picked up a paper. The door leading into Olga's bedroom was opened.

He looked up suddenly. Olga was there, in her room. She was standing with nothing on in front of her glass. She was even more beautiful than he had imagined she would be. He tried to hide behind his paper. He was in a very embarrassing position. He was sure she knew he was there, but he would never be able to say so. Whatever happened, he was always wrong. He never knew how he passed the time till she came in. She was wearing an indigo satin ciré that glistened wetly as it clung to her body.

'Sorry I'm late,' she said. 'Or were you early? And where are the cocktails?' She picked up a little silver bell and rang it.

Wilson drank his Martini. He needed it.

Then they dined. Dinner was very quiet. They talked of nothing, of Sebastian, of his own book, of Channel . . .

After dinner, she excused herself. 'Forgive me, won't you?' she said. 'But we don't treat you as a visitor. And I'm so tired.'

Back in the guest house he went over it in his mind. She can't have known I was there. She can't have known? . . .

It was beyond him. He picked up a book about Bornean leaf monkeys and threw it across the room.

Chapter 18

The RETURN

◆◆◆◆◆◆◆◆◆◆◆◆◆◆◆◆◆◆

THE MORE WILSON THOUGHT OF THIS EXPEDITION BENTINCK HAD arranged, the more he read about this particular part of the world, the less he liked it. And he had no desire to shoot an adult male gorilla. When he had agreed to Frazer's suggestion, he had not known that all this was included. And now he was stuck with it. When it was all over, he would give Frazer a piece of his mind. Frazer had not mentioned Olga. He knew about her, of course. He had also known or guessed that if he stayed here a few days he was likely to remain. His understatement amounted to actual deceit. Interesting people indeed! Lunatics, gorillas, beautiful nymphomaniacs, and certainly no place for a respectable, recently divorced young man. His story if he told it would not be credited. If he got into trouble, what would people think of him? What did they know about living in a house with a beautiful woman and a gorilla? Had anyone else ever done it? He wondered what Anne was doing, whom she was with. She would be with someone, of course.

He went back to his books again. If he was going to study, this was the best time. After breakfast one got some peace. 'Functional Affinities of Man, Monkeys, and Apes.' Chapter III began with a definition of primates: 'Unguiculate claviculate placental mammals, with orbits encircled by bone: three kinds of teeth, at least at one time in life: brain always with a posterior lobe and calcarine fissures: the innermost digits of at least one pair of extremities opposable: hallux with flat nail or none: a well-marked caecum: penis pendulous: testes scrotal: always two pectoral mammae . . .'

This had been written by St. George Mivart in 1873, and since it was quoted in this book, it must still apply. It was interesting to consider himself objectively as a primate who had three kinds of teeth, at least at one time in life . . . and all the other things. Hominidae . . . Man. He had lost his ability to concentrate. What he read struck him as either dull or comic. If dull, he could not remember it. If comic, it started trains of thought that were disturbing. But it was not really comic. It was like the giggle that ran over an audience at an emotional moment in the theatre. It was like some of the *New Yorker* jokes, like the stories of Dorothy Parker — more ironic than funny. A sense of humor was a mechanism devised by man to counteract his pain. Before the age of self-conscious-ness, in the Middle Ages for instance, there had been little humor as it was understood today.

He closed the book. The professor and Retief should be back tomorrow and Bentinck and he would be setting out three days later. Bentinck had sent up a boy to say he had everything nearly ready, including the porters they would need. He wondered how he would like all that walking. To go for a walk on the hillside was one thing, but this business was quite another. Frazer hadn't said anything about this either. He had thought, if he had thought about the matter at all, that one could do intelligence work in a car. There would only be two more meals alone with Olga before the pro-fessor returned.

He looked at the books on his shelf . . . 'Interbreeding Among Some Bornean Leaf Monkeys.' He had looked through it the other day: it did not seem to apply here. He wondered why Channel had given it to him. 'Some Considerations on the Host-Distribution of Parasitic Nematodes.' 'Experimental

Efforts to Transfer Monkey Malaria to Man.' 'Note on a
Hybrid Monkey.' 'Study of the Sexual Tendencies in Mon-
keys and Baboons.' 'Miocene Primates in British East Africa.'
'Development of an Infant Chimpanzee During Her First
Year.' 'Mentality of Apes.' 'Man's Place Among the Mam-
mals.' 'Fur Picking in Monkeys as an Act of Adornment.'

There were lots of others. But all had this in common: they
were subversive. They destroyed your confidence in yourself.
When he shaved or did his hair now, he thought of 'Monkeys
Picking Fur as an Act of Adornment.' The literature relative
to primates was not elevating, especially that which referred
specifically to the Pongidae. And now it was lunch time.

The trouble with scientists was that they had no sense of
humor. It struck him as he walked over to the big bungalow
that this was what was the matter with everyone at Mokala.
They were humorless. No one here, except Olga perhaps,
would think a mandrill's blue-and-red buttocks funny.
Channel would speak of them as sexual skin and refer to their
brilliant pigmentation as a manifestation of heat or sexual
periodicity which made it easier for the opposite sexes to
recognize each other as being in a receptive mood. Yes, he
would put it like that. Sebastian would immediately want to
paint them. Color sent him mad, whatever its location.
Owen would look away. Bentinck, if he had a gun, would
shoot it. The professor would not notice it at all. He would
be too busy looking to see what kind of tree it was sitting on or
the variety of fruit it was eating. Von Brandt would figure
out how he could capture it to sell to some zoo. Only Olga
and he would laugh.

Really, a mandrill's buttocks could be considered as a kind of
test. It might be amusing to write a monograph entitled 'The
Reaction of Man to Pigmentation of the Genus Mandrillus.'
It was a pity there were none here.

The difficult part of meals came when they ended. You

could not just have your food and run away. Especially if your
hostess knew that you really had nothing to do.

Lunch was over. The coffee was on the table. When the
house boys had gone, Olga said, 'Alone at last.' Wilson stirred
his cup. He hated to be teased. He got some comfort from the
book he had been reading about primates. 'Always two
pectoral mammae.'

She had got out a cigarette. He had to light it for her.
Women had so many advantages. He sat down again.

'Why are you so frightened of me, Wilson?' she asked. 'I
don't bite.'

'I don't know what you're talking about,' he said. 'I'm not
frightened.'

There it was again, this trick of putting him in the wrong.
'Oh, no,' the little boy in him said, 'I don't mind your putting
out the light. I'm not scared in the dark.' Lighting her cigarette had disturbed him. His finger had touched hers. She
knew quite well that he wanted to make love to her, and that
he was disturbed, because no opportunity had offered itself
and the professor would be back tomorrow.

'Listen, Wilson,' she said. 'You don't know what is going
to happen here. You think you do, but you don't.' She was
suddenly very serious. 'You don't know me either,' she went
on. 'You may not even know that I am a British agent. I
don't think you know how long I have been working for them.
I started before I was married. You are deceived by the outside circumstances: by the fact that I am not unattractive, by
the queer people here, by Congo, by the climate. But under
all this,' she went on, 'is the never-ending fight for the riches
of Africa.'

'I only said I would help Frazer because I thought it would
give me something to do.' It was impossible to follow her
change of mood.

'It will. And you wanted to forget certain things, did you
not?'

'Yes.'

'You were bored. Now with me you are not bored. At least I imagine you are not.'

'No.' Damn this woman!

'You want to forget your wife,' she said. 'Sometimes the best way to forget one woman is with others. You might think of that sometimes. You have the passion of your race for over-complicating things. You find me attractive. I find you attractive. We are here waiting for the end of the world — the world we knew, that is. The standards by which you have lived have no further application.'

Wilson was furious with her. She was trying to make out it was his fault.

Everyone seemed able to jockey him into positions invariably unfavorable to himself. One thing led to another. One position to another. He thought of last night. Of Olga naked in front of her mirror, of her turning and walking across her room. She knew that he had seen her. He had been meant to see her. And then after dinner she had excused herself. Had he been supposed to do something? Should he have said something? He had seen women naked before. Anne sometimes: girls in various theatres, girls at floor shows, and a few others. But that had been different. You knew you were going to see them. A beautiful naked woman should not be sprung on you on an empty stomach. And what did she mean, one woman to forget another woman, and then a third to forget the second, and a fourth to forget the third? His coffee was finished; he had sat here long enough.

'Going?' Olga asked. 'So soon?'

'Yes, I want to do some more reading.'

'Then I will see you at dinner,' she said. 'I will try not to be so late tonight.'

Wilson spent the afternoon in the garden reading and thinking. But he could neither read nor think. He knew he was waiting for dinner. He tinkered with his car a little. He rearranged some things in his room. He emptied his stud box. Why did one keep single links and odd studs and buttons? As a child he had had a passion for buttons. He had had a very fine collection, but why carry it on? There was a single gold and onyx link, two dress waistcoat buttons. There was another odd link, gold with his initials on it. He had been given them on his twenty-first birthday by his mother. He put it back in the box. But the other things could go.

He looked at his cameras, a Leica and a movie camera; at his two rifles and shotgun. Of course he could go over to Sebastian and talk to him, but he had had enough of Sebastian. Or Channel, but he had had enough of Channel too. Run down to see Bentinck? He was not in the mood for that. He did not want to go for a walk. He could not lie down and rest. He might write some letters, but there was no one he wanted to write to. The only person who seemed to take any interest in him was Anne's lawyer in New York. But 70 Pine Street seemed a long way off today. And how could he explain what he was doing here? I am engaged, he thought, in counter-espionage and in a clandestine affair with a married Polish woman. He was not actually engaged in either yet, but he was nearly . . . he soon would be. A world stake, Olga had said. And then parallel to it were his own private affairs. Not merely his own — everyone's. Behind the big public events of policy and war were the small ones of individual lives.

A boy came in to lay out his clothes and run in his bath.

'Here,' he said, 'want this?' He gave him the onyx link.

'Thank you, master.' He put it into his ear, threading it through the hole he had in the lobe. A funny place for it to end. It had come from Asprey's in Bond Street. Natives were lucky. They were so easily pleased. What would Olga wear? It was funny the way he wondered that every night.

She was wearing bright red. A sleeveless dress without shoulder straps. He had seen her first in red, but that had been dark crimson.

'You see,' she said when he came in, 'I'm early tonight. I did not want to keep you waiting again.' Almost at once the butler came in with the drinks.

'And did you put in a good afternoon's work, Mr. Wilson?'

'Yes,' he said. 'I read and tidied things.' He was not going to let her know she had upset him. But he was sure by the way she looked at her gold slippers that she knew. She had on no stockings. The red enamel toes showed through the open ends of her shoes. Her dress was slit and showed her leg almost up to the knee. She rearranged it.

'The professor should be home tomorrow,' she said. 'I do hope his little trees were all right. He will be so upset if they aren't.'

He followed her into the dining room.

'The party the other night was amusing, wasn't it?' she said. 'I am very fond of parties.' Then she talked about the mission and Owen. She said she had not asked him because of Sebastian.

When they had finished, she said something to the butler in Swahili. He bowed.

'He wanted to know if he could go,' Olga said. The boys left the house every night, but tonight she had underlined the fact. In the sitting room she went to the piano. She sang softly the song that Channel had asked for at his birthday — *Au clair de la lune, mon ami Pierrot.*

She sang it again and closed the piano. She was coming towards him. He rose to meet her. She seemed to float. He had no sensation of her coming nearer, only that she was coming, that she was nearer, that it was impossible for him to do anything but wait. Everything had led up to this moment. The scent of geraniums enveloped him, the scent of her hair, the rustle of her dress as it swept along the parquet floor, the tap of her heels. Her eyes were nearly black.

He was aware of a tremendous static urgency. This instant had no relation to any other, and then he held her. Rigid for a minute, both were resistant — charged. Then she relaxed, became soft, accommodating her body to his, fitting into it. Her lips were on his, her hands on him.

It was dawn when he left her. Light enough for him to see her body of ivory and gold.

Four hours later the professor and Retief returned. Their arrival woke him. They had come back too late.

In her room Olga woke, too. She thought of Wilson waking. No one could have slept through the noise of the return. She turned over in bed. Life was not as dull as it had been before the American had come. He was so easy to annoy. It was like teasing a child. She was tired of Fritz. He bored her. The American ... Henry Wilson ...

The professor came in.

'Darling,' he said, 'how beautiful you are!'

'Thank you.' She smiled at him. She was happy. He was happy. Everyone was happy.

Chapter 19

The ASSISTANT

〰〰〰〰〰〰〰〰〰

IN THE FOREST WITH THE PROFESSOR, RETIEF HAD BEEN TOR-
tured by jealousy and remorse. When he got back, he must
write down his thoughts, must try to explain himself to himself before he went mad. Write out the past and try, from the
past, from his record of it, to see into the future. How did one
write these things? It would no doubt take form as he began.
At least he would not be hampered by self-consciousness, since
it was only for himself. In his own room the day after their
return he began:

'I, who write, saw this thing from its small beginning,
watched it grow, became involved in it, first as a mere spectator and later in a more intimate fashion. It is therefore no
romance, but a private part of my life, bringing neither credit
nor discredit upon me, and finally coming near to overwhelming me.

'There are innumerable reasons for writing as there are an
infinite variety of writers. There are the great ones like Victor
Hugo, and the petits maîtres, the imitators; and those who
would be thought writers, but do not write; and the hacks
and the ghost writers, professionals who cultivate the gardens
of literature as assiduously as peasants. But I, Pierre Retief,
fall into none of these categories. I am no writer, but a scientist. In consequence, what I write must of necessity be
cold, objective, more of a thesis than a romance, though God
knows that of which I write is romantic enough and terrible

enough. Again I examine myself... my position in this strange and new capacity — at once the narrator and the hero — since each of us is the hero and centre of his own particular and individual world... the hero, I said, but also, I fear, the victim. It is this that has caused me to begin my narrative. But how does one begin? The locale — the *mise en scène* — is simple: The Congo. But the characters... How are they to be described? Perhaps the place itself must help to describe them. Mokala, set in the heart of the forest, is a backwater where human flotsam is washed up and stranded. There must be other such places resembling terrestrial Sargasso Seas. We — that is, the Professor, Olga, and myself — are thus easily explained. We are employed by the Government on botanical research. But the others? Channel the surgeon, Sebastian the painter, Owen the missionary, von Brandt the Nazi — what tide of circumstances washed them up and set them down in Equatorial Africa? What holds them here? What hope is there for them or for any of us? Can Owen's faith save him? Can von Brandt's arrogance save von Brandt? Can Sebastian's art? Can Channel's cynicism or his skilful fingers lead him back to a sane and ordered world? No, I say, for the world is no longer sane or ordered. And why should I write thus, since my words are for my eyes alone? Is this also a lie; that writing for myself I still hope that others will see? Is this another psychological device?

'I forgot to mention Congo. Or did I not forget? Is it because I fear Congo that I do not write of him? You will note — I note it myself as I look at these lines — that I speak of him as a man. That is terrible. It shows that I, too, a scientist, have succumbed to this strange cerebral anesthesia... that I too am no longer sane. Congo is not a man, but a gorilla.

'Having given this brief description of myself and my circumstances, I must begin — not that in anything can there be any real beginning, since there are too many factors of heredity and environment, of unremembered youthful conditioning.

In addition, after much thought about the form my story
should take, it seems best to me to present it as a romance, a
fiction . . . since as a direct testament it would be too incredible to be believed even by myself. I can indeed ask no one to
believe it, and shall obtain a certain masochistic satisfaction
in the irony of the fact that experiences, which have turned my
hair grey at the age of thirty-two, should after my death be
read as a pastime and amusement by those whose education
has been of such a simple and standardized type that they can
see no wonder in life and only accept the mechanistically ex-
plicable. The conversations are naturally not invented but
remembered in part, and reconstructed. The scenes are correct, for they are burnt indelibly into my mind and heart. So,
with some diffidence, I begin: But first, how I betray myself!
Obviously I write for others. For the professor, perhaps, so
that he will understand me to have been the unwilling tool of
circumstance.

'As a young man I was a pupil of the famous Le Blanc, at the
University of Brussels. By a lucky accident, he once selected
me to help him in a small experiment, and found me to be
sympathetic to him. I looked at the phenomena of life from
his own angle. We saw the same view, through different
pairs of glasses; his field of vision being enormous, embracing
subject after subject as though they were ranges of mountains;
while I saw only a small piece of it, but that I perceived very
clearly and with great intensity. It was this gift which en-
deared me to him rather than any particular brilliance on my
part, and led him to choose me as his assistant, in which
capacity I went with him to the Congo. Though at that time
I was studying medicine, and my work with him was extra-
curricular, I gave up my chosen profession, so great was my
admiration for this man whose happiness I was destined to
destroy. We had conducted sufficient experiments in the
Royal Botanical Gardens to obtain financial assistance from
the Société de Récherche Scientifique, and a grant from the

Aide Commerciale des Produits Tropicales; so, with what to scientists seemed unlimited economic resources behind us — for in addition the professor had a large private fortune — and armed with every kind of authority, we proceeded to this abominable country to continue our researches.

'Briefly, our work was concerned with latex, the sap of the rubber tree. Le Blanc had proved, in a small greenhouse sort of way, that this flow could be doubled by injection, corresponding roughly to the intravenal injections of saline solution into human veins. This experiment, which would revolutionize the rubber industry, being no more to him than a proof in a large way of an hypothesis already proved in a small one. He also wished to work with medicinal herbs, cinchona bark, quassia, senna, and trees whose wood was likely to be of value in industry. In brief, a Botanical Station was to be established.

'Mokala is mostly forest country, parts of which are so overgrown with great trees, some of them a thousand years old, that the sun never penetrates to the ground at their roots. The forest opens up into glades, where natives perform a somewhat desultory form of agriculture: growing bananas, millet, maize, sweet potatoes, pumpkins, ground nuts, and several varieties of bean. The earth is fertile, and the crops invariably good; wonderfully so, considering the way in which they are neglected. I speak now of the early days before we moved to the new Station up on the mountain.

'Occasionally elephants would devastate an area, but gorillas were the main trouble, and were both feared and hated by the aborigines. Their depredations were not always at once apparent, for with great cunning they would steal only a little at a time, and that so skilfully that, unless the very pods of the beans were counted, nothing would be noticed till it was time to harvest the crop. At others their devastations were terrible, with crops, even trees, being torn up and thrown about the little gardens. Incidentally, it must be stated that there is little confirmation of the stories concerning the abduction of native women by these creatures, though from the personal experience I am about to relate I do not imagine them impossible.

'When I say we went, it must be understood that there were four of us, for Le Blanc, before going, had married a young girl, his secretary. He had met her on the Riviera. She had no knowledge of typing and shorthand, but could decipher his handwriting. Olga Severenisky was her name. She was of Polish-French extraction, and had fair hair, so deficient in pigmentation that it was almost white. It was her habit to dress her hair — there were masses of it — in various ways, changing them from day to day — a habit which was disconcerting. She had a creamy camellia skin which was remarkably resistant to the bites of insects, and her form was slim and graceful, though well developed. From the first I considered her pretty and could see she would be a disturbing influence. It was impossible to ignore her, even when she was silent. Indeed, her silences called attention to her, and such a young woman was out of place anywhere except perhaps upon the stage ... a profession of which I have no knowledge. The professor was quite obviously enthralled by her. The fourth member of our party was the physician, Channel.

'We lived in a small whitewashed bungalow which had been built for us, and in due course Olga gave birth to a son. There was no particular difficulty about this, Channel being an excellent doctor and Olga a healthy girl.

'That we all lived and kept our health in that pestilential climate was due to the doctor, and we were undoubtedly the first white people to face the myriads of Anopheles Maculipennis, unperturbed by the fear of either malaria or blackwater; both particularly malignant in those parts, even natives dying freely.

'It will be the Channel serum which may eventually, if he can bring himself to put it on the market, open up vast tracts of swamp hitherto considered uninhabitable. It is possible that this was an additional reason for Le Blanc's desire to go to the Congo, to permit his friend Channel to try his experimental serums on three people of different types, sexes, and nationalities.

'Not only were we well; we were in what a layman would describe as radiant health; one of the three serums he used having tonic properties of the most powerful quality. It has occurred to me that the professor's potency may have been due to these injections, since up here where they are no longer necessary he appears to neglect his wife.

'The baby throve, putting on weight daily, and Olga was enraptured by it. Motherhood occupied her to such an extent that she did no other work, except the weekly report, which was urgent. By this time she had learnt to type.

'The professor's interest in the infant appeared to be more academic than paternal; though when it died he showed some signs of emotion. We were out together, measuring and weighing latex, when a native runner reached us with the news that the child had been bitten by a snake. Returning to the house, we found the baby dead, and Olga on the verge of madness. She was inconsolable, and could not be left alone for long. Even Le Blanc saw this after her second attempt at suicide. The interference this caused in our routine was considerable, for since we were working different sections of the forest, and the field and office work were inextricably mixed, neither of us could entirely take over the other's operations. However, the delay was not serious and our experiments proceeded. We took turns to go out to our respective areas, the professor going one day and I the next.

'She was not happy alone with Channel. Nor was he always at the Station. He was investigating sleeping sickness, and leprosy which was so common that no isolation had ever been attempted, and only when the leper was actually of a terrifying repulsiveness was any action taken. Then he was driven out of the village to die. Gonorrhea is almost endemic; syphilis the natives regard as serious. But I digress.

'About a month later, after the child's death, as we were eating our breakfast, the news came in that a gorilla had been trapped; and leaving Olga, who was in bed, we set off to see it.

'The distance was not great, and we soon reached the native land where it had been caught. The trap, an enormous affair like a cage of logs, tied together with rawhide strips, stood among the maize plants which had screened it, but which were now tramped down by the natives who surrounded their prize. It had been baited with a variety of banana of which these animals are inordinately fond. Already the gorilla was severely wounded in many places and bleeding profusely; this torturing being less a pastime than a religious rite among these people. They believe that by so doing they exorcise the devil which possesses it and reduce, for a time at any rate, the depredations of its fellows.

'Forcing our way through the crowd, we approached the cage. The gorilla was roaring with rage and pain. It was a female, heavy in young; a look sufficed to show us that. A further examination convinced us that the event was almost due, and it was then that Channel got his idea.

' "Pierre," he said to me, "I am going to have that young one, she can't live long."

'This was evident, a spear having pierced the gorilla's right lung.

' "Go quickly back and bring my instruments and chloroform. I will stop this spectacle." Le Blanc was seated on a log smoking a cigar. He was only interested in vegetable matter. The animal world he considered vulgar. That I had once studied medicine was almost the only thing he had against me.

'This was how Congo, as we called him later, came to be born. Channel succeeded in getting the natives to make their prisoner fast, and by the time I got back she was spread-eagled and lay gnashing her teeth with rage. To tie a gorilla down is something of a feat, but to enter the cage where she is tied is a thing I have done only once, and never propose to do again. The strength of these animals is phenomenal. They can take and twist the barrel of a rifle more easily than we can bend a pin.

'She lay there grinning up at us, blood and saliva running down her face. Her great canine teeth were bared like those of a snarling dog as she let out yell after yell. The pupils of her eyes were enormously dilated under the heavy brows.

'I had seen that look before, on the face of a homicidal lunatic; one who had killed several men. It was a mixture of ferocity and cunning. One felt that, though she had struggled mightily, she had not yet put forth her supreme endeavor. This she did when we got in. The whole cage rocked with her efforts, the mighty muscles of her swollen belly stood out like cords, and the milk spurted from her breasts. For a moment I thought she would break her bonds; had she done so, it would not have taken long to tear us, literally, into small shreds. I had imagined till that moment that I was hardened to anything, for I had seen many horrible sights; but that colossal animal lying there, chattering and coughing with rage, covered with blood, upset me. She had a man's arm beside her. We had come too late to treat him, and he had died. He would have in any case, for, coming too near, his arm had been torn from its socket as a branch might be plucked from a tree. It was not the neatly amputated limb to which one gets accustomed, but a gory lump; and Channel, in his white coat, with his instruments in his hand, was as calm as if he were about to examine a bacillus through a microscope.

'I do not believe the action of his heart was accelerated, or that he even contemplated the possibility of disaster. To him this enormous anthropoid was a scientific problem, but I felt otherwise. Perhaps, even then, I knew that evil would come of this unnatural thing.

'In the pursuit of scientific truth I have seen many strange sights, but never one to equal a Caesarian operation on a wounded gorilla in the heart of the Congo jungle.

'I should hesitate to say how much chloroform we used; some was spilt, of course, but there was not much left in a litre bottle when we had done. Needless to say, we put her out of her agony. She never woke from that sleep. The baby gorilla was wrapped up and given to a half-trained dresser; Channel had established a sort of clinic at our Station. He was bending over the dead mother, tape measure in hand, while I was helping him with his dissection before the rigor mortis set in, when to my astonishment on turning round I saw Olga with the baby gorilla at her breast. The professor was still seated. He had a fungus in his hand. It must have been on the log.

'The exact sequence of the preceding events I can only guess at. I think when she got up she sought us, and coming upon the native holding the young ape, its crumpled face so like a baby's, she took it from him instinctively. This was the more likely as the boy who held it had acted as assistant nurse to her own son, so the association of ideas would have been complete, and the gorilla, much stronger than a human child, had clutched at her. Anyhow, by the time I saw her it was done.

' "Look," I said to Channel, as he stood up with a detached muscle in his hand.

' "So," he said, "she has taken him."

'What his idea had been I do not know. Had he performed that astonishing operation out of mere curiosity? That I doubt. Had he meant to foster the child — I keep calling him that — on to a native woman? Or had it been his intention to kill it and preserve it as a specimen; one more, to be added to his already famous collection?

'And did Olga know what she had done? Again, what did we know of Olga, with her mixed blood, her strong instincts, and her veins full of experimental serums? It was a problem that could be dealt with later, Channel must have thought.

' "Take her back," he said, "and send me some bottles."
He had a storeroom full of them for specimens. "And spirits,"
he shouted after us as we left him.

'The professor accompanied us, carrying his fungus, a new
genus subsequently named after him.

'When Channel and I returned, the sun was setting, and
Olga, with the gorilla in her arms, said, "He is mine."

'That is how we returned to Brussels a year later. A professor, his assistant, his wife and her child. For that she insisted on. It was not a gorilla, but a child, and it was dressed
as a child. Only by using the great influence we had did we
succeed in getting a stateroom for them; the shipping company
maintaining that it was an animal, whereat Olga became
livid. She took her meals in the cabin, for the gorilla was very
noisy and screamed loudly if she left it.

'It is hard to describe the voyage, particularly in view of
subsequent events. Olga called it "Baby." The professor as
far as was possible never referred to it at all. If she had kept
it as a pet, it would have been different, but it slept in her bed,
Le Blanc and I sharing the next cabin. Channel had remained
in Mokala.

'The next few years I skip. There are some things one cannot write about.

'Our work, the professor's and my own, was successful beyond our wildest dreams. Of our life together with that
"thing," I will say nothing. I have already said that Olga was
beautiful, the professor no longer young, and at times absent-
minded; while I am in no way differently constituted from
other men — a fact that Olga had discovered without much
difficulty. And once it had begun, I was unable to get on without her. It is her abandonment of me, her faithlessness —
which is driving me mad.

'However, one thing was already apparent, even as early as
that — Congo hated us both; and already it was much
stronger than a man.

'How can I tell of it? — Dressed up like a boy, in a sailor suit, with socks and shoes, eating at table with us, its face like that of an old man. It still slept in the same room as Olga, and the professor in the dressing room adjoining. It had a brass bed with sheets and blankets in a corner. If it had been a child, such a thing would not have been permissible, but with the inconsistency of women Olga at those times chose to regard it as other women might a dog. But it, "he," was not a dog. Congo in his loves and hates was a primitive man; for if by heredity he was an anthropoid ape, by the environment Olga forced upon him he had made a jump from one geological era to another, and mentally must have corresponded to the Neanderthal man at least. And he was in love with Olga.

'I employ the term "in love" advisedly. That he should love her was natural, since she was his foster mother and had reared him, but it went far beyond this. His precocity may have been partially due to his feeding, which had always been the same as our own, much richer in concentrated proteins than his natural diet would have been; but it was an ugly business. Superficially his attitude towards Olga was that of an affectionate child. He clung to her hand, held her skirts. Putting his arms about her neck, he would kiss her lips with his mouth. The rest was only to be seen in his eyes when he thought himself unobserved; also there were times when, I am convinced, he was testing his strength. He did not do this by breaking things; he had got over that in his early childhood; he did it by moving them. I caught him one day with a trunk full of clothes above his head, he was holding it with both hands raised. Out of curiosity I noted its weight on the scales, seventy-five kilograms exactly. He held it as easily as a man would a parcel.

'In the meantime there have been changes. The new Station has been built. Congo is relegated to a room of his own . . .'

Retief paused. How hard it was to write! He had said

nothing about the other men. About Sebastian, of whom he had been jealous at first. About von Brandt, whose mistress Olga had become. About that ridiculous smug American whom she had no doubt seduced in their absence. That must come later. Later he would try to write of it all in the detached manner of Proust. He would get her back, he was convinced of this. The others would not last. The American would go back to America where he belonged. The German she would get tired of. The man was intolerable except as an animal.

Then things would be as they had been ... the three of them alone. Sebastian no longer counted.

But of his own feelings for Olga — could he ever write of them ... of the passion that was destroying him ... of his fear of Congo ... of his shame at the liaison by which he betrayed his benefactor? It must all ... all be put down clearly, not for others, but so that he could learn to understand himself. Today he could do no more.

Chapter 20

The EXPEDITION

〰〰〰〰〰〰〰〰

WILSON DECIDED THAT EVEN GORILLA-HUNTING MIGHT BE AN improvement on things as they were. Nothing more had happened with Olga. As far as she was concerned, nothing might have happened at all. Had that soft white body really clung to his? He thought of her lips, her breasts, her hair a pale golden rope between his fingers. He saw her again as she had been in the grey light of dawn . . . her eyes closed, her lips parted in a half-smile. And then — after such intimacy — nothing.

He had felt awkward with the professor ever since. And Retief looked at him queerly. Was he in love with her, too? Was everyone in love with her? Was von Brandt? Was the professor? It was hard to think of the professor with her.

Wilson had gone to Channel's house to say good-by to him. He was making an early start. Apropos of nothing, Channel said, 'Each man kills . . .'

'The thing he loves,' Wilson added. That was the way Channel always talked — in half sentences, in quotes, in psychological theories skipped like stones, or scientifically, or in great detail when it became a monologue. But much of his conversation was in bits, in flashes, like the passing of a bird between two trees. You soon lost it. Only the memory of what it might have been had you seen it better remained. Either that or lectures.

'Exactly,' Channel said. 'And what does a man love best?'

'A woman?' Wilson said.

'Himself. Yes,' he said softly, 'himself.'

He filled his glass.

'Himself,' Channel said again, 'his happiness. And then when he has it he destroys it. Do you know why?'

'No.'

'Because happiness is static. Man looks forward to it when he has not got it, but when he has, he fears it. It holds him up. He does not know what from ... he does not know why. So he destroys it. He rides over it — an army over a butterfly. For happiness is like that. You must not look at it too closely, you must not touch it. It is fragile ... and beautiful. So beautiful,' he added. 'I had it once.'

'Yes,' Wilson said again.

'It was long ago. I said it was not a woman, did I not? But it is only through a woman ... only by one that a man can see such butterflies. She was good,' he said. 'So good that it was embarrassing to me, and beautiful, though she did not know it. Beautiful as something small and perfect and neat is ... like a quail. Yes, she was like a quail. But it was not enough for me. I was successful. I had a name as a surgeon. I had money. I had the love of this woman, but I must torment her as a boy might torment a bird, holding it on a string.'

'And then?' Wilson said.

'And I lost it,' he said.

'Lost?'

'My happiness. After that, when I had lost her, there was nothing to stop me. I was more than successful. I was famous ... international. In Europe they still speak of me. But now I am here, where I have time to sit and drink and think. I lost, I gained, I paid. Soon after that it happened. Two of them died, and I was disgraced. I was tried for my life.'

So that was his secret. Disgraced ... two died. It was odd to think of him as an abortionist.

'A woman,' Channel went on, 'can perhaps be considered

a negative polarity, insatiable until she has found a positive polarity to equalize her desire; or a positive seeking a negative. The abstract conception is only possible to woman in exact proportion to her lack of femininity. Mentally sterile and physically potent, she challenges man to fecundate her, intriguing his mind with the pseudo-activity of her intellect, yet fearing his mind, since by it he can negate her. She thrusts the night, which is her time, into the day, which is his. Her conception of happiness is not to be forgotten. To be beaten is not to be forgotten. Man's conception of life is to forget, to lose himself in the dream of creation, the result of the dream being always less than the dream. Woman is fulfilled by action, man by thought. The love of a man can satisfy the body of a woman. But not her mind, which is filled with the fear that while he is not loving her he is lost to her; that while he is not caressing her, he has escaped her into a male beyond where she cannot follow. That he is thinking, to her means that he thinks of another woman — for to her it is inconceivable that there should be other thoughts, other aims, or other ends. That is why she says, "Tell me you love me" — "Tell me again and again — show me." She has no place in her mind for abstraction or for beauty — other than her own, the bright flower of it, that will attract the bee of man's desire to her honey.

'A sunset, to her, is not the mystery of light and shadow in the sky, not the suspended dust that causes it, but the red light which illuminates her hair; the strong shadows that will emphasize the provocation of her breasts: the fact that the sunset precedes the night, that the impact of its beauty may turn the man at her side to her. In her mind she is glad when the sunset has gone. What can one do with a sunset? In her mind when it is gone she says, "The sunset is gone, but I am here now, take me; I am reality," and the man, deceived, takes her, thinking that he holds the sunset in his arms, achieving it. Then only can she love the sunset, when it has given

her back that which it took from her: when it has placed the
man within her arms; because of this, the sunset is beautiful.'

Wilson was thinking of Olga: tomorrow he was leaving her.
The stuff was packed in his car. He would leave the car at
the store. That had been arranged. He kept seeing Olga
beside him — seeing her on her bed; seeing her at her piano.
He had said good-bye to her after dinner. He would not see
her again till he got back. How he wanted her! To hold her,
to feel her in his arms, to touch her!

Her hand when he had taken it tonight had been so cool, so
soft, so non-committal.

He went over Channel's conversation in his mind as he sat
watching him. His talk about himself: of how, as if regretting
his confidences, he had abandoned them and gone back to
generalizations.

I ought to go to bed, he thought. But he knew he would
not sleep. He might as well stay on. Over a month in terms
of time, but a lifetime in terms of events, though actually there
had been no events, no drama. Having an affair with a
woman was not a drama. It was even commonplace, or would
have been under other more ordinary circumstances. It was
not just Olga; it was ... He tried to think what it was. It was
no one thing, but many things, which had jarred him out of
his complacency. How happy I used to be! he thought. He
had been much happier before he came here, even in his unhappiness, because that had been, according to his ideas, a
natural state. Most men went through a period like this after
a divorce. They travelled and waited, then they got right
again, or nearly right.

He knew that all his talk of wanting to avoid women had
been only talk. His avoidance of them had only been provisional, and he had not actually avoided them, he had only
avoided entanglements. He had been emotionally used up.
He had meant to wait till the equilibrium was re-established.
But now he would never be as he had been ... Sometimes he

was elated by it. Sometimes depressed. The scales had
dropped from his eyes . . . the forbidden fruit . . . simile after
simile . . . cliché after cliché occurred to him. That they existed proved that there was ample precedent, but it was disconcerting to realize that he had lived like a blind puppy and
that suddenly he was beginning to see. Everyone here had
had something to do with it . . .

Channel was sitting back in his chair smoking cigarette after
cigarette.

'You have learnt a lot, I think, Mr. Wilson,' he said. 'Too
much, perhaps. But later it will help you when you have become accustomed to the pain of thought. Remember the variable, the unforeseen, the *imprévu* . . . that axioms are only axioms till destroyed by a new discovery. And if we live in an
unfortunate time, it is at least an interesting one.'

'Yes, it's interesting,' Wilson said.

'On your trip get me any skulls you can,' Channel went on,
'for my collection: gorilla, chimpanzee, monkeys, men . . .'

It was half-past one and time to go. Wilson got up.

'I shall miss you, Channel.'

'You will come back, my friend. You will permit me to call
you that? And you will be happy with Augustus Bentinck. He
is a philosopher.'

When Wilson got to the guest house, Olga was waiting for
him.

'I wanted to see you before you left. Oh, don't worry' —
she had seen his face. 'They are asleep.'

So it had not been a dream. It was about to repeat itself.
Man and woman forever, endlessly, repeating themselves.

Chapter 21

The FOREST

‸‸‸‸‸‸‸‸‸‸‸‸‸‸

WHEN WILSON DROVE DOWN TO THE STORE, THE PORTERS WERE camped round it. He left his car covered with a bucksail in a shed.

'Take us three days to get anywhere,' Bentinck said.

Anywhere meant the real forest.

Last night came back to him. Why was he going on this ridiculous safari when he might have been with Olga? Channel wanted him to bring back skulls. He wondered what Olga was doing. I am going on a gorilla hunt, he thought. But they might see none. He knew this wasn't the right spirit, but it seemed a very reasonable attitude. The idea, as an excuse, since they needed one apparently, was all right, but surely the idea was enough. It would be nobody's fault if they failed to encounter a gorilla.

They passed through two villages and halted at a third. The headman — an unpleasant-looking man with filed teeth — was a friend of Bentinck's. They greeted each other almost effusively.

'He's going to send a message for us,' Bentinck said. 'We'll soon find out if there are any gorillas about.'

The chief got out his drum. It was hollowed out of a log which had been emptied through a small vent at the side.

The headman stopped playing and listened with his hand cupped to his ear. The message had been picked up. There was a distant drumming to the north, another to the west. He seemed satisfied, and nodded his head.

Near the hut which had been allocated to them, Jan was breaking eggs. He had a basket beside him. The eggs were about the size of a pigeon's, and only one in ten was fit to eat. To the natives an egg was an egg, a day old or a month old, with a chicken in it or no chicken. Since they liked nestling birds themselves, the fertile eggs seemed preferable and the white man's prejudice against them an affectation. There were also some chickens, a fluttering heap, with their legs tied together, and two goats tethered to a tree. Jan produced a bottle of whisky, glasses, and some lukewarm water.

The villagers stood in a circle round them. The porters were talking to friends they had found and making passes at the women. Only the five Masai, who had decided on their sleeping place, were aloof, composed, squatting with their weapons beside them.

This was not the real wilds. It was a village just off the beaten track, but it was wild enough, puzzling enough, to find oneself here. And to have come so easily.

Wilson watched Bentinck pour another whisky, about four fingers. Jan brought the dinner. An omelette, Campbell's soup, and two roast chickens that tasted as if they were made of rubber. The boys were eating the goats.

After dinner they drank tea, more whisky, and stared into the fire. They could still hear the drums talking in the distance.

The chief came back to speak to Bentinck.

'He says there are gorillas everywhere, but that we had better go up the river by boat and then strike into the mountains; that's where they are thickest. He has arranged everything. There will be canoes above the falls.'

Now a boat trip was being added.

It was nearly dark. In a few minutes the night would fall, swiftly without warning, a black cloak dropped over them. The natives played their drums tentatively, but slowly the sound increased till it filled the forest, echoing and re-echoing

against its walls. Talking drums, war drums, sacred drums —
ordinary little drums to be tapped for pleasure. The drums of
Africa. A soft wind stirred the leaves, ghostlike wraiths of mist
twisted in and out of the huts, white against the blue smoke of
the fires. The natives had waited till the messages had been
sent before they began their own music. Wilson tried to concentrate on what he saw. For my book, he thought. He wondered if he would ever write it. The women cooking, moving
with totos on their hips. The men drumming, chanting, sitting passively waiting for nothing. The village was just a long
street with the forest behind it. The throbbing drums tore at
his nerves.

This was the real, unchanging Africa. And last night he had
been with Olga. He thought of her dresses, of her body undressed, of her voice as she sang, of the swish of her skirt, of
her golden slippers, of her green mules edged with maribou.
This was not just fifteen miles away from the settlement . . . It
was a thousand years away in time. Everything here had the
feeling of immense age. Wilson thought of the march today:
along paths wide enough for a single man, beaten into the
earth by a hundred thousand padding feet. The buzzing of the
insects had only intensified the silence of the jungle. The whole
place smelt of moist, green leaves; of rotting vegetation; of
death and growth; of that continual metabolism of which
Channel had spoken. Growing — dying. The thud of a
falling fruit, the crack of splitting seed. The occasional raucous cry of a parrot. A monkey's scream, then silence again
and the hum of insects. Sometimes a shaft of sunlight penetrated the jungle, lighting up the leaves. You saw yourself,
your life, a pin-point in space and time. You saw yourself as
nothing, and yet to yourself you were the world: the centre of
the universe.

The drums were still beating. The natives, their bodies
black satin shot with orange, crouched over the fires.

'The Belgians got a lot of rubber here in the old days,' Bentinck said. 'They killed thousands of niggers. Bad lot. Cut off their hands and nailed 'em onto their bungalows just to show the others what happened to the boys who didn't bring in rubber. But it got them in the end. The forest, I mean. Couldn't do anything against it . . . sent 'em crazy. Yes, they paid. In the end everybody pays. It's a comforting thought.'

When they reached the river, millions of fish were trying to get up the falls. Thousands jumped, thousands fell. The banks of the river were lined with tall elephant grass. Every few yards it was broken by a hippo path. Crocodiles lay on the sand shoals. They slept with their jaws wide open while little tick birds ran in and out of their mouths.

Above the falls the river flowed between the trees. Massive as walls, the masonry of the forest clothed the banks with green cliffs that leant perilously inward. Except for a village here and there, there was no break in the jungle. The water ran, a menacing, slow-flowing, ink-black current — an artery squeezed between the flesh of a vegetation rank, primeval, and impenetrable. Except for the dip and drip of the paddles, nothing broke the silence.

Hour after hour the river unrolled past the canoes. There was no change in the color of the water or of the green cliffs. What they saw now was indistinguishable from what they had seen an hour ago, six hours ago. More camps. Nights passed in huts put at their disposal by chiefs or headmen. Bentinck knew them all. Huts shared with scorpions, with enormous cockroaches that ate the calluses from your feet. Nights of sitting drearily before the fire — days and nights of utter unreality.

Then a three days' march and they came out of the lowland forest into that of the mountains. This was the last camp before the hunt began.

The gorillas were here all right. The natives in this village had a young one that they wanted to sell. It had a bad cough.

Channel had said they were very susceptible to pulmonary complaints as were the natives themselves.

'They say they heard them talking near the huts last night,' Bentinck said.

'Heard whom?' Wilson asked.

'Gorillas.'

'Talk?'

'That's what they call it. And perhaps it is talk. I've heard them myself.'

Among the bigger natives were Pigmies apparently owned by them.

Wilson was filled with a strange excitement. He still did not want to hunt gorillas, but he was getting nearer to the heart of this dark, steaming world.

He was up in time to see the sun burn away the mists of night. The people of the village were moving, carrying water, cooking. The women suckled babies at long black breasts. While they were at breakfast the chief brought a man to see them who had been bitten by a gorilla. He had gone into his garden one morning — the chief pointed to some bananas and paw-paws a hundred yards away — and the gorilla had leaped on him. It had bitten him through the calf — biting out the muscle like an apple. The man seemed proud of his wound.

This was the high rain forest: eight thousand feet above sea level ... a solid jungle of trees lashed together with tough lianas, veined by tunnelled gorilla paths that were like fish traps.

Sometimes Wilson could walk upright. At others he had to crawl. He was soon soaked with sweat; when he stopped he was cold. There were small clearings where tree ferns spread their fronds above his head: thickets of bamboo, monstrous lobelias thirty feet high, giant rhododendrons. A wonderland — a nightmare.

One of the hunters pointed to the left. There was a gorilla's nest. Near-by were his droppings. Bentinck touched them. 'Hot,' he said.

Hot gorilla droppings. In front of them was a deep ravine — a solid mass of verdure, a thick carpet that grew up from a black pit. Then came the noise Wilson had dreaded. A gorilla hammering the barrel of his chest. He had heard Congo do it. But Congo was young. This was an adult. Then it screamed. It was a terrible sound.

Bentinck raised his rifle. Wilson did the same, but a rifle seemed inadequate. There was little room to shoot. What was it Bentinck had told him? They charge and then run back . . . suppose it did not run back? The hammering ceased. The forest was silent. A branch cracked near-by. Bentinck lowered his rifle.

'Got away,' he said.

They returned to camp.

That night sleep was impossible. While Bentinck snored, Wilson counted sheep hopelessly. Then he gave up counting sheep. He gave up the idea of sleep. There were things he wanted to figure out.

He wondered how much men were affected by things that they thought were imperceptible . . . He had known he was near gorillas before he had heard them or seen the nest.

Were there unheard sounds, unsmelt odors? An owl was hooting. Twice the hoots coincided with Bentinck's snores. This struck him as remarkable. Then it alternated with the snores. Then the owl stopped.

He thought of liquor, sex, tobacco . . . Each was a single sensual pleasure. Each should be savored alone. But man was not satisfied with that. He mixed his sensations like a drink; he was in a state of continued emotional hangover: a state of neurosis. To cure himself, to keep going, he kept taking more of the hair of the dog that had bitten him. He never left himself time to think.

One should learn to separate things, to divide one's emotions, feelings, appetites, satisfactions. Bentinck said the natives had even two words for hunger. There was hunger, and hunger for meat when they were meat-mad for lack of it. But were things as simple as this ... as divisible? Did not even desires merge into each other?

To think of gorillas made him think of Olga. He wondered if he was jealous of her alone among the men at the Station. He decided he was jealous, but almost less of them than of the time that he spent away from her. He could not think of her as he had thought of other women. She was so different. Her life had been so different, which was why time was more of an enemy than men. She seemed apart from men, however much she knew of them ...

Bentinck was snoring louder now.

Chapter 22

The WIFE

~~~~~~~~~~~~~~~~~~~

OLGA THOUGHT OF WILSON AS SHE TURNED OFF THE RADIO. THE news in no way coincided with the opinions expressed in the two-months-old papers. The papers were sure there would be no war. Things would be arranged. Munich had proved how things could be arranged amicably. Hitler did not want war. He was a man of peace. The German army was the European bastion protecting civilization from the anarchy of Russian communism . . . The delusions of foreign correspondents, the policy of newspaper owners amused her. It was the old expediency; it was fear; it was whistling in the dark. But the radio — she had been listening to short-wave — told another story.

'You think, Olga . . . ?' the professor asked.

'War, Jean.'

'And here?'

'The repercussions.' She knew better than her husband what they would be. Risings of German planters; rebellion in South-West Africa and the Union. Sometimes she wondered if Jean did not know how well informed she was. This was one of the moments. His next remark proved it.

'There are some papers,' he said. 'Perhaps they might be safer with you.'

'That is for you to decide,' she said. 'I could put them in my safe.'

'Rubber is not as complex as is generally imagined, Olga.

It can be made from almost anything ... Cellulose,' he said, 'oil, coal, plants.' He paused. 'But it's a pity if it comes now. In another year I should have had what we wanted, or been near to it.'

'You are a valuable man, Jean.'

'I am a very happy one,' he said, 'with my work and with you; but if war comes again ...'

Olga lit a cigarette. Bentinck and Wilson might find out something. She wished there was some way of getting news of them. If there was war, they would hear of it and know what to do. If it came over the air, she'd tell the boys. Within a few minutes the drums would be tapping and the message relayed on. There was no danger of anyone being taken by surprise. The thought amused her. I'll get it by radio, she thought, and send it on by drum: the old and the new.

She thought of Wilson again. She wanted him back. She looked at her husband. He had readjusted his glasses and was once more absorbed in a story by Agatha Christie: the 'Murder on the Links.' He has his books and his discoveries, she thought. She had a tenderness for her husband. It was a pity that women should make nice men unhappy. If there was war, she would have her revenge on von Brandt ... she'd teach him to have affairs with colored girls ... She would teach him to respect women.

She went in to Congo, but soon had to leave him. Her nervousness communicated itself to the gorilla. She could always tell when he was getting dangerous. The pupils of his eyes became enlarged; he danced on stiff legs; he slapped his chest. She might be perfectly controlled outwardly, but she could never hide her feelings from him.

There would be war.

But meanwhile life went on with the same exactitude. Channel was coming to dinner. There were final orders to give: flowers to arrange. They would play bridge afterward. She wondered if she could bear Retief's reproachful eyes much longer. It meant so much to him: so little to her. And to Jean, even if he found out . . . probably nothing at all. Poor Jean was not defrauded.

Channel said a woman was a contemporary ancestor; that she was always looking inward and backward; that women hated machinery, finance, and were bored by complex manipulations. They did not even fall in love by their eyes as men did. The radiations of the male might affect them, but it was only cumulative when tactual. Actual physical conjunction had to take place — a touch of hands, a kiss. How funny that sounded to a woman! But he was right when he spoke of the psychic qualities of women. They were all to some extent psychic. Mediums, clairvoyants, witches, were always women. Wizards and sorcerers were much less common. One could laugh at all that sort of thing, but there was good reason to suppose that, despite the charlatanism, the swindling, the cheap palmists, there was something that went beyond the normally accepted. Channel had proved it beyond doubt with his experiments.

She tried to think when the last witch had been burned. It was not so long ago: the late seventeenth century, she thought. The witch, the gipsy, the wise woman, the ancient midwife, still existed in Central Europe . . . anywhere where the country people were untouched by civilization.

Perhaps it was foolish to think so much, to search for motive as she did. Sometimes she regretted her education: the fact that by her association with her husband, Retief, and Channel — above all Channel — she had learnt to analyze. And her French mother had had something to do with it. Educated French women had a tradition of love. They thought about it philosophically. They read about it. Though her mother had been killed when she was a child, she had been influenced by her. The yellow paper-backed novels on the shelf were the same as her mother's; not the same books, but books of the same type in the same bindings with the same pages that had to be cut with a paper-knife. The Nuns had been unable to eradicate her memories.

How strange that hardly any love stories were written about men and women, only about boys and girls. Why was it assumed that adults could not love? Why this arbitrary assumption? Up to thirty love was apparently charming and admirable; after that it became indecent, decadent. The charm, then, must lie in the ignorance, or innocence if you liked, of the lovers. Blundering love was beautiful. The love of those who had loved before was not. Carry it farther. Then the first flight of a young bird was lovely as it fluttered, afraid, in this new strange element, and the soaring flight of the adult beneath contempt.

One of the most beautiful love stories she had ever read was about a pair of birds, of ducks. De Maupassant . . . she got up to get the book. She turned the pages. There it was: 'Love.' The passage she liked came towards the end:

' "You have killed the duck," he said, "and the drake will not fly away."

'He certainly did not fly away: he circled over our heads continually. . . . Occasionally he took flight under the menace of the gun which followed his movements, and seemed ready to continue his flight alone, but as he could not make up his mind to do this, he returned to find his mate . . . he fell . . . it was as if someone had cut the string which held the bird suspended. . . .'

Olga closed the book. That was love. Something no one was able to explain. A glandular basis? What nonsense! That was sex, was pleasure . . . delightful while it lasted, but without significance. But love . . . was something else. That 'what else' might be the thing that drove you on. Perhaps one had to go on till one found it . . . perhaps the more one went on, the less likely one was to find it. What was love? What was love at first sight? Shakespeare had said: 'Who ever lov'd that lov'd not at first sight?'

Was it coincidence that in all de Maupassant, this story about the ducks was the only one which was without cynicism, without afterthought, without selfishness?

She thought of love again ... the ideal love of a pair of ducks. The so-called love; the mutual sexual pleasure of the ordinary man, '*L'homme moyen sensuel*,' and the ordinary woman. She thought of royal ladies who had satisfied themselves with their household guards. But there were plenty of little bourgeois wives who went to market with their baskets on their arms who were the same, only one did not read about them. They did not make history, only love. She had no confidence in cold women. It was because they had not been made love to. There were women who had had children, who had been married for years, and never experienced pleasure.

She put de Maupassant back on the shelf.

Channel was dining with them again. Jean was going to give her his papers to take care of.

She went to look at her clothes. If what she would wear was less important with Wilson away, the clothes themselves were important. Particularly those she had worn for him.

Chapter 23

The DOCTOR

CHANNEL HAD PERFORMED ANOTHER AMPUTATION UNDER hypnosis. He had just finished describing the operation in his case book. There it was, just another. No phenomenon, but something that he had come to expect. Yet it was because of these operations that he had been discredited. I, he thought, I, discredited when Paris is still full of surgeons who are abortionists. There was no danger in such a trade, provided you only helped the rich — the society women, who could not be bothered to have a child. That was in order. But help a working girl and see what happened. There was du Chêne the specialist ... Mon Dieu! He knew one of the cases he had had. A woman, the wife of a politician, who had been cured, yes, that was the word, of menstruation by means of local X-ray. She had hated her husband. She did not want to have a child, and it was a nuisance. Du Chêne had even thought it comic. But what had happened? She had met someone else. There had been a divorce. With her new husband, whom she had loved, she had wished to make a child and could not. And then finally a suicide. A young woman, beautiful. He had seen her: she had come to him, but too late. What could he do with her?

'You do such wonderful things, I hear, Doctor Channel.'

Fools, did they not see that he worked with nature, with God, and not against them? How dared a man do what du Chêne had done? How dared he interfere with the processes of life? What did man know of the checks and balances, of the finer metabolisms, of the relation of the body and the soul; of glands, of vitamins, hormones? Only the beginning, the edge of things, had been reached. Some day someone would penetrate the true mysteries. Some day someone would begin to understand.

First Mesmer. Then the brothers Puységur had confirmed his findings, but had proved that, though he was right in what he had found, he was wrong in his description of it. Experts who always hated any change claimed that, since the magnet was not necessary in hypnosis, hypnosis itself did not exist. Then the brothers, removing all physical contacts and continuing Mesmer's research, saw that they had come upon a new power. Electrical research proved that electricity was not fluid. It was this research on electricity which overthrew the mechanistic theory. Electricity, which had been considered a curious anomaly, was found to be the basic tie of the universe. Cohesion, magnetism, and gravitation were all seen as manifestations of this fundamental energy: matter itself was realized to be only the play of electric charges.

Therapy followed. Hypnosis was used to heal. No one went beyond this. Normalcy was the aim. No one inquired what normalcy was or why men became so tortured as to lose it.

Sigmund Freud's was no solution. It was only the partial development of an immense theme. Freud had only added the bedroom act to the conversation of the drawing room. He had not explained it. His concept of cause and effect was an oversimplification. The greatest mystery he had not touched. That mystery was 'the force,' of which sex was only a single manifestation.

Through the window Channel could see Sebastian's girls. They were sitting on the ground outside his house. They were just being. They were fundamental. They were more female than Olga because they were, as organisms, infinitely simpler.

The more civilized the race, or the individual, the more in
character or spirit did the two sexes approach each other.
A native man and woman were very simple. Warrior...
woman. All the relations between them were on that basis.
But a cultured man and woman in conversation often forgot
their sexual difference and approached each other intel-
lectually, as two brains in communion. Granted that as a
rule there were few friendships between men and women in
which there were no sexual possibilities, there were times
when these possibilities were forgotten. It was probable that
almost every man and woman who went out to lunch together
would, under certain circumstances, go to bed together should
those circumstances arise. Both were probably aware of this,
though neither sought the circumstance and might even avoid
it. But the Batanga girls were natural women. It was because of this naturalness that many white men who had lived
with native women never went back to their own race. Their
relations with these women was one which satisfied them,
because it was without other implications. A native woman
might destroy a man's soul through his own lust for her, but
she did not impinge upon it in other ways. He could live a
private mental life of his own parallel to that of his animality.
Either civilized men and women must come much nearer to
each other or they must break away from each other as was
happening in the Fascist countries.

How much he had thought and written on this subject!
When he died his manuscripts would be published. Indeed,
his publishers in America were looking forward to his demise,
which showed their appreciation of his work. They had told
him so very politely, disguising their wishes with flowery
euphemisms. 'They wanted to publish now or soon, they
hoped...' But his work would not be published now. It was
his justification, and no man still alive should justify. That
was contemptible. *Qui s'excuse s'accuse*... Besides, his hypnotic experiments had been carried to such lengths here that

they might be considered a felony. His own books proved what he had done. A few of his patients had died. That they would have died anyway would be considered no excuse, and he had had relations with local witch doctors. It had pleased him to find that Bentinck also believed in them.

It was amusing to discuss women with Sebastian and sorcery with Bentinck. Each was ignorant of theory and each advanced in practice. But the ends they had reached, by such dissimilar means, approximated his own. If he had done no more in his life, he had at least laid the foundation for further discovery.

He was dining with the Le Blancs. They would play bridge. It would be as it had been before the coming of the American — just the four of them. Sebastian rarely joined them. He despised dinner as function. They would have coffee and brandy and smoke cigars: the professor had good cigars. He had half an hour more, in which to rest and think.

Science was not the exact thing it had been considered. It was the study, not of mathematical exactitude, but of mystery. The scientist was the priest of today. His failure was that he had sold himself to practicality. It struck Channel that he spoke very rarely of his beliefs. It was easier to talk about women and write the other things. His books were interlocking. His book, of theory, entitled 'Force.' His book, of practice, detailed his experiments, and finally there was his daybook, a combination of diary and case book. In that everything was included — the factual and theoretical: his thoughts, his acts, and a description of his daily life for nearly fifty years. They would be attacked as inconclusive. But what did people expect? Did they really think there were conclusions? To conclude was to end. To end was to die. His books were an affirmation of life and a denial of actual death which was in his opinion as impossible as actual birth.

Birth and death because of their dramatic nature had been overemphasized. A baby was born. It became suddenly visible, actual; but it had been present for a hundred and eighty days. It had, in addition, been potentially present for a hundred and eighty million years, since the beginning of time. Both life and death had been removed from their context in the pattern of life as a continuous process. One in which the individual was supremely unimportant.

In a modern city few were aware of the process. This could only be accomplished by seeing birth and death: by hearing a woman cry out in childbirth, or by standing bareheaded as a funeral cortège passed. The old funerals had served a psychological purpose with their draped and plumed black horses going at a walk as they drew the hearse; with drivers in black wearing cocked hats upon their heads; with mourners in carriages and on foot. All that had gone, and with it had gone the idea of continuity. Man today was suspended in the vacuity of the immediate moment. Many, denying their psychic destiny, were on the verge of suicide. Man must have belief ... hope; the idea of something that transcended the material. War was mass suicide made possible by this uncertainty; because with so many means there were no ends.

Individualism was destroying man because he did not know how to profit by it. The Fascist tendency was reaction, a retrograde movement towards a tribal system that had been outgrown. Anarchy must follow unless man became cooperative by individual choice. Man's natural, instinctive cooperation had gone, but he was left with his impulse to combine, and if the economic system would not allow him to combine for peace, he would turn, furiously thwarted, and combine for war. If it came, it would not only be the end of an era, but of an aeon.

He poured himself a final drink. 'To the man of the future.' It was amusing to talk to oneself, to think aloud.

He was still laughing when he closed the door of his bedroom. He wondered how Wilson was getting on in the forest ... if he had shot a gorilla yet. He had thought about him a

lot. Coming from the outer world, he had disturbed them all.
Perhaps it was good to be disturbed.

Channel put on his decorations: his war medals, his *croix de guerre*, his *médaille militaire* with its green and yellow ribbon; his scarlet-ribboned *Légion d'Honneur*. They had taken this away from him, but he continued to wear it. The miniatures jingled on the lapel of his white mess jacket as he put it on. Medals, honors for service in war, for gallantry, for his services to humanity in medicine and surgery. These things were earned. They were like wound scars. They could not be taken away by the arbitrary act of a mentally defective academy; by a jealous faculty, by abortionists, by butchers, by ... cretins, morons, criminals; by politicians. This was Channel's last and final insult — to call a man a politician. He was working himself up into a rage. How had they dared to touch him with their Iscariot fingers! What regard had they for the Oath of Hippocrates? What kind of world was it where the 'ancient combatant' could be insulted by lecherous time-seekers, by sycophants, by the kissers of the public behind; by the powers of a church, which was now but a temporal Fascist organ ... by the mass of *petits bourgeois* ... by shopkeepers, scullions ... camels ... pederasts ... female dogs. How had they dared to pull him down? How had they been able to?

He touched his medals. Why had he put them on? Because he had been drinking? Because of the feeling of war in the air? One did nothing without a reason, but what was the reason? He hardly ever wore them. He had not worn them on the Fourteenth of July.

He pulled his short jacket down; pulled the military overalls up. They fitted his legs tightly. He was proud of his figure. Then he readjusted the scarlet cummerbund that covered his stomach. He looked down at it with pride: flat and hard as board. He had never had any trouble with his stomach. He was a man of moderate if catholic appetites. Most men ate too much, it became a habit. They distended their intestines and confused distension with repletion. They did not eat because they were hungry. They gorged till their great gut was full and pressing against the belly-band of their trousers. Both gluttony and drunkenness disgusted him, particularly if he had been drinking. A man could get drunk on food or women . . . drunkenness was not confined to over-indulgence in alcohol. Once gluttony had been condemned as a sin. Now all sin was contracted to the sexual act when it was not sanctified by marriage. Treachery, usury, the bearing of false witness were no longer condemned.

He adjusted his tie — a black butterfly perched at his throat. He pulled down his cuffs and looked to see that they were not frayed. His Wellingtons shone brightly. His hair — he looked in the glass — was tidy, his moustache was neatly waxed. In fact, he was ready — a credit to himself and to any place he went.

When he arrived, the others were waiting.

'We have been speaking of the war,' Olga said.

'The war?' He had been thinking of it himself. It was in everyone's mind.

'Yes, there will be war,' Olga said.

'I think so, too.' Channel took a Martini. 'But a new war will not be the war to me. The war is always the war you were in — that which came closest to you. The other wars have names, but that one is just *the war*. It stands isolated in your experience. It ranks with marriage, with the death of parents, or the birth of a child. It is the illustration in the book of your life. And that is because it has changed you. Not only physically by wounds or hardship, but mentally . . . afterward life seems very slow and quiet. In war you have no time to examine detail. Things move too fast . . . each hour a swirling vortex of action, of exhaustion, of boredom so intense that it becomes an active, palpable force against which you strive, wrestling with the minutes as you wonder when it will end: thinking of your home, of your young wife, hoping she is well and happy ... worshipping her, desiring her.

'You see her as you left her, being brave on the steps of the house, at the station, her eyes wide with withheld tears ...'

He drank his Martini, he nibbled the olive, holding it between his fingers.

'I think of France,' he said. 'A country suffering from overcivilization, a country of individuals, of peasants, of rentiers ... of people who demand only security in which to argue, to fornicate, to eat, to rear families, to save money, to drink wine. How beautiful the ideal of France, the idea of it! How decadent the practice of being French ... *la gloire* ... *la patrie* — *fraternité* ... *égalite* ... *liberté* — phrases, catchwords that have upon occasions almost come true.

'And myself?' He took another drink; he felt himself on the crest of the conversational wave. His mind was clear. 'I believe in Christ, in the Sermon on the Mount. But only as an atheist.' He was silent, lost in the implication of his own words. The Christ, for instance. He did not believe that Jesus was the Son of God, born of an immaculate conception. But why quarrel with those who did? Why not start from there, from Christ himself? There one found oneself in perfect accord. A good man. A wonderful man. A man with powers that were called miraculous because they were not understood. He believed in the miracles, but only with the corollary that others could also perform miracles. Cures by Christian Scientists and at Lourdes had been confirmed by competent observers. Since these were medically inexplicable, they were miracles. The interesting thing was not the method, but the principle ... the common denominator: the esoteric truth that bound the Pope of Rome to Mrs. Eddy; that tied Mrs. Eddy to the Lamas of Thibet, to the Indian fakir, and the Kaffir witch doctor. The philosophers of all nations, at all times, had been in agreement as far as principles

went, with only a few exceptions. Odd that the exceptions
should be German — Nietzsche, Spengler ... Good men of
any religion had everything in common but their dogma.
Where they differed was in the drill, the technique by which
they strove for a similar end. What quarrel had a good
Christian with a good Mohammedan, a good Buddhist, a
good follower of Confucius, a good Jew? Surely they had
more about which to agree than to disagree.

He thought of the spiritual aspirations of men as a country
— the Heaven of the Christians. That land was on the far
side of a river. On this side stood all mankind. Each religion
had built a bridge across that river. The river itself was time.
The waters that flowed down it — the days of a man's years,
the thousand months he might hope to live. The land on the
far side was the land of good, of hope, of the spirit and the
aspiration. The land on this side was the land of the flesh.
Good men of all races tried to cross the bridges, the bad ones
looked at them and spat.

Olga was staring at him. He should not dream like this.

'You are beautiful tonight, madame,' he said. He felt
himself old, tired. There was no virtue in him. He should
have known better than to drink after performing an operation.

Chapter 24

The LOVER

RETIEF'S AFFAIR WITH OLGA HAD RECOMMENCED. IT HAD GONE on intermittently for years — stopping while she had other lovers; starting again as she tired of them.

He sat in his room staring out of the window. It had begun again where it had left off nearly a year ago. And what did he get from her? Torment... relief from torment, and the days between while desire mounted uncontrollably. Misery ... oblivion ... more misery ... more oblivion.

Why was he drawn to her? Had she any sensibilities? Did she feel anything but a spasmodic desire which any man could satisfy?

Here he was, betraying the professor on Tuesdays and Fridays, running like a train on a schedule. Why Tuesday and Friday?

Wednesday and Saturday he was still content. On Thursday and Sunday he was ashamed. Friday he was ready again. Monday tormented. A strange rhythm, a cycle of adulterous satisfaction, of shame, of anticipation, of regret.

He picked up his pen. 'That American has gone,' he wrote. 'Von Brandt is apparently occupied and it has begun again. Congo knows. I feel that he knows. I feel that nothing good can come out of this evil. I am a rationalist. But I still know right from wrong, and this is wrong. It is destructive, symptomatic of the time in which we live. We give each other mutual pleasure. That is the way she puts it, but I am without confidence. It is only because the American is away. It is not that I am jealous of him. He is incomparably foolish, rich, smug, self-satisfied, and insensitive. He has gone to hunt gorillas in the forest with Bentinck. Could anything be more foolish than to destroy the great apes in their home? The destruction of gorillas, as of charity, should begin at home. Everything is due to Congo. Something happened to Olga that day. It was not just the loss of her infant. It is her preoccupation with the wild beast that she has nourished at her breasts.'

To think of a gorilla suckled at them was an obscenity. He put down the pen. To think of her caressed by those black hands... He put the end of his pen into his mouth. I must write, he thought. I must write or I shall go mad. Suppose the professor found what he wrote? Well, suppose he did? In a way he would be glad. It was written for himself, but if it was found... He was not even particularly careful of it. An end must come: an explosion. There were limits. He could not define them; he merely knew that there were limits to what he could bear.

It was Tuesday again. She had said after lunch: in the guest house. It was easy for him to get away... But Wilson's house! What cruelty... what sadism! Only a woman would think of a thing like that. He thought with longing of the bed ... of Olga. That was what she meant... to humiliate him, to destroy his pride. But to what end? To enjoy some distorted mental debauch, an orgy of the mind as well as of the body? Or did she just hate men?

He wished he knew more about women. His student days had been lived very correctly. If they had not been, he might have been better equipped to meet the situation which confronted him. But if they had not been, he would never have met the professor. Cause, effect; more cause, new effects... the squirrel cage of psychological action and reaction. He could not remember the beginning of this business. The first time, yes. Naturally. But what had led up to it? How had he become her lover? How had the American? How had von Brandt? How had Sebastian? She had made little attempt to keep them secret. In all this there was a hidden mechanism that he did not understand.

And the appetite came with eating. The more he had of her, the more he wanted. It disgusted him. Why should he wish to do this thing? Why did he watch the clock so carefully? Why did he move so uneasily in his chair? Why could he not write all this in his journal? It had been his intention to do so.

He paced up and down the room. Five minutes more. In half an hour he would be back here, nothing would be changed. The table, the chair, the pen: all would be the same. He would be the same. Olga would be the same. When they met tonight, it would be as if nothing had passed. And what would have passed? A consummation of the sexual act between a man and a woman. Everything . . . Nothing? It was everything before it happened. It would be nothing for a short time after it had happened. An appetite relieved. Then it would begin again. An act whose importance was variable in a direct ratio to the intervals between its accomplishment.

He could hear Congo shuffling up and down in his room. That meant she had gone. Congo always knew when she was out of the house.

Had the clock stopped? It was four minutes to two. He looked at the place where the hands would be when it was two-thirty. He would be back here then. As yet it had not begun. Then it would be over. His thoughts bore no relation to reality. He liked to think reasonably, scientifically. But this was beyond reason. Sebastian was wiser than he. 'Of God,' Sebastian would say. 'It is of God.' A strange God if this was of God. 'Of the Devil,' Owen would say. A strange Devil, if this was of the Devil.

Two minutes to two.

One minute to two.

Retief was back in his room. Everything was the same: the
table, the chair, the pen.

He had thought of its all being the same. He looked at the
clock: at the place where the hands had been when he left.
The hands had gone on moving while he was away. Time
had passed . . . irrevocably.

The clock was an accompaniment to life: the ticking
seconds a mechanical pulse which marked the passage of
what man called time. Actually there was no such thing. It
was a fiction. Man was better without it. Animals knew
nothing of time. They lived, bred, and died within time, but
without it. He thought of himself, of his ignorance. He was
like a child. The difference between a man and a child was
that the child was without precedents. Because a thing had
not happened before, a child had no way of guessing results,
no way of guarding itself.

He felt rested, without tension. His mind was freed. Only
temporarily, as he knew from experience, but for the moment
free. Had he harmed the professor? Olga was still the same.
He had taken nothing from her. She was not damaged. In
fact, she was better. She was always better afterward; happier; sleeker. Purring like a cat as it sat by the warm fire lick-
ing its fur, smoothing it; flexing its limbs, driving its claws
into the furniture and stretching.

There was no solution. Of God . . . of the Devil . . . of
magnetic attraction . . . of this . . . of that . . . A thousand
answers. No answers. Did everyone torture himself like this?
Did everyone seek an answer to desire, to lust, to love? He
picked up his pen again.

I was holding it like this before, he thought. He looked at
his hand. It held the pen. He looked at the clock. His hand
only a few minutes ago had been cupped on Olga's breast.
Now it held a fountain pen. Warm flesh. Black vulcanite . . .

I should be able to write now, to describe my sensations clinically, he thought. But he could not. He lay down on his bed. He experienced a delightful lassitude ... a wonderful clarity of mind. He thought of the professor's little Burma teak trees — not of his wife. They had done quite well. There had been no necessity to plant them except as an experiment. Such trees were not a commercial proposition. He thought of rubber; of the forest, silent and menacing; of gorillas; of Congo again; and then of Olga. He had not been able to think of her directly — only through Congo. He was astonished at the fact which he knew to be true ... that by Friday he would want her again.

The sexual urge had nothing to do with the desire for reproduction. The result of such intercourse was merely the by-product of desire. The Australian aborigines did not even associate the act and the result.

A man says to a woman, 'I love you ... I love you.' Then he loves her. Was this all he could do? Did this act, which, however much it might be disguised with sacraments and orange blossoms, remained an animal act, sum up the spiritual aspirations of his love? Did its utter inadequacy, save in terms of mechanistic sexual relief, have any bearing on his overwhelming desire to give, to become, to share? Could its repetition do more than repeat its inadequacy?

This is where I am lost, he thought, overwhelmed by the immensity of my cerebral conception. Because I am human, I fail as an animal. Because this thing I want to give ... to have, is not there. It never can be there. The idea is that of pure beauty ... absolute beauty ... an abstraction that could only be represented by a mathematical formula expressing the ultimate essence of all beauty, or by a poem. Yes, he thought, my love can be represented by an algebraic x. Against this adamantine x I shatter my life, spending it like a prisoner behind the bars of a dungeon.

'The symbol is all I have.' He was conducting an imaginary

conversation now. 'That is why I bring you a single rose, or six dark red carnations, or lilies of the valley. When I give them to you, I give you all beauty. Nothing I can do, no intimacy we may share, will be the half of this, for this is everything; that I should give them, that you should wear them on your breast.' The symbol greater than the consummation, the shadow greater than the substance.

'When I hold your hand, I hold everything. All of you, if you will. Between my hands and yours there runs a vital tide.' Man and woman . . . we hold hands and are silent. In our minds we consummate all beauty. But only because it is unstated; because this is the sunrise. We have no power to penetrate farther. After this we begin to disintegrate — again becoming two things — the mind and the body. The psychic balance is broken. In being two things we cease to be one. We become four. Your mind and body; my mind and body. No longer masters, we are slaves, with too much body to satisfy our minds; with too much mind to satisfy our bodies.

'I love you. I love you. The sun is setting, the silken sea is molten gold. It merges into the golden sky. There is the evening star alone: the first and brightest star shining in the lilac sky. The big fish jumps. The heron flies. Its neck is folded back, its legs stretched out. It is black against the sky. Then do I love you. I love you out there under the stars, upon the sands. I know you see them when you open your eyes.' Would the woman to whom he spoke these words in his mind understand? Would Olga have understood? But it was not for Olga or to her that he had spoken. It was to the woman of his dreams . . . the woman of all men's dreams. The ultimate woman, dream-sought and only found in dreams.

Tonight they would play bridge.
Friday he would make love to Olga again.
Retief turned over and went to sleep.

Chapter 25

The GARDEN

〰〰〰〰〰〰〰〰

OLGA WAS IN THE GARDEN WITH CONGO.

The garden was no longer what it had been when Wilson had come. Superficially it was the same, because there were no seasons here. The roses were out; the hibiscus and the bougainvillea were still in bloom. The Cape jasmine was still in flower; the blue flowers of the plumbago hedge were still blue. But the actual flowers had changed. There were new flowers, new buds; a new fragrance which resembled the old exactly, but which was not the same. Her situation, Olga felt, resembled that of someone walking along a river bank. It was the same river, but the water was different. It changed from minute to minute.

And she had changed with the flowers. She looked the same, but she was not the same. Love had come into her life. The incredible had happened. For the first time she regretted things... regretted Fritz, Retief, Congo.

A woman and a beast... in a world that was a garden. She picked a rose and threw it down.

For Congo things were changed, too. He picked up the rose and smelt it. The perfume of flowers gave him pleasure. He drew in the scented air and breathed it out. He did what Olga did imitatively. But he also had an appreciation, which ran parallel to his imitation. The perfume disturbed him. It hurt him low down in his loins so that he put his hand on

his belly and held it there. It made him sad. Perhaps the
pain in his belly ... the pain that he got from his pleasure in
the scent of the rose made him sad. Perhaps it was something
else. Perhaps it was that Olga was in love and he knew it.
Not that he knew of love, but he knew of pain ... of desire ...
of emptiness. It made him angry. She smelt different to him.
Her new scent killed the perfume of the rose. He threw it
down. He felt a barrier was raised between them. The new
scent of her love destroyed even her personal scent on which,
by her toilet, was superimposed the scent of geranium.

Congo put his finger into his mouth and felt his teeth. Their
size gave him satisfaction. He put his hand on a rosebush and
pulled it up. That was nothing. He wanted to pull up trees
... to break great limbs. His pain increased. It rose from his
loins to his liver and heart, it hurt his chest. He beat upon it
with the flat of his hand. As he beat, it stung him ... as his
blows stung him, he beat harder to strike out the pain. And
shrieked. He was in agony, tortured. More than ape, less
than man ... But man-like, man associated and woman, his
urge to be more than he was came upon him. For years it
had been growing.

His hands seized his jacket. He ripped it off. He tore his
trousers. If he could not become, he could destroy. He did
not know what he wanted to become: he did not know what
to destroy. He knew only frustration ... only physical
strength and intellectual weakness. He knew words; he could
understand them; but he did not know ideas. He had memories ... racial ones of an ancient gorilla past, and personal
ones, of his own life; but he had no conception of the future
beyond this feeling of unease and of pain.

She was coaxing him now, urging him with her voice,
forcing him with the prodder that he feared, threatening him
with the snake that he feared even more. She was going to
put him in his room. She was going to shut him up ... leave
him alone with his pain and those things in his head that were
trying to come out ...

Olga closed the door. How suddenly Congo's temper had come!... while she had been dreaming of Wilson. She had thought of the American and hated the gorilla. She had never hated him before. She had loved him in a way. She had liked to watch him: he was so like a man.

She went into her room. She stared at herself in the mirror and began to cry. She cried till she heard Sebastian shouting her name.

'Olga ... Olga! I want to paint you!'

It was like him to come now. Sebastian — the master of the inopportune. She washed her face, made it up, and went out.

'I want to paint you,' he said.

'I told you you couldn't.'

'Nevertheless, I wish to. It was only in the nude that you refused. I do not wish to paint you nude. It was a mistake to ask it. I am tired of the nude. Besides, if I wished to I could paint you nude from memory. I remember you nude. When I made love to you, I ...'

'Yes,' Olga said. 'No doubt you remember.'

'Very well, let us abandon this fruitless conversation. Sit there.' He pushed her down. He had an easel with him. He pulled a stab of charcoal from his pocket. 'Behold,' he said, 'I begin. Sebastian begins. That is something to see.'

Olga was thinking about Wilson. Where was he? What was he doing? What had his wife been like? He told her very little about her.

'As I work, I will entertain you,' Sebastian said. 'I will tell you about my experiences with women. Then later I will tell you the story of my friend MacMahon ... a relation of the Marshal and a painter in Paris of rich women. I, too, know that work,' he said. 'I have moved in expensive circles. I know the mink coat ... the Russian sable ... the chinchilla.

'In some places a mink coat is conspicuous,' he went on. 'In others, not to have one is conspicuous. Where there are many mink coats, you begin to classify them. Good and less good. For color, for texture, for gloss; for the way they are cut, the way they hang. It is as inconceivable in one place that one should not have a mink coat, unless one does not like minks, as it is in another that anyone should have one.

'Inside those mink coats there are women who are like all other women. A little sleeker, perhaps, a little cleaner. They have more time to be sleek and clean. And the quality of their fat is different. It is the rich fat that comes from rich food. They have the gloss of high feeding and grooming. They are on show: As much as a studhorse paraded with ribbons in his mane and tail; only their ribbons are orchids. Some of them have taken prizes at Nice, Cannes, Le Touquet, Deauville . . . at other places. They are in some curious way better than other women. Perhaps because, like the show horse, they are less practical. They cannot be used . . . only looked at. And they stare at each other with twitching nostrils. There are always men with them . . . generally old men, or very young men with the older women. It is very interesting to watch: this final distortion of eroticism; the final chord of a long symphony of spending, of women dissolved in the rich gravy of unlimited possessions, painted, perfumed, decorated, embellished, waved, massaged into wanton sullenness . . . for they are sullen, those women.'

He had his palette out now; he was working in venetian red and sepia. 'A method of my own derivative of the old masters, but an improvement,' he shouted.

'Yes, I have seen thousands of women — wives, mistresses, young virgins. I have been to those places where they congregate to drink chocolate with whipped cream, to eat cake, babas au rhum. How they smell of woman, of chocolate, of perfume, of the emanations of their own bodies, of their flowers — Parma violets crushed in their waistbands, pushed in between their breasts; of mimosa, of carnations — of sweet sweat, of lingerie, of sachets, of the rubber girdles that clasp their forms, of the furs of animals, of their natural harlot smell!' He held his nose. His brush was pointed towards her.

'Those women have no hearts. No woman has a heart unless she gives it to a man. And for all their scents, they smell hard. They smell like machines lubricated with perfume. They rustle like dry leaves as they move — as they tap about on their high heels. Pah!' he said; 'they Judas-kiss each other, they paw each other ... not as Lesbians, but as betrayers. They are disgusting, those women. Give me my little brown flowers. But even they I despise. Women!' he shouted. 'Women!' He picked up his easel and ran out.

Now she would have tea. Olga rang the bell. Poor Sebastian. He was not happy. She would have tea with a slice of lemon and think of Wilson; of his making love to her. She would wonder where he was; what he was doing. It had been an interesting day: interesting that Retief should have made her love Wilson; that being sorry for one man should make you love another.

It must have been coming on for a long time: since she had first seen him and decided that he must stay; since the Fourteenth of July, in fact. That accounted for her new feelings about Fritz: he had only come to see her once since then. It had thrown her back on Retief and that had been equally unsatisfactory. The rest ... the past ... had ceased to exist. She put it behind her. Jean would let her go. They had discussed this question before.

And Congo? He was getting dangerous. Today proved she had lost her power over him. He would have to be destroyed.

Chapter 26

The PHILOSOPHERS

CHANNEL BLAMED THE AMERICAN FOR HIS DISSATISFACTION. He had disrupted their lives. He was like a stone which had been set into a stream deflecting the current. How often had he done that as a child! — put a stone into a ditch of running water.

The victrola played *J'ai deux amours . . . Mon pays et Paris.* He was tired of the records. He was tired of these breakfasts with Sebastian alone.

'Masses . . . that is the way I see things, in masses of colors, arranged in battalions of beauty,' Sebastian said. 'Beauty is always terrible. It hurts . . . the wounds of Christ were beautiful . . . red blood, dry brown blood, white flesh against the black of the cross, a great sky behind him. His cry, "They know not what they do" . . . I hear it in my ears. Brown and red are the same . . . where does one stop and the other begin? The young green of a tree is terrible; it is irrevocable; it repeats itself each year, again and again and again . . . nothing can stop it. A man is born with the inspiration to paint. He learns to express his visions. I am terrible like a young tree. I grow and grow. Like leaves new pictures are born to me. They come out of me.' He was silent. He sat with his head sunk between his hands, staring at the ground beneath his feet.

What went on in Sebastian's tortured mind was instructive. Pursued by devils, he in turn pursued the angels of his inspirations in a never-ending race. The devils never quite caught up with him. He never quite caught up with the angels. This was what happened to everyone, but it was exaggerated and more clear in Sebastian. It was bigger, simpler in him as his body was bigger, simpler. To look at him, to consider his emotions, was to look at all humanity under a magnifying glass. Everything was easy to see. Details invisible in ordinary men stood out clearly in him.

That is what we are all doing, Channel thought: running away from devils, chasing angels. A fair woman, by the alchemy and distortion of the human mind, was turned into an angel ... all men had at some time or other pursued fair women. They were softer to touch than other women. They looked like those postcard angels that were given to you at Sunday School as a child, only they had bodies instead of white nightdresses and wings. It was funny to think that perhaps men were influenced in the pursuit of women by the religious pictures of angels ... You had them and then you got over them and the synthetic sunshine of their hair.

Men took the world as if it was made for them ... as if it was custom-made. This was man's assumption. He did not like to feel that he was just a little thing creeping about on a spinning ball; that he was invisible even to another man if he was more than a few hundred yards away; that except to himself he was entirely unimportant; that to a grasshopper, or an ant, or a mouse, a man was nothing at all except an obstruction to its way of life ... something it was as well to get away from, as a man got away from a storm if he could. Man was vain, eager, acquisitive, egotistical, stupid.

Yet each had a tendency to imagine himself more sensitive than others: to think that other people were better balanced simply because their faces looked calm. But what did we know of them? The turbulence of the heart, its pain, were not necessarily there for everyone to see.

Sebastian gulped his coffee and put down the cup with a bang into the saucer.

The relation of the sexes, Channel thought, was as present here as in the cities. In the cities sex walked the streets as it always had, made eyes in the bars and eating houses, concealed itself beneath the scanty subterfuge of social intercourse, became respectable in marriage, flaunted itself on corners, sold itself in the advertising copy of magazines; sneaked, in Freudian curiosity, behind kindergarten doors; disguised itself in a thousand stories, in gossip, in the social news of births, marriages, betrothals and divorces; came openly into countless murders; was an omnipresent power that seeped into every human action and activity, tying them together, joining the solitary acts of men and women as the cement run between stones joined them, tying them into a cohesive pattern of desire, fulfilment and fruition, which, though they might deny the cause, caught them inevitably in the consequence. It was sex that made homes and later broke them; that drove men to other women and women to other men against their wills, their interest, as salmon were driven, by their necessity, up-river, as stags in rut were driven, as everything that lived was driven, less to stay alive than to reproduce itself; less to exist than to produce more existence, more living matter, the quantity of today being the sacrifice to the quality of tomorrow — increase of such magnitude that the logical law of unjust selection could operate in its generous destruction to the benefit, not of the many born, but of the few destined to live and themselves suffer the pangs of further increase.

Increase ... the perpetual song of a dynamic force which had neither beginning, nor end, nor reason, nor method; which, consuming itself in a direct ratio to its own powers of multiplication, continued towards the consummation of an inconceivable destiny. Population, human, animal, or vegetable, increased up to the level of the means of subsistence, pressing continually against food supply in point and counterpoint. Increasing largely in good years, failing to increase in bad, but never, over a given period, able to exceed what the soil and water could support, not in the best seasons, but in the worst; the whole a pattern adjusted with such precision that the larvae were dependent on plants which depended on the rainfall, the birds on the larvae, and smaller carnivora on the birds . . . a delicate chain, whose balance could be upset by the elimination of a single factor . . . a storm that swept away the birds, allowing the insects to multiply till they destroyed the vegetal covering of the earth, a rain that washed away the larvae, a drought that desiccated the country.

By these events life was destroyed, the balance gone, but only temporarily. After a lapse of time it would be restored; in another form, perhaps, in a new design, but life as perfect, as complete, but more adapted to the changed conditions . . . life, always up to the optimum of possibility. Channel thought of the hundreds of thousands of Negroes exported as slaves from West Africa . . . today where was the gap? Was Africa empty? Hundreds of thousands exported, hundreds of thousands dead in the Middle Passage, terror, pain, and cruelty almost unimaginable to the individual, had done nothing to the stock. It was here, on these grounds, that the humanitarian ran foul of the eugenist and the statistician. The question of infant welfare was related to contraception, to sterilization; insanity, education, and nutrition were related to crime; politics, religion, and sex to economics.

Thought had gone far since Malthus wrote his essay and developed his theory that population tended continually to outrun its means of subsistence. Malthus, the abbé to whom contraception was attributed, had no idea of such a thing, at least no idea that went beyond continence which he considered unpractical. Yet from Malthus sprang Charles Darwin and Wallace; from them came the destruction of belief in the Bible as it stood, word for inspired word; and from there stemmed the present period of materialistic anarchy that rose out of a humanitarianism illogically and half-heartedly conceived in the last century.

Channel went back over his life in his mind. He thought of the things he had done . . . the things he had not done. There were always regrets at the things that had ended before their time. There was regret, too, at the loss of pain that was almost pleasure, at the pleasure that was almost pain. For many years these regrets had come back continually at the sight of a shop, a restaurant, a street, the name of a certain dish on a menu, a word found in a book, at hazard, as you turned the page; at a song, at a bar of music, at the turn of some woman's head in the street, at the color of a dress or the sound of a voice. All this because it was not done, because it had never been finished one way or the other, and your heart had been left dangling like a puppet on a string.

And what had you actually known of any woman, of her desires? What had she wanted of you? You only knew what you had wanted of her. You only knew your own desires, your own motives. And even those you did not know fully. You only knew what you were permitted to know of them, for your personality kept its secrets from your person.

How priggishly he had talked of love to Wilson! Man's actual motive was rarely the apparent one. Reality, the unknown force, cast its shadow in some conventional and acceptable design. The dream even had to be interpreted; it never stood intact, alone: it was derivative, suggestive . . . it was the writing on the wall, but writing in a strange tongue and in parable. There was no man who could accept himself as he was. The truth, the actual truth about himself would terrify him if he knew it, send him mad or into a monastery. When Luther saw the Devil and flung his inkhorn at him, he saw, not the Devil, but Martin Luther. Other experiences might have made Luther into something else, but that other thing that he might have become would have been different only in degree. On each man, as on every generation, lay the impress of the last.

He thought of his own father: he remembered him singing

him to sleep, walking up and down, holding him in his arms. He remembered him swimming with him sitting on his back, his legs about his neck, his hands in his hair. He remembered riding in front of his saddle. His father must have had similar memories of his father, and his father of his father, and so on, an interminable chain; each generation tending to repeat stories that they remembered from their own childhood ... fairy tales, folklore, superstitions that came down like this by word of mouth from the ancient past, were absorbed in the mothers' milk, transmitted by nurses, grooms, servants. His father had been born in 1844. His grandfather had been a boy at the time of Waterloo. And it went on like that, back into the past, each life overlapping another life, as tiles over-lapped each other on a roof. The more you saw of life, the stranger it was in its variety and differentiation.

There was no rest in the world; nothing was static; only change followed an inevitable pattern; and change was only change in degree, in form and not in actuality. Each man had existed since time began, as water, carbon, phosphorus, lime, iron, iodine ... He would exist till time ended — as matter. And his soul, that very speculative thing as yet undefined, might also continue to exist, rejoining some body of spiritual matter, some vast reservoir, from which new souls were drawn as they were needed. There seemed as good a case for trans-migration as there was against it.

Sebastian was still there, he was saying something. He looked hurt. 'You were not listening to me,' he said.

'Yes, I was, you were talking of beauty.'

'You would not have to be listening to know that. I always talk of beauty. But I drop my pearls before swine ... before scientists ... before women.'

There was silence while Laertes wound the machine and changed the record. It began again: the disk gained speed. *En voulez vous de la canne ... la canne de mon pays ...*

'I painted Olga yesterday,' Sebastian said. 'That is, I

began. I became furious. I gave up. I ran away. I am an
escapist.'

'That is what I have always told you, all artists are escapists. They hide from themselves.'

'I hide from no one.'

'You hide behind your work,' Channel said.

'I am my work.' Sebastian got up with dignity. 'I go to
my work now. You disgust me with your ignorance. If I con-
sort with women, it is because they do not disgust me. They
are natural — like flowers.' He spat over the terrace. He
stood to watch his spittle fall into the void below them. When
he could see it no longer, he left.

Channel was now alone with the breakfast table, with
Laertes, with the voice of Josephine Baker, with his thoughts
and Sebastian's dog.

*... Dis moi, Josephine ... Sur deux notes ... De temps en temps
... Partir sur un bateau tout blanc ... tout blanc ... Nuits de
Miami ... La petite Tonquinoise ...*

Record after record was played. Song after song, recorded
by Columbia, sung by the Negro woman in a desperate unknown nostalgia, swept over the terrace, over the mountain-
side and died.

Josephine, the African exiled from Africa. Channel, the
Frenchman exiled from France.

'If you have done thinking, I wish to speak.'

Sebastian was back. What had happened today? Why
was his mind working like this? He looked at the pile of
records that the boy had played.

'Go on,' Channel said; 'I am listening.'

'I can stand everything but not this,' Sebastian said. He
pointed to the dog. 'Not the seduction of Bernadotte. There
are limits to all things. The limit has been reached. Your
rudeness is not compensated for by your breakfasts. Me, I
despise breakfast. I do not mind your ignorance of beauty, of

the meaning of life, your scientific and childish pretensions, your collection of skulls and obscenities, your interest in ovaries, which are of God. But that my hound should be seduced shamelessly before my eyes, that you fondle his ears and rub his stomach — that is intolerable.'

The dog had withdrawn from Channel and gazed at his master with yellow, adoring eyes.

Channel raised his hand.

'Do not stop me, monsieur. I have more to say,' Sebastian went on. 'It is not necessary to ignore me because I am illegitimate. My father was a great man, there's no question of that.'

'Who was he?' Channel asked.

'I do not know,' he said, 'but he deserted my mother. Only a gentleman would have done that. My father was a duke or a lord — a great man. Then I starved in Paris and worked ... I met a girl; she kept me for two years; then I left her and went East, shipped from Marseilles before the mast, deserted in Saigon, stayed there awhile; then to Ceylon, the South Seas, Australia, South America. Working all the time at one thing and another and drawing and painting when I could get materials ... Then the Spanish War ... Africa. Here an orphan, alone, I seek to work. I strive to depict life, which I see as a big woman spawning ... spawning unceasingly. Life is female. I see her as a woman because I am a man. To me a woman is more female than a cow ... she is the female of my species. If I was a bull, I would not think of a woman. If I was a bull, a cow would be female to me. Woman to me is just the spawning part, the earth part. My woman is a great woman without a face ... a woman of billowing curves.' He swept his hands through the air. 'Breasts like udders, great haunches ... hams ... the belly of an elephant ... curve on curve ... convexity on convexity ... rolling, rounded with fat that quivers.'

He wiped his forehead. 'Now I will go,' he said. 'But

understand this: I demand an apology, and you will miss my conversation. It is my heart that has been hurt.' He put his hand on his chest.

'Apologize,' he said, 'within twenty-four hours in writing, or you will breakfast alone, monsieur.' Tears came to his eyes; he dashed them away. 'I will cook my own breakfasts,' he said. He drew himself up.

'Come, Bernadotte. We leave this place where we have been betrayed. We will work and think of our dreams.

'Apologize!' he shouted.

He turned and went back to his house.

The dog hesitated, looking first from his master to Channel. Then, picking up a fallen crust, it followed Sebastian.

The day was half-wasted. Channel lit a cigarette. And he had learnt a new version of Sebastian's past. There were at least twenty of them. It was a pity his feelings had been hurt, but he would recover.

The newly lit cigarette followed Sebastian's spittle. It described a curve in the air, then the forest swallowed it.

The hospital would have to wait; he was in no mood for it. He thought of his collection. If there was war, he would give it to the Royal College of Surgeons. In London he had been well received.

This decision had come suddenly. But it could not have, it must have lain a long time in his unconscious.

That it had come made things more clear. Something was going to happen soon ... he had never been wrong when he felt like this.

Chapter 27

The HEEL OF ACHILLES

~~~~~~~~~~~~~~~~~~~~

THIS TIME THERE WAS NO QUESTION ABOUT FINDING GORILLAS. Wherever Wilson looked, there were traces of them: dung, pieces of chewed vegetable matter — succulent wild celery that they had drawn along their teeth to strip — chewed bamboo shoots and discarded fruits...

They came on another sleeping place: twenty nests within a few yards of each other. Some were small, some big; some were single beds; and double where two had slept.

Natives from the village and some Pigmies had accompanied them. They had brought small fox-like dogs that were trained to gorilla-hunting. Since they ran mute, they wore wooden bells round their necks. But at this point, where they had actually come near the gorillas, the dogs hesitated and ran back to sit beside their masters. The gorilla dogs did not like gorillas. The wet gloom of the mountain forest was disconcerting. The foliage of the trees was grey, the branches festooned with Spanish moss. The feeling that though they were invisible the apes were watching was frightening. Bentinck seemed perfectly at ease. The Pigmies were fitting arrows to the strings of their tiny bows.

The path they were on was an elephant track. The spoor marks, as large as baths in the muddy ground, were filled with black water that crawled with life. Beside the elephant spoor was the spoor of the gorillas — their tracks and the marks of their knuckles.

They came to another bed. 'Big one,' Bentinck whispered.

The size of the beast was estimated by the pressure on the bed and the diameter of its voided excrement. High overhead there was the clattering cry of a bird. The huge trees were buttressed with triangular roots. Staghorn ferns sprouted from the trunks, lianas hung from the branches. Some of the trees were scrofulous with the fungous-like nests of termites. A butterfly with iridescent wings glittered for an instant in its flight among the treetops.

This was a brutal, subhuman place. This was where Congo belonged. And Olga, the height of sophistication, was, by some reversal in time, by some completion of a psychological and biological combination, allied to this atavistic world. Wilson grasped a tree to steady himself.

Bentinck was talking to the hunters. The hunters were talking among themselves. The Pigmies nodded their heads violently in agreement. Wilson gripped the tree more firmly. He felt ill. Fever? Fear? Emotion? Perhaps they were all merged . . . concentric circles cutting into each other as they swept over his personality. All he knew was that he felt ill and weak. Bentinck, the natives, and the Pigmies were apart from him. He was alone, isolated from them. He saw them . . . if he had stretched out his hand he could have touched the nearest Pigmy, but they were without reality. They were two-dimensional — like a picture in a book. He concentrated on the clearing in front of him, on the patch of sunlight that bored down between the trees into this little opening in the forest.

Bentinck came up to him. 'Going to camp here,' he said. 'They've gone and you've had about a belly-full.'

They were going to camp, and the gorillas had gone. We're going to camp, he thought. Never had he wanted to camp so much. Never had he been in a place where he wanted to camp less.

Some of the natives began to cut bamboos for the framework of the huts. Others brought leaves to thatch them; cooking fires were started. Jan was opening a can. It was still a picture, all distant, though only a few yards away. Wilson sat down with his back to a tree. Bentinck sprawled beside him and lit his pipe.

Wilson decided that it must be later than he had thought. Part of the clearing was shadowed.

'Old village,' Bentinck said. 'Gorillas drove 'em out.'

Wilson heard Bentinck speaking, but he was miles away. He was thinking of his home, of how he had left it.

A home was a slow thing. It had a slow growth. It grew round a nucleus of wedding presents, your own possessions before marriage, and your wife's possessions. It grew out of the memories of your old home: the home of your childhood. In each home were to be found the vestigial remains of other, older homes.

Each thing had a history. Given by friends, bought, inherited, each thing represented something other than what it was. They were objects certainly, some of them objects of art or value, but they were more than that. As you looked at them, memories of this man, of that woman, came up ... of this place, of that place; of this year, of that year. *We were there then.* We bought those little brass cannons on our honeymoon. We bought that picture on Fifth Avenue: that ivory Buddha in Paris. What was it they said about Buddhas? — That you should never use them for anything ... not as letter weights or doorstops.

A home was a collection of things — chairs, tables, beds, chests of drawers, china, silver, pictures, books, that had been integrated into a personality by their possessors; something built up slowly, to be suddenly disintegrated.

Much had been sold ... had become part of other homes. Much had been destroyed. He had destroyed his photographs, whole books of them: signed photographs of men he had lost sight of, of girls now married to other men. Their destruction had been hard to accomplish. They would not burn. They had had to be primed with kerosene; he had taken them to the country to do it. In burning them he had burnt something of himself.

The dog had worried him. They said that dogs helped you at a time like this, but they didn't. Their cold noses pushing into your hands meant nothing. They were only another living link with the past that must be destroyed, that must be given away.

And Anne's clothes. There had been lots of her clothes in the closets. It was curious how objective he had been about it: curious how little, and how much, they had meant. He still wondered why she had left so many clothes. It was part of the pattern of divorce, perhaps, symbolic — a sartorial washing of hands.

When I go, he had thought, I'll go naked, too. I'll take nothing. But it was hard to think of a home being over, of the life that had been lived in it being over . . . of beginning again naked in a brown lounge suit. That was the way he had gone.

With an effort he dragged his mind away from the past. He thought of the books he had borrowed from Channel and the professor. It was one thing to sit in comfort and read about gorillas; another to be camping in gorilla country.

He thought of the folklore of gorillas among the natives: tales of their raping the women, of their stealing infants and raising them. None were substantiated, but all seemed possible. There was the native he had seen who had lost his calf. There was the story about a family of gorillas caught raiding a banana garden that had turned on the men who were trying to drive them out and had torn them limb from limb: plucking off their legs and arms as a child might pull the legs off a grasshopper. Where you were had a lot to do with what you believed. No one believed in ghosts, but few people would spend a night in a haunted house.

Bentinck was smoking quietly. The Pigmies were playing their reed pipes. They had only one note, and the five who were playing waited for each other and blew on their pipes at the correct moment. In this way they produced a kind of tune. While they played, they hummed to themselves. This was surely the beginning of music. The evening wind swayed the treetops and icy water fell from the leaves.

Jan was beside him. 'Food, Baas . . . *scoff*.'

Still in a dream, Wilson took the dish.

Bentinck said, 'Tomorrow we'll get one.'

Always tomorrow . . . always yesterday. Last summer . . . next summer . . .

There was a fresh knuckle spoor. Bentinck pointed to a gorilla nest in the fork of a tree. It was made of moss, leaves, and small branches. At the foot of the tree was the male's nest.

'She must have a baby,' Bentinck said. 'Safe from leopards up there with the old man at the bottom.'

The bamboo at the foot of the tree was broken down and there were the usual discarded, masticated fragments. They came to a patch of wild celery. It reached to the shoulder and was almost impenetrable, except where the gorillas had broken a path through it. There was more dung, fresh, steaming in the cool of the morning.

The Pigmies disappeared into the undergrowth. They moved so fast that they were difficult to follow. They were able to stand up in the tunnelled trails that made Wilson and Bentinck bend over double and sometimes drop onto all fours. The track led upward steeply. They fought their way slowly through the creepers, over great fallen trees, past thornbushes that tore their clothes. They were stung by gigantic nettles. At times they had to wait while the Pigmies cleared a path for them.

Still climbing, they went on till they came to another

abandoned garden. The Pigmies froze like pointers. Wilson followed the direction of their eyes. Gorillas ... five of them. Two adult and three young ones. They were some distance away and standing their ground. Wilson felt Bentinck's hand on his arm. He was pushing him forward. As they moved towards the gorillas, the biggest one advanced towards them, the other big one — the female — and the young following him at a safe distance.

The big one stopped and began to beat his chest with his hands; the others did the same. Bentinck went on; Wilson followed him. They were now within thirty yards of the gorilla. His pitch-black face shone like polished leather. His lips were drawn back from his teeth. His eyes blazed with rage. He came on. He opened his mouth. He was immense. He came closer. He made no sound, but his belly rumbled.

As Wilson raised his rifle, the gorilla screamed. Beginning with a loud roar, it rose, pitched higher and higher. As it ended, he dropped onto all fours and charged.

As he fired, Wilson felt certain he had missed. He heard Bentinck's rifle go off beside him. There was a flash of spears. The gorilla turned a complete somersault and fell, not fifteen feet from them. Bentinck fired another shot.

The other gorillas had disappeared.

They were alone with the dead gorilla and the natives.

'Big chap,' Bentinck said.

'But I missed him.'

'Plenty of men miss their first. Make you nervous.' He polished his pipe against his nose, sat on a stump, and loaded it carefully. The Masai had withdrawn their spears and were wiping the blades.

'Go the best part of six hundred pounds and a nine-foot arm spread.'

Wilson went up to the dead beast. Bentinck had shot him through the base of the throat, the chest and heart. Its fore-arms were thicker than his own thighs. It was so clean that it looked as if it had just been groomed. It was silvery grey in color, but darker in front than on the back. Its chest was almost hairless.

'Get nearly white when they're old,' Bentinck said. His pipe was going now. He took it out of his mouth, looked at the bowl, and put it back. Wilson noticed that his rifle was still held across his knees and that it was at full cock.

'Well, that's done,' he said. 'Now we can get on with the real job.'

He went over to the gorilla and stared at it. 'Look, you nicked him.' He pointed to blood on its left arm. 'It's your gorilla. First blood,' he said.

'So it's my gorilla,' Wilson thought. His hand was still trembling so much that he could hardly light a cigarette. But if Bentinck had not been there? Von Brandt had said it's a good thing you are taking an experienced hunter with you. That had been the night that Olga had given the dinner party while her husband was away. He could not take his eyes off the gorilla. Prehistoric man must have looked like that. He thought of its savage eyes, of its crest, of its low forehead and heavy brows.

The flies were settling on it. They were on its wounds, on its mouth, on its eyelids; a green metallic fly was crawling up its nostrils. He sat down.

'Nice meat for the boys when I've skinned it,' Bentinck said.

When they camped Bentinck planned the trek back. 'We'll strike north,' he said, 'instead of going by the river; hit the road that passes near the mission and then have a look at Marais' dredge. From there we'll go on to von Brandt's, and then home. About a week,' he said.

A week more ...

'Want to see some people on the way,' Bentinck went on. 'They may have news.'

'Yes,' Wilson said. A week. They would be back in a week.

He wondered what had happened while they had been away.
So much could happen in so little time ... a week more to
wait ...

Bentinck was telling him how in the old days he had shot
a lot of gorillas and elephants for the boys working on the rail-
way. 'Shot them for meat. Contract job. Never liked it,
though. If they hadn't protected them, they would all have
been killed off by now.' He was silent again.

I'll be clearer about this when it's all over, Wilson thought.
Can't see the wood for the trees now. This was the place
where that cliché really meant something. When you were
in the forest, you could not see the forest. How good it would
be to get out of it!

That was all he could think of now: To get out of it; to
get back to Olga. The war, the reason of this trip, no longer
made sense to him. These tremendous trees had survived a
hundred wars. All events, past or future, were irrelevant to
them.

Marching through them, they took on a malevolent personality of their own. Though the route was different, it
seemed the same. It was as if he had watched a film and now
was seeing it run off in reverse.

Had they, by coming here into a world which had remained
unchanged for so long, stepped back into a timeless era?
Did you, when you became a part of such reality, cease to
be real yourself ... cease to understand reality? He knew he
was ill, of course; but he had not got fever. He had no dis-
turbance in his stomach; he did not even feel weak. On the
contrary, he was in harder condition than he had been for
years. What had happened had taken place in his head: in
his point of view. Bentinck's talk drifted past his consciousness. He heard it, he understood it; but it made no impression
on him. Had he reached the saturation point? Could you
have so many experiences, so many emotions, see and feel so
many things so suddenly that you became incapable of further

absorption? Could your soul, your spirit, or whatever it was, become waterlogged by a kind of capillary action?

Bentinck had just left him to go and shoot a buck for meat. He preferred hunting alone.

But it was good to be resting for a time. To sit like this in a village, thinking and watching — not life go by — that was what you did in a city. Here you watched it going on. These people were so unconscious of life that they were living it, but unaware of it in the civilized sense. Part of a tribe, of a village, of a family, of a group . . . they were like bees, part of a swarm and without individual self-consciousness. That was what Channel had been talking about that day, the new self-consciousness of man and his social and political disintegration because of it.

'Baas, Baas!' Jan was running towards him. 'Baas!'

Wilson jumped up.

'What is it, Jan?'

'Baas, it is the Baas. He is fallen. He is down a pit.'

'A pit? What could have happened?'

'Ja, Baas. A trap. He has fallen into it.'

Men were collecting round them. Jan sent one of them for ropes of woven bark.

A few minutes later, they were following Jan into the bush.

The trap was wide at the top, deep and narrow at the bottom. Wilson looked over the edge. There was Bentinck. A sharpened stake had gone through his leg.

He looked up at him. 'Got here quick,' he said.

'Quick as we could.'

Jan was fastening a rope to a tree. The end he threw into the pit and climbed down. More ropes were thrown. They were put round Bentinck's chest, under his arms. As the natives pulled, Jan eased him off the pointed stake. They dragged him up slowly. Wilson took his shoulders as he reached the top.

'Thanks,' he said. 'This is the end, you know. End of old Bentinck.'

'End be damned!' Wilson said. 'We'll patch you up and
get you back.' They would take him to the mission first:
to Owen, and then to Channel. Channel would save him.

'Channel,' he said.

'No, my boy. Nobody. Not even Channel. These stakes
are poisoned. Get me back to the village. Then we'll get to
Owen. I'll last a few days.'

Bentinck, as they carried him slung on a tepoi, was thinking
of the heel of Achilles. It had its application everywhere. His
own accident was an example. His certainty... that he
knew his way in the forest... had been his undoing. Von
Brandt's was women. Marais' might be his superstition.
Every man had a weak point — vanity, women, drink, love
of money, overconfidence. Hitler believed in astrology. Once
the stars went wrong, he would be finished: his confidence
weakened. Mussolini's was women. In their emphasis on
virility, the Fascists laid themselves open to women: belief in
the material predicated women. What was there more
material? What object was there in money if it was not to
purchase women, what object in power if it was not to dazzle
them? And as they forced women down, so did the women
drag them, deeper and deeper into the pit they had digged
for themselves.

Bentinck was reconciled to dying. His business on earth
was done. He had lived long enough. His friends, and his
wife, were dead. He had no further place among the living.

Jan came to tell him that a native had come after them.
So many Kaffirs had come to him in his life. He wondered if
this was the last. Black men bringing tidings of illness, of
death; coming to tell him of beasts they wanted him to shoot;
telling him... telling him. He had been told so much. He
had been told enough.

'Tell him to come, Jan.'

'You bring a message?' Bentinck asked.

'I come from Entobo. He says that he has done the bidding of the "Hunter of Medicine" and sends greetings.'

Entobo had come to him the night before they had started on this safari. A funny thought struck him. Their conversation had really been about this very question — the heel of Achilles. Entobo had said, 'Tell me what you know of them and I will make medicine to destroy them. For each man there is a special medicine, for as each has a strong part each has a weak, and against that weak place, once I know it, do I pit the strength of my art.'

Entobo was not interested in politics or war. He had come as a friend because he had asked him to. He had come also to get whisky to drink and obtain more packages of medicine from 'the hunter of medicine.' He had said, 'Tell me of your enemies, oh, my friend, and I will add my strength to yours.'

His enemies — von Brandt certainly, and probably Marais. He had told Entobo of the salt incident.

'This means, then, in your land that he fears the spirits. In that case I will make spirit medicine for him. I will bewitch him with a figure.

'And the "collector of animals alive." He, too, shall be dealt with, but by the flesh — subtly, by a woman.' Entobo had cast his bones on the floor of the store. 'I see it, my friend. I see a woman running, a man consumed.' Then he had gone out into the night as he had come, with many packets of medicine wrapped up in the *Times* and a bottle of good whisky stuck into his girdle. There was more whisky beneath it. He had said, 'When I have done my work, I will send you a messenger.' This must be he. He had come just in time.

'The Bwana knows?' Bentinck asked.

'He knows because it was I who told him of it.'

'Tell me how it happened.'

'Thus did it happen. I went to the house of Bwana by the boat that digs.' That was the dredge. 'I said to him, "Bwana,

an evil thing has happened. It is said that in a mountain village a doctor has made an image of the Bwana. This image
contains hair from the face of the Bwana. It is made of wax
and clay." '

'And then?'

'Then the Bwana was angry. For it is well known that he
destroys his hair and the nails he cuts from his hands and feet.
He did not believe me. So I told him how it was done. I
said that when he took the hairs from his face in the room
where he washes, it goes down the little pipe that runs out
into the garden, and that it was here that the hair had been
collected by a servant of Entobo. Then he fell into a very
great rage. His face became red and swelled. He made as if
to strike me, but I ran.'

'He was frightened?'

'Bwana, he was frightened. Why else would he have raged?'

'And Entobo works upon the figure?'

'He works, Bwana. He has made many of them.'

'And the Bwana who lives by the digging boat knows that
he works?'

'He knows ... all men know. They watch him out of the
corners of their eyes.'

Bentinck was silent. It might work. Anyway, it could do
no harm. Marais, if he lost even the smallest amount of
confidence in himself, might make a mistake: might forget
something. The funny part was that he did not really know
that Marais was in this business. It was only a hunch.

The boy went on. 'And the business of the other is done
also. It has been arranged.'

Bentinck looked at the native. 'Take this message to Entobo
the doctor. Give him greetings, thanks, and farewell from the
"hunter of medicine." Say he goes to the land of spirits; that
you have seen him; that he departs and in departing gives
greetings and thanks.'

'I hear the Bwana. It shall be done.'

The boy left him. In three or four days he would be back in the village and Entobo would have his message. The idea of Marais being attacked by witchcraft amused him. The idea of it — even if it did not work — amused him. The power of suggestion. If not, why would Marais be so careful about his hair and his nails? The weight of a little figure made of clay and wax might yet be a factor in the balance of international affairs. They had started psychological war, and he was turning it back on them.

Started be damned! It was old — so old that it had almost been forgotten. Nothing was new. The kind of pitfall he had been caught in was the oldest trap in the world. No doubt men had used them before they had weapons that could kill dangerous beasts. It was a fitting end for him whom they called 'the hunter.' The hunter dead. The hunter trapped. There was some satisfaction in not having died of fever, as Channel had said he would. But this was offset by the fact that he would not be buried with the other owners of the store. He had set his heart on that. It was disappointing.

His eyes met Wilson's. He had come to sit beside him. It was good of him to bother. Tomorrow they'd get to Owen's place.

'Good thing I've lasted to get you to the mission,' he said.

'Yes. I guess it's lucky.' Bentinck was a queer old man. His one idea seemed to be to save trouble. He knew he was going to die, but he wanted to die at the mission so that his death could be certified. 'Got to have everything in order. Might say you'd murdered me.

'About this other business,' Bentinck went on, 'better get the hang of it before I get too weak. Olga has got all the information: mainly suspicions. But they add up. Frazer's got the other stuff, but I wanted to run this down. Something big on ... it's on the other side of the mountains. No doubt about the rebellion: coffee planters all organized ... but Frazer knows it. It's something else. They've got dynamite, but I'm not sure where they're putting it.'

Wilson wiped the sweat away from Bentinck's face.

'Thanks,' Bentinck said. 'Bloody nuisance this happening. Upset Owen, too. He wanted to save me. Better prospect than the others. I'm so old, you see. No vice left in me. Kaffirs will be sorry, too. And the Masai. And it's spoilt your trip.' He was silent.

Wilson wiped his face again. 'How do you feel?' he asked. It was a silly question.

'Fine,' Bentinck said. 'No pain. Wonderful stuff that poison. Tell Channel; he'll be interested. Pity he couldn't watch it working. Clever man, Channel ... Interest him.' He was silent again.

Bentinck was the first man Wilson had seen die. Only a few days ago he had been thinking how strong he was, how tough, admiring the tireless way he marched, the ease with which he slept anywhere. Why, it was only a few days since he had shot the gorilla. He thought of his own life ... of Bentinck's. Bentinck had lived and was going to die a hunter. He thought of other men, of other professions: of how one man's work was another man's pleasure. All hobbies were work for someone else.

The commercial traveller worked in his garden ... the gardener wished he could travel. The business man made cabinets on the week end ... the cabinet-maker wished he could wear a good suit and commute to a comfortable office. A maid sewed seams ... her mistress did embroidery. Man liked to work, but he liked variety in work. A holiday was only a change of activity. Hunting was work for Bentinck.

Bentinck opened his eyes.

'It's funny that boy coming when he did,' Wilson said.

The funny thing about it was the way he had found them. You could not get lost in Africa. Wherever you went, you were watched ... a source of amusement, of conversation, of gifts, of meat. Again the paradox that Sebastian loved so well. Secrecy coupled with the observation ... knowledge joined to silence. The boys at the Station knew about himself and Olga, but would never say a word about it except to each other.

'Yes,' Bentinck said. 'Damn funny.'

'Finding us?'

'No, not finding us. That was easy. I was thinking of the little figures Entobo has made to scare Marais. And it has scared him: scared the life out of him.' He began to chuckle. 'Get the stuff from Olga and take it to Frazer. But I'm sorry about the gorilla. Looks as if we killed him for nothing. Things are moving too fast for us to catch up now. War, my boy. They get worse. Boer War was nothing compared to the Great War: Great War nothing to the one that's coming. I'd like to have finished up that way . . . in war with my boots on. Now I'll die in a bed at the mission. That's funny, too. Never thought I'd die in bed . . . never thought . . .'

Wilson couldn't hear what he said next. His voice faded. He closed his eyes. Perhaps they would be able to save him at the mission: if he wanted to be saved . . .

Bentinck was comfortable. That is, as comfortable as he could be made. Owen had fixed him up in his own house. Jan sat on the floor beside his bed. The Masai watched outside.

Wilson was on the stoep with Owen. He was looking at the little whitewashed church that Owen was so proud of. Everything was centred round the church — the schoolhouse, the dispensary, the living quarters of the children, the workshops and farm buildings. His respect for Owen increased. He had made all this himself, out of nothing, with very little money or help from home. It's funny, he thought, being . . . That was what Bentinck had said about the little figure, about himself being caught in a trap. Funny word, *funny*. It did not mean funny; it meant strange, queer, odd . . . it meant the unforeseen event. It meant in its widest sense the act of God . . . the inexplicable.

He poured himself out another drink. 'Don't mind, do you, Owen?' he asked.

'No, I don't mind. I don't drink or smoke myself, but I don't mind other people doing it. It's something you've got to decide for yourself.'

Wilson stared at the church again. He thought of Owen working on it with the unskilled boys he had got together when he began. 'What chance is there, do you think?'

'It's in the hands of God,' Owen said.

'You mean none?'

'None as far as man is concerned. He's beyond the help of man. Even Channel, if we could get him back. He'll die tonight or tomorrow, and he knows it.'

'Think we ought to go in to him?'

'He wants to be alone. And Jan is there. Jan will call us if he needs anything.' Owen looked at his watch. It was a cheap nickel-plated thing. 'If you'll excuse me, I've got to go.' He got up.

Wilson sipped his drink. The church bell began to ring. Service. Evening service. He saw Owen cross the grass between the house and the church. He saw the mission natives going towards it.

Augustus Bentinck is going to die ... die ... die ... die ... the bell said. Three days ago he had been alive and well. Now he was dying; tomorrow he would be dead. Owen took it calmly. Bentinck took it calmly himself. If there was going to be war, a lot of men would die.

Owen said nothing about the service when he came back. They had dinner ... chicken curry. The chicken was stringy and dry, the rice soggy. Wilson thought of the way Olga lived. After dinner they had coffee. It was bad. Owen seemed very depressed.

'Sometimes I feel things are hopeless, Wilson,' he said.

'I've never seen anyone die before.'

'It's not that — not Bentinck. He's not afraid to die. He

has lived his life. It's my life here. Everything I've done, I mean. And I wonder what I've done. So little. It's impossible to teach them morality. Impossible. I can't make them understand that it's important. They're like animals: worse than animals. They should resist, but they don't. They go out into the fields, in the courtyards, against the walls, in the barns and stables, even at the mission. I've preached to them for years, ever since I came here, and what good has it done? They say, "*Yes, Father,*" "*No, Father,*" and it goes on just the same . . . the same number of babies, the same women . . . Sometimes they do not even know the father's name. "A man," they say, "a man who came swiftly, like a storm at night, and bowed me down before him." Dear God, they're just like animals. You can't stop it because they can't see that it's wrong. They get hot working in the fields, they get excited dancing, or singing — even singing hymns; and then they're at it. Africans . . . wild with the jungle in their blood and a hand-to-mouth Christianity. That's what I call it. Christian because it pays them . . . the Church helps them, feeds them, clothes them. But are they Christian? At night when the moon shines they walk off into the swamps . . . I know some of the things that go on there . . . some of the things they believe. It's terrible. But what can you do about them . . . about it? I keep saying we are all the same in the sight of God, but are we?'

'They're happy,' Wilson said. 'Happier than us white folk.' He thought of Negro servants in America: serve a white man for a few years and be looked after for life by him. White folk still cared for their Negroes just as they always had. That was the burden of their superiority — that in a sense they were the servants of their servants, taking care of them when they were sick, getting them out of jail, pensioning them off like old hunters when they were past work. Whose nigger are you? That's what they were asked when they got into trouble.

'Yes, they're happy,' Owen said. 'That's what I can't understand. How can they be happy? How can they forget their sins? How can they forget that Jesus Christ died on the cross to save them? And then not care?'

'I don't know,' Wilson said. He had a lot of doubts himself. He thought of the deaths in religious wars, in massacres, pogroms . . . but you could not talk to Owen. It meant so much to him and he was fighting for his faith. He was a good man. A man who worked for others without thought for himself, without hope of reward or preferment, because he believed it was his duty to save souls. Not for anything would he interfere with his belief in God, in miracles, in an afterlife. In a way he was jealous of him. It must make life much easier if you could see it that way, mapped out like an ordnance survey — like a sort of Pilgrim's Progress . . . the little wood of fornication, the morass of adultery . . . It would be too hard to explain. That was the devil of it. You could never talk to parsons. You had to keep sheltering them from reality. You couldn't talk to them as you talked to either a woman or a man.

Look at the way the talk stopped or changed when a parson came into the room. And those muscular parsons, the good fellows who told stories cut pretty near the knuckle, were worse than the other kind, you couldn't even respect them. You felt it either unfair or indecent to speak of things that everybody knew if they were near. Either they had no children, or hundreds of children, and in a way the thought of them having children was abhorrent. But why should it be? — Unless it was because they seemed to be a sort of middle sex that in one's mind one felt should neither beget nor conceive. To make it decent they should increase by division . . . like protoplasm: one parson dividing into two parsons neatly, expeditiously, and without embarrassment to anyone. That was it. Parsons embarrassed you.

Jan came onto the stoep. 'Baas,' he said. 'Master . . .' Tears were running down his cheeks.

Owen got up. 'We had better go.'

Wilson followed him. He had forgotten Bentinck. How had he been able to? He was ashamed of himself.

'Not long now,' Bentinck said. I must make myself clear, he thought. This is about the last thing I shall ever say. He found he had no desire to talk. He had talked enough in his life ... seen enough ... done enough. And what good could come of more talk? He must tell Wilson. But really there was so little to tell him ... Von Brandt ... Marais ... He forced himself to say something.

'Go to Olga ... coffee planters fixed ... Frazer ... names and everything. Never should have let them come back ... Marais ... professor's formula ...' He was gasping for breath.

'Clever,' he went on, 'putting in a real Nazi like von Brandt, and then a man like Marais, if it is Marais. Tell Olga ... dynamite ...'

Owen opened his Bible. 'I'll read you something,' he said.

'God,' Bentinck said, ' ... Mary.'

'Mary the Virgin Mother,' Owen said.

'Mary ... Mary Bentinck. Going to see her soon. Been waiting a long time. I am not afraid,' he said to Owen. 'Had enough. Wilson can see to it now. Enough,' he said again. 'Enough of everything. I've been very lonely.' How lonely he had been! The dynamite. He saw it suddenly ... Lake Victoria! He gathered himself together.

'The bastards!' he said. 'Don't know if it would work, but it might. Thousands ruined. Egypt a desert ...' He shivered. ' ... no time ...'

Owen wiped his lips. He knelt by the bed. Bentinck had shrunken visibly as the poison took its final hold. He seemed much smaller. He made another effort to speak.

'Bury me deep,' he said. 'Don't want to be eaten. Dig you up. Don't want to be dug up and eaten.'

He tried to roll on his side. Owen helped him.

'Better?' he asked.

'Yes, but it won't be long. Wanted to be the twelfth.' He must be talking about the graves behind the store. 'Everything slowing up . . . slows up . . . then it stops. Seen it often. Animals,' he said. 'Big ones . . . elephants . . . Tell Channel . . . tell him . . . Olga . . . dynamite . . . the bastard . . .'

Foam formed on his lips, he gave a choking cry, tried to sit up, and fell back.

'He's dead,' Owen said. 'Bentinck's dead.'

Everything is up to me now, Wilson thought. He must get back to Olga. If there was war . . . Bentinck's death changed things. Everyone had said there would be war. Raymond Gram Swing had told him so last year himself, at a party with Anne. But he hadn't believed it. He had been too preoccupied with his own affairs. It had been just before the divorce.

He must get back to Olga. 'I must get back to Olga,' he said.

'You'll wait for the funeral?'

'Tomorrow?'

Owen nodded.

Of course it would be tomorrow. He wouldn't keep. 'I'll leave the gorilla,' Wilson said. It was funny how your mind worked. The gorilla was unnecessary now. Funny the hunter Bentinck caught in an animal trap. Funny . . . Owen . . . Funny . . . Did not want to be eaten . . . Egypt . . . What had he meant about dynamite? What had he been trying to say? Olga . . . the professor's formula . . . Marais . . . Anne . . . The carriers and the Masai . . . He would take the Masai with him. Pay the Pigmies off. He would give them salt and soap. Tobacco. Pay them . . .

The trek, shooting the gorilla, Bentinck's death, had pulled him up short. He had been removed from the realm of theory . . . Channel's and Sebastian's . . . into a world of dynamic fact. It had not affected what he felt for Olga: the two worlds were parallel, each self-contained. His hurrying back was not only because Bentinck had told him to get to her, but because he wanted her. Was this what Sebastian had meant when he spoke about women? About finding release and safety in them? Olga had become a necessity. To find her, to lose himself in her, to get up from her refreshed. My God! he thought, I'm thinking as Sebastian does. I'm going crazy.

Jan ... the porters ... Pigmies ... Masai. The gorilla skin and skull. How quickly the ants had cleaned the bones ... driver ants ate anything. He had wanted to be the twelfth grave ... tell Channel ... about how the poison worked ... that I did not die of fever after all ... Jan was to have his guns and other possessions ... Dump everything ... travel light ...

Chapter 28

The HOLLANDER

MARAIS TURNED DOWN THE RADIO, LIT A CIGAR, AND STARED at the list in his hand. So, it had come. The German army would march into Poland. England and France would declare war. It was a wonderful code: symphonies, marches, songs arranged in a certain order. There were perhaps a hundred men stationed in different parts of the world who could understand it. You had to have Kultur to understand it: to be musically educated; to know the names of the pieces and check them off. The time to act was near.

He went onto the stoep. Everything was the same: the thatched huts of the natives; the corrugated-iron roofs of the buildings, the stacks of timber; the cocoa pans travelling on their narrow rails; the dump of sludge; the regular beat of his dredges; strings of boys moving with shovels as they worked on a cofferdam. He looked at his watch. They were changing a shift. His white overseers. Everything was going on as usual; though nothing was changed, all was changed. It was war. He knew it. The others did not. There was something intoxicating about such knowledge. He had a sense of power, of drunkenness. He must see von Brandt: see him at once.

He called a boy. Then he went to his desk and sat down. First he addressed the envelope. Then taking a sheet of notepaper from a drawer he wrote a line, *Come over at once*, and signed it, *Hendrik Marais*. He gave the letter to the boy.

'Take it quickly,' he said.

The boy ran out of the room. And he would take it quickly. His boys were obedient. He treated them well and beat them well — coldly and without mercy when his orders were not carried out. It would take the boy two hours on his bicycle. It would take von Brandt an hour by car. Three hours. Say four to five, to allow for delays. But there was plenty of time.

From another drawer in the bureau he took an automatic. It was beautifully clean. It felt good in his hand. A weapon perfectly made and perfectly kept: an arm of precision. He laid it on the blotter with a box of ammunition. It pleased him to think of von Brandt coming, rather angry at the message he had received, at being so peremptorily summoned. But he would come. He would be here by dinner time at the latest.

Von Brandt was a fool. He liked women too much. He was too sadistic. His temper when roused was too ungovernable. Marais had no use for passion, for anything ungovernable. A man should be like a machine ... precise, accurate. This was the machine age: the age of iron lungs and hearts, of calculation, of action based on plans where armed force was synchronized with psychological propaganda to produce exact results. Of course von Brandt was young and the equator had done nothing to cool his blood or temper his disposition for violence. There were few men like himself who had complete control of their environment. He was an exception. Perhaps it was just as well.

Women were the weakness of so many. Money, luxury, power, all resolved themselves finally into women. That was where the money went. That was what the power was used to obtain. How lucky he was to have been born without any sexual feelings! He was not even homosexual. He was the ultimate product of his time — the man of calculation. One of the new type that was coming into being. Naturally later he would marry and contrive with some distaste to reproduce himself. This was a necessary indignity

required of all men for the perpetuation of the race. But to
place this absurd act first . . . to wish to lie with a woman, to
hold her and touch her — that was beyond comprehension,
an atavism. No, when the time came he would choose the
woman as one chose a horse or a cow: tall, blonde, with wide
hips, a big brood mare of a woman.

He looked at the ash on his cigar. There were four cen-
timetres of grey ash on it. A tribute to the grower of the tobacco, the maker of the cigar in Rotterdam, and to his own
nervous control. He had practised control since childhood.
His father had been a passionate man and he had seen the
absurdity of passion. Make the other man angry, yes . . . that
was good; but keep your own temper. A blow was no answer
to an insult. There was action and reaction, cause and effect.
Causes could be loosed like dogs to produce effects. His life,
which had not been unsuccessful, had been based on this. Impulse . . . you saw its results all round you. The impulse of
Olga Le Blanc to enslave all men. The impulse of that old
fool Channel to obtain a new-born gorilla. The impulse of
Sebastian to paint everything . . . the impulse of von Brandt
to possess women. There seemed to be nothing but impulse
in the world, which was why things were so easy for men like
himself.

Outside the dredge throbbed as it sucked up the river sand.
A boy was playing a Kaffir piano and singing to himself. A
sudden breeze shook a big mango so that the fruit fell to the
ground.

The boy he had sent must be halfway there by now. At
six o'clock he would have a drink and dress. Nothing could
change his schedule: not even war.

In addition to his dredging operations, Marais had other
interests. He had a share in several coffee shambas; he
owned two stores outright. He exported considerable quan-
tities of ivory, gum resins, copal, beeswax, mangrove bark,

ebony, logwood, palm kernels, kapok, skins, hides, and feathers.

For hundreds of miles in all directions his agents worked in the fine-spun web of his commercial enterprises. Nothing was too big for him to handle: nothing too small. He dealt in cotton, maize, ground nuts, rice, millet, tea, tobacco, and sisal. It made him laugh when people talked of Darkest Africa. In no country of the world were there so many roads. In no country had they been trodden for longer. It was simply that the European mind did not see, as roads, the little Kaffir paths that led over plain and forest, that joined village to village throughout the continent. Yet millions had passed along them: hundreds of millions for thousands of years: traders, slavers, black men and women visiting each other, men going to war, or returning from it. Why, you could put your finger down anywhere on the map of Africa and, if you sought them, you would find roads leading to that place. Africa was like the palm of a man's hand, netted with fine paths, criss-crossed with them. It had been his business — a part of it — to learn these paths.

At six-thirty Marais put on his white dinner jacket, straightened his tie, and went over to look at himself in the mirror. I look good, he thought. I look fine. I am a fine, healthy man. It gave him pleasure to look at himself — thick-set, very pink, and scrubbed, rather stout. Not fat, but well-fed and prosperous looking.

He touched his tie again and pulled down the jacket. He looked at his trousers ... at the knife crease ... at his shoes. Perfect ... everything was perfect. He looked just what he was supposed to be — a Dutch business man, a man of substance. This pleased him. He knew himself to be considered an honest man, one who had no wish to sail under false colors or appear other than he was. That was what he always said. 'The Dutch are a fine race and I am a fine example of it. Not too tall. So many Englishmen are too tall. Not too stout.

Many Germans are too stout.' When he said this, he laughed.

He was a very fortunate man: lucky both in his appearance and his health ... forty-four and only one tooth gone. For the rest he was as God had made him. Nothing had even been taken out of him: he had his appendix, he had his tonsils, he had most of his hair: only that one tooth which he kept among his studs. You could not be too careful about these things. His nails when he cut them he always burnt. His hair he had swept up when he clipped it, and destroyed. Not that he believed in witchcraft. It was just that he had lived in the tropics so long and had seen so much. One did not talk about those things.

And, after all, one was entitled to one's idiosyncrasies. He gave the room a last look — everything was very neat. He was a neat man, precise as a woman. His boy when he came in would have nothing to do but turn down the bed. He switched off the light and went out into the big sitting room.

He sat down and clapped his hands. His head boy came in with a tray ... schnapps, a tall glass, water and ice. The boy put it down on a little scarlet lacquer table.

He lit another cigar and poured out a drink. Now he could settle down to wait for von Brandt. Strange how everything had played into his hands: how plans laid years before in a hundred places and a hundred ways, had by the subtlety of his manipulations, been coordinated into this single scheme. Ephemeral, light as the strands woven by a silkworm as it built its cocoon, those threads were now a strong net thrown over all Africa, poised above it and ready to fall. Rebellion, revolt, sabotage, disorganization and direct attack, all synchronized. His work, when you came to think of it, was a masterpiece of espionage, a chef d'oeuvre of fifth-column activity. In the future people would speak of it ... in Germany ... The Marais Plan.

He smoked his cigar carefully, calmly. Everything was in order. He had only to wait. The day, the great day had almost dawned. Only one thing worried him: that affair of the witch doctor. How in God's name had he got hold of his beard? How had he thought of filtering his bath water? Who was responsible, and why? Yes, why? A white man's mind. But it could not be.

His cigar ash fell on the floor. I must be calm, he thought. Witchcraft. Phui ... What a fool to worry! He looked at the ash on the carpet. It infuriated him. His hand must have trembled. He must be calm. He must not let something like this upset him. He got up to go to his desk. He would write some letters just to fill in time. Go over some invoices, bills of lading. He stopped suddenly. What on earth was that?

In the middle of his desk, on the blotting pad, lay a little clay figure. He held onto the bookcase. It had not been there when he came in. He had not left the room. Only his butler had come into it when he brought the drinks. Everything going so well and then this. But it was nothing. He must not let himself get upset. He picked the figure up. He held it to the light. It even bore some resemblance to him. He looked to see if it had been damaged in any way — a string round its throat ... a wound. But there was nothing. He looked closer. Yes, there were hairs in it, some of them stuck out of the clay. Hairs from his beard and bigger curled hairs from his body that had gone down the bathroom drain.

He opened his mouth to shout. He would beat every boy till someone confessed. He would take the hide off them. He would kill them ... He closed his mouth. He would deal with them afterward: for the moment he would pretend nothing had happened. He would ignore the whole business. Picking the figure up again, he wrapped it in a bit of paper, unlocked a drawer, put it in, and locked it again. Then he went down on his hands and knees and cleaned the ash off the carpet. Everything must seem normal. For him to spill anything was not normal.

How his heart was beating! He poured out another drink.

Why had he this weakness . . . this fear? There was no such thing as the supernatural. All this Juju, this Voodoo, this Obeah, was nothing. The results they got were through fear. If you were not afraid, nothing could happen to you. But he had been afraid since childhood. He tried to think back. Stories of witches told him by a nurse he could not remember. A palmist once at a fair . . . his experience in the Far East, in Java and Indo-China. He had seen things there. His only weakness . . . It was in Java that it had begun seriously. It was there he had taken to destroying anything that came from his body after Hu Sing had died cursing him. That had been a near thing. Of course, he had killed Hu Sing. He had had to. Not kill — liquidate had been the word he had used in his report. But that it should follow him here . . . in the moment of his triumph. A manikin of clay and wax crudely modelled by a Kaffir witch doctor. Why should it upset him? It did not upset him. Nothing could upset him. And von Brandt should soon be here.

He thought of the armies massed on the Polish border. Danzig. Pah! that was a beginning . . . an excuse. In his mind he saw the tanks, the planes, the men.

What was a witch doctor's doll to this? The material was what counted. Men, machines, and the iron German will to conquer.

Chapter 29

The GERMAN

〜〜〜〜〜〜〜〜〜

VON BRANDT WAS THINKING OF SOUTH-WEST AFRICA. IN SOUTH-West there were nine thousand six hundred Germans — he had the figures — and their number would rise. He had lived there as a child, his father had commanded a post, and after the war — he had been too young for it — he had gone back. Then he had returned to Germany. Hitler had sent for him. He had stayed in Germany some years before coming back to Africa again . . . to West Africa, then to Tanganyika, Uganda, Kenya, and the Congo. He was happy. Only a German could be happy today. Only the Germans had a solution to life. It was war. It was the German sword that would bring world freedom and security: room for all to breathe and live an ordered life. There were the fools who said that the Führer only wanted peace. Naturally he wanted peace if he could get conquest without war. But it was known among the few, the elect, that war must come. He was one of the thousand cogs preparing for it. Germany today; tomorrow, the whole world.

That was why he was happy. He had something to live for. The pattern of his life was clear. It was simple; nothing was simpler than the will to go on till death found you. Death was the only thing that could stop a true German. They were a holy race, purged by the fire of war, freed from political schism . . . a nation of giants. To be one gave you a feeling of completeness and solidarity.

He sprang to his feet and raised his hand. 'Heil Hitler!' he shouted. He was quite alone in his house. The cry was an emotional expression, the crow of an exultant cock. The blood was running hot in his veins. He felt himself flushed by it. Things were going well. Everything. The planters were organized and armed.

His cages were full of wild beasts. They were thorough in the Third Reich. He had spent two years learning about beasts. In the Berlin zoo, at circuses, at museums. He had learnt to train a lion, going into its cage armed only with a chair and a whip. He had been taught the use of every kind of trap that would be helpful to him. He had been apprenticed for a year to Otto Friedland, one of the finest live-animal hunters in Africa. He knew his trade; it was no mere false front. His books proved that he made a living from it. There must be nothing imitation about your activities, he had been told by the Colonial Department. That is why we shall succeed, he thought, because we are thorough.

And there was Olga. She could not do without him now. There was also Maria, the younger of Sebastian's two girls. What a trick he had played on Olga with her, when he had agreed to her suggestion that she use her as a messenger! It was certainly a joke that Maria had been his when she was still at the mission school.

He looked towards the cupboard. His uniform was in it: he longed to put it on again. There also were other things — fuses, detonators . . . The last of the dynamite had been laid. Everything was ready. He was waiting only for the signal: he had been told that it would come. It was not his business to inquire how, but sometimes he wondered. 'You will receive your final orders . . . Meanwhile . . .'

And he was but one of them. There were thousands of Germans ready. They had been organized by a handful of men trained, like himself, for key positions. They would march everywhere. The Union of South Africa was prepared. The

Boers anxious to revenge themselves upon the English, and the natives ready in a hundred places to rise. They had no arms ... thousands would be killed, but what was that, provided the end was attained? Poor deluded fools. With the Germans ruling, they would assume their rightful place among the animals. He remembered, as a child, the Hereros' Rebellion of 1903. It had gone on till 1907. His father had said very little about it, but he had learnt things from the orderlies. They had talked freely in front of him, of the beauties of the Herero women; of how in the sergeants' mess they had had them waiting on them naked; of how some of the officers had played cards upon a girl's belly, making her lie stripped on a table. Young as he was, he had looked upon the beauty of those brown women. He had never forgotten them.

And soon those days of mastery would return. The days of freedom when a German could do as he willed. There would be no more of this absurd sentimentality, no more confused justice. The deprivations of his people would be justified by results. That was all that counted — results. He must go and see Marais again soon. He was a little afraid of Marais, though he was only a Hollander. There was something about his precision, his accuracy ... Nevertheless, he must go. He had been told to offer him every facility. There were some more cases of machinery to be conveyed to him. His transport system, perfected to move his animals to the coast, was to be used. His boys were to accompany the crates back. Naturally he had to send special boys with his consignments. The animals were used to them. Still, it was odd ...

At that moment a boy came in.

'A message, Bwana.'

'A message?' He recognized him — a boy of Marais'. He had just been thinking about Marais. He read the note.

Evidently Marais did not realize who he was. I am a man of some importance, he thought. When the time came, Marais would learn it. But he had been ordered to do what he could

to assist him. 'Put yourself at his disposal,' the actual wording
had been. But that was naturally a little strong. There were
limits. To be ordered to come at once when he had been having his evening rest! He got out his car.

Surely tomorrow or next day would have done. He had
been going to see him soon, anyway. What could Marais
want? What could have gone wrong? The last machinery,
four consignments of it, had been delivered in good order. He
had the papers in his pocket to prove it. It was six weeks since
he had seen Marais at Olga's. That was when he had met that
American. Maria said he had gone on a trip with old Bentinck. If he wasn't careful, all he would get was a dose of fever
for his pains. Writing a book, indeed! There were too many
books about the Congo already. No one read them.

There was the smoke of the dredge. He had driven fast.
But what the hell did Marais want? Anyway, he would soon
know. He'd stay for dinner, he supposed. He could hardly
not ask him, and then afterward he would drive back. It was
not amusing driving through the forest in the night. The road
was bad and there were lions and leopards about: not to mention elephants. They might be right in the road. But he did
not want to stay the night. He had other plans.

Leaving the car on the drive, he strode up to the house.
Marais was not on the stoep to greet him. He would soon put
this Dutchman in his place. He went into the big sitting room.
Perhaps he was sick. No, he was not sick. There he was
seated at his desk with his back to him.

'Well, I've come,' he said, 'and . . .'

Marais turned, pushed his chair back and sprang to his feet.
He stood still for a second, erect, staring into his eyes. Then he
raised his right hand and clicked his heels.

'Heil Hitler!' he shouted.

'Heil Hitler!' von Brandt echoed. What did this mean?
What was it all about? Why . . .

'Sit,' Marais pointed to a chair. He sat down and waited.

Marais was pacing up and down the room. He stopped suddenly.

'Well,' he said, 'it has come. It is war. We are about to march into Poland. The British and French will declare war on the Third Reich...'

'We...?'

'Yes, we, you fool. We Germans.'

'Then you also...?'

'Yes, I also. And now here are your instructions.'

Von Brandt sprang up and faced him. 'My instructions? Who are you to give me instructions? I am in charge here.'

'You are in charge?' Marais said. 'That is why they did not give you a radio. That is why you were detailed to bring me my guns. Look' — he pulled a paper from his pocket. He waved it in front of von Brandt. 'Colonel Hendrik Marais von Hohnlowe, Commandant of the Fourth Central African District.'

There was more, but von Brandt did not have time to read it.

'Now are you satisfied?' Marais said.

'Yes, but I don't see...' So this was how he was to be notified.

'You would not see.' Marais spoke patiently. 'You were here to do some of the work. I have reported on your conduct to Berlin. The work you have done is good. I have also with absolute impartiality reported your liaison with Madame Le Blanc and your interest in native women. For your information I will tell you that you were stationed here so that if anything went wrong you would have been the obvious agent. You are too simple to be trusted in the big things.' Marais' voice became very sharp. 'It is a pity you have not got over women. Mein Gott! you would find a woman anywhere if there was one within a hundred miles of you. But you are still puzzled. My mother was a Marais: a Hollander. I was brought up in Holland, but I never forgot my father or my race. Is that enough, or must I waste more time? There is much to be done.'

Von Brandt was dazed. They had been fooling him, then. He was no more than a pawn. He looked at Marais with new respect. A colonel in the Reichswehr. How well he had played his part! He began to regain confidence. It was after all an honor to serve under such a man.

Marais poured out two brandies. He added ice and water to both glasses and passed him one.

'To success,' he said.

'To success,' von Brandt echoed. The success of German arms: the reversal of the infamy of Versailles and living room for the master race. The die was cast. Success . . . there was nothing else. Germany was rising like a phoenix from the ashes of her past.

Confused with his dream of Aryan greatness was his desire for women: for Olga — he wished to master her; for the Batanga girl — he liked black women. They were insatiable, and the Batangas were among the best-looking natives. They reminded him of the Hereros of his childhood. Those stories had stayed with him. He liked the feel of their skin. Its texture was different. He liked the way they smelt: it was a feral smell, that of an animal mixed with the scent of hot gorse in summer. Nothing would be denied the German conquerors. He saw conquest in terms of women.

It was all very well for Marais to talk, but this was surely the true warrior ideal. And the leaders would get the best, the pick, willing or unwilling. He wanted them unwilling: to hold them struggling and force them back. His virility was titillated by the challenge of the moment, by thoughts of blood, of victory. This their great Führer had done. He had raised up their ancient forest gods, the great ones of Germany, out of their graves. War, women, loot, and victory were synonymous in his mind. His brain, misted by his thoughts and half thoughts, hardly took in what Marais was saying. He kept answering, 'Ja. Yes. Yes, Colonel,' but he had difficulty in keeping his self-control. He was itching to begin ... to show the world.

Fancy sitting here saying yes, yes, when the German legions were already marching, fighting, killing, pillaging ... raping. In his mind he heard the thunder of the guns, saw the tanks rolling, the Stukas diving on helpless columns, the flame-throwers searing human flesh: he smelt it burning. Germany avenged. Germany the destroyer. Thousands, millions of his folk marching rhythmically, their boots tramping the Polish roads. Young men hardened by exercise, by mountain climbing, by dangerous sports, for years, to this end. How wise their leader! How great! How magnificent it was to be a German, bringing culture to the world and a true everlasting peace upheld by the German sword! He felt implacable — iron-hard; great, as he had never felt before, and safe: like a child, warm in the womb of his heritage: a young warrior, descendant of warriors, once again at war. This was the natural state of man. The Leader had stated it. All else was decadence.

'You will stay the night,' Marais was saying. He did not want to stay, but if the colonel said so ... Maria would wait. She had waited before. She would be afraid not to. Sebastian ... That made him laugh now. Why, if Sebastian gave trouble, he would shoot him like a dog.

'Tomorrow you will go home and proceed to set the detonators and fuses.' How well he was informed! 'There must be no mistake: and remember, the man who does this will be rated a hero in the Reich. Look,' Marais said. He took a case from his pocket and pressed a spring.

Von Brandt stooped. There in its velvet bed was an Iron Cross of the first class with its silver edge and ribbon of black and white.

'For the hero,' Marais said. 'I have the authority. But afterward naturally it will be awarded officially by the Führer in Berlin. You will have to return for the real investiture.'

He put the case in his pocket. 'Strange, is it not,' he went on, 'what rewards a hero gets? Position, money...' he paused, 'women. All women. Any he wants are ready and waiting to oblige the man who has so served his Fatherland. There is no more of that sentimental morality today. Men once more are men, and women, women: the natural order has replaced the romantic nonsense of the past.'

Berlin. German girls. Von Brandt thought of the theatres, the lights, the clothes, the food, the music, the beer, the songs. The trees and mountains of his land. Before he had been relatively unnoticed, but now people would point at him... 'One of our African heroes.' He hardly dared to think of what he was going to do: an historic action; one that would change the history of the world; change geography. A nation would be reduced to starvation by the act of a single man. I am that man, he thought: I, Fritz von Brandt. He wished his father was alive; his mother. But no doubt they would look down from heaven and applaud.

Marais gave him another drink. How unmoved he seemed! How precise his action as he handled the ice cubes with a pair of small silver tongs!

'Drink,' he said, 'then we will eat. After that, bed, for you must rest well. Much depends on you tomorrow.' He spoke very seriously. 'Nothing must stop you. You understand?'

'I understand,' he said. 'Nothing will stop me.' He felt it in his heart. Nothing would stop him. His eyes rested on Marais' pocket. The little leather case was still in it. And as to risk: there was little risk. That anyone should do such a thing never appeared to have occurred to the English, though Professor Haupt's report had been made public some years ago and had subsequently been confirmed. They were fools. You only had to say what you were going to do and no one believed it. Look at *Mein Kampf*. The Führer had said what he would do. It was written plain enough, but because it was written, it was discounted. Now they would see.

Dinner was announced.

His host looked at the menu as though he had not written it himself. 'I hope you will like it,' he said. 'Turtle soup. Land tortoise, of course, but we call it turtle.' He laughed. 'Trout. How many people have their own trout in Equatorial Africa?' he asked. 'I am proud of them. They do well here. Then roast koraan stuffed with oysters. They are canned, but good all the same. Then strawberry tart. And hock to drink, Rhine wine, then coffee, my own growing, and a choice of liqueurs. Not bad, is it, considering where we are in the very heart of Africa?'

'It sounds wonderful. Wonderful,' von Brandt said. It was like Marais to have a dinner like this. He lived well. He had had many meals with him, but none so good as this.

'It is in the nature of a celebration,' Marais said. 'We must feast and drink to the success of our arms.' He stood and bowed. 'And to you, Captain von Brandt. Success to your mission ... and the rewards of success.'

The soup was served. They ate without speaking. They ate heavily, noisily, washing down the excellent cooking with three bottles of hock. Eating was in a sense a rite, a sacrament, for by eating did you gain strength to serve. To eat well, then, was a duty. Only the man well filled with blood could be reckless of it. As he ate, von Brandt felt his courage and desire mounting.

'Of course you will not wear uniform,' Marais said.

'Of course not.' But he was longing for the time when he could put on his uniform again. He hated civilian clothes. He felt naked in them.

The butler took away what was left of the tart and brought coffee. He passed liqueurs. They each took brandy. Cigars were passed.

'It is wonderful how long the ash lasts on these cigars,' Marais said. 'It is a test, you know.'

Von Brandt acknowledged it was a test, but he was thinking of Maria waiting for him.

'You are clear about your instructions?' Marais asked. 'Once you have made the demolition, return home, act as if nothing had happened. You will even be ignorant of the fact that war has been declared if you are asked. Later I will give you orders about joining the commando that will strike from the east at Nairobi. I am waiting for news from the Union and West Africa,' he went on. 'It should come in any time.'

'I was born in German West,' von Brandt said.

'I am aware of your place of birth.'

No doubt he was. He probably had his whole dossier. Von Brandt thought of the thoroughness of his own training. But even he had never suspected Marais to be anything other than what he represented himself to be. His host was evidently in no mood for further talk.

Von Brandt rose. 'Bed,' he said tentatively.

'Yes, bed,' Marais said. 'You will leave at dawn. There will be no need to see me again. Tomorrow will be a busy day for all of us.' He had not said what he was going to do, but one did not ask one's superior questions.

In his room von Brandt thought about his race. The Germans knew how to handle natives. In the nineties they had subdued the Wahehe. Some of the chiefs had committed suicide rather than fall into their hands. In nineteen-five, in the Maji-Maji Rebellion, a hundred and twenty-five thousand coastal natives had been killed. That was the answer to those who presumed to argue. That was the way to obtain order. There could be no order where there was argument. England and America and France were examples of this. Only in Greater Germany was there order, precision, culture, and true beauty. This was the machine age and mankind would be made to conform to the machine pattern. The Germans understood this because they were by nature soldiers and enjoyed the disciplined order of the army. It was only a matter of extending this principle throughout the nation, to the women, the children, to all the people ... first of the Reich, then by force of arms, if necessary, to the whole world. That was the way to obtain peace ... by the sword.

They were prepared to do this: magnificently prepared by sacrifice and devotion. They were a people dedicated. Von Brandt blew up his chest with pride at the achievements of his people. He thought of the iron cross in Colonel Marais' pocket. He knew his duty. He was going to do it. What a fine man Marais was! With what subtlety he had disguised his work! No one had suspected him. Even I did not, he thought.

At dawn von Brandt left. He did not drive fast. There was no great need for haste. Everything was planned. He allowed his pleasure to seep into him. The day had come: the time for action. He would enjoy it. That was where the Germans differed from the other nations, in their capacity for action: in their demand for it.

Still, it was a pity it had come today. He had had plans for last night. But no doubt Maria would still be waiting. Soon, next week, perhaps, if things went well, he would take her over completely and her sister, too. Then there would be no more presents. He would kill that communist dog Sebastian, who was always boasting of the way he fought for the Spanish Reds. When he got through with him, there would be one less communist. Only the Germans had stood between Russia and the rest of the world, and this was the gratitude they received. War ... Was it not said that those who sowed the wind reaped the whirlwind? The democracies would see. They would learn that they could not surround Germans.

He pressed his foot on the accelerator. The democracies had begun this, but there were many men in their governments

who believed in the Führer. It was only the masses that refused to see reason. He slowed up again, angry that his anger
had got the better of him for a moment. He wondered what he
would do with the animals he had now. There would be no
possibility of exporting them. Two lions, three leopards, a
young giraffe, some baboons and monkeys, a few buck, some
hawks, owls, a hyena, two Cape hunting dogs, and an okapi.
The best thing to do would be to destroy them. There was no
need for further deception. But it hurt him to think of killing
them, especially the okapi.

As soon as he came back from his mission, he would put on
his uniform, if Marais gave him permission, and take his rightful place in the African order. Perhaps he might get himself
transferred back to South-West. If he did, he would take the
Batangas and perhaps Olga as well — as Marais did not care
for women and he would have first claim on her.

He passed through a village. How idle they were! How
dirty! But soon all this would be changed. The Belgians in
old King Leopold's time had known how to handle them.
How soft the world had grown since then! Only the Germans
were hard: hard like steel, he thought.

He thought of his mission. Lake Tanganyika was more than
a thousand feet lower than Lake Victoria. The barrier that
enclosed Lake Victoria was slight and the lake was not more
than two hundred and fifty feet deep at its deepest points.
When he touched off the dynamite the lake would begin to
flood the flats, running south instead of north, the rush of
waters completing and enlarging the breach he had made.
Then the Nile would cease to flow. This was only part of the
greater scheme. There would be a holy war in the Near East.
A prophet had already foretold the drying-up of the Nile as a
sign. And when it ceased, the repercussions of war would
increase not only in the Near but also in the Far East, the
whole Mohammedan world would rise to throw out the infidels. The groundwork was all done: the rebellion fomented:

the charges laid; he had made many journeys over that area. Trapping and hunting, pretending he sought a particular variety of dassie in those rocks in order to plant them. In India, in Burma, in France, in England, everywhere there were similar plans all organized to fit into each other: all synchronized, all pieces of a tremendous scheme of sabotage that would utterly disrupt the world. And he, Fritz von Brandt, was about to do his part: do it, and get his reward. How simple a thing! — a small demolition job to be the lynchpin of a revolt and the ruin of a nation. It made one respect the planners of such schemes to see the artistry and scope of their vision.

At home, Maria would be waiting for him.

Chapter 30

The RIFLE

～～～～～～～～

SEBASTIAN'S QUARREL WITH CHANNEL HAD CONTINUED. THERE had been neither apology nor reconciliation. There could not be the one without the other. In addition, there had been no more breakfasts. Cooking it himself each day — the girls could not be trusted with so important a meal — Sebastian listened to the voice of Josephine Baker as it came, softened by distance from the terrace where Channel sat eating alone. Let him eat alone, Sebastian thought; let him suffer. Still, knowing himself to be missed by the doctor was poor consolation.

And when he could, Bernadotte sneaked away, called by the music which was also the call for food: the dog escaping: Sebastian bellowing at the dog: the screaming of the girls at each other, the soft wailing of Josephine, a solitary vulture circling the sky — that was morning: morning that had been so bright for him, with cereal, with bacon and eggs, with fresh rolls, with fruits and coffee. Channel had learnt to eat a big breakfast after the English and American fashion. He had accustomed Sebastian to it — and now nothing. He could not afford Channel's luxuries. He was too proud to beg from Olga. And when he fried an egg, it broke.

It astonished and amazed him that a man as dextrous with a brush as himself could not deal with such a simple thing as an egg: an egg — the ultimate simplicity. He was too great to fry an egg. That was all. In his mind this consoled him. In his belly it did not.

And there had been more trouble with the girls, more quarrelling: more visiting on the part of Maria. Last night she had not returned again. Why, if their father was sick, did only Maria visit him?

As the third yolk broke, he gave up. He would find out at once. He would get to the bottom of things. The time for action had come.

'Maria!' he shouted. 'Maria!'

She did not come.

He found her sister crouching in a corner of the house. She was weeping. Tears always infuriated him: broken egg yolks and the tears of a woman. What a morning! A woman never cried without reason and the reason always meant trouble for someone ... a new dress, an anniversary forgotten ... something ...

He seized her by the hair. 'Where is Maria?'

'I do not know.'

'Where is Maria?' He shook her.

'Our father is sick. She has gone to visit our father. She has not returned.'

'Why do you not go to your father? Do you not love your father? Are you so ungrateful to the benefits he has bestowed on you? When he dies, you will have no father.'

'He will not die,' she screamed. Sebastian was hurting her.

'Not die? Why will he not die? In the midst of life we are in death. Did you not learn that at the mission? The poor man is sick and you do not visit him.'

'Perhaps he is not so sick.'

'Then why must Maria go to him almost every day?'

'How do I know she goes?' Nina was angry. 'I only know what she tells me. And she gets presents. I get nothing,' she screamed. 'I must cook. I must work. I get nothing.'

'Presents!' Sebastian shouted. He picked up a stick. 'I will give you a present.' He struck her. 'And another present.' He struck her again. 'Do I not give you presents ... beautiful

beads of Venice? . . . a blue reboso? . . . a goblet of red Bohemian glass patterned and engraved with white? Who gives
Maria presents? Why does she get presents?'

'It is the German. He gives her presents for sleeping with
him.'

'More! Tell me more.' Sebastian was livid. Channel had
seduced his dog: von Brandt his wife. He threw the girl into a
corner. He was betrayed. He sat down. He jumped up.

'Stay there. I will paint you.' She had fallen just right.
The fold of her yellow dress caught the light; one slim brown
leg was extended. Her head was bowed over her breasts; her
hair hung down — a thick black snake over her shoulder. He
seized a big sketchbook and a stub of charcoal. The woman
sobbed. The sunlight poured in through the window catching
the yellow dress. The charcoal scraped against the rough tooth
of the paper. The beauty of desolation, of despair. The beaten
woman. The woman beaten, he thought. Light and shadow.
Beauty.

He felt it flowing from him. He was giving his art. It
poured from him, like blood or urine. It eased him to get rid
of it, it emptied him. His anger was vanishing as the picture
came. She was looking at him from under long black lashes
now. How sensitive these women were! How animal! She
knew he was no longer angry. Few civilized people were as
sensitive. He was exceptional in this, but most felt nothing.
He smiled at Nina. The yellow dog wagged its tail: it thumped
on the mud floor. If Nina had a tail, she would wag it, he
thought. It was a pity women had no tails. They would be
easier to understand.

He threw down the charcoal, it was used up, and picked up
another piece. Now he was calm. He had been foolish to beat
her. It was the other one he should have beaten. And that
Nazi: that German: that Fascist. Of course, he would have to
kill him. Tomorrow, he thought, I will kill him. The idea
gave him pleasure. The Fascist dead in his own blood . . . the

Fascist dead. The rescue of the maiden. His honor saved. It would be too late, naturally, to save hers. But to go now would also be too late. Since it had happened a hundred times with her and that animal, another time would make no difference.

He was showing remarkable common sense. He was pleased with himself ... with his restraint ... with his capacity for rational thinking. Later, when all this was over and he had killed the Fascist, he would paint a picture of a beaten woman. Nina could take up the pose again. He could duplicate the situation. Beat her again, throw her down again, beat her hourly till it was done. This was only a working sketch.

'Keep still. Mother of God, keep still.'

Nina kept still.

To Nina Sebastian was mad. Like or dislike did not enter into it. She was his. He had bought her. There was even a certain pleasuring in belonging to a mad white man. It gave you something to talk about: his funny ways, his pictures which were a harmless form of magic. But at the moment, as she lay huddled on the floor, the economic angle worried her. Adultery was no sin if you were not caught, but if you were it meant divorce ... divorce meant restitution of the price paid for the wife by the father. She did not think her father would pay easily. There would be trouble: arguments. She hated arguments. A quarrel was one thing, an argument another.

'How long has this been going on?' Sebastian asked.

'Has what been going on?'

'This abomination: this pollution of my nuptial couch: this betrayal: this, this ... In brief, how long has she been sleeping with the German?'

'Since she was a little girl,' Nina said.

'You mean before I got her?' Did she mean Maria was not a virgin? That her father had lied? That Channel had been mistaken? He was appalled at such betrayal.

'He did not like me,' Nina said. 'Only Maria. I tried, but he did not like me.'

'No doubt if he had you would have gone too.'

'Without doubt,' Nina said. 'He gives presents: perfumes, oil for the head, tweezers for pulling out hair, small mirrors.'

So he was being betrayed for a bottle of brilliantine, for tweezers . . .

'But when he whips her, he gives her more,' she said. 'Then he gives her money also.'

Sebastian put down his sketch and went out. He could not bear to hear any more. His anger had returned. Revenge. Honor. Betrayal. A great artist and a common cuckold. Oh, Mother of God. Oh, Mother of God. This, to happen to him! To a man who had been brought up by the good Sisters. Mother of God! That German beating one of his little brown birds . . . Tears came to his eyes: tears of rage, of frustration. Nothing could be done today. It would take him all day to compose himself and to plan.

Oh, Mother of God!

That evening the war came on the tapping speech of the drums; over the forests, across the rivers, over the swamps, the mangroves, over the silent emptiness of the steaming jungle: words tapped out by black men on pink palms . . . words: terrible words. WAR. IT IS WAR. OVER THE SEA. THE WHITE MEN ARE AT WAR.

The word of the drum . . . the word of the drum. Men in little villages hundreds of miles apart ran out as they heard the words. They could do nothing but kick their dying fires into flame. But they came with spears in their hands to relay the news. They tapped out the message: WAR . . . WHITE MAN . . . WAR . . . Gorillas sleeping in their nests turned and voided dung. The birds asleep on the trees ruffled their wings and slept again. The nighthawks flitted through the trees. The monkeys screamed and clasped their young to their bellies. And still the news went on; circling through the night of the forest, greeting the dawn, meeting the sun as it rose: greeting the burning heat of the daylight. WAR. THE WHITE MEN FIGHT. THERE IS WAR OVER THE SEA. THERE IS WAR. The Pigmies grasped their little bows. The Masai sharpened their spears. This was a white man's war. It did not affect them. But war was war. Their blood was stirred.

At the Station a houseboy came running in to Olga with the news. 'It is war.'

So, even with the radio, one had to learn from the natives first.

It was war.

Soon all Africa would have news of it.

Olga put down her knife and fork to listen to the boy. She had known it must come. He had come running into the dining room, where she sat alone, to tell her. Her husband and Retief had gone on their tour of inspection. The butler and the house servants crowded round her. It had come on the sound of the drum, out of the forest. Like Congo. Why must she think of Congo? Why did everything come from the forest?

'You may go,' she said.

The boys went.

She picked up her knife and fork. She put them down as the butler passed the vegetables again. Eggplant with a white sauce ... aubergine. They grew on vines. They were dark purple, almost black. They had shining skins. Her mind seized on details. In the other dish were small new potatoes cooked with mint and served with a butter and parsley sauce. Potatoes ... eggplant ...

She ate slowly. The food did not taste of anything in her mouth.

This meant ... What was the good of trying to use little things like eggplants as a device, as a temporary barrier against thought?

'Take everything away,' she said. 'No, nothing more.'

What did this mean exactly in personal terms? To her. To me, she thought. First, everyone would come back. Her husband would turn round and come back. He would get back tomorrow. Bentinck and Wilson would come back, and Retief, naturally, with the professor.

Everything was changed: suddenly. That they would change had been implicit, but there had always been the hope. And what was the professor's position? Would the Government in Brussels still be interested in his work? Wilson would go back.

These were the personal matters. But what would happen in the Union of South Africa, in Tanganyika among the German planters, and in West Africa? In Italian Somaliland? What was happening in Europe? In Poland? France and England were mobilized and perhaps in action. Great battleships were at their stations. And Frazer? Now that war was declared, he could come out into the open. If only Bentinck was here . . . His reports, fragmentary as they were, must be sent to Nairobi at once. Someone must take them. Wilson, when he returned? She did not want Wilson to leave.

She went to the radio and turned it on. Yes, it was war. England had declared war. France had declared war. The German armies were in Poland. She listened to the Oxford accent of the B.B.C. announcer. She turned the dial. Paris . . . The radio only confirmed the drums.

It was no use doing anything tonight. Tomorrow they would begin to come back: her husband and Retief; then in a few days Bentinck and Wilson. She must wait.

Should she go over to Channel? It would probably be impossible to make him understand. If he was not dining with them, he took things . . . piqûres, sometimes drugs. A man alone, an experimenter in dreams. No, he was of no use to her now. Use? Nothing was of use. Nothing could be done. So much could have been done before.

She got up to rearrange a vase of flowers. It was silly of her not to have finished her dinner: now she was hungry. She made herself some sandwiches and took a bottle of wine into her room. This was the moment for champagne. It should be drunk to celebrate an occasion or to mitigate disaster.

But war or no war tonight women were sleeping with men. More so perhaps because of the war. The long race memory of their blood, of women empty because the men had gone, called to them ... forced them. Desire was augmented by the thought of manless days and lonely nights, by the knowledge that a world denuded by death was a world only women could refill. And the men who would fight in this war were those who had been conceived in the last ...

She picked up the tray.

Olga had not begun her supper when she heard Sebastian calling. She went into the sitting room.

'Yes?' she said. 'What has happened?' The war ... 'It is no use coming to talk about ——'

'I want a rifle, Olga.'

She seemed surprised to see him, Sebastian thought. But, after all, what could be more natural than to come in the evening to borrow one of the professor's rifles. He had several and rarely used any of them. It was the most natural thing in the world. Also she looked very beautiful in the soft light of the sitting room in her green dressing gown with her hair rolled in a coronet about her head.

'But why, Sebastian? Why now? What are you going to do? Even if there is war. What can you do? We can decide nothing till the others are back.'

'To shoot,' Sebastian said. He hoped he did not sound excited. He smoothed his hair. 'Tomorrow I am going to shoot something. I am starting early.'

'When did you make up your mind?' Olga asked.

She understood nothing. No woman ever did.

'Just now,' Sebastian said. 'Had it occurred to me sooner, I should have come sooner.'

'Then why didn't you get Channel's? You knew I was alone. You might have frightened me.'

'I never thought of Channel,' Sebastian said. 'And he bores me. We are no longer speaking. You never bore me.' He was taking a .303 down from the wall.

'The cartridges are in the cupboard,' Olga said. She pointed towards it.

He took the bolt out of the rifle and held it up to the light. The rifling was in good condition. He returned the bolt, went to the cupboard and filled his pocket with the clips he found piled there. Channel, indeed! He was going to steal Channel's car; that was the reason why he had not disturbed him. Besides, he bored him. Those interminable books of his. You could express nothing in writing . . . only in pictures.

Olga still had her make-up on and her eyes did not look sleepy. He doubted if she really had been going to sleep. Why had she not been going to sleep? The question crossed his mind. How good the rifle felt in his hands! It was like being in Spain again. Spain . . . Fascists . . . his dead comrades . . .

How lovely Olga's hair was as the light struck it, brightening it with light and darkening it with strong, contrasting shadows. He looked at her breasts, he could see them through the lace of her thin nightdress . . . she was not careful with her dressing gown. He held the rifle in the crook of his arm. It felt good there. It gave one confidence.

'Thank you, Olga,' he said.

'What are you going to shoot?' She seemed to want to talk. But he did not want to, he wanted to get away. 'Won't you have a drink?' she said. 'I have some champagne on ice.'

Since he was here, he might as well talk. Why had she champagne on ice? A bourgeois drink. He was tempted.

'And a sandwich,' Olga said. Her dressing gown was fully open, though only for a second. She held it to her with one hand.

She was trying to seduce him. Sebastian was profoundly shocked. This was not the way it should happen. Nor was there time. His honor was at stake. His honor was a very ticklish thing. He was not very clear what it was. He only knew when it had been attacked. The situation in Spain, for instance ... Franco's rebellion against the Government had affected his honor so profoundly that he had gone there to fight Franco and his Fascists. He hated Fascists for making him fight them. That was their greatest sin. He had lost more than two years' work by this. True, he had seen some beautiful things, some terrible things. He had afterward made sketches, pictures which he considered superior to Goya's. But his soul had been damaged. He had also sustained two wounds, and been promoted to the command of a company, but these facts were accepted as a by-product only of the years, and uninteresting when compared to the time wasted and the spiritual damage done to his soul by war.

It was annoying that he could not make up his mind. He still wanted to paint Olga in the nude, though he had told her he didn't. And he wanted to sleep with her again. Both were to his mind the supreme compliments he could pay her. No man could do more, and few, if they were not artists, could do as much. But again, this was not the moment. He looked at her sitting on the arm of a stuffed chair: at the line of her shoulders, at her breasts, at her length from hip to toe. Most women were too long in the torso. They were like ducks with their buttocks too close to the ground. His fingers fondled the breech of the rifle.

'Yes, I would like some champagne,' he said. 'If you have some. It is refreshing if it is not too dry.' He did not like very dry champagne, it pricked his mouth. In his heart he disapproved of all champagne, not for its taste which he liked, but for its implications. Still at this moment he could compromise with his conscience. He could consider it medicinal. He had been upset by Maria's betrayal of him, by this attempted seduction, by the fact that he, the most peaceful of men, was being forced into action again; and it would serve Maria right if he was unfaithful to her.

'Come,' Olga said. She got up and went slowly towards her room. He followed her. She walked beautifully, swaying a little on her high-heeled slippers. At the door she looked back over her shoulder. It was the traditional looking back of the female: without subtlety. It annoyed him. He followed her, still with his rifle in the crook of his arm. That Olga should have the audacity to do this still stirred him profoundly. His world was crashing again. This was a further insult. And if he did not make love to her, she might be annoyed and want to take the rifle back. Women were like that, without a sense of the fitness of things.

He saw the champagne in a silver bucket on the floor and a dish of sandwiches on a tray covered with a napkin. The woman was shameless, and how had she known he was coming? He sat down and leant his rifle against the wall beside him. Olga sat on the bed. She was watching him. One thing was certain, he must get away before it was light if he was going to steal Channel's car.

Sebastian opened the champagne. He filled the glass.

'In Rheims there is a beautiful cathedral,' he said.

What had cathedrals to do with this? she wondered.

'Cathedrals and winged ships,' Sebastian said, 'are the noblest works of man. They are of God.'

Olga fetched a glass from the bathroom. How many couples had drunk champagne before going to bed together? Bacchus and Venus . . . Fritz would have said something like that: something banal, ordinary, to gloss over what he thought was the awkward moment. But no moment was awkward to Sebastian.

'It is too dry,' was all he said as he filled his glass again. Then he took a sandwich and put it into his mouth in one piece. A sandwich should be bitten at least in half, Olga thought. He took another.

'So the war has come, Sebastian.'

'War to the death!' he shouted. 'They cannot do this to me. It is death or dishonor.' He dashed the tears from his eyes, picked up his rifle, and ran out.

Olga ate the sandwich he had left and poured out another glass of wine.

The war had certainly upset him.

In the morning Sebastian was infinitely depressed. Even the old Ford starting so easily failed to cheer him. It was no virtue that a car should start downhill so easily. The dawn always made him sad, which was why he avoided it when he could. The valley below him was a solid, endless lake of woolly mist. He had almost allowed himself to be seduced. He was going to miss his breakfast later. He had, in addition, lost one of his virgin brides. He was engaged in the kind of adventure that he detested. His honor had been impugned. Today, and perhaps tomorrow as well, was wasted. The only thing that was satisfactory was the fact that he was finished with Olga. He was not even sure that he wanted to paint her now. But this again was double-edged. He had wanted to paint her. It was one of the things he had looked forward to. There was so little to look forward to: only the painting of a real masterpiece.

Driving in low gear he was enveloped in mist. It was folded over him like a blanket. The trees dripped with moisture. And perhaps he should have brought Nina with him. What was the good of going after one woman if you lost the other? Perhaps it was a mistake to have two women. You could not keep them happy; that was the biological basis of established morality. He was passing the place where he had told Channel he wished to be buried. But owing to the mist the magnificent view was obscured. It consisted of an ocean ... of an ocean of steaming clouds. He was not sure that it really was a suitable place. He hoped Channel would not need his car today. The last thing he wished was to cause him or anyone else any inconvenience. He was not a man who bore malice, but he must rescue his wife from a fate that must be worse than death for one brought up as she had been: consigned to him as a virgin by a doting father. And von Brandt, of all people — a Nazi who would have no respect for her.

Once the mist cleared, he would be able to go faster. He wondered how much gas there was in the tank. He wondered if the radiator was full. When he got down into the low country, he would see to everything — to the water, at any rate. There was plenty of water down there. He had been a fool not to think of food. He could have brought some from his house and a thermos flask of coffee. But all he had thought of had been his weapons — the professor's rifle, his own somewhat unreliable Belgian pistol, and the Moorish dagger. He was too impulsive, too reckless. He had so many defects of character. For a moment it occurred to him to turn the car off the road and allow it to precipitate him into the void beneath. What was the good of life when no painting even approximated the vision which had inspired it? Everyone betrayed him: his wife, his wives, Olga, Channel, his dog, even Wilson who had gone off with Bentinck without so much as looking at the nude he had commissioned. He missed going to the store with Channel for their discussions. To have them at home was not the same, and it was a great nuisance not being on speaking terms with Channel.

He began to think of his plan of action. He would get some food from the natives: bananas, paw-paws, some milk; he would fill up the radiator and if he had gas enough he would reach von Brandt's about ten o'clock. After that... Well, after that his plan would depend... Von Brandt's house, surrounded by its stockade, was situated halfway up a mountain farther along the range. There was waste land of lava to the north of it. He had often wondered why he had chosen that particular place. It was so far from the beaten track. Even natives avoided it as a rule, fearing the mountain devils that were supposed to inhabit its tortured peaks. His father-in-law's village was the only one in the vicinity. If I had a cup of coffee, he thought, I should feel better: something to eat and a boy playing the victrola. He had got soft living here. And now he was paying for it.

He thought of his near seduction. Had he been wise to resist temptation? The sexual act, as Channel called it, was so damned inconclusive ... a climax that was an anticlimax. A man never knew if he had achieved anything. He himself had never achieved anything. He wanted babies: many babies: fat ones that laughed and cried and gurgled and stole things and sent him crazy with annoyance. Then you knew you had done something. There they were, to fall over. The house littered with diapers and toys and baby carriages ... smelling of milk and powder ... of babies. He knew that if this were so he would probably leave the whole business in disgust, but at the same time it would be satisfactory, once it was over, in retrospect. That, after all, was the only satisfaction one ever got: the hope before and the memory after. Yes, he wanted babies, and breakfast.

A flock of guinea fowls ran across the road in front of the car. They were obscene like lice. They ran crouching on invisible legs. He hated them with their raucous cries, their bare blue and red crested heads, their white spotted feathers. He hated their idiocy and their cunning. Besides they were generally tough. Then he saw a snake, a big one. It was a python as thick through as his thigh. He hoped it would eat the guinea fowl, but this seemed unlikely. There was no justice. Some natives ate snakes. One day he would try one. He liked to try strange foods: snails, octopus, iguanas, ostrich eggs, penguin eggs with their opalescent whites ... anything new.

He kept thinking about food, which made him ashamed. This was not the moment for gastronomical recollection. He should be above such things. He was riding to the rescue of a maid. His was a mission of honor. He was ... Well, whatever else he was he was also hungry, which accounted for his thoughts.

Going round a corner he nearly ran into a truck. It was the professor and Retief. They shouted at him. He cursed them back and forgot them. He was hungry.

There was the village at last. The children clustered round him, sucking their fingers, touching the car, fondling their own protuberant little bellies. The girls and women followed them, laughing and chattering with more totos balanced on their naked, shining hips. He and the car were a centre of a mass of black, moving, almost unclad flesh. At least about these people there was no subterfuge. He had not got over his seduction . . . by now, he was convinced that he had been seduced. These blacks were honest even in their smell. They made no effort to disguise it. He was delighted as usual by their simplicity. They wanted money, clothing, anything they could beg or steal. A child was trying to unscrew the spotlight with its fingers while its mother stared at it with black-eyed approval. They wanted him to sleep with them; they wanted him to give them his hat. In brief, they wanted. It was very satisfactory. He was charmed.

A few men lounged about in the little mud compounds in front of the huts. One, a very big man, was engaged in dressing a friend's hair with a mixture of fat and red ochre. Every now and then he stepped back to admire his work. When he did this, he wiped his hands on his own head. How different it all was from Olga's bedroom and her iced champagne which had not been as sweet as he had hoped! She had deceived him in this as well. How different the women's little aprons from her green peignoir.

He asked for food. There was a stampede to get it. One by one they returned with paw-paws, sweet potatoes, yams, doubtful eggs, sour milk in calabashes, Kaffir beer, meat — days old and rotten — white grubs in an empty tortoise-shell, bananas and wild fruits. One moment he had been hungry and alone. The next, surrounded by these children of nature, these black Eves, he was faced with a surfeit. He descended from the car with dignity, and, picking up a little stick, put it into the gas tank. It was nearly full. Channel was the kind of man who would keep his tank full. His contempt for such men was mixed with relief.

He chose what he wanted from the women, paid them with some small coins he had loose in his pocket, and sat down to eat while the women stood round admiring him with that naive obscenity with which they treated all men. Knowing something of their language, it made him laugh. And what was it the English bourgeois Fascist poet Kipling had said about Judy O'Grady and the Colonel's Lady?

He found it easy to laugh now that he was eating. One of the dark ladies was pushing a little girl in front of her towards him. She wanted to sell her. He shook his head. His mouth was too full to talk. The child expressed relief, but her mother was angry at his lack of taste and initiative. She expressed it vociferously to the amusement of the other women. It was all very friendly.

When he had done he would go on and shoot the betrayer of his wife. Yes, he thought, I am about to commit my first crime of passion. It was amazing how his spirits had risen. One could do nothing, not even commit a crime of passion, when hungry. This would prove an interesting thesis for a discussion with Channel when the doctor had apologized to him and their relationship was resumed. He looked at the Ford. It was not much of a car. But Channel was curiously sentimental over it. He rolled a cigarette.

The little wind was heavy with the scent of men, of their dwellings, of their comings and goings, of the accustomed smells of the village; heavy with pollen that would fertilize the flowers on the swinging trees, with bacilli that would kill the men; with spores; fragrant with wood smoke, the smell of flowers, the smell of standing beasts. There were bees and flies and butterflies; young men, pregnant women, slim girls, dark-eyed slips that stepped daintily like deer, full men with heavy loins, slinking dogs, red cocks scratching for their hens. The breeze was heavy, weighted and scented with increase, charged with death and putrefaction, with beauty, with significance and the lack of it, thick with unseen dust — caressing, calling alike to man and to beast, to fowl and tree and flower; calling to the dove, the cock, the bull, the lion, and the young girl equally. Since time began, the little breeze had blown the breath of scented increase in its seasons.

It was all as it should be, each thing uncaring, each thing unknowing, each profoundly unself-conscious, servant only to accident and desire, ready only for the immediacy of its own fulfilment; ignorant of experience, careless of consequence, balanced precariously on the knife-edged moment, facing development that ended with extinction and left increase behind it, sown by the wayside of its passage. The crow, the coo, the roar, the neigh, the oath, the love word, all one with the little wind, all ephemeral, all of the moment, yet all charged with all previous moments; today, tonight . . . Thus was tomorrow born, with facility and without hesitation, without much pleasure or regret, out of urgency only, out of a little wind that blew, scented, through the forest, stirring the leaves of the trees, rustling them.

One day he would paint it.

Sebastian looked up. A group of men were standing round him. What were they saying?

'The war, Bwana. The white man's war. What is it?'

Why had no one told him about the war? Olga . . . Channel? Olga had said something, but he had paid no attention to her. His mind and heart had been too full. Even now he did not feel the full significance of the war. Later, he thought, I will consider it: after I have dealt with that Nazi.

But that was changed too. It was no longer purely a crime

of passion that he contemplated. No longer did he only appeal to the unwritten law for justification. His act of revenge, of justice, was also an act of war. By what had happened since yesterday it had become this. This thought spoilt some of his pleasure.

He got into the car and put his foot on the starter.

Chapter 31

The TIER GARTEN

~~~~~~~~~~~~~~

VON BRANDT CALLED HIS HOUSE THE *Tier Garten*.

The bungalow faced the lava valley between two volcanic mountains. He had chosen the site with care. It was designed for privacy. The natives hated this part of the foothills, considering it inhabited by the spirits of the dead. It was beautiful in a tortured, demented fashion. And it was private.

The house itself was large. A long sitting room was flanked at either end with a bedroom and bathroom. From his own room, the larger of the two, there was an extension which was his office. A nine-foot, fly-screened veranda surrounded the house. Behind it were the kitchen quarters, the compound and the kraals and cages where he kept his beasts and birds. In front was the garden. Beyond the garden the swirl of lava, rock-hard in some places, still boiling in others — cold or hot, with intermediate areas where a thin crust had formed over the molten stone. There were pools of almost boiling water and crevasses that exuded poisonous gas. There were stunted trees and patches of coarse grass, and then beyond, the volcanoes rose majestically, green-clothed in vegetation or stark with recent eruptions.

As he drove back from Marais', von Brandt was thinking of his home: of the animals he must destroy, of Olga — of Maria, who would be waiting for him. And it was war. War. He kept repeating the word to himself: War. Glory. The Iron Cross, first class. It was a shame to have to kill the okapi. It had been hard to get from the forests of the lower river, and Hamburg wanted it. The other animals were nothing: a job lot: easily replaced. Somehow he would save the okapi. And now he might get Congo: a half-grown tame gorilla: when he went back for his investiture. Suppose he could take them? That would be something: added glamour: hero, naturalist, explorer. Then there was his collection of whips: kibokos, sjamboks, whips made of rhino and hippo skin, whips made from giraffe, from buffalo hide. He would take them, too. He would give them away as presents in the right quarters. There was a use for whips in Europe now.

What a clever man Marais was! What an honor it was to serve under such a man! He thought of the leather case again, of the Cross on its bed of velvet. It was as good as his. He raised his hand from the wheel and touched his chest. He would spend an hour with Maria — Marais would never find out — and then get on with his part of the program. The detonators, a few metres of fuse... The battery which would explode the charge was in place. Everything was so simple, so beautiful; part of a world-wide design that was like a great painting in its perfection. Then honors, women, riches.

The blood pounded in his veins. This was the crowning moment of his life. From now on the pattern would change. He would come into his own. The Führer knew how to reward those who served him. The battle was to the strong. The race was to the swift. Only one thing counted... strength. He felt himself strong, indefatigable, undefeatable: Aryan, German, almost a god.

He was approaching his house. He wanted Maria's insatiable black flesh. He needed a woman — a black woman. The richness of that black ivory beneath him... the texture of that satin skin between his fingers. Olga's whiteness could wait. He would take her to Germany, and Sebastian's two girls, with the gorilla and the okapi. When he had done with them, he would give them away. They would serve their purpose till he

found a good German girl: an actress, perhaps: a film star.
Marais had said he could have anybody; that they would run
after him. Naturally there would be publicity. It would be in
the papers. The man who took Egypt alone. The man who
... There was no limit to his dreams. Dreams? They were no
longer dreams: they were realities: the act, the decoration, the
return to the Reich, the triumphal tour, the well-earned holiday. Then back to Africa, a Gauleiter, king over a country as
large as France.

Ten minutes more and he would be home.

Only the Germans were wise. Under their inspired Leader
they would conquer and reform the world. With the Jews and
communists and capitalists eliminated, the German race in its
rightful and master place, a new golden age would dawn. The
era of order without sentiment, of justice without mercy, of
strength, beauty, and the religion of blood. His tongue
mouthed the word *blood*, savored it. His own blood pulsed to
the thought, it suffused his eyes. It constricted his throat as
it pumped through his arteries. Blood crying to blood. Physical, actual blood rising to the thought of blood. The life stream
and death stream. It rose in a red tide, misting everything.
The blood of the soldiers falling gloriously in battle, of their
victims, of the women, of the children, of the Jews, running in
the gutters of their ghettos. Only in blood was there safety: in
blood, the blood of your enemies: in blood, the sacred blood
of your comrades: in the holy blood of the Leader.

So would the new Germany of the Third Reich rise. The
indignity of Versailles, the insults of the occupation, redeemed
in this hot, flowing, pulsing tide.

All other men were mad. Democracy was a madness. Security of the mind and body were dependent on the organized
leadership of a trained élite: the masters of the masters.

He was almost home. An hour, and he would have left
again upon his mission. The eyes of all Germany are upon
you, he thought. They know nothing of you now. Tomorrow

or the day after they will know. But unknowing, they watch
you. Maria... Heil Hitler... Blood...

Maria had waited for von Brandt all night. She had been
given food by his butler. She had exchanged gossip with the
other servants. They knew why she had come: to lie with the
white man ... to be beaten by him and rewarded afterward.
It was strange that he should wish to do this. They seldom
beat their women. A woman cost money. It was therefore
foolish to abuse a valuable possession.

In the morning Maria ate again. And went on waiting.
There was nothing on her mind. One white man was very like
another — inadequate and evil-smelling. All white men were
mad. And as to being beaten — he did not beat her very
hard. All he desired was to see her cringe and to hear her
screams before he pursued her and took her as she ran, sometimes in one room, sometimes in another.

What she had to do today was a little more complex... yet
simple enough, really. She knew her way about the lava of the
mountain. In her mind she balanced her fear of Entobo
against the gifts the German gave her. But as the witch doctor
had so wisely remarked, 'Gifts are useless to the dead.'

She chewed a stick of sugar-cane as she waited. She cleaned
her teeth with a little twig that she had made into a brush.
She examined her toes, holding her feet on her knees. She
combed out her hair and rearranged it. She waited.

When the car came, she would run into the house. He
would run after her waving his kiboko. Then...

The car was coming. She could hear it. The boys could
hear it, they were looking down the driveway. They looked
back at her. She looked at the road ... at the house ... at the
boys. A tremor ran over her. She might not like him, but he
was a man. Was he going to possess her again or was she going
to get revenge for the times that he had?

Maria was waiting for von Brandt in the big sitting room.
He seized her arm. She slipped from his grasp. Part of her
dress remained in his hand. She was frightened of him. She
had never been frightened before. But he had never hit her like
this before. The whip had caught her across the croup — a
hard, stinging blow. And his face ... He should not have her
if he looked like that, even if there had been no plan.

The sofa was between them, her bare breasts were rising
and falling, her nostrils dilated. She looked back at him.

He looked different. She had never seen anyone look like
this. There was no expression, even of lust, in his eyes. He did
not look like a man who would take a woman: he looked like
a man who would kill one. The eyes of a madman ... expressionless, blue stones that shone with a fury she could not understand. He looked at her, beyond her, through her.

He was swearing. He raised his whip and brought it down
on the sofa. The rawhide cut through the material. He was
swallowing hard, saliva dripped from his lips. His face was
red, his neck thick with blood.

She began to scream. He was still swearing at her. He
moved towards her. She moved round the sofa. The whip
whistled through the air again as he plunged forward. It cut
her wrist. It was like being touched with a red-hot iron. It
burnt. Blood flowed. She moved away from him; they moved
round the big sofa.

Without knowing what she did, she was feeling for the fas-
tenings of her dress. She must get free. She pulled: the silk
tore, she pushed it down over her hips. She was naked. Free
from the clinging yellow folds of taffeta ... naked as a brown
deer. Her eyes never left his face. As he saw her naked, he
sprang at her again. She slipped past him, through the window ... the door. If only she could get to the door of the
stoep. She felt the netting with her hand as she pushed it.
It banged back on its spring into his face.

Naked. Running. She had not run naked since she was a

child. *The buck* they had called her then. Like a buck she ran, bent forward, driving the ground from beneath her feet, spurning it. She heard him shouting behind her: heard him pounding after her. He had on heavy boots. She cleared a hedge of flowering shrubs. She ran towards the mountains ... towards her home that was beyond them — her father's house. The lava cut her feet; his boots would save him. She had slowed up. Entobo had said ... Did she dare? How light she was! ... how light! The buck, naked but lame. He was a heavy man. She swung left to the crust. It would carry her. It must.

Somebody was shooting. Maria heard shots and the crack of a bullet above her.

Shots. She was running naked. Her feet hurt her. The rock under her was spongy. She was on the crust — and running.

Chapter 32

MARIA

~~~~~~~~~~~~~~~~

SEBASTIAN SAW MARIA AND VON BRANDT THE MINUTE HE GOT
out of the car. He had decided to reconnoitre the position.
Now there was nothing to investigate. His wife, stripped
naked, was running from her seducer. It was a simple situation, one that had many historic precedents.

He found himself running, too. A wild joy permeated his
being. This is better than painting. This is the true release —
to pursue a Fascist. The Fascisti represented all evil to his
mind, all the things that he did not like he labelled Fascist.
Boiled mutton, which he had had in England, was Fascist.
Commercial artists were Fascists ... any artist who sold his
work was a Fascist. Dinner jackets, butlers, gilt furniture,
Dresden china, potted palms, orchid corsages, turtle soup,
motor cars less than seven years old, were all tarred with the
same brush. In a miraculous manner a car became less Fascist
as it got older, attaining a mystic political puberty at the age
of seven. At that age a respectable proletarian could own it
without loss of dignity.

He was a brave man running after a Fascist dog. He was a
Sir Galahad saving a maiden from herself, but nevertheless
saving her. He was an outraged husband. Meanwhile, it was
good to run with a rifle in one's hand. It proved something.
His courage, his manhood. It proved a thousand things and
was physically enjoyable as well. To run stimulated thought.
He liked the way his legs shot out and lifted him on in great

bounds. There was a certain magnificence about it. The charging lion ... the leopard ... the bull ... the stallion. He gave a neighing cry. 'Viva la Republica!' he cried. 'Viva, Viva ... Viva Garibaldi ... Viva Bolívar ... Viva the liberators!'

How he gained on him! He could try a long shot at him now. But he did not wish to stop. He was intoxicated with his own speed. He wanted to kill by hand. To kill him as he painted, with his thick nail-bitten fingers, closing them round his throat, tightening them, pressing his knuckles into his carotid arteries, cracking his spine, holding his head back, forcing it till it sagged there held only by skin and muscle bereft of all support. He thought of the blood suffusing that hated face, of the eyes starting out, of the tongue bitten and lolling. He wanted to sink his teeth into the brown sunburnt Fascist throat, to taste blood on his lips, to stamp upon the body and then to crow like a victorious cock ... resonantly; to beat his chest like a gorilla, to spurn with his heels kicking like a horse, to trample and roll upon the cadaver, to kneel upon it trumpeting like an elephant. His rage boiled joyously within him. It was so long since he had killed a Fascist. I had forgotten, he thought, how beautiful it was. Tears of regret at his lack of memory came into his eyes, clouding them, so that he almost fell over a small bush. Now he could again revenge his dead friends, his own wounds: acting at the same time within the unwritten law which permits a man to protect his women, and the international law of war. He was free to work his will upon an enemy.

He slid down a gully and clambered up the other side. There they were still running. Von Brandt was gaining on Maria. She must be letting him do so for some obscure purpose of her own. And he was gaining on von Brandt. The girl was swinging to the left. Von Brandt would cut her off ... she must be mad! If she had not been mad, she would never have left him for such a creature. Had she understood nothing of

what he had told her? Had he failed in converting her to the
principles of Christian anarchy?

Only when a man had been brave did he dare to acknowledge fear. And only he himself was the judge of this. His
courage was a matter between himself and his heart. A time
always came when he could show courage. Every man got his
chance. Every man was tested, and if he passed the test he had
the right to be afraid afterward if he wanted to. He had often
been afraid and did not mind saying so. He had proved himself when he had taken a machine-gun post in Spain. He had
taken it alone and unaided. It had been a terrible, a fearful
thing to attempt. He had attempted it. He had accomplished
it. People had respected him for it. He had made a name for
himself and could then acknowledge fear. He was terrified of
cows. A cow was a terrible animal. A bull was worse. He had
the greatest respect for bull-fighters of all kinds — matadors,
picadors, all who dared to face bulls. After taking that gun
post, it had been a great relief to be able to acknowledge this.
I am afraid of cows, he had said . . . and bulls. People had not
said 'Sebastian is a coward.' They had said 'Sebastian is a
brave man. Is it not strange that he fears cows and bulls?'
It was agreed that it was strange and no one had expected him
to approach them after that. A machine-gun post — he
rushed forward; a cow or a bull — he rushed back. It was an
eccentricity, no more than that. It was reasonable too. It was
even religious, this not liking things with horns. The Devil
had horns as everyone knew. The good Sisters who had
brought him up had been afraid of cows, perhaps for this very
reason. Women, though fools, were sensitive to these things.
They were very aware of sin and the Devil, who was always,
according to them, wishing to get into bed with them and
make them sin. The sin was that they all enjoyed it. A good
woman was one who was very much afraid of anything she
enjoyed which was why she kept away from men, and all
horned creatures who were by their nature related to the
Devil.

He stopped to gain breath. How that German could run!
The result, no doubt, of his early training in the strength-
through-joy movement. The good Sisters had never taught
him to run; and that foolish virgin — he still thought of her as
that — had stopped and was looking back: like Lot's wife.
Could a woman never run without looking back? Did she not
know what would happen if he caught her? She must know.
He had often pursued her himself. And in this matter, this
alone, there was little difference, as far as results went, between a woman caught by a good proletarian or a bad Fascist.
Communist, some had called him. His heart was hammering
and he gasped for breath. How could an artist ever be a Communist? He was above all an individualist. No, he was no
Communist. He was a Christian Communalistic Anarchist.
They were very rare, only the most advanced type of man
could understand such a political credo of cooperative, proletarian freedom under God. Meanwhile, his little brown
wife, his buttercup, would get herself raped, and then when
he had killed the Fascist he would have to make love to her
out there under a tree. Poor child, he would console her. He
would, by his love-making, obliterate the other and terrible
memory. If he did not do this, she would no doubt suffer from
some psychosis. It was his duty as her husband and protector.
He began to run again. It would be very pleasant.

Now he was near enough. Two hundred metres. He knelt
and fired. Maria was running lame. It would give her time.
Von Brandt slowed up and turned to look for him. He fired
again. Von Brandt ran on. He was going to cut her off, just
as he had thought he would. Why had she turned? Why had
she not gone on running straight? What had happened to her
yellow dress? It had been expensive.

Sebastian got up and walked on. He must get his breath, if
he was going to hit him. Still those shots had done something.
And with him arriving so opportunely Maria was safe.

There were more people on the opposite ridge: a white man,
some natives with spears. It was Wilson.

He looked down again. Maria was running, but going very lame, and she had lost a lot of ground by changing direction. Her foot must be badly hurt. Von Brandt was ploughing after her. The going seemed to be heavy. Then it happened. Von Brandt sank up to his knees. He threw out his arms and fell. He was screaming. Maria stopped running. Sebastian stood still with his rifle butt on the ground. Wilson and the Kaffirs had stopped halfway down the hill.

Von Brandt's fall had arrested everything ... and his screams. They were much fainter now.

Suddenly he had it. Von Brandt was burning in the lava. He had gone through the crust. That was why Maria had swung round. To lead him over the treacherous, molten quicksand. How clever she was! What a credit to him! His little brown bird to think of a thing like that. And the Nazi was dead or would be in a few minutes.

Maria was picking her way back towards him. Treading lightly, leaping here and there. He held his breath. She was safe now: on hard ground. At least she had sat down. You would not sit down unless you were safe. Besides, it would be hot. She was looking at her foot.

Wilson was quite near her. She was waiting for them to come up to her. It was not right that Wilson should see his wife naked. The men with Wilson were pointing at von Brandt. They were Masai. He could recognize them now by their painted shields and long thin spears.

What a morning it had been! His resistance to Olga; stealing the car; shooting von Brandt; rescuing his wife. And now he was about to effect a meeting with Wilson and his savages on a volcanic mountain. Von Brandt dead. What a day! He ran his hand through his hair.

What a good thing war had been declared: it would clear up any little difficulties about von Brandt's death.

And that was why he had met the professor and Retief on their way home again as he had come down the mountain.

It had seemed funny at the time. It was only two days since they had left and they had been going to stay a month. They had shouted at him, but he had not paid any attention to them. He had thought they must have forgotten something. But that was it. The war had come. That was why Wilson was coming back, too. But where was Bentinck?

He wondered if there was enough gas in the Ford to get them all home.

Wilson had left the mission in the morning with two of the Masai to guide him. The others and Jan had waited to see Bentinck buried. War had come in the night. Owen had come in to tell him. So Bentinck had been right. They were too late to do anything now. *Get back to Olga. Get the stuff to Frazer.* He tried to make head or tail of Bentinck's last words: The Bastards ... dynamite ... Egypt ...

The Masai stalked in single file in front of him.

It was an accident that they had come out onto this valley, as far as he was concerned. The original plan had been to pass by von Brandt's ... to visit him. But that had been abandoned with Bentinck's death. That they were here now was simply that it lay on their line of march.

When he had seen the house and kraals, he had recognized it from Bentinck's description. Then he had seen a woman running with a white man running after her. The man must be von Brandt. Then shots. He had not seen where they had come from till one of the Masai pointed with his spear. Then he had seen another white man.

Von Brandt had fallen. Wilson had recognized Maria. But why was she not dressed? And the other man ... Sebastian. Wilson found himself running towards von Brandt. Sebastian was running. The girl was standing poised with her finger in her mouth like a child watching. Then she sat down and looked at her foot.

Von Brandt was no longer moving. After his fall he had

screamed, had flapped his arms, and then had lain still on his face.

'Wilson!' Sebastian shouted. He was waving his rifle. 'We have arrived in time. It is due to the grace of God.' He crossed himself. 'She is safe.'

Does he imagine I knew about all this? Wilson was bewildered. Sebastian had put down his rifle and was stripping off his shirt.

'Put this on, Maria,' he said. 'Cover your nakedness, my love, my little brown bird.'

She put it on reluctantly, drawing it over her head. The sleeves were much too long. Funny how you noticed these things.

'The Fascist is dead,' Sebastian said. 'He cooks.'

The significance of the remark dawned on Wilson. That was why ...

'Are we going to leave him there?'

'Why not?' Sebastian asked. 'And, besides, it is not practical to get him. He cooks,' he repeated. 'I know of this place. In a few days nothing will remain. Come, Maria, we will go back. I will drive you back,' he said to Wilson. 'I have the car here.'

He had the car. It sounded as if he was offering him a lift home after the theatre.

Maria said something to Sebastian. She was pointing to the house. It looked very peaceful. There was smoke rising from the cookhouse. Wilson could see some boys moving about. Either they did not know what had happened to their master or did not care.

'She wants her dress,' Sebastian said. 'She says she left it there. It was a good dress, of yellow taffeta. You remember it, I expect?'

One of the Masai was investigating the lava, testing it with his spear. The other had sat down to wait. Maria was looking at her foot again.

'Come,' Sebastian said. 'We will go down and get the dress, and I will wash out your foot. I think we will have coffee, too. I want coffee. Von Brandt had good coffee. I forgot my breakfast.' He picked up his rifle.

Wilson followed him to the car: Bentinck dead: von Brandt dead: a gorilla dead: the war had come. The picture was changing quickly ... a play. The curtain of the second act was going up. *Lift home. I've got the car ...*

Sebastian drove them to the house. He shouted to von Brandt's servants, 'Bring food, bring coffee. The Fascist is dead.'

Maria exchanged Sebastian's shirt for her yellow dress and joined them. The place was in an uproar, everyone talking, Sebastian shouting for food. Maria, flaunting her yellow taffeta, gesticulating.

'His boys are glad he is dead,' Sebastian said. He banged on the table with his fist. 'Now food and coffee. Mother of God, bring food!' he shouted. While they waited, he examined everything ... the collection of whips ... the S.S. uniform.

In von Brandt's bedroom they found a box of detonators and some lengths of fuse. They excited Sebastian. It appeared that he understood explosives. He had worked with them in Spain.

'You see, Wilson,' he said, 'what a good deed we have done. A good man does not have engines of destruction in his home. A good man does not seduce innocent maidens ...'

Here was proof that Bentinck had known what he was talking about. Sebastian, with Maria on his knee, was fitting a length of fuse into a detonator and clamping it with his teeth. 'If we could find the explosives, we could blow something up,' he said ... 'I should like to blow something up again.'

It was a good thing they could not find explosives. Wilson did not feel that Sebastian in his present state of elation was to be trusted with demolitions.

Maria was very silent in the arms of her husband. Her silk dress was torn. The giver of gifts was dead. She was growing more and more uncertain about getting a reward from Entobo. And she would have to offer some explanation of her presence here. She considered the Masai speculatively. They were very beautiful young men. They were preparing to leave, one ride in a motor car being enough for them. She wished she could go with them. She wished her husband would put her down. She wished the German was still alive. She wished she could join the houseboys in the kitchen . . . And her foot hurt her. Someone should have looked at it. Was she not the heroine, the cause of all this confusion? This was her only satisfaction. What had happened had been caused by her. And now they were going home.

Tears filled her eyes. She had been unable to steal anything.

Chapter 33

The RETURN

CHANNEL WAS AWAKENED WITH THE NEWS OF WAR AND THE theft of his car. Laertes was most disturbed about the car which he had gone to clean and had found gone.

So war had come.

Yesterday evening he had taken something new. Even to himself he would not acknowledge that he took something too often. There were so many things to try, and the only way to see how they worked was take them yourself.

Obviously, it was Sebastian who had taken the Ford. There was no one else on the Station who could drive, except Olga. Other things were queer, too. There was only one Batanga girl outside Sebastian's house . . . Nina, the less frivolous of the two. This confirmed his suspicions that Sebastian had gone in search of her sister. After he had had breakfast, he would speak to Nina. He hoped Sebastian would not damage his car. It needed special, almost tender handling. For instance, it did not like to take corners rapidly, owing to a slight defect in the steering. It had to be coaxed round them. The feed pipe had a tendency to choke, and on a hill the hand brake was not strong enough to hold it if you left it standing without stones behind the wheels. And there were various other little things which made driving more interesting. One thing was certain, it was no use worrying. Sebastian would bring it back or he would not. Meanwhile, he must have breakfast.

He breakfasted. Josephine Baker sang. The yellow dog came for scraps.

In the night war had come, his boys said; his car had gone.
Sebastian and Maria were missing. There was plenty to think
about.

The mist in the valley below was lifting. He lit a cigarette
and walked over to Sebastian's house. Nina was sitting in the
shade eating a mango and weeping.

'Where is your master?' he asked.

'He has gone to seek my sister, lord,' she said. 'My sister is
bad. She has gone to another man — the German hunter of
beasts. He promised her six dresses of silk.' She had no idea
what Maria had been promised, but six dresses of silk occurred to her. To go for less would have been foolish. 'To me
he promised nothing, so I stayed. My sister is bad. Our father
will be angry if the painter of pictures claims back her price.
My father will beat me for not stopping her. The painter of
pictures, our husband, has already beaten me. My heart is
sore.'

'Why did he beat you?' Channel asked.

'Because I would not tell him where Maria was till he had
beaten me. Then, when I had told him, he beat me again.
He beat me with a stick' — she pointed to it — 'and not with
a whip. Our father will be angry when he hears that. A
woman should be beaten with a whip.'

'Yes,' Channel said, 'of course a whip should be used.' How
conventional people were! He tightened the belt of his
blue dressing gown, bringing the heads of the white dragons
closer together on his chest. Now for Olga. If she was not up,
she could get up, or he would see her in bed. She looked
charming in bed. He wondered how many men had thought
that. That there was war would not change her appearance.
He left Nina. She reached for another mango and began to
cry again.

In a world armed to the teeth and actually at war, this was
a comedy — a teapot storm: the running away of a native
woman to her lover; the petty fornications of the fair Olga;

Sebastian's feverish painting; his own book; his experiments and the few medical services he had been able to render in this pin-point of the universe. Yet to all of them their own lives were important, to be lived out in detail against this immense background of political unrest. Man's hopes and efforts were for the small things, the personal, and no matter how he was swept along in the tide of political or economic change, he kept fighting his way out of it towards the personal and the small, towards his own microscopic ends. A soldier fought in a war, but he thought of his home, his wife and children, his shop or his farm. A woman thought in terms of her children, her husband, her lover. In the end everything came down to man and woman; to their relation to each other; to the family to which they had given birth or belonged. How different Olga would have been if her child had lived, or if the professor had been younger and more ardent... if... there were a thousand if's to each question. He stood for a moment outside the professor's house and then went in. She was still in her room.

He called, 'Olga! Olga!'

'Yes. Come in. I'm still in bed.' What a pretty voice she had! A world at war and the mind still registered the beauty of a woman's voice.

She was altogether charming as she sat up in bed to greet him. Her golden hair was down, her face flushed like a child's with sleep. She put her knuckles into her eyes to rub them and stared up at him. Innocent as a child, he thought. More innocent because of her knowledge; more satisfied than any child could be because she has arrived at a point where she thinks she understands.

'Good morning,' he said. 'You look very well.'

'Good morning, Doctor. I am well. And in no need of your services. But I am glad you have come... I want to ask you something. What has happened to Sebastian? He came in last night to borrow one of Jean's rifles. I told him of the war

and he took no notice. He said he was going to shoot something. I have never known him to shoot before.'

'There has always been some question of Sebastian's sanity.
Anyway, if it makes you any happier, he has stolen my car.'
He sat down.

'Fancy taking your car,' Olga said.

'Nina says he has gone after Maria. She has run away to
von Brandt.'

'Von Brandt . . . he . . .'

'He what?'

'Nothing. Only I can't understand the way men like these
black women.'

'Are there any others? After all, Olga, you are the only
white woman here, and you are married. How they must
regret it,' he said. 'How I would regret it myself if I were a
younger man.'

She looked up at him. Innocence, when one analyzed it,
was no more than lack of desire . . . something achieved by the
ignorance of childhood, the satiation of the adult, or the exhaustion of the aged. Satisfaction and innocence were then
synonyms, while satisfaction lasted.

He was interested in the ambivalence of his mind. The war
was the essential thing. These reflections were beside the
point . . . an escape from the reality which was about to overwhelm them all.

Olga handed him her cigarette case. He took one.

'What were you thinking?' she asked.

'Of men and women, my child; of my youth, perhaps; of
how beautiful you are. Blondes are always beautiful in bed.
They look so clean. It is possible that the war entered my
head, but I dismissed it.'

She laughed. 'What a compliment!' She was silent, and
then said, 'Do you think Sebastian will shoot von Brandt?'

'How do I know what he will do? I doubt if he knows himself.'

'He took a rifle. He said he was going shooting.'

'And you hope so . . .'

She shrugged her shoulders. 'I hope nothing. It is not my affair.'

'No,' he said. 'It is no one's affair.' He got up. 'I must get back.'

Olga sat up straight. 'What are you going to do, Channel?'

'Do? The war, you mean? Not much today. Begin to pack, perhaps. You realize that it is over here' — he made a gesture — 'that all this is done.'

'Yes.' Channel was right. Her work here was finished now. Not that there had ever been much in it beyond reporting the gossip she heard and arranging for a man like Bentinck, who knew the natives, to work among them. Modern espionage consisted, as far as the agent was concerned, in collecting every piece of even apparently irrelevant information . . . in reporting trends and rumors. Her position as the only woman in this part of the world had made the Station a social centre where inevitably almost everything came to be discussed.

Where were Bentinck and Wilson? When would they get back?

As he went round his hospital, Channel thought how interesting it was that they had consciously, almost self-consciously, put the war out of their minds this morning. Olga had mentioned it. He had spoken of it, naturally. But neither of them had really said anything. They had talked so much about it before it came. Now there was nothing to say: one could only accept it. They had not spoken of it because it was too big, too far-reaching, too important. They would get used to the idea in a few hours and listen to the radio and discuss the news; but now . . . no. In Europe they were conditioned to thinking and speaking of it as a reality, but here, in this paradise — this evil paradise — the discussion had been academic. Like a discussion of hell.

He looked up. A truck drove in: the professor and Retief were back. Of course they were back: the war: it had come to them in the forest; come on the drums in the night.

The professor and Retief were getting out of the truck as he reached it. They all shook hands. It was many years since they had shaken hands.

'So it has come, Channel.'

'Yes, it has come.'

They went into the house together. Olga was waiting for them.

Le Blanc kissed his wife. 'We should have been back sooner,' he said, 'if we had not had a breakdown.'

'A breakdown? Where?'

The conversational level interested Channel. How casual they were keeping it!

'Soon after the village, Olga, ma chère. We had just passed Sebastian driving like a lunatic the other way.'

'Sebastian borrowed one of your rifles, do you mind? I could not stop him.'

The professor patted her hand. 'I mind nothing. It is good to be back. I was afraid for you.'

Chapter 34

The COLONEL

AFTER HE HEARD VON BRANDT LEAVE, MARAIS WENT OVER TO look at the dredges. This phase of his life was over. The war had ended it.

A born organizer, he had made this place. He was a manager, one of the new types of logical men: a producer, thinking in terms of product, to whom human beings meant less than nothing except in relation to production or to the consumption of products.

He went round his garden, savoring its beauty, looking at the flowers, at the shrubs and trees. He had made all this, too. He had given this small section of the wilds an air of civilization, of sophistication. He had cleared it, planted it, stamped it with his mark; worked it up from jungle into its present superneat perfection. It could be done everywhere, the world could be tamed. But only by administrators. The British had no idea of exploitation. They believed in rights. Rights had vanished with the machine gun, the tank, and the bomber. Rights — he spat out his cigar stub — were something you had to put up with when you were without the means of suppressing them.

By this time von Brandt would be well on his way. He smiled as he thought of von Brandt's vanity. How that little black Cross had affected him! And the implications of the Cross . . . glory, women, riches, position. An interesting man, von Brandt. Almost homosexual, and like so many of his kind, overcompensating his defect by his affairs with women: not knowing that he hated women. A sadist who confused all issues. He might have loved a boy: a woman he could only brutalize. Yes, he was an interesting case: a human violin to be played by anyone who understood the mechanism of his mind. Von Brandt, who slept in a hair net ... with his collection of whips about him.

The rhythmic throbbing of the dredges gave Marais pleasure. He stopped walking up and down to listen to them. Engines sucking mud and gold out of the river bed. It was symbolic of the New Order. Most men were mud, less than nothing. For the moment, till events further crystallized themselves, there was only one thing left to do. The Station and that ridiculous professor must be cleaned up — his formula was needed; and Olga, who thought she was fooling everybody, must be put in her place. Fritz could have her later. It was a small job, almost without risk: a mad painter, an old doctor almost equally mad with his passion for hypnotic investigation. The professor and Retief were away, but they would be home by this evening. Everyone knew of the war by now. It was not necessary to be a student of psychology to be able to deduce the action of the professor. He would return to his wife. Bentinck was dead. That had made him laugh when he heard it: a hunter caught in a trap. Of them all Bentinck had been the only one of any significance. He had respected him.

He lit another cigar. Men were moving in Africa. Moving all over the world: men like that fool von Brandt. Other men, German planters, farmers, were collecting, getting ready for the moment of attack. Everything was planned. Der Tag had come again, but this time failure was impossible. What was it Napoleon had said? ... Planned to the last button on the last gaiter.

He spent the morning and early afternoon resting comfortably; he had trained himself to relax. Only fools wore

themselves out. By an effort of will he put the little figures
out of his mind. There had been no more of them.

On his way to the Station Botanique, Marais passed von
Brandt's. He did not stop; there was no need to. Von
Brandt would report to him on his return. He looked down
the driveway that led to the house. There were fresh motor
tracks crossing each other. There would be three lots, naturally: he had come to see him, he had gone home again, and
he had left on his mission. Automatically, without slowing
down, he checked them.

Marais laughed. He was going on a visit: on a formal call
that would turn into something else. He thought of himself
bowing over Olga's hand, raising it to his lips. *How nice of you
to come . . . a drink, of course!*

Of course! Then he would steer the conversation.

He drove at a reasonable speed. He always did unless there
was reason for hurry. To drive faster than you needed was
not efficient.

He passed Bentinck's store. He turned up towards the
mountain road. He gave the car more gas as it climbed. He
was amused. Yes, he was very amused. '*Here comes old Papa
Marais,*' he thought. '*Here he comes to call.*'

The professor, Retief, and Olga were in the sitting room
when he came in. Where were Sebastian and Channel?

'Why, Meneer Marais, how nice it is to see you,' Olga said.
He bent over her hand. They had been gathered round the
radio. He waved to it.

'So I bring you no news?' He smiled. He had never felt
more friendly towards them: children, caught in the web he
had woven.

'Of course we are neutrals,' Olga said. 'But it is bound to
affect us.'

'You are neutral by marriage, madame, and you were
born in Poland?'

'Yes, but it is long since I was there.' In her mind Olga saw her country. She thought of her home: of the Polish army. 'It will not be easy to conquer Poland,' she said. 'They have a fine army, and there are England and France.' It seemed silly when she had said it. How were they to get to Poland?

'The Poles must meet something new, madame: a mechanized force such as the world has never seen. Can men fight monsters of steel?' Where were Sebastian and Channel? He must sit so that he commanded the door.

'And our painter friend — the good Sebastian?' he asked.

'He is away,' Olga laughed. 'He has lost one of his wives.' Retief was putting ice into the cocktail-shaker.

Marais brought a cigar from his pocket. 'You do not mind?'

'Of course not. You always smoke them, don't you?'

The professor sat with his elbows on his knees, holding his hands in front of him, fingertip to fingertip.

'A war will interrupt your little experiments, Professor,' Marais said.

'It will also increase their importance, meneer. This is a war for raw products: for oil and meat . . . for rubber, for fat. A war of imbeciles, for how will war increase them?'

Retief filled the glasses and handed them round. It was a friendly scene. Olga beautiful, poised; the charming hostess. The savant, her husband, leaning back in his chair. The admiring assistant dispensing hospitality. How lucky he had arrived just at this moment! Lucky that the professor was at home. No, not lucky. Nothing planned was lucky. He had known they were on their way back. He had calculated for it. He had arrived as he had known he would arrive. Evidently they did not know of Bentinck's death yet. Why had they not been told? It was like the natives to say nothing about it. They probably did not wish to bring bad news of a friend.

It was a charming room: the furniture; the skins on the

floor, the rugs, the pictures, the objets d'art... everything good, in perfect taste, and the feminine touch — the vases of flowers, the scattered periodicals, a book or two lying about on tables. He sipped his cocktail. In a minute all this must end. He thought of his own dredges — so many things would stop. Nearly ended... actually ended in fact. What he saw was a picture which was about to fade: an unfixed photographic print.

Till it disappeared, he would taste it as he tasted his drink. A connoisseur in living: an artist: one who conducted circumstance as though it were an orchestra. Von Brandt must be nearly there by now. His heavy automatic was pushing into his hip, pressed into it by his chair.

'Another cocktail?'

'If you please.'

Retief refilled the glasses and sat down.

This was the moment. They were nicely grouped. He sat in a position where he commanded them; and the door, if Channel came in, was covered.

'I have some news for you,' he said.

They sat forward. Did they think he had news about the war? He had that, too, but it was private. 'Bad news,' he said. 'I am surprised you have not heard it. Our friend Bentinck is dead.'

'And Wilson?' I should not have asked that, Olga thought. It would have come out, anyway.

'Mr. Wilson is on his way back, I understand.'

'How...' the professor began.

'He fell into a game pit. He died at the mission. It is hard, is it not? And something of a paradox that a hunter should be caught in a game pit.' Marais raised his glass. 'Let us drink to the memory of our friend. To Augustus Bentinck the hunter.'

They all stood up. He was holding the glass in his left hand. His right was behind him. His fingers were on the butt of his Lüger.

As they sat down, he pulled it out. Only Olga noticed it in his hand. She made a movement as if to get up, and sank back again.

'And there is something else,' he said. The pistol was now in full view. 'A little information, if you please.'

'Information? ... And what do you mean by drawing a pistol in my house?' The professor was angry.

'Perhaps I should introduce myself,' Marais said. 'Colonel Marais von Hohenlowe, of the German army and at your service.' The friendly fat business man had disappeared. Here was a soldier: a colonel. As he spoke, his whole bearing had changed.

'Yes, information, Professor,' he said. 'Your formula ... and you, madame,' he included Olga, 'the papers that our dead friend confided to your care. Not that they are of importance now, but I wish to include them in my dispatch.'

If there was anything in Channel's belief in telepathy, this would surely prove it. Olga was calling for him in her mind, calling his name ... willing him to come. *Channel ... Channel.* It was extraordinary how cool she felt: as if she were a spectator. Her husband was, too. So was Retief. Everyone ... at least they looked it. Even Marais with his pistol in his hand.

She looked at herself in the mirror. I look very nice, she thought. It was like a play, like acting in a melodrama. Only as yet it was not melodrama. It was all so quiet, so restrained, so good-tempered. Marais' arrival, his giving them the news of Bentinck's death and then holding them up, like a bandit. No, not at all like a bandit. Her hand went up to her hair. She felt for a hairpin that was loose and pushed it in. So she had been right in suspecting Marais. It was so easy, now that she knew. How easy it was to be wise after the event ... to lock the stable door after ... His continual good temper, his geniality, his neatness that was even greater than Channel's, his interests here and there that took him on trips.

Everything pointed to him now. Von Brandt had been no more than a stalking horse: so obvious that he had not been really dangerous.

Marais was speaking to her. Only with the greatest difficulty could she make herself concentrate on his words.

'Yes, Olga,' he was saying, 'it would be best if you could persuade your husband to hand over his formula: best for everyone.' He was smiling. 'Then there would be no ill feeling, no regrets.' He spoke quite softly, almost caressingly. 'It is war,' he went on. 'The most distressing things can happen in war. Even to charming women . . . perhaps more to charming women than to anyone else.'

He was threatening her. He turned to her husband.

'Don't you agree with me, Herr Professor? She is so beautiful. So young, so full of life, and it is so long since some of our men have seen a white woman.'

The professor had jumped to his feet. Marais' pistol covered him.

'It is best to remain calm. Sometimes a cigarette has a calming effect upon the nerves. No, do not mistake me. I have had many happy evenings here' — he glanced round the room. 'Olga is a charming hostess. I can do no more than advise.'

'Give him nothing, Jean,' Olga said.

Retief was grasping the arms of his chair. He was getting ready to spring. She stopped him with her eyes. He relaxed. Marais was perfectly at ease. He stood balancing himself on the balls of his feet. He is much stronger than he looks, Olga thought. He is hard. That bulk is not fat; it is muscle.

'You must understand,' Marais went on, 'that resistance is useless. This is not an isolated instance. Everywhere our people have struck. We are organized. What is the good of arguing with Fate? We could become allies . . . become friends again.'

He was enjoying himself.

'At this moment,' he went on, glancing at the clock, 'we have launched an attack on Egypt. Perhaps you do not know that Lake Victoria can be drained . . . emptied . . . a little explosion.' He turned to the professor. 'You can guess what will happen then. The Nile will cease to flow. The water will run south over the flats into Lake Tanganyika. No Nile . . . no Egypt. So simple, so easy. And von Brandt is doing it. The preparations have been made for a long time. He will press a button and . . .' Marais blew the air from his cheeks. 'Pouf . . . it is done! the good von Brandt: a simple child of nature, but a valuable servant of the Third Reich.'

Retief could apparently restrain himself no longer. 'I am a Belgian,' he said.

'Yes, monsieur,' Marais said, 'but then you have concerned yourself with things which are our affair. You have secrets that we require.'

Olga bit her lip. This was what Bentinck had hinted at: the big thing: Egypt . . . no Nile floods . . . famine . . . pestilence . . . And she had slept with von Brandt.

Then she laughed. 'And me?' she said. 'Why me? What have I got to do with all this?'

'I have often wondered. A woman's love of intrigue, perhaps. I do not know.'

'It could not be hatred of the Germans, of course,' Olga said in her lightest voice. 'It could not be any resentment that you should have marched into my country. That is assuming that I was concerned in this. I wish I had been,' she went on. 'Dogs . . . Prussians.'

'Dogs, Prussians,' Marais copied her. 'Perhaps. But is there not a proverb about every dog has his day? Today is ours. Our German hounds are pulling down the Polish boar.' He permitted himself a smile. 'The papers, Olga, and quickly: the ones Bentinck gave you, and the professor's. If you have not got them, at least you know where he keeps them.'

'No . . .' *Channel*, she prayed. *Channel, come quickly.* Had he forgotten Channel?

Marais went towards her. She backed away from him. If she could lead him on a little, so that Retief was beside him or behind him ... But he was too old a hand. He was laughing.

'No, Olga. You do not catch me like that. Why,' he said, 'I have been at this work for twenty years. But do not agitate yourself — there is no hurry. We will stay here comfortably — a friendly group till our doctor comes. Then, having captured him, I will lock you up and wait for Sebastian and the so charming Mr. Wilson.' He looked at Olga.

So he had not forgotten Channel. Olga went on moving towards Jean.

'Yes, go to your husband, my pretty one, see what he can do.'

Marais might be prepared for Channel, but he had forgotten something else. Olga thought of her husband's detective stories. Didn't the books say people always forgot something? She kept her eyes on Marais, but her hands were behind her on the wall. There it was, she could feel the moulding of the door ...

'If we agreed, meneer ...' Her husband looked at her. He was afraid she was going to betray them.

'If you agree, there is nothing more to be said, Olga. In fact, there will be rewards. The Führer needs men like your husband. In the New Order the scientist will take his rightful place. He will have honors ... money; and a woman like you will ...'

There it was. She had her fingers on the bolt. It was moving slowly, silently. How lucky she had oiled it the other day! The bolt was out now ...

'You promise, meneer,' she said. 'We could go to Berlin ... to the city, away from this dreadful place?'

'I am glad you are beginning to see sense.'

Marais was still standing. His pistol held in his right hand. His left hand was on the back of a chair. He held it tighter. He hoped no one would notice. Things were not going right.

He had an intolerable pain behind his right eye. It frightened him. It was agony. It was as if his eye had been pierced by a long needle that had penetrated his brain, partially paralyzing it. Only his training, his iron will, saved him. His whole body was rigid with resistance to pain. With his mind he was trying to isolate it.

Fool, fool, he said to himself, God-be-damned body, hold on. It is I, the mind, that governs you. As I say, so will you do. As I say ... But the pain went on, the needle went on driving through his eye socket, twisting and turning within him — burning, tearing. He was beginning to sweat. He tried to think what it could be. He had never known any pain before except that of a wound: never known illness.

'What's that?' Olga said, pointing. 'My God ...'

For a moment Marais' eyes flickered in the direction of the window, but he did not look round.

'What an old trick, Olga! That is what comes of reading your husband's detective stories.'

But Olga had pushed the door open a little. It opened inwards. She could feel it gripped. She had succeeded. She raised her hands to her face. She began to cry. That always sent him mad with rage ... It always had ...

There was a rush of air as the door swung open.

Congo's moment had come. He did not know whom he was about to avenge. He knew nothing. His unused muscles were suddenly released into the action for which they longed. For half an hour he had been growing more and more uneasy ... had, for some curious reason, not expressed his anger by screams or the beating of his chest. For half an hour he had crouched by the door, his fingers against it till he had felt it move and seen her hand.

A big man, a stranger, faced him. His black lips drew back from his white fangs, his red mouth opened and he charged.

Oh, beautiful strength! There was nothing to stop him: no prodder, no snake; nothing. Only the man. Taller than

he, but a small thing in his hands, a thing that broke as he
took it by the arm. Then, as it fell, his teeth sank into its
neck. Hot blood, soft flesh, muscle. It was good to bite.
There had been a noise as he sprang and a stinging pain.
But it was nothing. He could not be stopped. He would kill
them all. Then he would be alone with her. With everyone
dead, she would smell right again. Smell of geranium — of
woman.

He leaped at the professor. Retief tried to interpose himself
between them. She was screaming at him.

At last he knew power.

This was the moment for which he had been born. He
knew it: as his ancestors had known it: the instant of battle
with other males.

The pain and her screams only excited him.

Chapter 35

The THORN

CHANNEL SPENT THE DAY PACKING UP. A FEW SPECIMENS HE had discarded, but most were wrapped in newspaper, labelled, and already crated. They would be a nice addition to the Royal College of Surgeons in London. It was interesting to speculate about what would happen to them. With England at war they might never reach their destination; or, having reached it, might be bombed. Naturally London would be bombed. Still, these things were out of his hands. He had collected. He had done his best. He was sending them where, if they were not destroyed, they would be most appreciated. It was an act of finality one way or the other: symbolic of the times. An ending of something, which carried the implication of a new beginning.

Some of the papers he used for wrapping amused him. The old headlines: the old wishful thinking that had led to the débâcle: papers printed in Paris and London wrapping skulls. The news was as dead as the skulls... as the bottled surgical specimens.

The future was now separated from the past. He must start again for a third time. First in Paris, where he had reached his zenith and also his nadir. Then here, where he had in another way attained certain ends. Now this, too, was cut away from beneath him. He must go on from here. To France? No, on the contrary. He would not be well received in France. Besides, he was too used to Africa and the Negroes. Abyssinia. That was the place to go. The war there was by no means over and would flame up again. He had a man in the hospital now — a refugee from Ethiopia: a lesser chief who would lead him back.

He had got out a lot of his clothes: spare surgical instruments, and a Webley-Fosbery pistol that he had not looked at for years lay among them on the bed. An English officer had given the pistol to him in the last war. On a chair were his field glasses, Zeiss, that he had taken from a dead Prussian.

His manuscript was done up. That was going to America. They could be trusted not to publish it till after his death. Du reste ... it was in the hands of the Bon Dieu. Funny how you thought in such terms: God ... Fate ... Nature. In the hands, anyway, of that which transcended the purely human. He put his medals on the bed. They would go with him. Though the Abyssinians might not know what they meant, they would know they meant something, and if they did not ... he would know. Yes, he thought, to me they mean something.

A car went past the window. He looked up. Marais. So he had come, too. No doubt before long everyone would come — Sebastian, Wilson, Bentinck. For an instant he had hoped it was Sebastian. The old Ford had assumed a new importance. He would need it for his trip. He would take a lot of gas. When it ran out, he would abandon the car. He would march on foot. Use horses, camels. It would be very interesting. An old civilization unchanged for thousands of years. He had done enough for today. He found it somewhat astonishing that he should be so ready to make a new life; that he should experience relief at parting with his collection, at dismissing his patients and leaving the hospital he had been at such pains to build.

He lit a cigarette. He sat at his desk to write something; an idea that had come to him. He could send it to America later. All the time he would be sending things ... fragments, pieces. He might even get over there to coordinate them one day; if not, someone else could do it.

Nothing was of value till it was stated. A thought was useless. How much knowledge had been lost because the original thought had escaped the thinker; had not been put down! Thought begot thought. The idea stated might be foolish, might serve no apparent purpose, but someone reading it might take it farther: develop it from a fragmentary idea into a composite whole. The very thing that had been deemed negligible might be the missing link to a chain that some other man had formulated. A tree must spring from a seed. Those who had seeds, it seemed to him, even if many of them were sterile, should sow them. Then at least they had done their best. Others could carry on where they had left off; or need not. The responsibility lay less with those who wrote than with those who refused to write.

'... Men are gregarious,' he wrote: 'as gregarious as horses. Separate one horse from the troop and it will endeavor to return to it. Kill one and the others will gallop away, but suffer no regret. Man likes to be with other men, but he does not love them; what he loves is the proximity of others, the implication of security they give.

'Today is an example of this. The return of the professor and Retief; Marais' coming; Bentinck and Wilson no doubt on their way.'

He stopped writing. He had better go over to the house and see Marais. He might have news ... I'll go at once, he thought. He picked up the pistol from the bed. They might try it; put up a can and shoot at it. He broke the gun. It was loaded. And the professor had some forty-five ammunition.

He was hardly out of the house when he heard a scream and a shot. Was Congo out of control? One day he had known it must happen; he had warned Olga. More screams. They were human. He began to run. He dashed through the door into the living room. Congo had the professor in his arms, he was holding him like a baby, cradling him, but the professor's neck was broken. Olga stood backed up against the wall. Marais was dead, his arm torn off; it lay beside him. Retief was on the ground beside the professor's chair.

So it had happened. The ape had run amok. The balance between Olga's psychological power over Congo and Congo's fury had reached the final crisis; growing slowly over the years, the weight of the past had been too great. As Congo turned towards him, he fired. The heavy bullet took Congo in the face. His head was thrown back by the impact of the bullet, but he did not fall; dropping the professor, he charged forward. Channel fired twice more, thanking God for the automatic action of the revolver. It was enough. Congo threw out his arms towards Olga and fell.

'So you came,' Olga said.

'Yes, I came.'

'I willed you to come.'

Channel took her by the arm and led her into the bedroom. He went back for brandy. He poured out two stiff drinks. What a mess! The room was a battlefield. Three dead men and a dead gorilla. What would have happened if he had not come? What had prompted him to take his pistol with him? And what had Olga meant: 'I willed you...'? He supported her as she drank.

'Someone has got to get to Frazer,' she said. 'Nairobi... von Brandt must be stopped.'

'Yes,' he soothed her, 'someone will go.' Who on earth was Frazer? He knew the name, but what had it to do with Olga? Why must von Brandt be stopped? What was he going to do? He looked at her. Was she going to break down? What she had seen was enough to make her. He tried to reconstruct the scene... Marais on a friendly call: no doubt, they had been talking about the war over a drink. Then Congo. The shot. That must have been Marais. He had probably hit him, and

then the gorilla, mad with pain and rage — destroying everything. Would he have turned on Olga if he had not come in
time? He had his fingers on her pulse. He looked at her eyes.

'There is no need to do that, my friend.'

'Do what?'

Olga smiled at him. 'Use your eyes . . . your power on me.
I am calm. I shall remain calm. It is over.' She was staring
at the Empire mirror. In her mind she was saying the words
over and over again, repeating them. 'It is finished. It is
over. Mokala is finished. Jean — poor Jean — Retief . . .
Congo.' 'Congo is dead?' she asked. 'You shot him?'

'He is dead.' That mess must be cleaned up. He had better
get her to his house. She could not stay here.

'I am glad Congo is dead,' Olga said. 'It was a mistake.
How one pays for one's mistakes! I was mad when I took
him. I think he changed my life,' she said simply. 'A thing
of the forest . . . A woman should not take a thing of the forest
to her breast.'

Let her go on talking. That was the best thing. Let her
talk. Her eyes were dreamy.

'Evil,' she said. 'A woman is too near to evil. I feel different with him dead. And Jean . . . Do you think I was a bad
wife to him?' She did not wait for an answer. 'If I was, he
did not know it.' Bentinck, Jean, Retief, Marais, Congo —
all dead.

'If you could cry, it would do you good,' Channel said.

'I have no desire to cry. I can only feel that a weight is
lifted from me. I feel different. You should not have done it.
You should not have let me take him.'

'I have often blamed myself, but how was I to know you
would come before I killed him. I wanted him. A beautiful
specimen, a new-born gorilla.'

'Did you know that we were going to be divorced then?'
she asked. 'After the baby died. He was good to me, but it
was not enough. Then taking Congo changed things. Can
you explain that?'

'No, ma chère, but there are so many things I can't explain.'

'I gave him milk, and what did he give me? He gave me sanity. I was almost insane then. But he also gave me something else, that gorilla that you cut from his mother's womb, that I took still wet into my arms.'

Channel lit a cigarette and gave it to her. She inhaled deeply. 'Thank you,' she said.

They smoked in silence.

'He was a German agent, you know.'

'Who? Von Brandt?'

'Of course, von Brandt, but he did as he was told. Marais was the brains, and we never knew it.'

'But what happened?' She had better tell the story now.

'He was holding us up. Then I let Congo out. He killed him, and then I could not stop him. Do you think he was jealous of Jean?'

'Yes,' Channel said. 'He was your husband. He was very near to you. That was why he killed him.' It was also why he had killed Retief, but he would not say so. She went back to an earlier remark.

'Frazer must have the news. We've got to get him a message. If only Bentinck were here, he would know what to do.' But Bentinck was dead — then Wilson. 'Von Brandt has got to be stopped,' she said again.

'Von Brandt? What's he doing?'

'He's going to blow up Lake Victoria. They have discovered that it can be done. The Nile would cease to flow.' She covered her face with her hands.

'I'll go,' Channel said. Then he remembered that Sebastian had stolen his car. 'My car,' he said.

'Take Marais'.'

'Yes, that's an idea.' It was a good car, a new Chevrolet. He stroked her arm. 'Will you be all right alone ... at my house, I mean. You can't stay here.'

'I'll go to your house.' She got up.

'The back way,' he said.

They went out through the pantry. They passed Marais' car; its door was open. Out of habit Channel went up to close it: a reflex action, he thought. You see an open car door and close it. But why was it open? It was unlike Marais. He looked into it. What was that? . . . On the rubber floor mat lay a little figure of clay: a child's doll. It lay on its back. A long white mimosa thorn had been driven through its right eye, its right arm was torn off and lay beside it. He banged the door quickly. He did not want Olga to see it in her present state. Marais' right arm had been torn off; he had lain on his back.

'Anything in the car?' Olga asked.

'Nothing, my dear. I was just looking.'

He sat on an armchair in his room. 'Excuse the mess,' he said, 'I was just packing. It is finished here.'

'Yes, it is over.' How they kept repeating it, as if to convince themselves! She stared at the packing cases. 'I called you,' she said, 'and you came. I wonder what would have happened if you had not come.' She shivered. 'Alone with Congo . . .'

They heard Sebastian shouting.

'Olga! Olga! . . . Channel! Where is everybody? Mother of God, what has happened? Is everybody dead?'

'Come here,' Channel called. 'We are in here, Sebastian, in my house.'

Sebastian, Maria, and Wilson came in.

'Thank God, you're safe, Olga,' Wilson said. He went up to her.

'I brought back the car,' Sebastian said. 'It is a bad car. You should get the steering fixed.' He held Maria by the wrist. 'You must forgive me,' he said. 'It was for my wife. She had been abducted, but he is dead.'

'Who is dead?' Olga said.

'The Nazi. Dead, the Fascist dog. And how she fought for her honor! I am proud of her.'

'What happened here, Channel?' Wilson asked. 'We have been into the house.'

'You had better let Olga tell you. Come with me, Sebastian, we will go and tidy things up a little.'

'I am at your service,' Sebastian said. It was good to be friends again. The apology was forgotten.

'Laertes will make you tea? Wilson, you know where to find drinks. Please forgive the appearance of my house. I was packing,' Channel said.

'Then there is no hurry for Frazer. Egypt is safe.' Olga sat down on a box.

'Egypt, Olga?' That was what Bentinck had said. Dynamite . . . Egypt . . . the bastard!

Wilson looked round the dismantled room. A short time ago he had been a guest here. Olga had just finished telling him of von Brandt's plan. She had told him about Marais, and Congo. She had told him at some length and without reservations. All the time she had talked, she had smoked one cigarette after another. There was an ash tray full of the stubs beside her. He had told about the trip and Bentinck's death.

This was going to be a different kind of war. He must get back to England: they would need everyone. This was the end of everything. Mokala was indeed a microcosm of the greater world. Already so many dead . . . von Brandt, Retief, Bentinck, Marais, and the professor: so many changes. And this was just the beginning.

Olga was staring at him. She had changed. He could not say how, but she looked different. All this had happened to-day and she was calm, almost cold. No doubt the reaction would come in a day or two. Just now she was numb, bruised by the suddenness of it all.

'Henry,' she said — it was the first time she had called him by his Christian name— 'there are some letters for you. I forgot them.' She was opening her pocketbook.

He took them. Two bills . . . it was funny to get bills here, to realize that he had bought things in shops, regular shops. The third was from Anne. The American stamp, her handwriting, made him feel ill: he would not open it. But what was the good of putting it off? He knew he must open it. He slipped his finger under the flap.

What a lot of letters he had had from her . . . that rounded free hand that hardly anyone could read. It was decorative, but illegible. She had a trick of dividing words in the middle and adding the pieces she detached to the preceding and following word.

'Dear Henry,' he read. 'You will be glad to hear that I am married. To Jim. You remember Jim . . .' There was more, but he read no farther.

He thought of the last time he had seen her. He had been going to the dentist, walking down Forty-Eighth Street, when he had seen her coming towards him on the other side. He had often thought of its happening . . . it had been bound to happen; but somehow he hadn't been ready. They had passed each other without looking back. At least he had not looked back. She had been dressed in a tomato-colored coat and skirt, and wore a black halo hat. He had thought, 'If I had been with her, I should not have let her wear that hat.' She had changed very little: as pretty as ever and rather slimmer than she had been. He had seen all that as they passed each other. It was strange to pass someone like that when you had lived together: it was funny to see your wife in clothes you did not know. It was very soon after she had left him. The dentist had put in two fillings, and had tried to sell him a dachshund. It was a mistake to have a dentist who was a dog fancier. He had tried to make a joke of it on the way home.

Funny, sitting here with Olga and thinking of Anne in her

red suit, of the dentist, of New York; and to know that it was done ... that having come into his life Anne had passed out of it.

Married yesterday. Jim. Who was Jim? At any rate, that was something else settled. Perhaps, as old Bentinck said, things were simpler than they seemed ... perhaps things did settle themselves. He found himself glad that Anne was safely married. She needed someone to take care of her. He was free at last from Anne. She was Jim's responsibility now. But who the hell was Jim?

Me and Olga, he thought ... Olga and I. He began to see things clearly. It had always been Olga. All his life long, before he met her, he had been living to meet her. And since he had met her, he had been in love with her: not merely physically — he was sorry about that now — but in love. It was an extraordinary thing to realize suddenly that Anne had never meant anything to him. He had thought she had, but she hadn't. What had meant something was his idea of her ... that was what he had loved; not Anne, but the figure of Anne he had built up in his mind. When it had become impossible to overcome the difference between what she was and what he thought she was, it had been finished. Olga was the woman he had thought Anne was. Her qualities were those with which he had invested the theoretical Anne. Jim ... Jim. He had it now — there was only one Jim — Jim Bradford it must be: a serious writer on economic and social subjects. It must have been going on a long time, then. That was why she had wanted to improve her mind — why she had changed and said she was tired of going out all the time. And he had thought that things might have gone better if he had tried to understand the same things ... read more, talked more seriously. But it had not been for him at all. It had been for Jim.

Olga was still watching him. She knew that the letter he held was from Anne.

'Bad news?' she asked.

'No. Good. Anne is married. My wife,' he said.

'Yes, your wife. And that makes things better for you?'

Wilson lit another cigarette. 'Yes,' he said.

And how much better it did make things! Somehow until she was married again he had felt responsible for her. It was partly that which had held him back with Olga. He had not wanted to have an affair with Olga. There had been other affairs, women he had been fond of, friends; he had never been promiscuous. But Olga was not like that. There could never have been a light affair between them. The one thing he had determined was not to let himself be hurt again: not to love until he was sure he would be loved. You could only be in love just so often... something happened to you each time...

Olga was examining her hands. Her lashes lay over her cheeks as she looked down.

'I'm going to Nairobi tomorrow; the papers must go to Frazer at once. Will you come with me, Olga?'

'Me?'

'You can't stay here, darling.'

'I must stay for a little while. There will be an inquiry. I was the only witness, you know.' She smiled at him. 'Even in Africa such things have to be explained. But you ought to go. Frazer must have the news and Bentinck's notes. My husband's papers you can give to the Belgium Consul.'

'And you?'

'I'll come later, if you care to wait.'

He went over to her. She stood up. He took her in his arms and kissed her. It was a different Olga that he kissed...

'We'll be married in Nairobi,' he said, 'and then go home.'

'Henry,' Olga said, 'my husband was only killed this afternoon.'

'I'm sorry, Olga.'

'I did not love Jean, you know that. Yet I did love him.

He was more my friend than my husband. In that way I loved him . . . a good, kind, clever man who never hurt anyone.' She paused. 'But I will come. If you are still there, we can talk of this again.'

She turned her face up to him. 'Kiss me, Henry. I am going to lie down now. I am tired — oh, so tired.'

Everything in Olga's drawing room was cleaned up. No trace of the battle was left. The bodies had been carried into the professor's study. He lay beside Retief on the big desk. Marais was stretched out on the sofa. Congo, carried by four reluctant boys, had been put into an outshed on a trestle table. Marais' arm had presented a problem. It had been solved by wrapping it up separately and laying it beside him. All the bodies, including Congo's, were covered with sheets from Olga's linen cupboard . . . they had embroidered monograms on the corners.

The quantity of blood on the floor had been immense. 'He bled like a pig,' Sebastian said, as they moved Marais: 'litres of blood, the thick red wine of life, spilt upon the ground.'

The lion and bongo skins were washed and put out to dry on the lawn behind the house. A few buckets of water had soon cleaned up the floor.

'Nothing shows on this red granolithic, Channel.' Sebastian was proud of his work. The houseboys had been unwilling to help him. 'And I will take his pistol.' He wiped it carefully. 'It is a better one than mine, and fortunately of the same calibre.'

Channel had spoken very little while they worked. Now that it was done, he sat down. The damage to Marais' eye had not been done by the gorilla. It puzzled him.

'A drink,' Sebastian said. He got brandy and glasses. He shouted for ice.

'Now,' he said, 'we must have everything in order. We

must inform the Administrator, we must send for the priest —
for Owen. We must dig graves. Everything must be official,
with stamps, statements of witnesses. I understand these
things. I have been concerned in many crimes. A friend of
mine was murdered once. They thought that I had done it,
but I had ceased to be her friend, so what interest would I
have had in it? "On the contrary," said the police, "that is
what makes the motive." Now here' — he drank some brandy
— 'there are many motives, yet they are accidental, irrelevant
to the crimes. Did I push that Nazi into the lava?' He struck
his chest. 'I did not. Did Olga pull off Marais' arm? She did
not. Did she kill her husband and Retief? She did not. I shall
affirm that she did not.'

'You weren't here.'

'Nevertheless, I shall affirm. Let us write the letters,' he
said. 'I had better write them. I write a fine, flowing hand.
The good Sisters instructed me. My writing shows character
... in addition it is beautiful.'

He wrote the letters.

'Dear Mr. Owen ... Please come over as soon as it is
convenient. We have had a slight mishap here. There
are three men to be buried: the professor, Meneer Marais,
and our friend Retief. It is not necessary for me to com-
ment on the climate or to suggest that a certain expedition
is necessary.'

He signed it.

'Now for the Administrator.'

'To His Excellency ...' He looked up. 'They always like
that. But it is a pity the Administrator is still on leave. This
man, being an underling, will give more trouble.'

'I, Sebastian, beg to inform you of the death of Captain
von Brandt, German spy, killed by falling into a bed of

lava while pursuing an innocent, indigenous maiden. Mr. Wilson, citizen of America and patron of art, and I, the artist, and some servants, witnessed this act of retribution by an always just God. In addition, Professor Le Blanc, a Swiss subject, his assistant, Doctor Retief, a Belgian citizen, and Meneer Marais, another German in the service of his Government, have met with death at the hands of a tame gorilla belonging to Madame Le Blanc, which suddenly ceased to be tame. The gorilla is also dead, killed by the admirably aimed bullets of my distinguished friend, Doctor Channel, citizen of France. These gentlemen and the gorilla will be interred as soon as the missionary, the Reverend Mr. Owen, subject of the United States of America, arrives to perform the ceremony.

'We, the undersigned, will be obliged if Your Excellency will conduct the necessary investigations concerning these sad, except in the case of the Germans, events. Believe me, Excellency, your obedient servant in Christ,

'SEBASTIAN, painter.'

'Sign that.' He brought the letter and pen over to Channel. Wilson came in quietly.

Channel looked up. 'Olga?'

'She is asleep.' Wilson sat down.

'That's a good thing,' Channel said. 'Rest is what she needs. I thought I might have to give her something.'

'I want something for Maria,' Sebastian said. 'She is much disturbed by what she has been through.'

Sebastian took the letters. Writing them had been in a sense a formality, as the news would have spread already, but they were also in the nature of a legal cover. No one would be able to say, 'Why did you not notify the authorities?' if there was such documentary evidence. He had made a duplicate of each. When he came back, Channel and Wilson had not moved.

'I had to send two boys with each because of the ghosts. Even together they do not like to move at night.' He had seen them leave, but it was more than likely that by now they were back again. Still, if they were, they would leave at dawn.

Wilson turned to Channel. 'I'm going to Nairobi tomorrow. Will you take me down to fetch my car?'

'Naturally.'

'And what are your plans? You were packing?'

'I shall go to Abyssinia,' Channel said. 'The country is nearly unknown. I think it might be interesting. New people, new diseases, new country. I am without honor in France. Even in war they would remember much against me. And I have no legal right to practise there.'

'Abyssinia!' Sebastian shouted. 'What an idea! I will paint the Negus. We will come with you. I, Sebastian, with the girls, and Bernadotte. We will travel in your miserable auto . . . till it breaks down. We will become chiefs, kings . . . I will find that Fascist who never paid me for his wife's picture — the red-headed one. I will kill him with many tortures to repay him for his treatment of that so charming woman.' He strode up and down. 'It is settled, my friend, my comrade. Only death will part us.'

He turned to Wilson. 'If you are going tomorrow, you must have the picture. I will take it off the stretcher and roll it. It will travel better that way. Of course, you have never seen it, but it may be better that way . . . a masterpiece, a chef d'oeuvre . . . a Sebastian to make the mouth water.'

'Picture?' Wilson said.

'The nude you commissioned. Sheba, I call her. Two hundred francs. It is a gift at that price. A parting gift . . .'

'There is something I must get,' Channel said. He picked up a flashlight from the table.

A moment later he was back.

'What do you think of that, Wilson?' He put the little clay figure on the table.

Sebastian picked it up. 'A pity it is broken,' he said. 'A work of art. It is of God. And why the thorn?' He looked at it closely. 'It resembles our dead agent,' he said. 'It resembles him greatly.'

'Yes, it is Marais,' Channel said. 'Do you notice the arm. It is the right arm. And the eye.'

'The thorn . . .' Wilson said.

'There you have something. But suppose it caused pain to Marais. Note I say only, suppose. But something must have happened to him. If not, how could he have forgotten Congo? It is my opinion,' Channel went on, 'that Congo did not damage his eye. I examined it carefully.'

'Bentinck did it,' Wilson said. The old man's words came back to him.

'Bentinck could not model,' Sebastian said.

Wilson ignored him. 'Bentinck arranged with a witch doctor to do it. He said, "It may do nothing; on the other hand, it may help. It may make him forget something."'

Channel's voice was serious. 'There are matters we do not understand.'

'You really mean that?' Wilson asked.

A boy was laying the table. How extraordinary it was to be here without Olga! To think that only a few hours ago three men and a gorilla had been killed in this room. Except that some of the skins were missing from the floor, nothing was changed. It was Channel who had ordered the food. Olga was best left alone in his house to rest.

Wilson found it difficult to eat.

'The intolerable thing about life,' Channel said, 'is not that it is so short, but that it is so narrow . . . that we can only lead one life. My God, a longer life . . . No, nor would I go back and have what I have had again unless I could go back with my present knowledge. That is why the Devil is por-

trayed as an old man in a young man's body . . . the strength
of the youth and the knowledge of age. Trial and error, and
the correction of error . . . experience. But as you gain in
experience, so you lose in power . . . the poise and the counter-
poise. You have shot at those balls that go up and down on
a jet of water at a fair, Wilson?'

'Yes.'

'When you shoot, you watch them go up and wait for the
instant where they are stationary before they begin to descend.
You know that since they have gone up, they must come down,
and you know that before they do this, before they change,
they must hang poised. It is then you shoot. There come
such times in the lives of men. Today is such an instant.'

It was obvious that Channel was trying to distract him.
But Wilson could not forget what he had seen. He still heard
von Brandt's screams getting thinner and thinner as he died.
He still saw the bodies in this room, the disorder, the blood.
And Olga: the change in her that had come with Congo's
death. The little figure . . . Bentinck's words, *He may forget
something.* What had Channel's metaphysics to do with all
this? He looked at Sebastian. He had just taken a third helping of chicken and was breaking the bread between his hands
into big chunks. The sensitive artist was unaffected . . . Channel was still talking — about youth, now.

'Youth,' he said, 'consists of the illusion of permanence.
If you are happy, it is forever . . . if you are unhappy, it will
last till you die. That is the agony of youth — its belief in
permanence, in unchanging security; a hangover from the
childhood home, from parents, nurses, servants, from school
— the feeling that whatever you do wrong you have only to
tell someone of it and they will put it right. Youth knows
nothing of the ball rising and falling on the jet of circumstance . . . nothing of the ups and downs of life.'

His chair scraped as he got up.

'Olga! is anything the matter?'

They were all standing.

'Nothing,' she said. 'Please sit down. I have come for the papers. They can't be left in an empty house.' She shivered. 'How empty it is!'

'Where are they? I'll help you.' Wilson went to her. He put his arm round her shoulders. She came closer to him.

'In the wall safe in Congo's room. I thought they would be safest there.' She had a key in her hand.

Channel had put the little figure into his pocket as she came in.

'I'll burn it,' he said.

'Yes, burn it,' Sebastian said. 'That will make sure. Let him burn as he will in hell, as the Fascist rapist burnt upon the mountain.'

'I will get you something to make you sleep, Olga,' Channel said, when she came back. He gave her a cigarette.

'I want something for Maria,' Sebastian said. 'I will accompany you. The poor brave child — and something should be done for her foot. Mother of God, how did I forget her foot?' he asked Wilson. 'Why did you not remind me?'

He held out his hand.

'Two hundred francs, Mr. Wilson: a gift. The picture will make you think of Sebastian.'

Channel came out of Olga's room as Wilson went in to say good-bye to her. It was the room that he had occupied while he waited for the guest house to be made ready. He had the papers she had given him in his pocket. His car was loaded. He had said good-bye to the others. Only this, the last good-bye, was left. Olga sat up as he came in.

She said, 'Sit down, Henry.' She pointed to the edge of the bed.

'So you have come to say good-bye. That is always sad. Au revoir. But only to say adieu is really sad, for then, when we say that, we know we shall not meet again, and commend

our friends to God.' She lit a cigarette. 'In a few days you
will be in Nairobi. You will see Frazer. You will be in a different world. Once there, you may feel quite different. You
may wonder at what will then appear to be your madness at
Mokala. You will think of the woman Olga, no longer
prejudiced by her presence. A thousand thoughts will present themselves to you. You may think that she is an ad-
venturess; that since she was not faithful to one man she will
not be faithful to another.

'Now perhaps you see why I want you to go alone. When
everything is over here, in a month I will come. And either
you will be there or you will not.'

'I'll be there.'

'Then good-bye, Henry.' She raised her face to be kissed.

When he had gone, she sat still, waiting for the sound of
his car: she heard it start. She heard the wheels grip the
gravel of the drive. Now that he had really gone, her body
ached for him. She thought of him as he had sat there looking
like a schoolboy — unhappy, awkward, embarrassed. She
had wanted to take him in her arms: to comfort him; to let
him love her. But nothing would have been gained by a protracted good-bye. He would wait for her or he would not.
That was what she had said to him. And she needed time,
too, to reorganize her life. Whatever happened with Henry,
everything here was finished. She would take nothing away
but her clothes. She saw the death of her gorilla as the turning point in her life. Her association with Congo had merely
been the acceleration of a process begun in childhood and his
going out of it had ended a phase of her life that had been
purely physical. Oddly, his death affected her more than
that of her husband, or Retief, or the coming of war. Both
men belonged to a past which had been dominated by Congo
... to the life of the woman that she had been.

Channel had told her about the figure in the car. Henry
had told her what Bentinck had said to Entobo. She won-

dered what Frazer would think of it all: she hoped she had made it clear. She thought of Fritz von Brandt. If he had taken her warning and kept away from black girls, he would have been alive — and perhaps have accomplished his mission. She thought of how she had told him to leave them alone ... of his going to have his bath, of his bowing over her hand, of the muted click of the heels of his tennis shoes ... of her own thought that night about the transition from social to sexual intercourse ...

Chapter 36

The CEREMONIES

~~~~~~~~~~~~~~~~~

CHANNEL SUPERVISED THE DIGGING OF THE GRAVES. RETIEF and the professor he had decided to put side by side, Marais a little distance from them. Congo he had already buried. Sewn into his own blanket he lay under six feet of earth at the foot of a cluster of banana plants. Channel had been unable to resist making an examination of Congo. He had removed and preserved his heart, appendix, and kidneys. His brain, unfortunately, had been damaged. It would have been interesting to see if the specialized existence he had led had affected it. He had also had another look at Marais' eye. It had been pierced by a sharp instrument — the leg of a compass, a nail, or a long thorn. One thing only was certain: it had not been done by the blunt fingers of a gorilla.

Meanwhile, everything was ready for Owen. The bodies had been enclosed in rough plank coffins. The boys who would be required to carry them and fill in the graves were standing by. I have done all that is possible, he thought: all the practical things. Now we wait for the mystic putting away which is the concern of priests. Ashes to ashes ... dust to dust ... the panoply that followed all death; the propitiation of the gods by priest, medicine man, or witch doctor. The service Owen would conduct was the Christian form which had been built upon foundations so ancient that none knew their origin. Built, as many churches had been built, upon the ruins of the temples that had preceded them: all a part of a single religious pattern which, having begun as a fear of devils, was now changed into a love of God. But this was devil country, filled with spirits that no Owen could exorcise or control.

He would be glad to get out of it. They had all paid too highly for the life they had led — the beauty, the ease, the comfort. How right he had been to long for pigeons flying in a cold, blue sky . . . tumblers falling with a flash of wings. How right Sebastian had been with his premonition of death, even though the death had not been his own.

Olga had said he could have the big truck and anything else he wanted. All this was hers now. His specimens would leave for London today. The porters were ready. Owen would inherit his hospital equipment and presumably his patients as well. He was also going to get the contents of the other bungalows. Olga was giving him everything. Owen would inherit the earth, and if he was not careful it might destroy him. He thought of Owen playing his Josephine Baker records on the victrola; but of course he would not play them. He would play hymns and classical music. He saw him coming now. He was leading his bicycle.

'So you have come,' he said: 'a bad business.'

'Yes, it's a bad business, Doctor. A bad business to bury your friends.'

'I have them ready.' Channel led him to the house. Sebastian arrived with his two girls. Olga followed them. She was wearing a light-weight white flannel suit.

The three coffins were laid out on trestles in the big sitting room. The pallbearers stood in the doorway. Someone — it must have been Olga — had draped the caskets of the professor and Retief with the Belgian and Swiss flags and piled them with flowers. Marais' coffin stood bare of ornament.

They waited while Owen put on his vestments in Olga's bedroom. Nothing was too strange today.

Olga remained calm throughout the service. She followed

them when they carried out the coffins. There were no tears in her eyes as they were lowered. She bent, picked up a handful of earth, and threw it into each grave. The boys began to shovel.

As she turned away, she put her hand on Channel's arm. 'Where did you put Congo?' she asked. He pointed. She nodded her head.

They went back to the house. Coffee was served and a cold collation. Whatever happened, Olga would remain the perfect hostess. Owen added details to Wilson's account of Bentinck's death. They told him of the tragedy. Sebastian's girls had accompanied them into the sitting room. They sat perched close together on a low stool like two little brown birds.

To Channel it was all a fantasy, an unreality. These people, the room, the memories of the last ten years . . . the end of the life they had led here and the beginning of the greatest war the world had ever seen. There could be little conversation under such conditions. They ate, and drank coffee.

Owen put his cup down suddenly and pointed at the Batanga girls.

'You should marry one of them,' he said to Sebastian.

'Marry? I am married to them.'

'He means marry one properly,' Channel said.

'All right. To please you, Owen. Come, Maria. Maria, get up. I will marry you. But it must be at once, Owen.'

Channel wondered why Sebastian had given in so easily. It was not because he was conscious of any wrong he had done.

'To please you,' he had said. Perhaps Owen had just caught him in a marrying mood.

Sebastian led Maria forward. 'I choose you, my little brown bird, because you are bad. This will cure you of being bad. Mr. Owen the priest, as you know, being from the mission, is a great doctor. He will curse you. You will burn in hell if you are unfaithful to me again.' He shook her. 'Your sister I do not have to marry. She is a good girl.'

When it was over, Olga wept. 'It was so beautiful,' she said, 'so stupid.' She laughed and wept again.

Sebastian informed Owen he was going to Abyssinia to hunt Fascists with Channel.

'Perhaps I shall find that count whose wife I painted. He never paid me.'

'And Nina — will you send her back to her father?'

'Nina, my little brown bird? No, Olga, she must come. We are married.'

'You are married to Maria. Surely you remember.'

'Ah, that. That was to please our friend. He has so little to make him happy. But I am also married to Nina. She is my wife by the law of her people. They are my wives in common law,' he said proudly. 'That I put an extra bond on Maria is to hold her. She is frightened now and she will be good. Will you not, Maria?'

She did not answer. She was crying in her shame.

'You see,' Sebastian said, 'she is frightened. And I need them both to carry my things when the car breaks down. Channel is bringing Laertes and the Ethiopian chief. We are all going together . . .'

'It will be charming,' Channel said: 'a family party.'

Burials and a marriage, a last supper in the big bungalow: the priest bewildered, the women crying. Now even the illusion of rationality had been abandoned. The play was over. The scenery which they had used so long, having served its purpose, was about to be destroyed. A few more formalities and then only the empty stage would remain, waiting for new players.

How little regret there was for the dead! How little he felt himself! The bond that had held them to each other had been fortuitous, the result of circumstance rather than affection. How few dead men would be welcomed even by their families if they came back after a few months! And this had been no family. It had been an arrangement that was now disarranged, and each of them was thinking less of the past than planning a new pattern for lives which had been disrupted but not broken.

Sebastian was delighted at the turn of events. It was all very dramatic, colorful. The death of Retief and the professor was offset by that of Marais and von Brandt. He had acquired a new and legal wife: a possibility that had never occurred to him. How he would treasure her in sickness and health, in goodness and badness! Maria charmed him: his naughty brown bird whom he had saved. Owen must give him a certificate.

'I demand a certificate. If I have none, who will believe me?' He presented Owen with a pen and paper.

Today was a wonderful day. Sebastian felt himself full of virtue: strong with the desire to paint. His girls were beautiful to him. Olga was beautiful. Channel was his comrade, their quarrel forgotten in the press of events, and he was tired of being here. They would move on together over the face of Africa, fighting, painting, working, making love and discussing the love they made ... that he made. He slapped Owen on the back. 'A great day!' he said. He picked up his wife in his arms. 'Do not cry, little one. I will be a good husband to you. I have always been a good husband.'

But Maria still wept. She did not understand this wedding. He had said she would be cursed if she betrayed him. And Entobo had threatened her if she did not destroy the German. Her fear of the German had gone now, forgotten in the memory of the gifts which were ended by his death. She was also doubtful if Entobo would give any reward for her work. Her sobbing increased.

'You see,' Sebastian said, 'she is overcome with remorse.' He put Maria down and took Owen's hand. 'It is a fine thing you have done. I will never forget this day.' He picked Maria up again and strode out with her in his arms. Nina followed them, also weeping.

THE CEREMONIES

383

Channel smoked and looked at Owen, who sat bent over the table with his head sunk in his hands. Olga had gone to her room and was taking her clothes out of the closet and laying them on the bed. From where he sat, Channel could see her. How quickly it was ending! How quickly men adjusted themselves to change! It delighted him to watch Olga. Wilson had gone. Soon she would follow him. He looked at Owen.

Owen was watching Olga, too. Poor Owen. There was no man living who would not, if he could, be more potent than he was. Even Owen. Even the priest, for it would give him a bigger devil to wrestle with. Life was based on conflict. It remained the same, whether your conflict was with women in an effort to obtain the greatest number possible, or with the Devil to prevent him tempting you with any.

When Olga said good-bye to Owen, she kissed him. It was the first time she ever had. He knew it would be the last.

'You are a good man,' she said.

But was he? He had never been kissed by a woman before. He stared over the handlebars at the road in front of him. How often he had ridden over this road to see them ... to see her! His mind refused to accept what had happened. He could not believe that it was all gone, that so many were dead, that it was war.

Chapter 37

The AGENT

~~~~~~~~~~~~~~

WHEN HE REACHED NAIROBI, WILSON WENT STRAIGHT TO FRAZER.
'So you're back.'

He had not seemed surprised to see him.

'Quite a little show you had up there,' he went on.

That was one way of putting it. 'So you know about it.'

'Roughly. No details, of course, but I hear of most things.
Bush telegraph, you know.' He shrugged his shoulders apologetically.

'Well, I've got the details for you and old Bentinck's notes.
Olga ... Mrs. Le Blanc said I was to bring them to you at
once.'

Frazer held out his hand. 'Glad she's all right,' he said.
'Charming woman.' He lit a cigarette and stared at one of his
hunting prints. He seemed to be talking to a gentleman in
pink whose grey horse had just sent him over his head into a
stiff thorn hedge. 'Kept you from brooding, anyway. Now
make yourself comfortable,' he pointed to a chair, 'while I
have a look at them.'

Frazer looked at the papers carefully. There were notes in
Bentinck's crabbed tight hand ... in Olga's writing: the tale
of the comings and goings of von Brandt, the reported opinions
of the Administrator, of Marais. How innocuous they were!
... just like the others that had kept coming in for years; and
finally her description of Marais' attack and von Brandt's mission. He got up and unlocking a drawer took out a file.

Yes, here were the missing links.

Amin el Hussein the Grand Mufti had prophesied in Iraq that the Nile would cease to flow. When it did, the Moslems would take it as a sign from Allah and rise up to throw the infidels from the East. This was to be the sign from God and the signal. It had seemed a mad prophecy at the time, but how nearly it had come off!

He thought of the series of accidents which had prevented it: Sebastian's pursuit of his girl; Marais forgetting Congo; Channel having his gun in his hand when he ran over to the Station. How the little unforeseen things stepped in! The Germans calculated on everything but the variable which defied all calculation ... the human factor, the lag or slip of time.

But it could have been done. Victoria could have been drained. And the dolls of an old witch doctor might have saved the Empire. He looked back at Olga's report.

'I did not see the figure, but Channel did,' she wrote. 'And Mr. Wilson told me that Bentinck had arranged with Entobo to have them placed where Marais would find them. But this does not explain the figure in the car that he cannot have seen, nor the fact that Marais' right eyeball was pierced and his right arm torn off. Von Brandt's fate is easier to understand. This, too, was Entobo's doing, Wilson says. It was arranged that he should be killed by the girl, since girls were his weakness, and living in that vicinity she must have known about the lava crust.'

He put down the paper.

Somewhere in another file he had a confidential report that might have something to do with the case. Soon after he came, von Brandt had struck Entobo with a whip. The trouble had been hushed up because of the complications it would have caused. That blow, given two years ago, might have been his death warrant ... More things in heaven and earth ... more things in Africa. Here only the ordinary was strange. He thought of the long dispatch he would write. No one would

believe it. Couched in the stilted language of officialdom, it
would be pigeonholed and forgotten. 'Poor old Frazer,' someone might say. 'It's the climate, you know. Living at that
altitude on the equator...' It was easy enough to dismiss
such things in Whitehall. He smiled.

He turned to Wilson. 'You'll stay with me, of course.
And what a good thing you bought a Ford! You'll have no
trouble getting rid of it. Any plans?' he asked.

'Get back, I suppose, and see what I can do.'

'Any idea when you want to go?'

'Soon, but I'll stick around a bit. Mrs. Le Blanc is coming
as soon as things are sorted out. The inquiry, you know.'

'I'll see she has no trouble. And the Administrator will
have some explaining to do ... Got rich a little too fast. But
I'm sorry about Bentinck. Good old chap.'

Frazer was a difficult man to talk to. Nothing seemed to
disturb him. How much had he known all along? At dinner
— it was excellent — they spoke of trivialities. Wilson inquired about some of their mutual friends. Frazer gave him
the local gossip. After dinner they went back to the sitting
room and the hunting prints. Only then did he begin to
question him.

'What are the doctor and the painter going to do?' he asked.

'Going to Abyssinia, apparently. Channel can't go back
to France. He got into trouble there over an abortion, I
think.'

Frazer laughed. 'Do you really think that? He got into
trouble, all right, but it was because he was too advanced.
He did some hypnotic stuff that the other doctors did not
like ... operations; and some of his patients died.'

So that was it. Wilson was relieved.

Life in Nairobi was superficially the same. There were
no soldiers about, they had moved north. There were less
retired colonels. They had joined various irregular outfits

or had gone back to England. But there were still parties, still racing, still polo tournaments. The luncheons and dinners blurred into each other, into a social round that was dominated by Wilson's mental pictures of Olga. Wherever he looked he saw her. His conversations, his visits, his motor drives were without reality. He could not write to Olga to tell her where he was and what he was doing. She had told him not to. She had said she would come. All he could do was to wait.

Frazer told him the inquiry had gone off without a hitch. The immaculate young man from whom he had bought the Ford told him to bring it back any time and he would be glad to buy it. The blonde girl, Lady Soames' niece, had married her boy friend Reggie and rode his ponies all day, because Reggie had joined the army. The only difference in Nairobi was that now, instead of only a few people wanting to sell a few things, everybody wanted to sell everything. 'Clearing out, old man; no point in hanging on, is there?' Well, he was clearing out himself as soon as Olga came. They would go home. To England. He would park Olga and join something. After all, he had been in this thing before any of them, and his friends had been killed. Someone was going to have to pay for that.

When he told Frazer he was going to marry Olga, he said, 'Congratulations. Charming woman.'

'You knew she was there, of course?' Wilson asked. It was an unnecessary question because Olga had told him about Frazer.

'Oh, yes.'

'But you didn't tell me.'

'No, I thought it might put you off — social life, and all that. Besides, I thought it would interest you to find her for yourself out there in the bush.'

The conversation had ended on that note. He could hardly explain to Frazer how interesting he had found her.

'She had better stay here when she comes,' Frazer said. 'Save a lot of trouble. I'll tell them to get her room ready.'

It was difficult for Wilson to reconcile the normalcy of this life — the regular meals, the expert service, the banal conversations, the whole social routine — with world events or with his own immediate past in Mokala; with Channel the dabbler in the occult, Sebastian the mad genius, the professor, Retief, the two Germans, the gorilla ... Olga. He thought of them all continually: of their striving towards certain ends; towards what they imagined to be security: Owen for the security of God; Channel the security of esoteric power; Sebastian the security of art; the professor the security of pure knowledge; Olga the security of the flesh; the Nazis — von Brandt and Marais — the security of a prehistoric religion of the blood. He thought of what Olga had told him of her past, of the influence of Congo on her.

Inexplicable as the pattern of their lives remained, it fitted into a general and inexplicable pattern: Old Bentinck's love of the animals he hunted; Channel's devotion to medicine; Sebastian's to art; von Brandt's to war. His own thoughts were confused, his ends confused, for he, like the others, sought life, sought oblivion and achievement: sought the infinite here, in Frazer's house, while he waited for Olga.

And this seeking, this world-wide psychological unease, was the cause of war. Here, in this lack of ends and superfluity of means, in this new and undirected self-consciousness, lay the key to everything. All men were seeking furiously, failing furiously; and, furiously thwarted, turning against each other. Neither Sebastian, nor Owen, nor Channel, nor the professor, nor Olga was right. Nor were any of them wrong. Each had a half-truth. The full was a physical life that was spiritual, in an art that was an expression of God, in a religion which was the love of man. The esoteric sexual joined the political and the religious to the psychological. Man was

THE AGENT

plunging into the abyss. He would come out of it fully humanized or remain in it a beast. Man was, it seemed to him, bursting out of bondage, out of the womb of a time that had been warm, darkened with false security. Now he must gamble all to gain all ... or lose all. In his lifetime, if he lived, he would see man reborn or die.

Olga drove Marais' car to Nairobi. There had been a little trouble over it. Sebastian had been against it. Such an act, he said, was not correct. He had become a great stickler for convention since his marriage. But Olga knew that behind his protests had been the desire to steal the car himself. Not having a car except for the big truck had been one of her husband's eccentricities. He had claimed that the Government should supply transport. The argument, begun when they came, had ended only with his death.

A month. And what a month it had been! The inquiry; the packing-up, the giving away of everything, the paying-off of servants, the good-byes to Channel and Sebastian, the discussions, the exhortations, the promises. And above all, coloring everything, her thoughts of Henry Wilson and her hopes for the future. Would he wait for her, or would he go back?

She knew she had changed, but would anyone else? And had she really changed or did it only seem that she had? Could anyone change? Certainly she felt for him what she had felt for no one else. He seemed to be the answer that she had been seeking all her life.

Her luggage was in the back of the car with her boy. That was all she had retained of her old life. I am going to begin again, she thought. They were all beginning again except Owen. She saw them in her mind as she drove: she saw the fêtes and the parties, she heard her husband's gentle voice, she saw Retief's pathetic eyes. But that was the past. In front of her was Nairobi — and Henry, if he had waited.

Olga's plan for finding Henry Wilson was simple. She drove straight to the Ford agency. An immaculate young man said, 'Mr. Wilson? Oh, yes. Mr. Wilson is staying with Mr. Frazer.'

She had guessed he might be, but had wanted to make certain. If he had left, he would have sold the car. So he has not left, she thought. He has waited. Nothing else mattered. She drove to the house.

There he was in the garden, sitting under a tree reading a book. He saw her at once.

'So you've come, Olga.'

'Yes, I've come.'

'Everything is settled?'

He had not kissed her. 'Yes, Henry.'

'Then come in. The boys will see to your things. Frazer has your room ready. I told him you were coming.'

He led her along a passage and opened a door. 'Your room, Olga.'

For a fortnight Wilson had kept fresh flowers in this room: red roses, the darkest and most fragrant he could find. For a fortnight he had thought of her being here, adding her perfume of geranium to that of the roses. The moment had come. She was here. In his arms, close to him. Warm and soft against him, her lips on his.

'It has been a long time, Henry.'

'A long time,' he said. 'A very long time.'

Chapter 38

The DISPERSAL

^^^^^^^^^^^^^^^^

IT WAS NEW YEAR'S DAY.

Owen leant his bicycle against the wall of the main house of the Station Botanique. Everything had been taken out of it. Olga had given him everything. All the things that had been here were now at the mission. He was inundated with luxury. He had not wanted the things, but he had not been able to refuse to take them. Even many of the plants and flowering shrubs had been transplanted from her garden.

Why had he come over today? There was nothing to see... no one to see. He looked towards the graves. He had buried these men. Then he had married Sebastian to Maria. They had had no business to bury Congo so near the others. But he had been as helpless over that as he had over everything else.

That marriage! That mockery! Yet he had brought it upon himself. It had been his suggestion. He, a minister of God...

They had left here in the old station wagon and in the five-ton truck. They had even stopped at the mission. He thought of them as he had seen them last, Channel driving the professor's truck with the Abyssinian chief beside him and Laertes sitting on the piled gear: Sebastian following in the station wagon with his harlots and his dog. Pointed north into the unknown of Ethiopia, abandoning everything, they had gone gaily, waving to him, shouting their good-byes. He saw Channel in his mind, neat as ever with his red silk handkerchief stuffed up his sleeve; he saw Sebastian rolling a final cigarette with clumsy fingers before he started.

He thought of Marais and von Brandt; of Congo whose evil spirit had dominated Mokala. He thought of the years of his association with these people; he saw their work and his own as nothing, as a scratch made upon the waters of Africa, as a faint wound upon the integrity of the forest. And still they all went on. Those others to the north while he stayed here. They went on because they must, because there was no drawing back from life. Scientist, painter, hunter, playboy, adulteress, and priest. All fashioned in the image of God, they lived or died ... they lived to die. Some of their graves were here. There would be other graves in other places. Each, one day, would lie still: his life ended, his effort ended: all that he had ever been or done a fading memory soon to be forgotten. Good or bad they died.

To the north, Marais' dredges were rusting while a guard placed by the new Administrator watched over the buildings and equipment. To the west, von Brandt's Tier Garten had gone up in flames, destroyed by his servants, who had hated him. His animals were killed.

Bentinck's store with its eleven graves — he had wanted his to be in the twelfth: 'to make a round dozen,' he had called it — was tottering on its hardwood legs. The great marula alone remained. And here at the Station the vegetation and the ants had already, in three months, almost destroyed the slow work of years. Flowers had seeded themselves, roses and creepers had sent out long, tender shoots that had turned into strong, gripping arms that throttled the buildings. No native would come near the place. The riot of jasmine, of honeysuckle, of wistaria, of potato creeper, of bignonia, was sinister in its beauty.

He walked through the house. Memories assailed him. Olga, in her cool beauty, Sebastian, Wilson, Channel ... the parties ... the marriage scene. His footsteps sounded very loud on the cement floors. A scorpion ran in front of him. He looked up to see a snake in the rafters — a big mole snake. It was the one Olga had kept to intimidate Congo. He opened a cupboard. A cloud of moths flew out. The flags. This was all that was left of the flags she had used to decorate this room.

He went back to the graves. Congo's was near a big clump of red-brown bananas. There were three fingers of fruit. The bananas pointed upward at the sky, like hands . . . like brown gorilla hands. Pendent from every bunch was a flower, a solid dark purple ball, heavy, with a bloom on it like a grape. Each had a petal turned back — scarlet as blood; the leaves of the plants were great green flags that rustled in the breeze. Elsewhere the fruit had been ravaged: the bananas, the mangoes, the citrus fruit, the guavas, the paw-paws; but not here. This clump had been passed by. The gorillas were back at the Botanical Station, but they would not go near Congo's grave.

He looked at it more closely. It had been disturbed. It bristled with bamboo pegs. He pulled at one — it came up. Not a peg, but a six-foot stake that stank of putrefaction. The point had been buried in Congo's body. He threw it from him in horror. More devil's work, more poison, more witchcraft. Wherever he went, he encountered it.

He walked on over the overgrown drive. There was the guest house that Wilson had had. There was Sebastian's house where he had lived with his women. Beyond that, the hospital — its roof-tree was broken. Channel's house . . . He went over to the terrace where the doctor had breakfasted so often. It was amazing to think of him in Abyssinia with Sebastian. He did not know if they had reached their destination; he only knew that they had gone with a native chief to guide them. Olga and Wilson were in London: married. Olga had written to him. Wilson was in the army, and likely to go abroad. Those were the others of this company.

He went into Channel's house: empty, of course, except for a

few things that had not been worth moving — specimens, obscene, bleached white by the alcohol in which they had been
preserved; human organs; growths that had not been rare
enough to send away. The whole place was empty. Everything was at the mission: tables, chairs, desks, pictures —
everything. He had inherited the earth. He walked through
the rooms. He looked into a cupboard. Why was he here?
Why this searching the cupboards?

There were some papers in it, and a box of matches. Something Channel had written in his neat French writing that
leaned over from left to right. How pointed the letters were!
— sharp, neat. They reminded him of the doctor. He must
have written it after his typewriter was packed and then forgotten it. He sat on the window-sill to read.

'This is a testament of failure,' Channel had written; 'of success built upon failure, and the ultimate failure, that of success. Being personal, it remains public in the sense that any
man, at any time, is a product of his times . . . a reflection of
them. And at no time have public and personal failures been
more common; at no time the ends achieved been more futile.
At no time publicly or personally has the doctrine of good
will so defeated its own ends. The condition of the world is
due to the cumulative effect of the personal failure and futility
of all those separate individuals who make up the world. The
single man or woman cannot be separated from the conditioning of their environment, nor from the impact from without of those forces which govern public movement. Neither
rationality nor cynicism has led to circumstance. And unprin-
cipled good will — the faculty that imagines good can be done
by evil methods or that good can be done within a specified
framework without due consideration of the full context —
can be as bad or perhaps worse than actual malevolence, since
it builds up no resistance against it. Having the means, we are
without ends and act from day to day, provisionally, thinking
the good of today enough; not seeing that the good of today,

thoughtlessly performed, may do harm ... may set in train circumstances which, lacking the control of spiritual certainty, may be evil. In the end nothing can be achieved but bitterness by cerebration alone.

'Man is not the master of his destiny: not even master of himself. The widest limits of his wisdom remain provisional in that, able to gauge and measure empiric fact, he is unable to gauge or measure spiritual reaction ... utterly unable to understand either himself or anyone else. Hence what he deems a benefit for another may, from that other's point of view, prove to be a disaster ... and what he thinks a kindness become a cruelty. It would seem that the basic fact of existence is its solitary nature and that no man has rights over another ... almost that no man should impinge more than very superficially upon the orbit of another's personality. It seems possible that, much as it may be desired, there can be no merging ... can be no giving or taking; that there is no race for the swift nor battle for the strong; that without spiritual, psychic certainty there is only the law of diminishing returns that operates geometrically and often inversely. To him that hath shall be given ... so much that he hates what he has and is smothered by it. To him that hath not shall be taken away that little which he hath, so that he too dies. Plethora and scarcity are just two of the names of destruction. War is another name. And the man at war with himself is at war, though he sits in a garden surrounded by flowers and singing birds. ... He can sit quite still and yet destroy himself and those about him for whom he has nothing but good will. Those whom, because of his good will, he has betrayed, not for the thirty pieces of silver of Judas, but for a lesser price — that of his own self-esteem which, fearing all issues, sought the path of appeasement, of a pseudo-morality based neither on fact nor truth, but upon expediency ... the expediency of the moment ... that good will of the moment which is the mark of all weakness since it is measured out and circumscribed ...'

The three pages of manuscript ended as abruptly as they had begun. They were a part of something Channel had been writing of himself, but what he had written applied to him, too ... to all men.

Channel had gone north into the wilds ... to amputate, to heal, to cure, to save. They were all gone utterly: as they had come: out of nothing into nothing. Back into the world ... into death.

But over the mountainside, over her despoiled garden, the spirit of Olga lingered. He knelt to pray for her.

This was an evil place ... beyond prayer.

He thought of his mission, luxurious with gifts, with imported furniture, with books — detective novels and scientific works, with yellow paper-backed French novels that he would not read and had not been able to destroy. He had packed them in a box. He thought of the gilt Empire mirror with the eagle above it ... of the bed ... Olga's bed; of the white polar bear skins.

He thought of Olga.

He prayed for strength and wept.

The whirlwind ... surely it had swept him up. Surely he was caught in it: in the memory of his temptations. I did not come to save her, he thought. I came to see her ... to be near her. O God, how he had deceived himself! He was a man like all other men and had not known it.

Life here was over. Only death remained — putrefaction and corruption. Already the buildings were falling into disorder. They had sown the wind and reaped the whirlwind. Their fathers had eaten sour grapes and the children's teeth were set on edge. Those who were dead had died by violence ... brutally, suddenly. But why had Olga been spared? Why had Sebastian the libertine? Channel the cynic? Why had he been spared himself, since he, too, had lusted in his mind.

Hardly knowing what he was doing, he felt in his pocket.

There were the matches he had picked up. He struck one. He held the flaming match to the thatch of the roof of Channel's house. He went to the hospital, to Sebastian's house, to the guest house, to Olga's. All were flaming. Columns of smoke rose into the sky. Arson. He had committed arson? Or had he purified by fire? He stood watching the flames, standing as near as he could to them. Something fell beside him. Olga's mole snake had crept from the roof. It slid over the ground at his feet and disappeared into the bushes. Neither he nor anyone else could destroy the snake that personified all evil. Even this, his last gesture, the destruction of this place and his memories of it, was without such irrevocable finality. It was the snake he must conquer. The snake, as it crawled on its belly, symbolized all evil, all cruelty, all wickedness. It was the snake that had counselled Eve to tempt Adam in the garden.

And what had prompted him to burn? To what strange gods was he offering sacrifice? Had he done right or wrong? If I had not picked up the match box, he thought ... If I had not come here today ... If ... If there were answers in life, where were they to be found?

And when he got home there would be more fires. Everything that had come from here — even the plants that he had tended so carefully — he would tear up and burn: the furniture, the bed, the pictures, the boxes of books — everything. Olga had begun a new life. These things that had been hers must be destroyed, for they held within them the memory of evil. Of what had been the Station Botanique, nothing must remain but the graves of its dead ... nothing but the folklore that would surround this hillside.

It was war that had brought this devastation to Mokala. It had come because man had tolerated evil instead of fighting against it.

The heat of the burning houses was intense. Swirls of heavy smoke drifted round him and rose in columns into the sky.

The green flags of the banana leaves wilted, turned brown, curled and burst into flame. Through the smoke he could see the crosses on the graves and the bush beyond.

A figure was coming towards him. It came slowly through the smoke, fading and reappearing as the smoke thickened and cleared. It was his enemy. It was Evil itself. It was Entobo the witch doctor. He was close to him now. He had stopped and was staring at him. An old man, small, shrivelled, with hard, black eyes.

'I see you,' he said. 'I see you, a foolish man who thinks to destroy with fire.' He held up a bamboo stake. 'A foolish man who tears up a poisoned stake and throws it to the ground, unthinking of the foot that might strike upon it. There are men, servant of the white spirit, that merit death; only for them do I make my medicine in the festering body of the beast that dwelt here.' Entobo held the stick point forward towards him. 'There is death in every splinter of that point. There is death if I put one in a man's shoe or in his bed. What can you know of medicine, or life, or death, or the forces that dwell here? What can any white man know?' He was half-hidden now in the thickening smoke. The houses were burning down, their roofs crashing, the flames whipped by a sudden wind. To save himself from the sparks, Owen covered his eyes with his arm. When he looked back, Entobo was gone. And he was trembling: a man alone: a man alone in an Africa whose significance he saw at last: the giantess, the dark, spawning womb where all men were Pigmies dwarfed by her immensity. Africa the untouched . . . the untouchable . . . the beautiful. Men came and went. Bentinck was another hunter, dead: just one more. The two German adventurers, the professor and his assistant, were joined to the rest in death, to the thousands who had died violently in Africa: their new graves marked with wooden crosses, with cairns of stones, would soon be overgrown and forgotten.

Africa was guarded by her fevers, her little forest paths

saved by the beasts that trod them, her rivers watched by saurians. Her secrets were forever guarded ... forever safe.

This was the Congo song: the song of the sluggish rivers, of the mountains, the forests; the song of the distant, throbbing drums, of the ripe fruits falling, of the mosquitoes humming in the scented dusk; the song of Entobo, of the gorilla and the snake.

The song no white man would ever sing.

THE END